THE
CHOICE

THE

CROWN PUBLISHERS, INC.

CHOICE

Barry Reed

NEW YORK

F OR M ARIE

AUG 2 8 '91

Copyright © 1991 by Barry Reed

Published by Crown Publishers, Inc.,
201 East 50th Street, New York, New York 10022.
Member of the Crown Publishing Group.

CROWN is a trademark of Crown Publishers, Inc.
Manufactured in the United States of America
Library of Congress Cataloging-in-Publication Data
Reed, Barry.
    The choice / Barry Reed.
        p.   cm.
    I. Title.
PS3568.E36475C47   1991
813'.54—dc20   90-48217
                                                       CIP

ISBN 0-517-58124-8
10 9 8 7 6 5 4 3 2 1
First Edition

Book design by Deborah Kerner

Who can be wise, amazed, temperate
and furious,
Loyal and neutral, in a moment?

MACBETH, ACT I, SCENE III

THE
CHOICE

1

She was seated on the wine leather couch in the inner foyer pretending to read something from the current issue of *Forbes*. Her eyes, dark and luminous, peered over the magazine as Galvin entered. A painting by Caravaggio framed her tawny silk hair, and her soft amber features blended easily with the antique tones of the old master. Galvin paused, checked his watch—although he knew the time, 7:30 A.M.—then continued past her toward Julie Hedren's station. His leather heels resounded with an intimidating click on the polished marble floor.

"Good morning, Miss Hedren," he greeted the receptionist, who had fixed a smile on him the moment he entered. Galvin would hone in on that smile, like radar. He grasped her hand and returned her smile with one full of Irish charm, a raffish glint in his ocean-blue eyes.

"Good morning, Mr. Galvin." She handed him a sheaf of messages. "Lunch is reset for one-thirty at the Bay Tower Room. All other appointments stat." She drew an imaginary line with her ballpoint pen. "Depart for Logan Airport at four. The chauffeur will meet you out front. Arrive at National at five fifty-five. Accommodations for four days at the Capitol Hill Hilton."

"Fine." Galvin scanned the incoming roster, noting that every member of his thirty-man litigation team had checked in. He picked up his briefcase and turned to go.

Julie Hedren always fought for little swatches of attention, especially from Galvin. She had expected some discourse on the Washington meeting.

"One other thing." Her pen jabbed the air toward the seated visitor. "There's a Miss Alvarez here. Says she's a lawyer. Needs to see you today."

Julie leaned forward and cupped her hand to her mouth. "Cape Verdean, I'd say," came a smug whisper.

The conceit was not lost on Galvin, who avoided it by again checking his watch. "No appointment?"

"No appointment." Miss Hedren spoke with renewed authority, like a gatekeeper, loud enough for all to hear.

Galvin hesitated. It was unlike him. He had learned the Yankee art of delegation. And he was immersed in the tax fraud case of the nation's fifth largest bank. The next few days would be grueling. He was guiding a billion-dollar client through a Congressional investigation. He should have dismissed this early-morning intrusion. But he was curious, even a little intrigued. Maybe it was the visitor's Latin presence or the way her hair cascaded in glossy swirls about her shoulders.

"Give her an appointment for sometime after I return from Washington," Galvin said.

"I tried that, Mr. Galvin, but she wouldn't leave. I suggested she see one of the junior associates or even Andrea Schneiderman."

"Andrea who?"

"The firm's new apprentice. Columbia. Summa cum laude. More quals on her res than a federal judge."

"Schneiderman, Schneiderman." Galvin smiled inwardly. Who would take a Schneiderman, let alone an Andrea, into the male WASP enclave of Hovington, Sturdevant, Holmes & Hall? Maybe they're getting pangs of conscience. Or practicality. "Yes, have her see Andrea Schneiderman."

Galvin flicked an imaginary speck from the lapel of his tailored blue serge suit and headed for the double oak doors of his new world.

Hedren's thoughts trailed after him. There wasn't much about the machinations of Boston's most prestigious law firm that she didn't know. She did, after all, receive and at times monitor incoming calls, and she could detect a pattern as the red buttons flickered when the senior partners were on their private lines. All personnel, including 280 of Boston's best barristers, passed her desk. And the incoming mail was sorted under her inquisitive eyes. After five years as receptionist and now approaching the age of thirty, she felt twinges of mortality. She had dated some of the junior associates, but Frank Galvin was a different matter. She knew his story, about his earlier bouts with alcoholism, his womanizing, his downward spiral and curious redemption. In his darkest moment he had refused to be bought off and against impossible odds had won the largest medical malpractice case in legal memory. Now he was sober, polished, quite rich, and quite inaccessible. She liked the square cut of his jaw, the furrows that time and experience had etched in his ruggedly handsome face. His smoked silver hair, once scruffy, was now carefully coiffed. He had a commanding presence that awakened a primal urge in Julie Hedren.

Galvin headed the firm's litigation department and was accepted and even feared by his stuffy partners. Most important, he had the loyalty of the junior associates. Litigation, once the firm's stepchild, barely tolerated by the more lucrative commercial departments, was now a money-maker. And with cash flow came respect. Frank Galvin went for the jugular and won. To a gilded clientele, where price was no object, that was all that mattered. And he ran with the Brahmins as if he had always belonged. Yet sometimes, despite his cool self-assurance, Julie Hedren sensed a hint of vulnerability. Lately he seemed to be harboring some inner disquiet, when his eyes, icy blue at times, would soften as he relived some wound from the past. It was particularly noticeable when his former mentor Moe Katz would call. Julie Hedren suspected that the Frank Galvin of old was never far away.

Galvin put his hand on the polished brass doorknob, caressing it lightly. After pushing the door open he would plunge into the pressure cooker of corporate law: twenty-hour workdays, crunching deadlines, overbearing clients, vying, playing odds, skirting disaster. Buttressing it all was an unbelievable array of talent who could match his pace. Galvin was well aware that basic to the firm's success was its gifted cadre—Ivy League, young, law-review brilliant, most steeped in family tradition with political, fiscal, and social connections. No commercial compound or government agency had such backup. When a client entered the blue-chip cloisters of Hovington, Sturdevant, Holmes & Hall, he could be sure of two things: He would get the best counseling possible and the bill would be exorbitant.

And it was an elitist world. Senior partners had million-dollar salaries, summers at Oyster Harbor, weekends in the Hamptons. The women were elegant and the men powerful. Heady stuff, and Galvin relished every moment. He liked the hum and the rhythm and the smell of it. Five years ago he was a washed-up ambulance chaser, spieling off-color stories to cronies in dingy barrooms. Now he was sought after, consulted, admired, and feared. No longer was he the tough Irish kid yearning to become a member of the establishment. He was the establishment.

Galvin met Cy Sturdevant at the edge of the polished oak staircase that spiraled up to the library and conference rooms and down to several floors that housed the firm's junior associates and support staff. Already the computers were drilling their staccato rhythms, while the charcoal-gray legions of young lawyers, clutching yellow legal pads and accompanied by consultants and secretaries, streamed toward their assignments. No one ambled or lolled at Hovington, Sturdevant, Holmes & Hall, not even the cleanup crew, not even Cyrus Sturdevant, the oldest surviving partner, who was nearing eighty. There was always a sense of urgency about the place, an ordered frenzy that added up to "billable hours"—the heart and soul of corporate law.

"Galvin, my boy." Sturdevant was in a rare expansive mood. "That was a good one young Trimble pulled off last week." Sturdevant had rolled up his *Wall Street Journal* and slapped it into the palm of his hand.

It was Sturdevant and Hovington who had hired Galvin five years ago after watching him dismantle Boston's premier trial lawyer, J. Edward Concannon, in the celebrated St. Catherine Laboure case. It seemed an unlikely relationship at first, the Irish Catholic has-been, a graduate from a third-rate law school, and the old-line firm where echoes of Oliver Wendell Holmes, Louis Brandeis, three Governors, two United States Senators, and ten Superior

Court justices still reverberated within the corridors. The anomalous relationship proved a gold mine. The firm prospered. Galvin, after years of frustration and floundering, finally found his stride. And this year Francis X. Galvin, the truant from the brick bottom of South Boston, was to scale the heights of State Street; the ultimate honor—a full partnership. Or, as Moe Katz would say, "splitting the pie across the board."

"I'm sorry, Cy." Galvin stopped momentarily. "I've been working on bailing out Pilgrim National. Hadn't heard about young Trimble."

"Ingenious, Galvin, simply ingenious. That kid's a doer. He'll be a shaker before long." Sturdevant tweaked the wisp of his white mustache. "Billed twenty-seven hours in *one* day to Comp-Tech Computer in their takeover by Delaware East. Can you believe it?" He gave the *Journal* a resounding whack on the bannister.

"In one day?" Galvin thought the forty-eighth floor was getting to Sturdevant.

"Damn right!" Sturdevant broke into one of his rare smiles. "Worked around the clock here in Boston, then took a plane to L.A. and logged three additional hours. Wait until Comp-Tech gets the bill. Hell, Galvin, I'll bet no one will ever top this. Twenty-seven hours! I mean, that is really something!"

"Yes, Cy, that's something," Galvin said quietly.

The double oak doors behind Galvin were electronically controlled. But slipping in alongside two secretaries came the dark young woman with the beguiling eyes, the one he'd seen in the reception area, trailed by Julie Hedren.

"You can't go in there!" Hedren shrieked.

"I'm sorry, Mr. Galvin," the interloper said, "but I must see you."

"Look, Miss . . . ?" Hedren's authority was challenged.

"Alvarez!"

"You must leave immediately! This is a law firm, not a subway station."

"I'll handle this, Julie." Galvin half raised his hand and Julie Hedren retreated.

"Now, Miss Alvarez." Galvin consulted his watch for the third time in ten minutes, a dismissive trait picked up from his Brahmin associates. "You have exactly thirty seconds."

She stood there for a moment. Everything about her was fresh and tailored—the russet suede suit, the white ruffled shirt with cordovan lace at the collar, the soft Moroccan leather boots.

"Mr. Galvin," she said apologetically, "I bought this outfit at Saks to impress you." Her hands swept in half-arcs toward her knees. "Cost me over a thousand dollars. I can't afford this any more than I can afford my law books, my part-time secretary, or my answering service. I have a case. In fact, eight cases, and I need your help. Give me a half-hour so I can run it by you and go over some of these documents." She patted her briefcase. "If I can't convince you by then, I'll be on the next bus back to Fall River."

"You have thirteen more seconds." Galvin was intransigent.

In one last defiant shot, Tina Alvarez looked Galvin square in the eye. "I watched you try the St. Catherine Laboure case," she said, "and you lectured to our graduating class at Governor Bradford Law. You told us that the purpose of the law was to represent people, not things. I can still hear your words. 'You men and women are officers of the Court—' "

"Look," Galvin interrupted. "I'd love to discuss the verities of the law, but some other time."

She shook her head. "I guess I made a mistake." Her eyes moistened.

If the cool, unassailable Frank Galvin had an Achilles' heel, it was women. One woman not too long ago almost led to his destruction. There had been others. Galvin was aware of his susceptibility. And he knew this misty appeal could all be a con, a play on his weakness.

"Okay," he said gruffly. "I haven't got thirty minutes, but I'll halve it with you. First you promise me you'll heed my advice, whatever it is, okay? Even if I tell you to board the . . . the . . ."

"Cape Verdean Express," she injected. "The next one leaves at ten—I'll be on it."

"You must be a mind reader." Galvin tightened his jaw in an attempt to remain serious.

"I hear pretty well."

"Cape Verde. That's south of County Kerry?" asked Galvin.

"By about eighteen hundred miles," she said. A trace of a smile disclosed white, even teeth.

"You now have fourteen minutes," Galvin snapped. "Come with me."

In Frank Galvin's office, Tina Alvarez exhaled slowly as she eased into the rich leather chair in front of his desk. She had somehow survived the rigors of the morning. Courtney Evans, Galvin's secretary, brought coffee, and Galvin told her to buzz him in ten minutes for the meeting with Judge Stone.

Galvin sat on the edge of his rosewood desk, arms folded on his chest. Tina sipped her coffee from the Wedgewood china, then took a quick peek at the surroundings as she tried to steady the cup to keep it from rattling. Everything in Galvin's oversized corner office, from the panoramic view of Boston Harbor to the elegant Chinese rugs on the teak parquet floor, exuded wealth and power. A stone Buddha squatted nearby, an enigmatic curl to its lips that seemed to impart a knowing grin in her direction. Several terra-cotta figures with sphinx-like eyes peered from beneath bamboo fronds, and along an entire wall were gold-leaf panels depicting temples and goddesses. She wondered if the IRS approved.

Galvin reached for his coffee cup.

"Well, my dear Portia, what can I do for you?"

"Have you ever heard the word *teratogenesis?*" asked Tina.

"Can't say that I have. Sounds ominous."

"It is. Comes from the Greek. Literally, it means 'monster-producing.' "

"Greek and Latin were never my strongest subjects." Galvin paused to sip his coffee. "I was so bad in Latin that Sister Mary Joseph kicked me out of altar boy class and made me promise never to become a priest, a promise I've kept to this very day."

Tina wanted to laugh. But time was not on her side, so she continued.

"Well, a teratogen is a drug capable of producing congenital deformities in the newborn. Like thalidomide back in the sixties.

7

That's the classic example. As you will recall, thalidomide was touted as a sedative prescribed for women during pregnancy. The drug was whipped onto the market without sufficient testing and generated over twenty thousand malformed children that we are aware of before it was withdrawn worldwide."

"It produced a lot of litigation," Galvin remarked.

"Litigation, but little money was recovered for the afflicted families." Tina placed her cup and saucer on the ebony and teak table. "The pharmaceutical firms hid behind the old 'state of the art' smoke screen. They weren't legally responsible unless the injured parties could prove that the manufacturers had unmistakable scientific knowledge before marketing the drug that their product was capable of harming people. The courts saved the manufacturers' rear ends. '*Caveat emptor*,' they said: Let the buyer beware."

"Like every dog's entitled to one bite before the owner gets tagged with responsibility," said Galvin.

"Precisely. Well, the law has progressed a little since those *caveat emptor* days. Today if a drug manufacturer puts something on the market and it causes damage, like birth defects, and the manufacturer knows or should have known its propensity for injury, then the company's liable."

"An excellent dissertation," Galvin said, his voice getting edgy, "but how does this involve me?"

"Have you ever heard of the drug Lyosin?" Tina tried to keep calm. Time was running out.

"Lyosin—who hasn't heard of Lyosin?" Galvin said. "It's going to let us all live to a hundred and five. That's the new miracle drug that dissolves blood clots, prevents heart attacks and strokes. Greatest find since penicillin."

"Maybe. Maybe not. It also can kill and maim. I have eight cases of children of Portuguese families in the Fall River area, with birth defects ranging from cleft palates to absent limbs, some too hideous to talk about. All are mentally retarded. I can prove these defects were related to the ingestion of Lyosin."

"I hope you make a zillion dollars," said Galvin. "So why are you talking to me?"

"I mean, Mr. Galvin." Her voice faltered. "I *think* I can prove it.

8

I want to leave you my file. In it is a narrative of a lot of strange events uncovered by a reporter from *The Fall River Times* linking the drug with birth defects."

"I still can't see how this involves me."

"Quite frankly, I'm in over my head. Lyosin is distributed by Gammett Industries, a big New Jersey corporation, but the manufacturer is Universal Multi-Tech, a British-based conglomerate."

"You've got your work cut out for you," said Galvin.

"I thought I could handle it. The fact is, Mr. Galvin, I work on two-bit cases—domestic quarrels, sewer abatements. I earn a hundred dollars here and there on drunk-driving cases and go to court to save tenants from getting thrown out into the street. I can barely pay my rent. I told the Portuguese families I'd take their cases on. I've been data-gathering for eight months. The more facts I accumulate, the more I realize how much I'm at sea. Spent four thousand dollars already just checking things out. I can't bankroll the case. I don't know what to do next—and the statute of limitations runs out next Tuesday."

"You mean you've sat on these cases for eight months and next Tuesday you and your clients could be out of business?"

"That's why I'm here. I need you to take over the case and bring suit immediately."

"Look, Miss Alvarez. I'm simply too busy. I've got one hell of a job to do keeping a respected member of our financial community out of jail. I can't get sidetracked on trivial litigation."

"Trivial litigation!" Suddenly the fire flashed in Tina's coal-black eyes. "God, when you tried that Catherine Laboure case, you had such beautiful anger." Her voice became stronger. "I never missed a day of that trial. And you lectured us about fighting for justice. 'There's too many lawyers trying to save too much money for too many rich people. Don't sell out,' you said. 'Don't become a paper pusher for the ruling class.' " She shook her head. "I hung on every word."

"Well, that was good advice and I hope you follow it. Bring suit yourself."

"But I haven't the foggiest notion of how to get service of

process on Universal and Gammett, particularly Universal. It's a foreign corporation."

"That's why you went to law school. Look, I just can't get involved. It's as simple as that. If the statute of limitations is running out, sue anyone. The prescribing doctor. The pharmacy. At least you'll have a viable suit before the statute expires. You can amend and add parties later. Bring suit in state court—right down there in Fall River. And say a prayer to St. Jude that you get the right judge."

Galvin extended his hand. "Good luck, Miss Alvarez."

She sighed and shook his hand half-heartedly.

"I must be going," he said.

"Mr. Galvin." She started replacing her file in her briefcase. "One last thing. I've been reading about Pilgrim National and Judge Stone—how they've been laundering money for years and now is accounting day. U.S. Attorney Brown and the Feds are bringing up some pretty heavy artillery."

"Yes, I am well aware."

She stood up. Their eyes locked for a final instant.

"I hope you make a zillion dollars," she said. Then she was gone.

■

Courtney Evans called Galvin on the intercom to remind him that Mr. Hovington had arrived and that he and Judge Stone had been waiting for over half an hour.

"What was that murder case down in Fall River years ago where a young woman took an axe to her parents?" Galvin asked.

"Lizzie Borden," she said. "The Lizzie Borden case."

"Oh, yes." Galvin's voice had a curious lilt. "Courtney, check to see if the Borden homestead still exists, and book me for next Friday night at some good motel in Fall River. There's something about that case that I want to check out."

2

alvin stood with Carter Hovington near the bank of
television cameras that monitored the terse exchange
between Judge Webster Stone and New York Congressman
Eduardo Carrerras.

"Now, Mr. Stone." Carrerras studied some notes, then his eyes
narrowed as he peered out over his glasses. "Representative
Enwright and the members of this House Banking Committee
would like some straight answers, if you please.

"Were you aware, at any time during the year 1989, that you and
your banking institution were in violation of U.S. Code, Title 31,
Section 5313, namely failing to report to the Internal Revenue
Service over two million dollars in withdrawals from the account of
a particular depositor, to wit: Offshore Development Corporation,
from January first to March thirty-first of that year?"

From his position in the pit-like amphitheater, Judge Stone bent
forward toward the microphone in front of him. He cleared his
throat raucously, then glanced at the ceiling.

"Cut!" came a command. "Hold it!" A man in shirt-sleeves
waving a notebook stepped out from the last row of spectators.
"Mr. Stone," he barked in a curt, directorial tone, "don't clear your
throat or blow your nose, especially into the microphone. Remember, you'll be on national television. Look straight at Chairman
Carrerras. The answers are not up around the light fixtures."

The speaker was image-maker Elliot Bauman, hired by Frank
Galvin to refashion Judge Stone to fit the mold for his forthcoming
confrontation with U.S. Attorney Roosevelt Brown.

"And, Mr. Stone." Bauman's voice softened. "You are the chief executive of the largest bank in New England. You didn't get there by *not* having the answers. Your replies should be concise and to the point. Okay, time for a short break, but everyone stay in place. We'll try it again in ten minutes."

"I don't know." Carter Hovington nodded toward their client, who had suddenly slumped forward in his seat. "Everything sounds too rehearsed. It lacks spontaneity."

"The last thing we want in the courtroom, Carter," said Galvin, "is spontaneity. An unprepared witness can destroy you. That's a bitter lesson most lawyers learn when it's too late. Look, we're not telling Stone what to say, but how to say it."

"I know," said Hovington, "but we seem to be getting a lot of style with not much substance. I wonder if Stone will make it?"

"He'll make it," reassured Galvin. "He's come a long way in six weeks. Do you recall when we first met him? Imperious. Garrulous. Black frock coat, string tie, diamond cuff links. Insisting he be called 'Judge.' Sure, we have some buffing to do, but look at the progress. Just the right shade of gray around the temples, conservative blue suit, modulated voice. He even looks like a banker."

Hovington wasn't so sure. Nor was Galvin. But Galvin was trading for a psychological standoff. Stone was a wounded animal at bay, but he had to stand his ground. "You've got to have the balls of a lion," Galvin counseled. "And a lion never leaves his life, he loses it."

To Lion-Balls Stone, the alternatives didn't look too appealing.

The conference room at the Capitol Hilton, hired by Bauman, had been redesigned to simulate, down to the closest detail, the Congressional Hearing Chamber. This was the dry run. Galvin was leaving nothing to chance. There would be no surprises, no ambush. Even those acting the parts of committee members looked down from the bench with the proper amount of judicial disdain.

"Stone will win or lose it all on Thursday," said Galvin.

"Oh, a loss won't be all that bad." Hovington managed an

12

impish grin. "There will be appeals, petitions for rehearings, requests for a change of venue. The firm's bill will be substantial. No, strike that," Hovington said, his smile broadening, "it will be outrageous."

The entourage to Washington included twenty of the firm's most trusted employees. There were to be no leaks of the mock-hearings, especially since Carter Hovington had secured a copy of the committee's list of questions. And only he and Galvin knew that a friendly Congressional aide had returned a long overdue favor.

"Chip is doing one hell of a job," Galvin said to Hovington, referring to Carter Hovington's twenty-six-year-old son, who had become immersed in Stone's defense and was presently portraying the acerbic inquisitor Eduardo Carrerras. "Even Carrerras would be impressed." And Galvin meant it.

Chip Hovington was a young Frank Galvin and more. It was no accident or stroke of favoritism that Chip was Galvin's first assistant. Like a star quarterback, Chip brought out the best in his associates, enabling Galvin to set up strategies, confident that they would be executed flawlessly. All of this teamwork did not go unnoticed by the senior Hovington. And even if Carter Hovington rarely complimented Galvin openly, both men understood that the admiration was there.

◘

Elliot Bauman bristled with credentials. A former CBS anchorman, he now ran a national consulting firm that prepped key executives, such as Stone, for hot-seat confrontations. If "60 Minutes" was in town to do a number on some marginal entrepreneur, Bauman's crew would tape the interview, making sure in the interests of journalistic integrity that nothing was left on the cutting-room floor. Bauman was well worth the enormous fee that Pilgrim National was paying him.

Galvin recalled Stone's exact words when first introduced to Bauman: "No goddammed song-and-dance man is going to make me into something I'm not. You'd better get that straight from the start."

Bauman agreed. He listened to more of Stone's railings, a few swipes at that "Puerto Rican snake" Carrerras and that "coon" ambulance chaser Rosie Brown. Unfortunately, the slurs surfaced in local papers and in the *Washington Post*.

Galvin smiled inwardly as he recalled Bauman's cosmetic surgery. "Stone's no different from other captains of industry," he had told Galvin on the plane to Washington. "I just engaged that macho ego of his and channeled it to work for itself. The Juan Perón approach usually does it," Bauman continued. "Perón had a penchant for white shoes, white duck pants, and the finest dark-blue blazers money could buy, with more than a few medallions embroidered into the breast pocket. But Perón was no dummy. His image maker, Sidgo Castellana, was a hard-boiled pragmatist. He got Perón to don a crumpled shirt, sleeves rolled up, black pants, and ordinary street shoes, no shine. When Perón campaigned for President of Argentina, to the peasants, the farmers, and the workers who made up ninety percent of the electorate, he was a folk hero.

"And you know, Galvin," said Bauman, "Stone listened."

Galvin recalled Stone's subtle surrender.

"We have less than two months to work," Bauman had told Stone. "First, we shed fifteen pounds. I have you programmed with a physical therapist at the In-Town Racquet Club. She's quite nice."

"What?" Stone sputtered, his arrogance fading.

"And you'll like the diction coach."

The actual hearing went better than expected. With Galvin and Chip Hovington seated as counsel at Stone's elbows, Stone, with a clear, dignified voice, resounding in quiet confidence, carried it off as if he were Lee Iaccoca.

It was Carrerras who exhibited a lack of judicial restraint, causing several members of the press corps to shake their heads as Stone calmly parried Carrerras's badgering and caustic repetition. When Stone corrected the Congressman, he did so like a seasoned debator, tempering each reply with proper deference and civility. At no time during the two-hour grilling did he invoke the Fifth Amendment. Unlike bank officials in similar circumstances, Stone refused to blame others. He candidly admitted being unfamiliar with the particular Federal Reporting Regulations designed to spotlight laundering of illicit funds. For such dereliction, he did not attempt to absolve his conduct, adding that to the extent that the law was Constitutional and if the Government, as contended, did in fact prove that he was in *knowing* violation of its provisions, then he, Webster Stone, stood ready to accept the consequences. Galvin had seen to it that this refreshing bit of candor had a built-in safety valve—the subtle threat of prolonged litigation was not lost on Carrerras, nor on U.S. Attorney Roosevelt Brown.

Carrerras finally zeroed in on Stone personally.

"Mr. Stone," he began, carefully enunciating each word, "you have been quoted in various media sources denigrating the racial background of members not only of this committee but also of other federal officials who have been lawfully constituted to act as the investigatory and prosecutorial arms of the citizens of this nation."

Galvin was surprised Carrerras would resort to such low-road tactics. Yet Galvin had prepared his client for this very contingency. Stone waited patiently for Carrerras to tuck every inch of humiliation into his question.

"In the March thirteenth edition of the *Washington Post*"— Carrerras held up a newspaper clipping, then removed his glasses and tapped them forcefully against the exhibit—"you referred to me as a 'Puerto Rican snake.' Have I quoted you correctly?" Without waiting for a response, Carrerras continued. "And you used similar derogatory language to describe United States Attorney Roosevelt Brown. And, Mr. Stone, I'll extend to you the courtesy that you failed to render Mr. Brown. I will delete your exact words. Let's just say you characterized him as a 'blank,' "— Carrerras raised two sets of fingers—" 'ambulance chaser.' Were you the author of these defamatory slurs, or have you been misquoted? I think you owe this panel an explanation. You see, my forefathers didn't come over on the *Mayflower*."

"Nor did mine, Mr. Carrerras," Stone replied deferentially. "All I can say, sir, is that I am thoroughly embarrassed over these statements. Unfortunately, I made them. I offer no excuses and I am saddened that they were ever uttered. It was reprehensible. . . ." Stone's voice trailed off. He started to choke and asked for some water. "I sincerely and publicly apologize to you, Congressman Carrerras"—his voice was husky with emotion— "and to the members of your committee and especially to United States Attorney Roosevelt Brown." Stone sat motionless. Nothing, not a sound or a movement, disturbed the moment of contrition.

"Perfect, perfect," whispered Elliot Bauman to Carter Hovington.

Even Carrerras nodded approval.

◻

Galvin had been waiting outside Congressman Carrerras's office for forty-five minutes before a matronly secretary told him that the Congressman would see him later in the day and to come back in three hours. Galvin accepted the heel-cooling and returned later as instructed. At five minutes to five, he was ushered into the inner office.

"I was impressed with your client, Mr. Galvin." Carrerras tucked his head into his chest and leveled a gaze over his glasses. "It was almost as if you had an advance copy of our agenda."

Galvin said nothing. Right now he was less a lawyer than a salesman. Silence was part of the package.

"Now, Roosevelt Brown is his own man, mind you." Carrerras was quick to jump into the conversational gap. "He's the country's top prosecutor. I don't know whom he hates more, child pornographers or white racist bankers who have their hand in the till. My committee can only make certain recommendations to the Justice Department. Assuming, for the moment, Mr. Galvin, that Justice is favorably inclined to forward *my* recommendations to U.S. Attorney Brown, and that in the interest of avoiding protracted litigation Brownie goes along, then we're at square one. Follow me?"

"I'm with you." Galvin sensed the deal would go down.

"Now, as a lawyer, Mr. Galvin, you are well aware that final disposition rests with Federal Judge Chester Baron. That's square two."

"I understand," said Galvin.

Carrerras took off his glasses, removed his lapel handkerchief, and polished the lenses with great ceremony. Several seconds passed.

"What fee is your firm charging for all this defensive opulence?" He held the glasses up to the light, inspecting them carefully.

"Want a ballpark figure?" asked Galvin, who saw the opening he was looking for.

"Ballpark," said Carrerras.

"Including costs, I'd say one-point-five million, give or take a hundred thousand." Galvin didn't flinch. Neither did Carrerras.

"Okay, Counselor." Carrerras pressed a forefinger against the desktop. "Here it is. Stone and Pilgrim plead guilty to a misdemeanor. No criminal sentence, but civil penalties will be assessed in the amount of one-point-five million. Stone will issue a statement that you and Brownie will work out jointly, the appropriate penitential froth. Now let me tell you, Mr. Galvin." Carrerras lowered his voice to a raspy whisper and looked up at Galvin from beneath his black bushy eyebrows. "If Stone's name was Julio Mendez and he originated from Medellín, Columbia, he'd be wearing the denims until he cashed. You tell him that for me. Agreed?"

"Agreed," said Galvin.

"And, Mr. Galvin." Carrerras rose to let him know the meeting was ended. "Those were pretty expensive acting lessons."

3

They hadn't spoken for over an hour. Galvin sat on a sagging Naugahyde sofa engrossed in newspaper clippings, diaries, photographs, investigative reports, affidavits, and reams of red-ribboned documents from the Food and Drug Administration and the Atlanta Centers for Disease Control.

"Another cup of coffee, Mr. Galvin?" Tina Alvarez glanced over her shoulder as she reached for Styrofoam cups in the small cabinet that housed various condiments, plastic kitchen utensils, and outdated law books.

"That would be fine." Galvin closed a blue-backed manuscript on a pencil to mark his place and wiped his eyes with the back of his hand. "And please," he added, "call me Galvin."

"Okay, and I'm Tina. That's short for Antonia." She approached with a small salute of the coffee cups, her lips parting as she tossed him a sympathetic smile, edged with gratitude. They had spent five tense hours since Galvin had driven from the Holiday Inn to Arruda Street, where Tina's office was squeezed between a line of gray triple-deckers, located a flight above the blinking neon of a 7-Eleven store.

Galvin studied Tina as he took the cup. She was young, late twenties. She wore a plaid flannel shirt tucked into stone-washed jeans. A pair of jogging shoes had replaced the Ferrangamo boots. Yet she looked more attractive than when he first saw her. Before, there had been something about her eyes. Gypsy eyes. Seductive. Beguiling. Now she was fresh, appealing, like a college sophomore. It was the warmth of her smile, the deep dimples that formed in her cheeks, the olive smoothness of her skin against the whiteness of her teeth. He loved it when a woman smiled, especially in his direction. There were so many shades to a smile—open, friendly, childish, carnal, deceptive. This one had integrity, a certain naïveté that spelled trust, one that Galvin would almost stake his life or his career on. Almost.

Tina's office reminded him of his own when he first started in practice—cramped, books stacked in boxes on the floor, a gun-metal desk in the secretary's alcove, an outdated Remington typewriter. Yet unlike his old quarters, which had always had the look of impermanence and lack of scholarship, Tina's small rectangle was neatly arranged and with taste, from the gilt-framed diplomas on the wall to the row of file cabinets and the fresh flowers on her walnut-veneer desk.

"The whole thing intrigues me." Galvin sipped his coffee. "You've raked a hell of a lot of leaves. Now you have to pull it all together in one tight bundle that translates into dollars and cents. You put shekels in the clients' pocket. Siphon a few off for yourself. That's where it's at. There are no brooding issues in the law anymore."

"I know," Tina sighed, "but right now I'm stuck in a legal quagmire and I'm about to be sucked under. There's an old Portuguese saying, *'Mais olhof que barriga.'* "

"Let me guess." Galvin steepled his fingers under his chin. " 'Bit off more than you could chew'?"

"Something like that. You know, Galvin." She shook her head. "I've been lawyering for four years. Working my buns off. When I took this case several months back, I said to myself, 'Tina—this is it. The big one. The lawyer's dream. And it's all mine. No referral fee to split. The light at the end of the tunnel.' Was I ever fooled. The light turns out to be the Montreal Express coming straight toward me. I'm about to be throttled." She drew the flat of her hand across her throat.

"My older sister, Viera, owns a beauty salon, not far from here. She has money, a new Porsche, boyfriends, goes to some hedonistic retreat in the Caribbean every winter. Right now she's off the Algarve waterskiing. Keeps after me to take a crash course in hairdressing. Get with the real money. Tell you the truth, Galvin, sometimes I seriously think of packing it in."

Galvin drained his coffee cup, the way he used to drain Scotch glasses. He waited several moments to gather his thoughts.

"Okay, so you're disillusioned with your apprenticeship. Everyone is. Law is the hardest game in the world when you first start out. And the field is overcrowded. There are more lawyers per square inch in this country than anyplace in the world. You're a people lawyer and there simply aren't enough people to go around."

"Boy, and just what Fall River needs is another Portuguese people lawyer." Tina laughed. "Especially one in skirts."

"In a way, every field is overcrowded," said Galvin. "But don't get me wrong; the cream rises to the top in any profession. All you need is staying power. There are peaks and valleys, but if you hang in there, demonstrate the exuberance that you've displayed in this case"—Galvin's hand swept toward the boxes of documents he had been wading through—"you'll make it. Clients need someone like you." He felt it was time to disengage gracefully, before it was too late, and it was time for some parting advice. "I'm impressed with the work you've done. Really." He pointed toward the documents.

"When did the FDA approve Lyosin as a marketable drug?" Galvin asked.

"March twenty-second, 1980," said Tina.

He was captivated, too, by her memory. She could narrate the drug's history, from chemical inception, through market buildup, to final approval, with instant recall.

"Tina, let me be brutally frank. Okay?"

"Okay." She sat opposite him with her knees propped up, her arms around them, as if to brace herself against rejection.

"I think you're spinning your wheels. This case is a loser. In the end the clients will hate you, then bad-mouth you, and you'll be at least a hundred thousand dollars in debt." Galvin pretended to take another sip from the empty coffee cup as he waited for his message to sink in. "Tina, believe me, stick to the small stuff. You can be the best people lawyer in Bristol County."

"I don't want to be even the best lawyer in Bristol County,"

Tina snapped. "Right now I've got clients who are up against the wall and I'm not going to quit. I made commitments to these families."

"Okay, then, let me tell you where you're at. Lyosin goes through all the rigors of a new-drug application: animal studies—"

"Too bad the mice weren't Portuguese," Tina injected.

"Look." Galvin suppressed a grimace. "They screened, tested, human studies, peer-group analysis, subjected to the scrutiny of the world's greatest scientists—Rocklei in Australia, Strechausen in Vienna, LaRoche in Paris—endorsed, even touted by the Royal College of Physicians in London. These are not just paid consultants, mind you, but world-renowned. Christ, they had everyone but Mother Theresa and Albert Schweitzer in on this one. It's the greatest medical find of the century. Cardiovascular disease is the world's number-one killer and Gammett Industries finally found a way to combat it. Are you hearing me?"

"I'm listening." Tina's dark eyes moistened.

"Tina, do you know how many dollars Gammett and Universal shelled out to get this far?"

"Quite a bit, I'd assume."

"Try a hundred million! And that's probably conservative. Now, do you think they're going to stand around and watch some neophyte Portia, a few years out of a third-rate law school, try to make a ripple on the great moat that protects their investment?"

"I'm not." Tina sipped her coffee and eyed Galvin carefully. "But I'm looking at the guy who's going to bring Gammett down to size—Frank Galvin."

"Are you crazy?" Galvin sputtered. "You didn't hear a word I said."

"I heard and felt everything you said." Tina's eyes plumbed his. "But you wouldn't be here if you didn't care for this kid." She picked up a photo and passed it to him. "This is Hector Ramondi."

Galvin studied the Polaroid as carefully as Tina was studying him. He saw a boy with an impish grin, cross-eyed, mongoloid. The kid would never play Little League baseball, never carry some girl's schoolbooks or walk on a fence like Huck Finn. He would be ridiculed, pitied, then—when his parents died—institutionalized, devoid of love and laughter. Temptation passed through Galvin like a sigh. Then it was gone.

"You know, Tina." He tried to avoid her gaze. "Let me give you some advice. When I started out in this business, everyone's plight was my plight, everyone's fight was mine. Causes—you name them, I took them on. I could give you stories you wouldn't believe. Then it finally dawned on me that there were two sides to every story, and most of the time I was on the downside. I learned the hard way. Clients con you. You wind up cynical and distrustful."

Tina sighed. "Yet you tried the St. Catherine Laboure Hospital case against impossible odds and you prevailed."

Galvin shook his head. He wasn't getting through to her. "Sure, I took on the whole world in that case. But I did it because I knew something was rotten. There was a cover-up. I just knew it. And yet it was a stroke of pure luck that I won the case. Everyone was lying—the defendants, the doctors, the nurses—but doing it quite skillfully. The jury was believing every word they said. It was my old partner, Moe Katz," he said, smiling wistfully, "who journeyed to New York City and finally ferreted out the admitting-room nurse, who ultimately blew the doctors away. The nurse testified that the doctors had told her to change the hospital records. But it took a lot of prodding and even chicanery on my part—first to find her, then to get her to testify. She knew that the defendants had stolen my client's life and, by altering the medical records, conspired to steal her children's only chance for justice. And they damn near succeeded. That's the point, Tina! The nurse didn't bang on my door. She didn't come forward for four years! Even then, she did so with great reluctance. You don't cross the medical mafia easily, believe me."

"Well, why is my case so different?" Tina asked.

"First of all, I don't think you have a case. Who's to say medically and scientifically that this child's deformities"—Galvin held up the photo of the Ramondi boy—"are even remotely connected to Lyosin? You've collected a lot of data, and I've been over most of it. The one thing that pops out at me is that there's not *one* shred of medical or scientific evidence linking Lyosin to the boy's problems. Not one."

22

"Do you think it's pure coincidence that *eight* families are involved, all with the same ethnic extraction, all within a geographical proximity?"

"Maybe it has something to do with those very factors—ethnic background or some contaminant in the area. Have you thought of that?"

"But what about the *Fall River Times* article? Do you think the reporter picked that stuff out of thin air?"

"Okay, what medical school did the reporter go to? Did he win the Nobel Prize for genetic research?" There was a peremptory edge to his voice. "There are a few things in his article that he forgot to mention. Like Lyosin is the greatest medical breakthrough in this country since Walter Reed isolated the parasite for yellow fever. Countless people will be saved because of it.

"Tina, have you ever lived around someone who had a stroke?" He didn't wait for an answer. "It macerates the brain. People who seconds before were vibrant human beings, capable of productivity and intellectual discourse, suddenly are cut down—like that." He snapped his fingers. "Wallowing for the rest of their days in wheelchairs or in special beds. Some without bowel or bladder control." Galvin paused to allow the graphics to sink in.

"These are the victims that Lyosin is going to help—would-be cripples, thousands upon thousands. There are side effects to any drug—even aspirin can precipitate a heart attack in certain people. There's no such thing as a perfectly harmless drug—and the law doesn't exact perfection. Any war has its share of innocent casualties.

"Now your reporter writes an article bad-mouthing Lyosin," Galvin said testily. "He not only does a disservice to the people dependent upon the drug but also works a cruel hoax on these families whose children are supposedly affected. He builds up false hope that they'll win millions of dollars. Tina, you have about as much chance in this case as a can of gasoline surviving a forest fire. . . ." The words trailed off. A reluctant smile flickered across Tina's face and faded into silent understanding.

"Hey!" Galvin suddenly looked at his watch and jumped up. "It's ten to twelve. The witching hour. Let's pursue this *mañana.*

The week's been a cruncher and I'd better get back to the hotel."

It suddenly occurred to him that in addition to being exhausted, he hadn't eaten since the morning snack on the plane up from Washington. "Better still," he said, "do you know anyplace open at this improbable hour where two starving lawyers can get some eggs over easy with, maybe, home fries and Canadian bacon?"

Tina thought for a moment. "Yes," she said. "It's a lovely Portuguese café overlooking Taunton Bay—candlelight, soft music, the whole bit. We'll have *ovos fiambre*, an old Gypsy recipe from Mondego. My treat. I'll pull my car around and meet you out front. Better follow me. The kids around here are Mondegoans, and they just love silver wire hubcaps, especially after midnight."

Galvin waited in his Jaguar and listened to the cushy swish of the windshield wipers fending off the cold March rain. The street was deserted, even the 7-Eleven sign was dark and stilled. Galvin wondered why he was where he was, inventing problems for himself. If anything, he should have sent Rhys Jameson down in his place. In the firm's lineup of young talent, Jameson was just a step behind Chip Hovington and, like Chip and Stuart Trimble, was up for junior partnership at the April board meeting.

"Hello!" came a yell to his left.

Galvin cracked open his window. "I'll follow you!" he shouted.

"Okay!" Tina cried above the rain that suddenly had increased in intensity.

"Where to?" Galvin also competed with the downpour.

"My place!" she yelled, jabbing the air straight ahead with her finger, and her Datsun moved slowly ahead on Arruda Street.

◻

Saturdays at Hovington, Sturdevant, Holmes & Hall were no different than weekdays, possibly even more intense. Briefs had to be proofed and finalized, trial schedules met, diaries updated, billable hours logged, and time sheets totaled. There was a change in the clerical crew, but the main work force, especially the junior associates, beavered in their alcoves or in the library under the watchful eye of superiors, *all* hoping to impress the senior partners.

If a lawyer didn't make junior partner within six years and full partner within ten, he was headed for the door.

It was 10 A.M. when Carter Hovington was notified by Galvin's weekend secretary, Allison Crane, that U.S. Attorney Brown's office had called to schedule a 4 P.M. conference at the Federal Building.

"Okay," said Hovington, "confirm that we'll be there and make sure Mr. Galvin is notified immediately. By the way, Allison, where is he?"

"I'm not really sure." She hesitated. "The diary indicates he's staying at the Holiday Inn in Fall River on new business."

"Fall River on new business?"

"Yes, sir," Allison Crane reconfirmed. "Fall River."

"What in the hell . . ." Hovington muttered, then caught himself. "Okay, Miss Crane, thank you. Better connect me with Mr. Galvin on a two-way call."

"I tried just as soon as I heard from the U.S. Attorney's office. That was five minutes ago. He's listed in Room 340, but no one answered. I had him paged, but he wasn't in the lobby or in the dining room. He's still checked in, so I left a message to call, said it was urgent."

"Okay, try again in fifteen minutes—and put him through to me just as soon as you reach him."

◘

Cy Sturdevant came into Carter Hovington's office unannounced. He caught Hovington off guard, with his feet propped up on his leather-topped desk reading *Sports Illustrated*.

"First of all," Cyrus said, beaming, "let me congratulate you. That was one fine job you and Galvin accomplished down in D.C. Fine, Carter, simply fine. My spies tell me that Congressman Carrerras was quite impressed and that the deal's going down. Needless to say, Judge Stone is elated. He can't sing the firm's praises enough. Not only are we reentrenched with Pilgrim National, but Stone tells me the Bank of Boston and Suffolk County Savings are getting disenchanted with Auerbach and Dray. You know what that means, Carter?" They exchanged intuitive nods. It was a moment to relish.

"The other thing is minor," said Sturdevant crisply, "but it has to be dealt with. It concerns Rhys Jameson."

"Jameson? He's Galvin's protégé; his right-hand man." Hovington deliberately omitted mention of his son. "What about Jameson?"

"Well, Stanley Fairchild of Mayflower Laboratories called yesterday afternoon and gave me some information about Jameson that I just couldn't believe. It'll pose a problem for Galvin, but it's got to be dealt with forthwith. I'll give it to you straight, Carter." Sturdevant's face became deadly serious. "Jameson apparently is dividing his loyalties."

Taking on outside legal work without clearance from department heads, or receiving referrals from lawyers in other firms without full accounting to the partners, were grounds for immediate dismissal. The rule covered the senior partner right down to the greenest law clerk. It was sacrosanct.

"Yes, it seems that every Saturday and Sunday night Jameson plays drums in some dive in the North End."

"Drums?" Hovington didn't know whether to burst out laughing or to match Sturdevant's grim expression.

"That's what I said." Cyrus Sturdevant simulated a drumming motion with his wrists. "In a waterfront bistro called the Windjammer. A hangout for yuppies and cocaine snorters."

Carter Hovington suddenly realized the seriousness of the situation and the logic of the longstanding rule. Years ago Sturdevant and Hovington had agreed that recruits were to be gleaned from law schools with established reputations. Galvin was the only exception they had ever made. To lure such talent, they paid premium salaries and promised to promote from within. In return they exacted undivided loyalty. The firm came first; it was to be the associate's life and soul. There were no part-time practitioners. All business was the firm's business. Sturdevant, Hovington, Holmes & Hall was not unlike a military base. Cultural, recreational, and social activities revolved around the firm. The young associates were destined to meet the right kind of people. Even marriages were arranged.

"I'll take it up with Galvin," said Hovington. "It's not as if young Jameson was moonlighting or siphoning referrals into his pocket."

"Not far from it." Sturdevant did not agree. "First of all, it holds the firm up to ridicule. Suppose some gossip columnist wants to have a little fun at our expense—*like we don't pay our help*. . . . Our starting salary is higher than the best firms in New York City. That's why we've been attracting the top graduates from Yale, Harvard, Columbia, and Stanford for the past twenty years. Second, suppose, just suppose, the joint is raided. It's the firm's name that will draw the headlines. Can you imagine the front page of the *Herald*?" Sturdevant paused for a moment. "Where did Jameson go to school?"

"UCLA and Texas University Law School," said Hovington. "Number one in his class at both schools, and he won the National Moot Court competition his senior year. Also, plays five musical instruments." Not only was Hovington an equal partner with Sturdevant, but he was also responsible for personnel development. He had instant recall when stats were requested on any employee, be it full partner or photocopy-machine operator.

"The board meets next month," Hovington continued. "We should settle it before then. And speaking of the board meeting, Cy, you know and I know that Turner Hall has been nothing but a pain in our side for as long as we can remember. The only reason he's here is the Alicia Arnold Henderson trust. His great-grandmother was somehow related to Benedict Arnold. History and the stock market haven't been too kind to Hall. Moreover, he's effeminate. He might get nailed chasing young boys. Talk about fodder for a gossip columnist. I think it's time we asked him to relinquish his partnership. The corpus of the Henderson trust is just a few million. He can take it with him."

"I agree," said Sturdevant. "He's an embarrassment."

"I propose Hall's name be deleted from the firm's letterhead and Frank Galvin's added, and that Galvin be elevated to full partner."

"Let me think about it, Carter. You take care of the Jameson affair and let me struggle with 'Sturdevant, Hovington, Holmes and Galvin.' Quite frankly, it doesn't quite have the old ring to it. It'll take some getting used to."

Both men knew that Frank Galvin was too good to lose. Other firms had made overtures. Sturdevant and Hovington were each a year away from retirement. With Galvin aboard, their golden years were guaranteed to be golden.

◘

It was a voice from somewhere far off. Soft, lapping at him like lake water caressing the shoreline.

"Senhor Galvin."

He tried to awaken, but seemed to drift. He felt warm, too comfortable. The aroma of fresh-brewed coffee and the homey sizzle of a frying pan caused him to open his eyes and stare at the ceiling.

"Where am I?" he murmured contentedly.

"Senhor Galvin, you're here with me. Lawyer Alvarez. *Bom dia, amigo.* How are you this fine morning?"

Galvin awakened with a start. He was conscious that he had been sleeping in a chair. His shoes were off, as were his tie and jacket, his watch was gone, and he was covered by a shaggy fur-lined blanket.

"Oh my God, what time is it?"

"Ten-thirty Saturday morning." Tina Alvarez adjusted the digital clock in Galvin's direction. "You sat down here last night and you were asleep in ten seconds. Your jacket and tie are hanging up, your shoes are in the closet. Your watch and wallet are safe and your car is still outside, even with the hubcaps in place."

"What happened to the café?" Galvin shook his head and sheepishly pulled the blanket up around his chin, quickly checking to make sure his pants were still on.

"This is it." Tina smiled. "Café Antonia de Oliveria Alvarez. My place."

"What's that I smell?" Galvin inhaled deeply as he slowly came to his senses and tried to recall the evening.

"*Ovos fiambre*—my special Gypsy recipe."

"Smells like ham and eggs." Galvin grinned.

"That's what it is. *Ovos fiambre* is Portuguese for ham and eggs."

She set a large glass of fresh-squeezed orange juice and a porcelain mug filled with hot coffee on a table to his right.

"You take a shower, gringo, and I'll whip up some hot buttered rolls and banana fritters to go with the *fiambre*. You'll find everything you need—shaving equipment, towels, even a bathrobe—all laid out."

"It's as if you had an advance copy of my agenda," Galvin laughed as he headed for the bathroom.

4

Galvin gazed out the passenger window at the brackish waters of Rhode Island Sound, again wondering why he had agreed to meet the Portuguese families. Tina maneuvered her Datsun past the dockside piers and out onto the Cape Cod Expressway.

"That's 'Big Mamie' down there." She pointed to the battleship U.S.S. *Massachusetts*, its slate-gray hulk riding at quiet anchor, its turrets and sixteen-inch guns still facing aft and seaward. "Perhaps our greatest tourist attraction."

"I know. I was on it the night before we invaded Iwo." Galvin said it too quickly, with a hint of bravado.

"Wow!" Tina exclaimed. She had sensed Galvin's reticence,

now his introspection. She needed to generate enthusiasm. "That was quite a war: the 'last good war.' I forget who wrote that."

"Studs Terkel," Galvin said quietly. She had allowed him the answer.

"What was it like?" She looked out of the corner of her eye, trying to gauge the effect of her opening.

"What was it like?" Galvin frowned.

"I mean the night before going into battle. Eight thousand miles from home, from your girl. What were your thoughts?"

"Oh." Galvin waited several seconds. "Thinking about Yvonne De Carlo and June Haver and Carole Landis, I guess, and how I'd never see them again."

Despite his stab at self-effacing charm, Galvin shivered as he recalled the days before Iwo Jima. He was a tough eighteen-year-old leatherneck, six weeks out of Camp Lejeune. During the day he swapped lies with his buddies, played poker, and polished his M-1 rifle. At night he slept on deck with his pack and helmet as a pillow, gazing up at the inky firmament. Secretly he fingered his rosary beads in the pocket of his fatigues.

Only the thrum of the tires on the macadam now disturbed the silence. "We just have a few more miles," Tina said. "You'll get a chance to meet everyone. The children won't be there, but the parents can describe the problems. Hector Ramondi should be at home, though. He goes to a special school five days a week just to keep him occupied."

She turned onto a dirt lane off the main highway and headed toward a cluster of Fords, Chevys, and Plymouths parked near a weathered Cape Cod cottage.

◘

Galvin sat on a worn sofa next to Tina Alvarez, facing a group of suspicious yet hopeful faces. These were hardworking people to whom nature had dealt a cruel blow. Manuel Ramondi, mid-thirties, short, swarthy, mustachioed, a fisherman working trawlers off the Grand Banks, gone four months at a time. He chatted with Frank Galvin and his other guests as if it were a christening or some

30

other social gathering. Thalia Ramondi nodded graciously to those assembled as she served grilled sardines and Madeira Red. The others—Juan Martinez, who painted houses and drained septic tanks, his wife, Annucia, who drove a school bus, three bricklayers, a postman, a bartender, some unemployed—sat in stoic silence. All led marginal lives, a paycheck away from poverty.

They exhibited great courage. "You are blessed, with one selected by God," Father Emmanuel Correira had addressed them at Santa Lucia's School for Special Children. "Yours will be a life of special praise to the Almighty, also of great personal sacrifice." The padre reminded them that "their kingdom was not of this world."

But the numbing truth was that their kingdom *was* of this world, and they were its vassals, tethered to a life of misery and defeat. Some blamed their affliction on past transgressions. Bitterness was replacing love and helplessness was replacing hope. Now they were assembled for their final effort. They believed in Lawyer Alvarez; she was one of their own. She had promised them a way out of their bondage. She had promised them a captain. Frank Galvin. He was here.

Galvin listened carefully as each family chronicled its woes, supplemented with grim photographs of helpless offspring. He studied the bottle of Lyosin, emptying several gelusel tablets into the palm of his hand. They looked no different from ordinary cold medication. He read the packet insert. *In minutes their lytic properties enter the bloodstream, course through the vascular system to attack the sludge of arteriosclerosis, dissolve clots gathered in the blood vessels, from the aorta down to the tiniest capillaries.* It was a golden promise, worthy of Madison Avenue.

He held one of the green capsules between his thumb and forefinger, studying it as he listened to Magdalena Cabral recount her troubles. The eight mothers had many things in common. They were all fairly young, ranging in age from twenty-three to thirty-six, and they each had three or four children, one or more of whom had been born with severe birth defects. All had a family history of cardiovascular disease, all were Portuguese, and all had been on full-strength Lyosin for several years.

31

"Where did you get this prescription?" asked Galvin, still studying the capsule.

"From St. Luke's Ob/Gyn Clinic," Mrs. Cabral replied. "At their walk-in pharmacy."

"And you, Mr. Cabral, do you take Lyosin?"

There was an affirmative nod.

"How about you, Mr. Lopez?"

Again, an affirmation.

"Why are you still taking the pill, Mr. Lopez, when you believe it can do harm?"

The shrug of his shoulders had ancient origins. Lopez looked toward Tina Alvarez. They spoke together in rapid Portuguese.

"Galvin," she said. "These are simple people. The doctor says take Lyosin—it'll add years to your life—they take it. They are like children in these matters—as dependent upon the doctor as upon Father Correira."

A nice piece of sophistry. Galvin let it pass.

Galvin was about to wind things up when he glanced out the window and saw Hector Ramondi lurching between the cars parked in the gravel-and-dirt lane. It was difficult to believe he was only nine. He looked like a hulking teenager. Hector was bundled against the cold March wind, with mittens, a poplin mackinaw, corduroy trousers tucked into rubber galoshes. His knitted woolen cap was tugged down over his ears. Galvin noticed three older youngsters kicking a soccer ball on the muddy front yard. He assumed they were the Ramondis' other children.

He tried to listen to the discussion as he gazed out of the window at the kids. Hector Ramondi sat down in the mud and watched the soccer ball bounce off several cars and roll to his feet. He picked himself up, tried to kick the ball, missed and landed on his back, splattering in the mud—much to the delight of the other children, who pointed and laughed, and the exasperation of Thalia Ramondi, who had the same view as Galvin.

"It's getting late," Galvin said, nodding to the group. He picked up the bottle of Lyosin and put it in his suit coat pocket—a symbolic gesture, like a detective preserving a crucial piece of evidence. "Let me be candid with you." He began as if he were delivering a summation to a jury. "You wouldn't expect anything less from me or from Miss Alvarez. It would be next to impossible to prove Lyosin was the cause of your children's problems. The drug has FDA approval and is prescribed by your physicians. Most of you are still taking it! Your lawyer, Miss Alvarez"—he nodded toward her—"has done a remarkable job at her own expense to investigate your claims to see if you *had* a feasible case."

He looked into their open faces and could read fear and defeat. He had addressed many juries and was a master at the art of persuasion. This jury needed no convincing. He was backing away and they knew it.

He glanced out of the window again. Hector Ramondi was smiling at him. He was caked with mud, sitting on the cold ground, unconcerned about his present predicament or future fate. Galvin smiled back. Eventually, Hector would be stashed away somewhere. Galvin tried to shrug it off. He gathered his papers and notebooks.

"I'll tell you what I'll do," he said, hesitation creeping into his voice. "I'll study all this data over the weekend. I promise you. And I'll get back to Miss Alvarez by Monday. I'll take everything under advisement."

It was a legal cliché. But it ensured that he would feel less guilty on the ride home.

◘

There was one last stop. Galvin parked his Jaguar in front of the National Park pier. The attendant told him that visiting hours were over, but if he just wanted to peek at the main deck, he could have a few minutes.

Galvin stood on the starboard side beneath the turret guns and saw the sun die somewhere out beyond the Sound. He leaned over the teak rail and watched a shrimp trawler making its way toward Sakonney Point, its purple stern light glowing eerily in the gathering dusk.

Alone now, he was lost in the evocative twilight of forty-odd years. Events came flooding back. He was Marine Corporal Frank

Galvin, a rawboned eighteen-year-old who could kill a man with his bare hands. He had stood on this very deck, fingered the same railing as he had scanned the coral puffs on the horizon for signs of Japanese kamikazes.

They would hit the beaches the next day on a small spit of sand with a volcanic rampart called Suribachi. He shuddered now as he recalled running up the debris-strewn shoreline toward the craggy escarpment protecting the enemy lines. He had long blocked from memory the young Japanese soldier, barely sixteen, head shaved, making his way out of a bunker, a white flag tied to his cartridge belt, hands aloft. It was too late. Galvin blazed away. In the heat of battle, carnage was erupting everywhere and his buddies were falling. He was about to race on. The lust of the kill was upon him. Then he heard a groan. For a moment he wavered. He put down his M-1 rifle, cupped the boy's head in his arm, and as blood gushed from abdominal wounds, he gave him a drink from his canteen.

"Naze," the Japanese soldier moaned. Then his eyes rolled back and he died.

Galvin never talked about it. Others felt the war held a special romance and wore their exploits as ribbons and medals on festive occasions. Galvin tossed all his mementos in a box, never to be seen again by anyone. And only a short time ago, while representing a Japanese manufacturer, did he learn the meaning of the word *naze.*

"It means 'why,' " said the client, wondering what was behind the question.

Galvin didn't explain.

◘

He had checked out of the Holiday Inn and headed along the Fall River Turnpike toward Boston. There had been three urgent messages from his office. He'd tend to those en route. He called Tina's office but got her answering service.

"This is Frank Galvin." She would hear the tape later. "Tell your clients I'll take the case. I'll discuss it with the firm Monday and get approval. Just a formality. Start drafting the complaint. I'll send Rhys Jameson, one of my best men, down Tuesday to check it and get the litigation started. And, Tina, never be a paper pusher for the ruling class. Always keep that in mind. Over and out."

Galvin replaced the cellular phone and smiled to himself. A new and heady energy seemed to envelop him, almost erotically. He whizzed past several cars, the speedometer edging eighty-five before he eased down.

Ahead the orange neon of a Howard Johnson's came into view. He still had a two-hour drive to Boston. But first, he'd stop for some *ovos fiambre*.

5

Galvin was ten minutes late for the business brunch at the Ritz Carlton. It was more than just a Sunday breakfast. For Carter Hovington, Cyrus Sturdevant, and selected partners, it was a pious ritual, carefully monitored by the Brahmin nobility who sipped Bloody Marys at nearby tables and exchanged polite nods. Which partner, associate, client, or newsworthy figure made up the mid-morning ensemble also caught the eye of various members of the media, sprinkled strategically throughout the posh dining room.

At the lobby newsstand, Galvin purchased some mints, reserved the *New York Times*, and, with a twenty-dollar bill curled discreetly in his hand, headed for Pierre, the tuxedoed maître d'.

"Monsieur Galvin, bonjour!" greeted Pierre. He helped Galvin out of his topcoat with all the familiarity of a family butler, quickly pocketing the tip with seasoned dexterity. "Right this way," he said, lapsing into perfect English. "Mr. Hovington is waiting." He picked up an oversized velvet-backed menu, snapped his fingers at two waiters in red waistcoats, and paraded across the rich burgundy carpeting.

Galvin nodded to several of the guests. Old money, he thought—handsome sculptured men on the silver-haired side of middle age, elegant women with taut bronzed skin. There were no Thalia Ramondis or Magdalena Cabrals to be found here. They'd never make it past the kitchen.

They eyed him carefully, the men a little envious, the women from an intrigued distance. Galvin's entrance never went unnoticed. He had an air of risk and adventure about him. He'd been born on the wrong side of respectability and had the reputation of the rebel. But he was their rebel. That made the difference.

"Sit down, Galvin," Carter said when Galvin reached the table. He glanced from the menu to his watch. Tardiness was a fault seldom forgiven, even in himself. "Only you and me today. Have a few matters strictly between us."

Galvin nodded deferentially.

"The usual, Galvin?" Hovington returned to the menu.

"Yes, Carter, the usual." Galvin looked around. Old World strains from a cello and violin mingled with subdued laughter and the clink of crystal. Waiters moved with the silence and grace of underwater swimmers, lighting cigarettes, dispensing rolls and butter, chilling and pouring the Château Margaux.

As if by magic, Pierre appeared. Carter Hovington tolled the order. No notepad was needed.

"Orange juice and a croissant for Mr. Galvin. I'll take iced cantaloupe, eggs Benedict, unbuttered toast, and bring a pot of coffee."

With a continental click of his heels, and a "Bon appétit," Pierre reached for the menu, placed it under his arm like a swagger stick, and strode off toward his lectern.

A law firm, particularly one as highly successful as Hovington, Sturdevant, Holmes & Hall, is essentially a dictatorship. There are no stockholders, voting rights, options, or proxies. It was Carter Hovington's firm—no one ever doubted that, not even Cyrus Sturdevant. Like most dictators, Carter Hovington was predictable,

36

particularly to Galvin. And Galvin was prepared for Hovington's breakfast agenda—the gruff compliment on the Judge Stone case, the admonition that final disposition was still unsettled, the mild chiding on his lack of communication over the weekend, especially the missed appointment with U.S. Attorney Brown, rescheduled for 8 A.M. Monday. All of these Galvin anticipated and handled with tact. There were few surprises.

Hovington patted his lips with the white linen napkin. As if on cue, the waiter was there to pour coffee from the silver service and freshen the Perriers with ice and limes.

"There's a few further items I'd like to discuss, Galvin. One might seem unimportant, but upon reflection it concerns the very lifeblood of the firm." Hovington selected a cigarette from a silver monogrammed case, tapped it several times, then snapped the case shut.

"How is young Jameson doing?" Hovington asked, lighting his cigarette.

"Jameson?" Galvin leaned toward Hovington. "Jameson is one of the finest lawyers I've ever worked with. With Chip and Jameson on the roster, I can even go to Saturday football games. What about him?"

"You know he's West Coast?"

"Wouldn't bother me if he were Appalachia. He's got the mind of a computer, with energy to burn. Carter, at eighty thousand a year, he's a steal. He could return to Silicon Valley tomorrow and be general counsel for any number of firms for six figures, with all the perks thrown in."

"I'm well aware of his legal ability, Galvin." Carter didn't want to be sidetracked. "But what do you know about Jameson's outside activities? I mean how he spends his leisure time?"

"Leisure time? Are you kidding, Carter? He works around the clock. I don't even think he has a girlfriend."

"Well, when he gets time off, does he sail, play tennis, polo? Things like that?"

"He gets two weeks' vacation a year," Galvin said. "He took Christmas off and New Year's. He's the firm's representative for the United Fund, has an apartment in Back Bay, and plays softball with some townies." Galvin knew Hovington was concerned about something other than the professional merit and private pastimes of his first assistant.

"Galvin, you might think what I'm about to say is petty—*I* thought so when Cy first told me about it. I've checked it out. It's true."

Galvin waited.

"Rhys Jameson plays *drums* in some rock dive on the waterfront every Saturday and Sunday night, has been doing it for the past six months."

"You're kidding me." Galvin held his napkin to his mouth to keep from bursting into uncontrollable laughter.

"No, I'm dead serious, Galvin."

"Never would have guessed it," Galvin said. "Jesus, Carter, that kid has more talent than I ever imagined."

"Galvin, I think you've missed the point."

"No, I don't think so, Carter." Galvin was never a yes man. "You want me to tell Jameson to stop playing, right?"

"Not exactly." Carter knew it was a delicate situation. "He also plays wind instruments. Look, he can play those in his apartment to his heart's content. But certain protocol, Galvin, must be observed. We can't have one of our associates standing on a street corner tooting a saxophone."

In a moment it was over. Galvin quickly assessed Hovington's position. Protracted discussion would be futile.

"I'll speak to him," Galvin said.

"Fine." Hovington ground his cigarette into a silver tray. "He's a bright lad with a great future in the firm. Tell him that comes from me."

The cellist and violinist were playing *Intermezzo*, and the prattle and laughter had picked up along with the refills of Bloody Marys and Dom Perignon. Galvin and Hovington ate in sedate silence for several minutes.

Feeling that the Jameson matter had been put to rest, Hovington moved to a new subject.

"What was so important Friday night and Saturday that you kept everyone in the dark as to your whereabouts?" Hovington reached for his wheat toast.

"A new matter, Carter. Tell me, how much *pro bono* work does the firm do, say on an annual basis?"

"*Pro bono?*"

"Yes. Free legal work. Counseling clients without remuneration."

Carter looked at Galvin. "Are you serious?"

"Carter, our litigation department earned fees totaling sixty-eight million dollars last year; just my department alone. Aside from loaning out Rhys Jameson to the United Fund and Chip to the Mayor's Committee on Public Justice, I can't say we logged *one* billable hour for an indigent client."

"Look," Hovington said defensively, "we encourage all our lawyers to engage in community activities."

"Well, I want us to take on a case, Carter. It'll need a good slice of time and a great deal of seed money. I'm proposing it tomorrow afternoon to our New Business Committee and I want your endorsement."

"Galvin, I'm sure whatever it is, you have the firm's welfare at heart. You have my unqualified backing, you know that. You recommend it, the committee will go along—especially after your coup with Carrerras and Judge Stone."

Hovington paused and glanced from side to side. And then he caught Galvin completely by surprise.

"As of May first, you will become a *full* partner and the firm's name will be changed to Hovington, Sturdevant, Holmes and Galvin."

Galvin sat in stunned silence. "But Hall?" he said.

"Turner Hall's resigning next week and taking the Alicia Arnold Henderson trust with him. Everything's been worked out. It's for the good of the firm."

Hovington patted his lips once again with the linen napkin. "Galvin, we've been together for five years and I've seen what you can do. You took litigation, a dying department, and infused it with new life. Your presence has taken a stodgy old-line firm and thrust it into the twenty-first century. Oh, we all would have made a generous living administering estates and catering to our banking clientele, but look at the accounts you've generated."

Galvin smoothed the tablecloth in front of him.

"Cy and I discussed this at length last night. Cy retires in six months and I'm not getting any younger. Galvin, I'm stepping down in January. Madge and I are going on a world cruise and"—Carter glanced at his watch—"you, Francis Xavier Galvin, are going to run the firm. Cy and I will draw up certain agreements.

"One thing Cy and I know, Galvin," Hovington went on, his eyes misted, "is that you have integrity. I always thought loyalty beat integrity—but you have both. The firm, Galvin, is *yours*." He rolled his hands outward.

Galvin watched Hovington make his exit, then stared out the arched window at the frog pond in the Public Garden. The tones of early spring were returning to the pink laurel and dogwood lacing the Common, and the flower stalls along Arlington Street were alive with vibrant hues. The events of the week had been tumultuous. He was tempted to order a drink.

"Leon," he said to a waiter, "give me a plain soda."

"With lime, monsieur?"

"With lime," said Galvin.

6

Rainmakers" are guaranteed longevity in any law firm. Hovington, Sturdevant, Holmes & Hall was the exception. Carter Hovington felt that the firm had all the business it could handle. Associates were discouraged from attracting new clients. High-tech industries, media communication companies, foreign and domestic corporations, and other gilded clienteles sought the firm because it provided the best legal counseling that money could buy. New accounts, occasionally, were generated by associates. This was inevitable. One didn't graduate from the Choate School, Princeton, and Harvard Law without connections. But new business belonged to the firm; the credit to its procreator was nominal.

Carter Hovington and Cy Sturdevant were unimpressed with someone claiming political influence or touting "courtroom connections." "Knowing the 'right people' is transitory at best," as Hovington put it succinctly at the annual meeting. "A law practice dependent on such an approach is unlikely to retain permanence. A case is won on the merits, not because the pleader curries favor with a friendly judge. One who boasts judicial influence oversells his wares."

Yet new business came in daily and had to be carefully computerized and channeled into proper categories of expertise, be it taxation, corporate mergers, or litigation.

The New Business Committee was made up of the six senior partners: Ian Campion, Charley Joiner, Calvin Williams, Reed Smythe, Cyrus Sturdevant, and Carter Hovington.

At exactly 4 P.M., the heavy oak door to the partners' room eased open, like that of a bank vault, and Carter Hovington, trailed by the five partners, all impeccably dressed in dark blue or pinstripe gray, made their entrance. This was the inner sanctum, where office policy, management and legal issues, and the evaluation of associates were decided, often quite summarily.

The scenic panorama of Boston Harbor didn't distract from the business at hand. The oval-shaped room was decorated in heavy baroque, carpeted with the finest Orientals, and completely insulated from exterior sounds. A fire crackled in the Italian marble fireplace, and Jennings, the black attendant, stood at the portable table waiting to pour tea or coffee from the silver service. A large portrait of Oliver Wendell Holmes, robed in judicial black, peered down with benign approval upon his successors.

Galvin entered at exactly four-ten. If the senior partners were envious of Galvin's meteoric rise, pettiness evaporated when they thought of their burgeoning portfolios. To the six at the top of the pyramid, their million-dollar salaries were assured.

41

"The formula is quite simple," Hovington had once explained to Galvin. "Pay associates eighty dollars an hour and bill the clients three hundred. The more associates, the more billable hours. It's short division. We're not running a mom-and-pop law firm. Our bills have to be extravagant. The client expects it."

Galvin's entrance was always electric. There was a forward lean to his stride, a driven quality to his movement. "Gentlemen," he acknowledged, nodding to the seated partners. They returned his welcome. He took a plush swivel chair at the far end of the room. The Wedgwood cups had been cleared, and Jennings discreetly retired.

Carter Hovington rose from his position at the head of the polished rosewood table. It glistened with mirror brilliance, reflecting the crystal chandelier and the oyster-hued scroll of the ceiling.

"Gentlemen," he said in an expansive tone, "you all know that Frank Galvin and I met with United States Attorney Roosevelt Brown this morning. Well, the government is accepting the plea of our client, Pilgrim National Bank and Judge Webster Stone, to a *misdemeanor*, like, uh, spitting on the sidewalk." There was instant laughter. "And, gentlemen"—Hovington held up his hand to subdue the humor—"the firm's fee is one-point-four million dollars. Our account was credited at twelve-oh-one this afternoon." He glanced at his watch.

The partners rose in unison and applauded. Hovington extended both arms, palms up, toward Frank Galvin before waving them quiet.

"Now," he said pleasantly, "I want you to listen to Mr. Galvin as he proposes a new piece of business. You all know the success we've enjoyed because of Frank Galvin. Please give your undivided attention."

Galvin stood up, embarrassed, and surveyed the partners. "Many thanks for the accolades," he began. "I couldn't have accomplished what we did without the approbation of all of you and the combined confidence you place in my staff. Actually, the compliment should be theirs. I'll make sure it's extended.

"What I'm proposing is a little unusual." He paused. "Eight families in southeastern Massachusetts have been afflicted with children born with deformities that may well be attributable to the drug Lyosin."

"Wait a minute," Reed Smythe broke in. "Are you proposing that somehow the firm become engaged in a lawsuit over Lyosin?"

"That's exactly what I'm proposing." Galvin tried not to show his annoyance at the interruption.

"Well, apart from the probability that everyone in this room," continued Smith, "perhaps even you, Mr. Galvin, takes Lyosin, *our* Washington office represents Gammett Industries, the distributor of Lyosin. As a matter of fact, it was Kyle Trenton who was the driving force behind FDA approval."

It came as a complete surprise. He should have checked it out. He also realized the futility of further discussion. *Conflict of interest.* The bane of every law firm.

"Well, this is why we have a New Business Committee," Hovington injected quickly. "I'm sorry I didn't know this in advance. If we represent a client, even remotely, we sure in hell can't take a case against it."

Galvin remained standing. This was not a defeat. He appreciated the firm's position. He suddenly felt sorry for Tina Alvarez and the Ramondi family. But a rule was a rule. Pulling out would be embarrassing, but even Tina Alvarez would understand. Suddenly he thought of Moe Katz, his old mentor. Sure, Moe would help. He was well on his way to recovery after a severe stroke. This would be right up Moe's alley.

□

Rhys Jameson entered Galvin's office shortly after the evening clerical crew had changed its roster. Galvin was signing checks and Courtney Evans waited by his desk so she could make the 9 P.M. mail.

"Come in, Rhys." Galvin gestured toward a seat. Courtney Evans reminded Galvin that he and Hovington had to be at Federal Court at ten the next morning for final disposition in the Pilgrim National case. A press conference was scheduled at the Parker House for eleven. At noon he and Chip Hovington were to fly to

New York City to meet with lawyers from Sterling & Moss on the Rhyolite Corporation merger. The takeover threatened to be hostile. A fight loomed—for each side, a law firm's dream.

For Galvin, the next day was cut out. As was the present evening. He'd be home, perhaps, by midnight.

"Rhys." Galvin tried to make his assistant feel comfortable. "We've been on the run so much around here, I don't think we've ever had a chance to rap. Like a Coke or a coffee?"

"No thanks, Mr. Galvin. I'm already over-coffeed."

Galvin moved from behind his desk and sat on the edge of it.

"Rhys," he said, "how did you happen into the law? Your background is science. Number one at UCLA. I would have expected you to have gone into that field somewhere in California."

"I thought so too, Mr. Galvin, but the sciences just didn't grab me. My dad was a scientist of sorts. Into aerodynamics. Worked for Hughes Aircraft in Culver City. He died in '73, and Mom worked at the checkout counter at Safeway to make sure I got to college."

"I understand you play several musical instruments." Galvin worked into it slowly.

"Well, I almost didn't go to college. In my third year of high school I got bitten by the music bug. Became an obsession. Ricky Nelson had his own group, and I used to sub for his drummer. Boy, did I get wrapped up. Learned guitar, piano, several wind instruments."

"I understand you play with a rock group here in Boston," said Galvin.

"The Beacon Hillers," Rhys said enthusiastically. "Four guys— one's an M.D., an orthopedic resident at Beth Israel, plus there's a stockbroker and two lawyers. The lead singer—she's easy on the eyes—goes to Harvard Med."

"Quite a professional cross section," Galvin remarked.

"We got together six months ago. Started out as jam sessions. Now we're booked at a place called the Windjammer on weekends. I love it. As they say around here, Mr. Galvin—it's my retreat, my Walden Pond."

"That's what I want to talk to you about." Galvin paused.

"You know, Rhys, this is difficult for me to say—but I have to say it. I might even be tempted to do the same thing you do, believe me, if I could play an instrument. But you've got to recognize the position that you may find yourself—and ultimately the firm—in. I'm asking you to confine your playing strictly to the amateur ranks. I don't want to lose you, Rhys, but you have to quit your present arrangement. It's firm policy, and even though I don't agree with it, I must respect it."

Rhys Jameson sat stunned for several moments. The directive was like a blow to the solar plexus. He admired Frank Galvin and he loved the challenges and the faith that Galvin had placed in him. It was because of Frank Galvin that he stayed with the firm.

"Mr. Galvin," he stammered "what you're asking me to do is to give up being an individual, to give up a part of myself. Look," he said, anger creeping into his voice, "I've worked my butt off for this firm. They pay me eighty thousand, and I logged nine hundred sixty-seven thousand in billable hours last year. Me alone. That's a hell of a lot of productivity. I like it here. I like Boston. Most of all, Mr. Galvin, I like you. I'd follow you to hell and back. You know that. But the *firm* doesn't own my soul. It never will."

Galvin wondered if there was a way out of this "all or nothing" directive, some compromise.

"Rhys," he said slowly. "Let me tell you a story. Happens to be true. All I ask is that you listen carefully before you make any decisions. I can't recall ever telling this to anyone."

Galvin walked toward a small framed photograph hanging incongruously among Oriental paintings and silk scrolls. It was his old Marine Corps squad from Camp Lejeune—kids from Ohio, New Mexico, Georgia; Oakies and Arkies. They were young—eighteen or nineteen—with crew cuts, brandishing carbines and 45s and macho death-defying grins, hands on hips, helmet liners tilted back on their heads.

"This is my old World War Two outfit," he said, examining the faded photograph. "We were pinned down on Red Beach at Iwo Jima for two days. Nothing was moving. I was petrified. I carried a Browning automatic rifle. Do you know the life expectancy of the guy lugging the BAR?" Galvin didn't wait for an answer. "I knew

I wasn't going to make it. The Jap machine guns had us in the cross hairs. We burrowed into the sand like moles, deep as we could get. Suddenly the lieutenant gives the order to move out. He was a tall lanky kid. Played football at Texas Christian.''

Galvin glanced over his shoulder at Jameson.

"Well, I knew, and the squad knew, and even the lieutenant knew that it was a goddammed ridiculous order. We were sitting ducks. We were on a ridge about a mile up the beach. I looked back. We were landing tanks and artillery and half tracks.

" 'Lieutenant, this is crazy!' I yelled. 'We need support. Take a peek behind you. In an hour those Jap guns will be cleared.'

"He looked at me. I can still see the freckles across his pug nose, his gray smokey eyes. He was chewing a chunk of tobacco and spit it at least five feet. It was his last act of disdain. He confronted death and spit in its face. Hell, he was no more than a year or two older than me. But he had brass balls. I'll never forget his words.

" 'Corporal,' he said in his slow Texas drawl, 'when I give the signal, we move out. And we keep movin' and shootin' until those fuckin' mothers out there are silent. Understand? Now, you fuckin' no-good assholes,' he shouted, 'let's blast em! *Now!* ' ''

Galvin was getting choked up. He turned from the photograph and walked slowly back to where Rhys Jameson was sitting.

"The lieutenant was the first to go," Galvin said huskily. "He was right in front of me. Had his face blown away. We all hit the sand. But I was in command now. I gave the order to move out—language a little *stronger* than the lieutenant's. We lost half the squad that day. They're still buried at Red Beach." Galvin's eyes misted. "But we took our objective. It took me forty years to come to grips with it.

"I don't know if I'm making myself clear, Rhys?" Galvin said it half-apologetically.

"Mr. Galvin," Rhys said quietly. "I understand your position and that of the firm perfectly. An order is an order. My resignation will be on your desk in the morning."

Somehow Galvin knew this would be Rhys Jameson's decision.

"You know, Rhys," Galvin said, extending his hand, "I wish you luck. You'd have made one hell of a Marine."

After Rhys left, Galvin sat at his desk for several minutes. It had not been a good day. Losing a superb lawyer over a stupid rule was exasperating. Yet he knew it was too late to salvage Rhys Jameson.

He walked to the window. Below, the city twinkled with life. He watched the late-night commuters, like phosphorescent insects, threading their way to the north and south shores. Across the Charles River basin the rigging of "Old Ironsides," the U.S.S. *Constitution*, was decked in streamers of white light. He wondered about the lieutenant, about his old squad, about the young Japanese soldier. Little beads of sweat stippled his forehead.

"Mr. Galvin." Courtney Evans's voice interrupted the silence. "Miss Alvarez on line three."

He reached for the phone, then hesitated. "Tell her I've gone," he said into the intercom. "Say—I'll call her first thing in the morning."

He went to his office washroom, rinsed his face and hands, patted them with paper toweling, looked in the mirror, and straightened his tie. He was feeling a little unsure of himself. Suddenly he felt alone. "Moe Katz," he said to his reflection. "Moe will know what to do."

7

Galvin checked with Moe's wife, Miriam, on the car telephone.

"My God, Galvin!" she shrieked. "I'll get the knishes and schnapps and whip up your favorite corned beef on rye. Will Moe ever be glad to see you."

Despite the late hour, Miriam Katz greeted Galvin at the door of their modest home with warmth and goodwill. She kissed Galvin, tears in her eyes, then stood back and grasped his hands. "Let me look at you," she cried like the good Jewish mother she was. "My, don't we look handsome—and look at those threads!" She fingered the rich texture of his cashmere coat. "I told Moe, just today, Galvin. 'Moe,' I said, 'I have this strange feeling that Galvin is going to drop by.' "

It was a kind lie, one that Miriam allowed Galvin to hide behind.

"For you, my lovely darlin'." Galvin produced a dozen yellow roses he had bought at the all-night florist in the Copley Shopping Mall.

"Oh, I love yellow roses." Miriam smelled them deeply. "I used to tell Moe not to waste money on fresh flowers—they'd be dead in a few days. I told him to buy silk ones at Bloomingdale's. But you know, Galvin, I love the fragrance of roses."

"Galvin, my boy," came a raspy voice from the living room. "Miriam, take Galvin's coat and get the knishes. Come in! Come in!"

◘

They sat in silence. In the half-closed eyes of memory, the reminiscences were played out. Galvin sometimes saw his ex-wife. His four grown children were scattered. Moe's daughter, Rhonda, who years ago had had a wild crush on Galvin, was married to a doctor in New York—an ob-gyn. She had two children—one a boy named *Francis*. Francis Leventhal.

Moe slumped in his wheelchair, looking old and crinkled. He was positioned near the fireplace, where tongues of flame licked at pressed-wood logs, the glow casting eerie shadows about the room. Moe's balding pate glistened in the reflected light, and his eyes were like two black jelly beans encased in jars behind his thick-lensed glasses. Moe had never looked young for as long as Galvin could remember—and that went back thirty years. Moe had to be in his eighties, but despite his age and the ravages of a stroke, his mind had never lost its acuity, nor his spirit its zest. Now, as always, he was a man without artifice. Integrity and honor were as important to him as his name. To Moe Katz, the law was religion, the courtroom a temple. And he had schooled Galvin in these principles, taking him under his forensic wing, teaching him the basics of trial technique, the fine art of persuading a jury, and the more pragmatic art of survival in a business dominated by the Brahmin aristocracy. You've got to ally yourself with the client, Moe had counseled, relive his plights and ordinary ambitions, his hurts and anguish. Only then can you become the true advocate.

"Now, Galvin." Moe clapped, breaking the awkward silence. "I know you've given up the hard stuff, but I've got some soda and bitters. And, Miriam!" he yelled to his wife. "How's the corned beef coming? Remember when we were trying the St. Catherine Laboure case? Corned beef on rye. We lived on it."

Moe wheeled toward a book-lined wall, pushed a button, and a tier of buff-colored law books pivoted on their shelves. The result was an instant bar. Moe hummed as he cracked the ice, pouring a healthy Scotch for himself, lacing Galvin's soda with a twist of lime. Miriam served the sandwiches and condiments, and put some quiet music on the stereo, something from Mendelssohn. Moe closed his eyes and breathed a contented sigh.

"L'Chaim." Moe's bony fingers grasped the glass. He placed it symbolically on his breast, then raised it in a reverential toast. It was Moe's tribute to his alter ego, the son he yearned for but never had.

"L'Chaim. My dear friend," Galvin said quietly.

They sipped their drinks. A benedictive smile softened Moe's craggy face, and his jelly bean eyes danced with contentment. The fire had died and the red-chalky glow of the embers signaled a tranquil end to a frayed day.

"Moe, if you wanted to refer an impossible, way-out case," Galvin said, relaxing in the comfortable stillness, "I mean to someone with balls, someone who wouldn't quit, who comes to mind?"

"How 'way out'?" Moe sensed something coming.

"Pretty far," Galvin said. "A product liability case against an industrial giant, a foreign corporation with unimaginable clout and money to burn."

"Trying to prove someone's got lung cancer from whacking Marlboros for forty years?" asked Moe.

"Something like that."

"Try Mel Belli in San Francisco. I understand he's suing the hell out of Union Carbide for the Bhopal disaster in India."

"Well, Moe," Galvin said, "in it's own little way, this is just such a disaster. It involves a pharmaceutical firm that manufactures a drug that might cause birth defects."

"That's expensive litigation," said Moe. "I sued Baer, Froelich ten years ago, trying to prove that their birth control pill caused a cerebral thrombosis and brain damage in a thirty-seven-year-old housewife."

"I remember," said Galvin. "I watched you try it. You damn near pulled it off."

" 'Damn near' isn't good enough in this business, Galvin. Second place only counts at the racetrack. You either win or you don't eat."

"I recall the case well, Moe. We were on the outs then, you and me. I had left to form my own firm. You were outgunned in that case, and outmaneuvered," Galvin continued, "but you still did a masterful job."

"C'mon, Galvin." Moe shook his head. "I came up bubkis. Spent thirty thousand of my own money. Jeeze, I died when the jury came back for the defendant. I looked at that poor woman. In a wheelchair, couldn't talk. The jury turned her out. I broke down and cried."

"State of the art. That's what beat you, Moe."

"State of the art, my ass. Baer knew that giving this pill to women over thirty-five was a death warrant. I just couldn't prove it. Bastards. And the judge sided with them every step of the way."

"I watched it." It was Galvin's turn to shake his head.

"Judge Kelleher did me in. I was the little Jew boy who took on these impossible cases—who didn't deserve to win." Moe's eyes glistened, his voice husky with emotion.

"I remember," Galvin said.

"Moe." Galvin reached over and touched both his hands. "How would you like to take on one last case? I mean one of substance."

"Me?" Moe laughed, jiggled the ice cubes, and took another drink of Scotch. "You must be on the sauce again. I'm too old for one last big case, Galvin. These days I just like to putter. What about you?" he offered. "Or do those Ivy League cohorts of yours detect a strange whiff in the air whenever the word *plaintiff* is mentioned? I wondered why they always walked downwind with their noses in the air."

"Moe, I've been over the case. It's a long shot. But it's there. It needs development. Perseverance. Your expertise. Eight Portuguese families have children born with severe deformities. As bad as thalidomide."

"Thalidomide? Hell, that never got FDA approval."

"Came within an ace," said Galvin. "Merril-Richardson manufactured it under the trade name of Devadon. It was being ramrodded through for FDA approval when the morbidity findings in Europe started erupting."

"Well, why can't you and your pals with the three last names take it on?"

"I said I would, then just today I learned that somehow our firm has a connection with the manufacturer. It's a classical conflict of interest."

"Sounds like a cop-out," Moe said. "Where's the case, anyhow?"

"Fall River."

"Fall River? That's the end of the earth. Next you'll tell me that the statute of limitations runs out in a week."

"No. It runs out tomorrow."

"Tomorrow! I knew I shouldn't have had Miriam answer the door."

Galvin said nothing.

"What's the drug?" Moe asked.

"Lyosin."

"Lyosin. For Christ's sake, Galvin, that's the drug that pulled me through, dissolved the sludge in my arteries. I'm on it three times a day."

"Well," Galvin sighed, "who else would you recommend? Do

you think Ed Concannon over at Powers and Cross or Charley McGlaughlin might take the case on? Charley hasn't had a hit in years."

"I didn't say," Moe replied gruffly, "that I wouldn't take the case on. Give me the number of the *goy* I'm supposed to call."

8

Julie Hedren placed the call to Tina Alvarez and lingered long enough to monitor Tina's opening greeting.

"Galvin," came an exuberant voice, "am I ever glad you called. Tried to reach you several times last night." Hedren punched the OFF button.

"I did as instructed, Professor. Stayed up all night and finished the legal complaint. If I say so myself, the counts against Gammett Industries and Universal Multi-Tech are textbook perfect. Also, sued St. Luke's Clinic and Fernandez Pharmacy—negligence, strict liability, breach of warranty, gross negligence, wanton and reckless conduct, punitive damages. The legal beagles at Gammett and Universal will start scurrying."

"Look, Tina." Galvin tried to interrupt. "I've got to tell you something." He tried to marshal his thoughts, unconsciously running his index finger along the inside of his shirt collar. "I can't take this case!" he finally blurted out.

He was met with stony silence.

"Listen, Tina, we somehow represent Gammett and Universal. Ethically, we just can't get involved. Conflict of interest."

Several seconds passed.

There was a weak, deflated response. "Thank you, Mr. Galvin, for your kindness. I'll handle it myself." The "good-bye" trailed off like a regret.

Galvin stared at the receiver, then shrugged.

He pressed the receptionist page button. "Miss Hedren, tell Mr. Hovington, Jr., we'll meet in the lobby in ten minutes to catch the noon shuttle to New York."

As Galvin gathered his notes for the encounter with the Sterling & Moss litigators in Manhattan, he thought about Tina Alvarez. And on the noon shuttle, as he tried to organize his game plan with Chip Hovington, he thought about her again. Later, as the cab they'd taken from LaGuardia inched its way through traffic toward Park Avenue, he could see a resemblance to Tina in some of the young professionals striding smartly along East 63rd Street.

It wasn't until he and Chip were ushered into the glass-and-bronze conference room of Sterling & Moss and formally introduced to their legal opponents that Galvin shrugged off his lethargy. Their adversary's trial team sat at parade-rest, barricaded behind stacks of imposing documents, their eyes quickly appraising Galvin and Chip as they entered.

"Mr. Galvin." A tall, square-shouldered figure stepped forward. He was Hollywood handsome—dark, well-groomed hair, tan, and, like Galvin, with penetrating ice-blue eyes. He extended his hand and forced a tight smile, causing his black mustache to curl slightly upward. "Welcome to Sterling and Moss. Hope we can get together." It was a crisp, incisive, no-nonsense greeting.

Galvin had book on his opponent. Ted King was Sterling & Moss's top litigator and one of New York City's most successful trial lawyers. And he looked it; he radiated energy and confidence, held his chin slightly ajut, dressed expensively. The skull-and-crossbone cuff links on his Turnbull & Asser shirt reflected the afternoon sun.

Galvin shook hands with professional distance. He recalled when Ted King's name had been Thadeus Kinkowski—an All-East linebacker in his collegiate days at Penn State. King also had an impressive war record. A much-decorated Green Beret captain in Vietnam, he still retained the look and bearing of the jungle mercenary to whom the hunt was perhaps more important than the kill. He ran his litigation team as if they were on night patrol in the Mekong Delta. He would be tough to ambush.

◘

The Clerk of Court, Emmanuel Taveras, studied Tina Alvarez's legal complaint with a trained eye. He whistled softly to himself and nodded affirmations as he scrutinized the thirty-six-page document for even the slightest imperfection.

He glanced at the old Seth-Thomas clock that ticked away on the municipal gray-green wall above his rolltop desk. "You just beat the statute of limitations on some of these claims," he said. He adjusted the date stamp and banged the papers into the court docket.

"That'll be, let's see, four defendants, eight plaintiffs, twelve co-plaintiffs, six hundred and eighty dollars in filing fees, Tina. I'd say you've got your work cut out. We've never had such a lawsuit here in Fall River as long as I've been Clerk, and that goes back forty years. I'll have the Bristol County Sheriff's Office serve the complaints on St. Luke's and Fernandez tomorrow, but you'll have to serve legal process on Gammett Industries at their principal place of business in Patterson Heights, New Jersey. Universal may be a problem."

"I know," sighed Tina as she wrote out a check for the filing fee. "Universal is a Dutch-English corporation with offices in London and in Amsterdam. Getting jurisdiction over them here in our little corner of the world, as you say, may be a real problem. They manufacture Lyosin, but they'll probably say they conduct no business in Massachusetts and their responsibility ends at the Southampton docks. I might spend my legal lifetime on this case, Manny."

"And your dowry." He smiled as he stamped the court's endorsement on the back of her check.

Tina had to pass through the main courtroom on her way from the clerk's office. It was late afternoon, and shafts of sunlight filtered through the dusty arched windows above the empty jury box. She walked in front of the judge's bench, pausing for a moment at the jury rail. The deserted courtroom added to her sense of loneliness. She fingered the walnut lacquered rail, pitted with age, and wondered about the famous lawyers who had argued here—Louis Brandeis, Oliver Wendell Holmes—and of the jurors of long ago who had sat and listened and judged the frailties of human conduct. The fixtures, the worn spectators' benches, the criminal's dock enclosed with black metal tracery, portraits of past judges scowling down from the green plaster walls—all of this had changed little since Lizzie Borden was acquitted here and the poor fish peddler Bartolomeo Vanzetti was convicted for a mail-truck robbery a year before he and fellow anarchist Nicola Sacco stood trial at the dock of world opinion.

Tina said a little prayer to Saint Rosa, patroness of fishermen, first for her father, who was off the Grand Banks, and next for herself; if anyone was at sea with little hope for a landfall, it was she.

"Gracious Saint Rosa," she whispered, "please send me a safe current and a guiding star."

◻

Tina sat with her feet propped up on her secretary's gunmetal desk, reading a law book that she had checked out of the courthouse library. Her one-day-a-week secretary had gone. The neon from the 7-Eleven penetrated the office with its fluorescent glow. The more she read, the more she realized she needed the intercession of Saint Rosa. Service of process on Gammett by registered letter might stick, but trying the same maneuver in London or in Amsterdam was fraught with legal pitfalls.

With dejection bordering on despair, she contemplated the difficulties involved in simply gaining access to Universal. And then when she got there, if she ever did, the case still had to be won. She knew she might need to enlist counselors both in London and Amsterdam, perhaps even institute new proceedings in both countries. If so, the statute of limitations might well expire. And it would take money. Gobs of it. But both time and a bankroll were in short supply. She was about to reread the case annotations under the heading "Suits Against Foreign Corporations" when the call came in.

"Hello," said a gravelly voice. "You don't know me, Mrs. Alvarez, my name is Moe Katz. I used to be Frank Galvin's law partner before he became rich and famous."

"Mr. Katz," Tina replied abruptly, "I'm not sure why you're calling, but let me *assure* you and Mr. Galvin that I'm in no need of charity."

Moe had spent a lifetime dealing with people. He had to convince Tina Alvarez somehow that he could be trusted.

"I'm sorry, Mrs. Alvarez."

"It's Miss."

"My apologies. I'm getting old, I guess, and a little forgetful. But I think I might be able to help you."

"Please, Mr. Katz," Tina snapped. "It's late and I'm in no mood."

"Okay then, I'll be brief. At my age I don't need the aggravation. I told Galvin I'd call. I called. I can now go back to my cigar and brandy knowing that tomorrow at the office I can look forward to a slow and easy week—maybe draft a will, settle a case or two over the telephone, read Cardozo or Clauswitz. From what I hear, you have a near-impossible case. I wish you luck."

"Wait, Mr. Katz, don't hang up. I do need help. Bad."

"I know," said Moe, his voice losing its gentility. "Can you be in my office in Boston at nine tomorrow morning?"

"I'll be there," Tina said.

"Okay, bring your entire file. It takes me a while to get moving. Jim, my chauffeur, brings me in about seven. That way I don't run into traffic and the elevators are clear. I have to spin around in a wheelchair," he said. "And, Tina—mind if I call you Tina?"

"Please do."

"Jim will rustle up some breakfast. He's a short-order cook *and* chauffeur—plus he paints the house and mows the lawn. Of course, for the IRS I got him listed as a paralegal."

In the banter, Tina Alvarez saw a slight glimmer of hope.

"You like *Vorsht mit ayer?*" Moe asked.

"Vorsht mit what?"

"That's old Russian for salami and eggs."

9

"itigation reflects society's deep dissatisfaction with life,"
Moe Katz used to say while trying to shape Galvin's early
career. "It's unfortunate, but nowadays the law is a rollick-
ing game of chess. Lawyers can move to a new game, but clients
are stuck with the result. We've lost our ability to sit down as
gentlemen, give a little if we have to. Sometimes I have more
respect for the hooker," he would add. "If she can't get five, she
takes three."

As Galvin faced Ted King across the conference table, Moe's
words came tumbling back. Litigation was the last resort. A costly
spare-no-expense struggle for the clients, a lucrative ongoing war
for the law firms. None was better equipped for the battle than Ted
King and Frank Galvin.

The afternoon was spent in parrying, conceding innocuous
points, occasional incursions and strategic retreats. By day's end,
both King and Galvin would dictate their terms. Each needed to
gain the psychological high ground.

Galvin was now in control of the gist and thrust of the case. He,
Chip Hovington, and Rhys Jameson had logged countless hours in
preparation of the Sterling & Moss visit. His client, Rhyolite
Copper Corporation of America, was the largest producer of copper
and copper-related products in the world. Yet Rhyolite had come
on hard times. "No one seems to want copper bathtubs anymore,"
Chip Hovington had mused as he briefed Galvin. "Six years ago,
Rhyolite closed at forty-seven dollars a share. In today's bull
market it's ten. In dire need of funding, Rhyolite sold one of its

subsidiaries, Atlas Ball-Bearing, for nine hundred million dollars. Shouldn't have posed a problem," said Chip, "but it did. They were flush with cash. What to do with all that money? The shareholders, of course, felt it should be disbursed as dividends. What the board of directors didn't know was that someone, onto the cache, was quietly buying up Rhyolite's outstanding stock."

Galvin knew the rest. The mysterious stock gatherer turned out to be New York financier Werner Graf, who now controlled thirty percent of Rhyolite's stock and had made over-market-price overtures to the shareholders to buy them out. Among a host of charges, Graf accused Rhyolite's chairman and directors with dereliction of duty, inflated salaries, and gross mismanagement, conduct demanding dismissal. And then he threw in the kicker. If he took control, the nine hundred million dollars would be distributed as dividends. To disenchanted shareholders, this was a golden promise.

When Rhyolite's chairman, Robert Barr, finally realized who was on his trail and why, he did what any frightened board chairman would do under similar circumstances: He ran for his lawyers. Not to be outdone, Graf enlisted the Wall Street legions of Ted King and Sterling & Moss.

The relationship between Carter Hovington and Robert Barr went back a long way, to Princeton, class of '32. Over the years, in good times and in bad, Hovington, Sturdevant, Holmes & Hall had been Rhyolite's all-purpose law firm. And to Barr and Rhyolite, the threatened takeover by Graf was Armageddon.

When Galvin headed for the confrontation at Sterling & Moss, he was mindful that Rhyolite's annual meeting was two weeks away. By then it might be too late to halt Graf. Barr and the current board would be out.

"Time. We need time," was Barr's last plea to Galvin. "A court order enjoining Graf's solicitation, anything. Just get us past the annual meeting."

Galvin and his staff had worked round the clock trying to figure out a way to stop Graf. It had been Rhys Jameson, a few days before his resignation, who found the answer. He studied Graf's vast holdings, analyzing intertwining zones of commerce generated by either Graf or Rhyolite. If any business or competition would be diminished by Graf's acquisition of Rhyolite, then certain antitrust regulations might be violated. Jameson outlined the strategy. One of Graf's corporations manufactured smog arresters—a gas-filter contraption installed in automobile exhausts to neutralize toxic fumes. It was a cottage industry. Only four manufacturers existed nationwide. A Graf takeover ostensibly would reduce the manufacturers of smog arresters from four firms to three, a violation of the Clayton Anti-Trust Act.

It was a long shot, but it might force Graf to negotiate. And slow hostilities. Sterling & Moss might listen. That was the plan before Galvin met Ted King.

After six hours of deliberation, and an opportune lull in the maneuvering, Galvin played his high card—threatening suit if Graf persisted in invoking a proxy fight. King seemed unperturbed. It was late and King suggested adjournment.

Galvin had used his best shot. He could see no signs of concern in King's eyes and demeanor.

"Gentlemen, I think we've gone as far as we can," said King. "For today at least. Let me apprise my client of Rhyolite's intention—the threatened lawsuit—and we'll commence at zero eight hundred hours tomorrow morning. All right with you, Mr. Galvin?"

"Fine." Galvin nodded.

"Mr. Galvin. Mr. Hovington." Ted King rose to his full height and squared his shoulders. "Let me drop you off at the Carlyle."

Chip Hovington said he would walk. He was meeting someone at the Oak Room bar at the Plaza and it was only five short New York City blocks.

Ted King sat with Galvin in the back of the plush limousine as it headed up Madison Avenue in the early-evening traffic. Galvin declined a cigar. King unwrapped one with deliberate care, lit it with a flourish, and smoked in silence.

"I wanted us to talk alone," he finally said. "That antitrust ploy—the smog arrester." King removed the cigar from his lips and chuckled for several seconds. "You know, by God, that was a good one. Who in the world ever dreamed that up?" The chuckle grew into hearty laughter. "Oh, it'll delay us a little; just a little. Graf has the money, Galvin, and the time. Not bad cards."

Galvin listened.

"Now, just a tip." King paused for several seconds and flicked an ash from his cigar into a chrome armrest tray. "Check into your client's background, you might find something interesting." He glanced sideways at Galvin. "Like his four children recently purchasing Atlas stock. I think that's the company that Rhyolite sold for nine hundred million. Now, any suit against Graf . . ."

The rest was anticlimatic. Galvin swore to himself. If it was true—and it probably was—all negotiations would certainly blow. Insider information. What a hell of a note. Barr didn't purchase the stock. But his children did. How the hell did King ever find out?

"Okay." Galvin feigned nonchalance. "As you say, it'll delay things a little. Assuming what you say is true, what's the bottom line?"

King studied the lighted end of his cigar. "These come from Turkey, Galvin," he said. "Beat Havanas all to hell."

"I'm sure you didn't invite me along to discuss the relative merits of smoking tobacco." Galvin allowed just enough irritation to creep into his voice.

King folded his arms across his chest and parried Galvin's annoyance with a sardonic half-smile. "Let's resume our little skirmish tomorrow morning," he said. "You want to check out my story on Barr. What I'm telling you is gospel. Right now I've got a handball date."

They stopped in front of the Carlyle and a uniformed doorman in white gloves reached for the door, hesitating discreetly.

"Tell me, Galvin," King said, "did you ever whack any gooks in that war of yours?"

"Any what?" Galvin frowned.

"Gooks, Japs?" King smiled, but his eyes had the glint of blue steel.

"There were no gooks in my war." Galvin's jaw tightened. "Only soldiers. Good night, King. We'll resume at zero eight hundred."

"Zero eight hundred." King snapped a quick two-fingered salute.

They parted, the Marine Corps corporal and the jungle mercenary. The game would be played. Both would win.

◘

"I'm not putting the blame on anyone, Carter," Galvin said after paging Hovington at the Boston Pops and relating King's bombshell. "This never occurred to any of us. If anything, I'm at fault."

"It's extortion," fumed Hovington. "I thought Sterling & Moss was above this sort of thing."

"Sure, it's blackmail," Galvin replied curtly. "But what about our little smog-arrester caper? Carter, the situation is serious."

"What do you advise?" asked Hovington.

"I want affidavits from Barr's children that they had no advance knowledge of the Atlas buy-out. I want details—who put up the money, how much, and so on. I need them tomorrow."

"Galvin, that may take some doing."

"Then it'll have to take some doing," Galvin said curtly. "I can stall maybe twenty-four hours. Plead other business. Right now, Carter, I want you to call Barr and get him down to meet me at the Carlyle at noon tomorrow. I've got to go over the whole thing first hand. No time to massage the client. Barr's got to know the downside."

"Okay, we'll do our best. And, Galvin, I heard about Rhys Jameson. I hated to lose such a talent."

Galvin sucked in and held his breath. "So did I, Carter. Maybe you can arrange to have Stu Trimble switched over from Trusts to my department."

"Again, that'll take some doing. But I'll talk it over with Cy. Oh, by the way"—Hovington threw it in as an aside—"Jeremiah Wilson, general counsel of Gammett Industries, called today, told me they were served with suit papers on those Fall River children you were talking about. We're to defend the case."

"What?" said Galvin. "Are you sure?"

"It'll be a good piece of business. Wilson's cleared it with their insurer. He faxed the documents this afternoon. Wants to know what we advise Universal in London if they receive similar papers."

Galvin wanted to protest the involvement. But he had too much on his mind. "Put it on hold until I get back to Boston. Right now Chip and I have our hands full in keeping Barr afloat. You know, Carter, if Graf takes over, Barr is out. We're out. And Sterling & Moss is in."

"I understand. I'll call Barr right away."

After the hours spent coming up with the antitrust gimmick, it turned out to be just that—a gimmick.

And in the back of Galvin's mind, like a cinder in his eye, was the Alvarez suit.

At the Plaza he found Chip Hovington in a candlelit alcove at the far end of the Oak Room bar, chatting and holding hands with a smartly dressed attractive young woman.

"Galvin." Chip looked up, surprised. "I thought you'd be doing a few laps around the pool. . . . Oh, Dana," he said, "this is my boss, Frank Galvin, the one I've been telling you about."

She nodded graciously.

"Galvin, this is Dana Weatherbee, a dear friend and one of the top newscasters here in Manhattan."

"Very pleased to meet you, Dana," Galvin said. "But I'm afraid I have to steal my associate for the rest of the evening. Something very important has come up."

Chip looked up at Galvin, who remained standing. "It can't keep?"

"Afraid not. It involves Rhyolite. Barr is due here at noon tomorrow, and I've got to see you back at the Carlyle in, say, half an hour."

"Okay, half an hour," Chip said with a shrug.

They watched Galvin make his way along the brass and mahogany bar toward the front entrance.

"You know, Dana," Chip said, searching out his friend's hand again, "there goes one of the finest men I've ever met in my life. I'd follow him anywhere. He's one tough nut, yet he's got the one quality that's hard to find these days—in your business and in mine."

"Integrity," she said as she ran her soft fingers along the back of the hand that gripped hers.

"Yeah, integrity," he agreed. "But something more. He's got a sense of honor. A kind of quirky idealism."

"I can see you respect him quite a bit," she said.

"More than my own father," Chip replied.

◘

During the cab ride back to the Carlyle, Galvin smiled to himself. He wondered how the senior Hovington and the gray tigers of old Nassau would react to Chip's new friend. She was beautiful, all right: creamy smooth skin, gleaming white teeth—and as black as the ace of spades.

◘

They got on a three-way call with Barr at his Marblehead home.

"It's blackmail!" spewed Barr.

"That's what I said," Carter Hovington agreed. "We should file a complaint with the SEC or the FBI. It's extortion."

Hovington was making a crucial error, telling the client exactly what he wanted to hear—which could be embarrassing, since later advice might dictate retreat.

Galvin thought he'd better bring Barr down to earth and regain control of the conversation.

"Let me see if I have this straight, Bob. You say—and I believe you—that your children borrowed a hundred thousand dollars *without* collateral from the Yankee Cooperative Bank, where you are on the board of directors, so they could purchase Atlas stock, and your children had *no* inkling, whatsoever, of Rhyolite's intended buy-out?"

"I'd swear to it," Barr fumed.

"You might have to, and so might your four children, under penalties of perjury. And, Bob, I doubt that a federal judge would believe any of you."

"What?" Barr's voice was now less domineering, tinged with a new uncertainty.

"Listen," Galvin said, cradling the telephone between his neck

63

and shoulder, "forget the Feds. This information was communicated to me as a threat. But nothing's in writing, the mails weren't involved—and besides, what King told me is the God's honored truth. Now, I got a funny feeling that he wasn't doing me any favors. He could tell from my reaction that it took me by surprise. But I have a hunch he was sending me a message—like 'Call off the dogs.' "

"Do you think our antitrust-suit strategy is working?" Hovington asked.

"I don't know. Maybe. Maybe not. Graf has more money than God, and he didn't become king of the hill by tossing it into the air. And maybe he knows that no one really wins a pissing contest."

"But he'll plunder Rhyolite," Barr protested.

"Maybe that'll happen—eventually. But right now we need time. Say we put Graf, plus a few of his henchmen, on the board of directors—who knows, Bob, you might even grow to like the guy."

"Never!"

"Okay, Bob," Galvin said. "I'll meet you in the Carlyle lobby tomorrow. By then we'll know if we have to hit the trenches. And I want those affidavits from you and your children."

Galvin paused several seconds. "One last thing."

"Yes?"

"I'm going head to head with King tomorrow morning. I might have to make some immediate commitments. I need blank authorization to put Graf on the board of directors, and two of his cronies, if necessary."

"I'd resign first," cried Barr.

"Think it over, Bob, we're running out of options. Gentlemen, good night."

◻

Galvin and Chip arrived an hour late. The receptionist ushered them into the conference room where the Sterling & Moss litigators fidgeted and paced, like a firing squad awaiting its victims.

No excuses were offered. King knew the tardiness was deliberate. And Galvin knew that King knew.

"Can I see you for a few minutes, Ted, maybe in your office," said Galvin.

King pressed a button. "Joycelyn, is the Charles Evans Hughes suite available?"

"Yes, Mr. King," came the crisp response.

"Reserve it for at least an hour. Charge it to the Rhyolite case."

Billable hours, Galvin thought. My God. They're even more computerized than we are back in Boston.

Sterling & Moss had been featured in *Architectural Digest*. Hovington, Sturdevant, Holmes & Hall had a touch of Bostonian baroque, but the glass-and-crystal prisms of Sterling & Moss had the touch of New York class, the trappings of power. Ted King had come a long way from Hackensack. And Frank Galvin had come a long way from brick bottom.

They faced each other under an intimidating portrait of Charles Evans Hughes, the thirty-third Governor of New York, Supreme Court Justice, and guardian of the Sterling & Moss legacy.

"Funny," said Galvin, appraising the painting, "you have Hughes. We have Holmes. Tell you what," he digressed. "After today's session I'll take you on in a friendly game of handball. You reserve the court."

"You know how to play the game?" King looked at Galvin with a no-bullshit stare.

"Schoolyard champ back in South Boston," Galvin said.

"When was that?" King didn't wait for an answer. "I must warn you, Galvin," he said seriously. "I'm a tournament player. I'll play you, but I won't waste my time. I'll play you left-handed, okay?"

"Fine," Galvin accepted, knowing the concession was minor, that any tournament player had to be ambidextrous.

"Okay, you're on! Four this afternoon. I'll reserve all the equipment you need."

Galvin was playing a long shot. He figured that King had tipped him off the night before for a reason. King had the Barr deal down cold. That was a given. There was something else. Was Graf really nervous about the smog arresters?

"Okay, Ted, four o'clock. You play left-handed. I'll play left-handed. I want this to be fair." Galvin moved out from under the baronial stare of Charles Evans Hughes and looked out of the massive glass window at the purple haze enveloping the East River.

"Now." Galvin turned and faced King. "You and me. Can we agree on an amicable settlement of Barr versus Graf, or do we go to the mat and make tons of money for both of us?"

"You know, Galvin." King slipped into a predatory smile. "I like you. What do those fuckers know? Graf. Barr. Shit, for all we know they traded secrets with the enemy. Galvin, we fought at different times, but it was the same war. You in the Pacific. Me at An Loc and Khe San."

For a moment King's eyes misted. Galvin spotted the thin glistening. "Sometimes, Galvin, I get a strange feeling, sort of déjà vu, like I was with the French at Dien Bien Phu. Maybe it's happened to you. As if we were there, Galvin, actually there. With Leonidus at Thermopylae, Chinese Gordon at Khartoum, Foch at Verdun."

Somehow, somewhere, Galvin had heard it before. Sure. George C. Scott playing General George Patton. Reconjuring past wars. But in all the bravado, Galvin spotted a weakness. King had tipped his position like an overzealous quarterback, giving away the signal for a forward pass. If Barr needed time, Graf needed even more.

"King"—Galvin dropped the Ted—"let's cut the bullshit. If we can't get together right now, you and me, we'll make a fortune. Four years down the road, if I'm still around, we'll be running up to some federal judge for a restraining order or an injunction. The cash registers will roll like taxi meters. Right now, Graf can afford it. But times change. You know that."

"Okay." King placed both hands on his hips. A dominant stance. "Here's our deal. Barr remains chairman. His crew retains a *one*-man majority on the board of directors for at least one fiscal year. Graf ceases and desists from acquiring further Rhyolite stock. And, of course, we forget about Barr's kids getting that insider windfall. Tell you what," he said, his arrogant smile becoming boyish. "I'll spot you ten points—a twenty-one-point game. If I win, Graf gets a deadlocked board *four* and *four*. If you win, it's just Graf. No playground champ can turn down those odds,"

"Fifteen points," countered Galvin.

"Shake. Fifteen points." King extended his hand.

King applied a cruncher, but Galvin applied the old South Boston parry. Spread the fingers. Drop the thumb. No one was fooling anybody.

◘

"Gentlemen," King addressed his associates, "we've reached an agreement. Mr. Galvin and I will work out final details at four this afternoon. Right, Mr. Galvin?"

Galvin nodded.

"I'm sure no one will go back on his word," King added.

The gray and beige cadre of Sterling & Moss displayed no emotion. They gathered their papers, clicked open their briefcases, and began the orderly transition that marks the end of any case. The settlement was expected. Galvin noticed that, too.

◘

Galvin could see King through the small oval window in the white metal door leading to the gym. King, wearing a black tank top and black spandex tights, was hammering a tattoo on a punching bag with the practiced rhythm of a trained boxer. Galvin stood for several seconds watching King's gloved hands dart and flick just above his head. King's body was as lean and as hard as his demeanor. For a visceral moment, Galvin had serious misgivings about the match.

He joined King at the punching bag. King cast a sweaty grin, quickly assessed Galvin's lithe physique, dispensed with preliminaries, and led him toward the handball courts. It was a posh athletic club, with the latest of equipment—stainless-steel universals, bicycling machines, computerized treadmills—each equipped with shapely young women in aerobic tights, measuring, weighing, and counting calories. Above, a balconied running track tested the feet and hearts of portly stockbrokers, wheezing lawyers, and an array of corporate types, all trying to stay the inexorable hand of time. The resonating slap of handballs hitting hardwood walls sounded like rifle fire. Galvin had never quite gotten used to any form of combat. He pretended to. Even before opening to a jury, the butterflies were always there. This time was no exception.

The preliminary volleying was not half-bad. "It's like swimming," Galvin would later tell Chip Hovington. "Once you learn, you never forget."

Galvin played the straight shots and caroms reasonably well. Yet for just a warm-up, he knew he was getting winded. King was scarcely breathing, lobbing slow methodical shots like a batting-practice pitcher.

"Okay." King was now all business. "You serve, Galvin. The count stands fifteen to zero. Your lead. Twenty-one is out. Win by just one point."

King settled back near the far wall and Galvin advanced a few steps. Galvin bounced the hard black rubber ball several times off the floor, tugged at one of his gloves, and smashed the ball with every ounce of energy he had. The ball smacked the main wall, caromed off the side, seemed to gather speed in an upward arc, and bounced in the corner near King. King waited for it to land several feet ahead, and with one graceful motion stepped forward and slapped it for a killer, inches above the front wall. Fifteen to one.

At fifteen to eleven, with King still moving easily and Galvin stopping, starting, punishing himself to keep in the game, King let up. A few missed shots, setups sent Galvin's way, allowed Galvin to gain five unanswered points. Twenty to eleven.

King now came on with a rush, sending the ball spiraling and spinning in all directions. He employed a variety of cuts and hooks and slices. The ball at times seemed to stop, then reverse itself. Galvin grasped at air. King applied a series of subtle body checks, physically blocking out returns. Galvin was soaking wet, exhausted, and could feel the sting of sweat running into his eyes.

"Okay, it's twenty all. Match point." King delivered it like a death threat. "You know, Galvin, for a novice, you didn't do half-bad. But this is where I put you away."

Galvin barely got his hand on King's powerhouse serve, which must have been ricocheting at a hundred miles an hour. He lunged and managed to send a feeble shot toward the wall. It died, but not until it hit, then dribbled to the floor. Pure luck.

It was Galvin's serve.

He feigned a hard smash, instead sending a soft lob that hit and bounced well ahead of King. King pounced on it like a panther, slashing it back, but skidded out of control and crashed to the floor.

The ball came back to Galvin at waist level and he was about to drill it home. King, unable to spring back into action, watched hopelessly as Galvin, cocking his arm for the final swing, stepped forward. Then, in a startling moment, Galvin reached out and caught the ball. King looked up at him like a felled gladiator being given a reprieve.

"We'll play the point again," Galvin said.

"No, we'll call it," King cried, scrambling to his feet. "It'll go into the books as twenty all."

"The board of directors?" said Galvin, bouncing the ball against the floor.

"Only Graf." King nodded. "You get Barr and seven."

Galvin smiled.

They shook hands.

"Some other time, Galvin," he said, "our paths will cross. And for an ex-Marine, you're too fuckin' soft. You'd be eaten alive down here."

"That's why I'm not down here," said Galvin.

◘

They flew back to Boston in Rhyolite's Lear jet. Barr was particularly jubilant, getting sloshed on his fifth martini. "I'll handle Graf," he said. "Hell, Galvin, I guess I ran scared this afternoon. Imagine me agreeing to a deadlocked board. You really stuck it to that bastard. Our threatened antitrust suit really did it."

Chip caught Galvin's mischievous grin and shot it back like one of King's handball serves.

The Lear whispered through its dark corridor of air, and Galvin could see the lights of Providence and Greater Fall River off the right wing. He thought about Tina Alvarez and wondered if Moe

Katz had gotten in touch with her. Too bad Alvarez didn't have a fire-eater like Ted King in her camp. But King would be too smart to get involved. Jameson? Sure. Somehow he'd nudge Jameson in Tina's direction.

10

News of Galvin's coup crackled along Barrister's Row and among the blue-chip firms of State Street and Beacon Hill long before Rhyolite's jet touched down at Logan. There was even talk of some sort of handball game. Galvin would later dismiss it with a broad smile. But some noted that he never actually denied it.

Julie Hedren placed Galvin's Friday-morning call to London. "I have Heath Mallory on the line," she told him. Mallory was Universal's vice president of marketing.

"Thank you, Julie." Mallory then came through as clear as if he were next door.

"Heath. Mind if I call you Heath?"

"Please do, old chap. Good to hear from you, Frank."

"Call me Galvin."

"Right-o. I chatted with solicitor Hovington earlier. We received a piece of certified post from a lawyer Alvarez in the States addressed to our president—that's Ruuden Gore—and per Hovington's instructions, we refused to sign for it and returned it unopened."

Interesting, Julie Hedren thought as she listened on the line.

"This is no big deal, Heath," Galvin said. "Hovington gave you sound advice. This was an attempt to get jurisdiction over Universal by utilizing Massachusetts's long-arm statute. Once you or your secretary sign for the letter, whether it's opened or not, Universal would be stuck with a lawsuit right here in the colonies."

"The colonies." Mallory chuckled. "That's a good one, Galvin. Right, Frobie?"

Galvin was startled to hear another voice cut in.

"Hello there, Mr. Galvin. Stan Frobisher here. Solicitor general of Uni—head legal beagle, as you would say. We've a knack at spotting these things. Even take a peek inside before we ship them back, if you know what I mean." There was mirth in Frobisher's voice.

Galvin knew what he meant. Some postal clerk was in the bag.

"I see," said Galvin. "Putting the old steamer to use?"

"Good heavens, man," Frobisher laughed, "we're a piece more sophisticated than that. Didn't even have to open the envelope. It's called spectrographic monitoring. I have a facsimile of the plaintiff's complaint and covering letter in front of me right now. I'll fax you a copy."

"No, you keep it," Galvin stammered, trying to suppress the anger that was creeping into his voice. "Look, lawyer Alvarez can't get jurisdiction over Universal unless she invokes the Hague Convention. This she hasn't done. At least not yet."

"She? A Portia? Taking on Universal Multi-Tech Limited?"

Galvin was in no mood for transcontinental banter.

"She might already be out of luck because of the three-year statute of limitations here in Massachusetts," Galvin said. "Where are you actually based—I mean your home office?"

Julie Hedren smiled as she listened. It sounded to her as if a few laws were being broken.

"We're actually *incorporated* under the laws of the Netherlands. Our residential office is Amsterdam, but our principal place of business is here in Bromley Green, just north of London."

"Okay, fax me your charter and incorporation papers, including a list of officers, and ship all the marketing data you have covering the last five years."

"Will do," said Frobisher.

"What's the connection between Gammett and Universal?"

"Well"—Mallory came back on the line—"Gammett's the marketing arm for Universal in the United States and Canada. But Gammett's an entirely separate business entity chartered under the laws of New Jersey and run exclusively with stateside personnel. Legally, they're as different as Chrysler and Revlon."

"Service of process upon Gammett as agent of Universal will be Alvarez's next move," said Galvin. "You'd better send me any agreements you have between the two. If there's an interlocking directorate or if Universal exerts substantial control over Gammett, we might be stuck."

"We'll get them off," Frobisher chipped in. "These documents will be on your desk first thing Monday morning."

"Send them to my attention, personal and confidential. That way we'll save some time."

Like Alice, Julie Hedren was getting curiouser and curiouser. What was so special about this lawsuit? Was Galvin playing both ends against the middle?

"One last thing, Frobie," Galvin warned, "you may next receive a letter by certified post directed to your president that looks innocent—maybe pink stationery with the stamps upside down, say from Joan Smith or Mary Jones. That'll be a ploy to accomplish what the first letter failed to do."

"My dear Galvin, you are absolutely psychic. That's exactly what happened, right down to the pink envelope. In fact," Frobisher said smugly, "it came the same day. Back it went—again unclaimed and unopened—but we retained a copy of the contents. It's a watered-down version of the initial legal complaint."

"What's that machine you gentlemen use to accomplish all this . . . ?" Galvin almost said "illegality."

Frobisher laughed. "Well, it's what you might call a little walking-around money for the postal clerk. A few bob for him and the missus and he goes on his merry way. Comes back an hour later, picks up the post, and no one's the wiser. Pays for a fortnight in Cornwall. Then we have the spectrograph. Developed by British Intelligence during the war; refined by the Air Ministry and Interpol. 'Sneaky peepy,' we call it, Galvin. The bloody thing can see through walls, around corners, or poke into tourist bags. Envelopes are de rigueur. Quicker than you can say Henry the Eighth, it computerizes, decodes, analyzes, and spits out a printout of what's inside."

Galvin's stomach was turning. He had the visceral feeling that he was wading into shark-infested waters. Suddenly Mallory came back on the line.

"Mr. Galvin, how is the security back there?"

"Security?"

"Well, right now, old chap, there should be three of us on the line. You, me, and Frobie. Our wattage snooper indicates that someone else at *your end* is plugged into this conversation."

"What? You can tell that four thousand miles away in London?"

"Oops. There it goes! Some little busybody just got off the line."

"Well, I'll be." Julie Hedren must have been listening in. Jesus! "Okay" Galvin decided to sign off. "All our people are totally loyal. But I'll check on it."

Galvin thought about how to deal with Julie Hedren's eavesdropping. Perhaps best to ignore it. Julie was basically decent. If he pretended to forget it, so would she.

He sat at his desk for several seconds, his fingers steepled against his lips. The pink letter must have been Moe's idea. It was a good try. But Moe had never played in this league before. Alvarez had actually accomplished service of process on Universal but would never be able to prove it. Ethics. Legality. Were they just faint echoes of things heard in law school long ago?

He wondered if Moe had gotten in touch with Rhys Jameson, as he'd suggested. Alvarez, Katz, and Jameson. They'd make worthy adversaries. But in the end Galvin knew they'd lose. First the money would run out. Next the bombardment—an avalanche of papers with short court deadlines. He thought of Robert E. Lee after beating the Union Army at Chancellorsville. "I'll victory the Confederacy to death," said the courtly general. For Alvarez, Katz, the beleaguered Fall River children—it was just a matter of time. And attrition.

They met in Moe Katz's office early Sunday morning. The city was in a festive mood. Souvenir hawkers and T-shirt vendors were setting up stalls along Commonwealth Avenue and in the Lafayette Mall. Tour buses vied for parking space. Visitors had congregated to sample the rites of spring and anticipate the Boston Marathon one week away.

Rhys Jameson, wearing Adidas sneakers, a green satin Celtics jacket, and faded chinos, looked incongruous carrying a leather briefcase.

"Mr. Katz, I presume." He extended his hand to the balding gnome-like figure seated in a wheelchair in front of him.

"You're Jameson." Moe Katz returned the greeting. "Come in, my boy. We've got a long day ahead of us."

Rhys glanced past his host and saw Tina Alvarez descending a portable ladder in Moe Katz's law library. He had talked with her on the telephone earlier in the week after receiving a note from Frank Galvin suggesting that he might want to assist her. Alvarez was beguiling in her pink pullover and form-fitting matching corduroys. Her auburn tresses bounced as she stepped down from the last rung and flashed a welcoming smile.

"This is Tina Alvarez." Moe Katz spun his chair around and wheeled toward her.

"Thanks for coming." Tina extended her hand. "Though you might regret it. I think we're all bonkers. We've got a hopeless situation, but Galvin told me that if anyone could plug the dike and prevent us from being washed away, it was you and Moe Katz." She nodded in Moe's direction.

"Okay." Moe rubbed his hands together. "That's enough prattle. Sit down, take off your jacket, and let's see what we're up against. Coffee?"

"Black," Rhys said, still appraising Alvarez.

Two hours later Rhys Jameson had digested four volumes of files and four cups of coffee.

"Think I got a handle on it." He sighed as he put down his

yellow pad on which he had been scratching case law and legal precedents. "We've got two, maybe three options and we might as well fire everything we have. All at once. There's no tomorrow if we lose on jurisdiction. You tell me you sent registered letters to Universal in London and in Amsterdam?"

Alvarez and Moe nodded.

"I'll bet my bottom dollar that everything will be returned unclaimed," Rhys said. "When I worked for Hovington and Galvin, we used to defend Datsun and Volkswagen. You can't get service on foreign nationals if they don't want to play in your ballpark. Those letters will come tumbling back as clean as when they were sent. Datsun always claimed their commitment ended at the docks in Yokohama, Volkswagen at Hamburg. They could manufacture firebombs and death traps with impunity. I can't recall one case we defended where the plaintiff survived the jurisdictional issue."

Tina frowned. "We've sent registered letters on other than legal stationery to Universal's home office in Amsterdam, as well as to their principal place of business in Bromley Green in the U.K."

"Look, you're fighting submarines with a flamethrower," said Rhys. "I'm telling you, those letters won't even be claimed."

"How about the pink one?" Moe inquired.

"Won't work. They're too cute to be sucked into litigation. You sue one of Hovington's clients, you pay."

"We could sue the bastards *in* Holland or *in* London?" Moe Katz asked, quickly realizing the bind they were in.

Rhys shook his head. "No way. The U.K. statute of limitations has already run out. And the Dutch don't cotton to Yanks like us disturbing the status quo. Their law favors the manufacturer, not the consumer."

"*Caveat emptor?* I thought that went out with the Industrial Revolution," said Moe.

" 'Let the buyer beware.' There's no such thing as consumerism in the foreign market. That's why the Japs and the Krauts are beating us all to hell in exports—ships, planes, cars. They don't have to factor consumer safety into the price."

"What about the Hague Convention?" Tina asked.

"That's the last resort. It's complicated, and even that avenue might be shut down. We have to draft letters rogatory, serve them on the agent or general manager of Universal, complete with translation, and appoint foreign barristers. Believe me, there's the rub. They've got an old-boy network over there that makes ours look like amateur night. Dutch and English solicitors probably belong to the same fox and hounds society. It's all very formal. And very expensive. They won't even don a wig unless they get paid up front."

"We may have no choice," Moe said.

"You're probably right," Rhys agreed. "So we might as well get started. I'll call Berlitz first thing tomorrow and get someone to start on the Dutch translation."

Tina liked Rhys's decisiveness. "You say *we*" she said. "Are you in?"

"Hey, it might be our funeral," Rhys said, "but we'll have one hell of a wake. Sure, I'm in!"

"What's your estimate on the initial outlay of money?" Moe asked.

"I must confess, I'm broke," said Tina.

"That makes two of us." Rhys held up two fingers.

"Okay, okay." Moe pushed his wheelchair back from the conference table. "Forget about costs. I haven't been whacking out two-bit cases for forty years without squirreling something away. I'll bankroll the case—at least for now."

"One last thing we might try," offered Rhys. "Sue the American corporation—Gammett—as resident agent for Universal. If Universal exerts some form of control over Gammett, a local judge might listen."

"Thought of it already," Moe said. "Legal process was served on Gammett at their home office in Patterson Heights, New Jersey, by the Ocean County constable's office just the other day. We sued Gammett as the seller and distributor of Lyosin and as resident agent for the foreign manufacturer, Universal."

At 4 P.M. they were still at it. The Alvarez-Katz-Jameson combine split for a thirty-minute, long-overdue lunch. Jim, the chauffeur, made sandwiches and served coffee.

"We may have overlooked one thing." A small smile crinkled the corners of Tina's dark eyes. She paused before taking the last few bites of her tuna on rye.

"What's that?" asked Moe.

"Settlement. Maybe Universal will settle. If their attorney—"

"You mean if Frank Galvin recommends it," interrupted Moe.

"Precisely."

"Look. Galvin doesn't call the shots for Universal," Rhys pointed out. "This case will go the full route. I think we all know that. Universal won't offer a dime, believe me. The bleeding hasn't even started. And it'll be our blood on the floor, not Hovington and company. They'll make a fortune out of all those billable hours."

"Okay." Moe clapped his hands. "No one said that life or being a lawyer was easy. Back to work. I know these Yankee defense firms. When it comes to paying some poor son of a bitch, Hovington throws half-dollars around like they're manhole covers. And he's a shrewd old codger. Wouldn't tell you if your pants were on fire."

□

Galvin could feel the approbation resulting from the Rhyolite case as he headed toward Hovington's office. Cy Sturdevant greeted him effusively, telling him that Stuart Trimble was being assigned to his unit.

The partners and junior associates nodded approval. But as Galvin entered Hovington's office, he was troubled.

"Sit down, Galvin." Hovington could sense Galvin's mission. "I just got a call from Jerry Wilson, general counsel for Gammett. Thinks you're a miracle worker. He heard about the Rhyolite case and wants you and your team to be their guest next Tuesday to meet with the president, tour the plant, the usual get-to-know-the-client routine. We'll take the company plane to Trenton."

Galvin remained standing. He had always liked the old-world comfort of Hovington's office—the Winslow Homer paintings on the wall, the expensive sandlewood interior, yachting memorabilia placed throughout its broad expanse, and the feeling that confidences disclosed remained as discreet as the fixtures.

Galvin came right to the point. "Carter, I want off the Lyosin case. If the firm has to handle it, let Chip be the attorney of record."

Hovington was a master tactician and had anticipated Galvin's request. "Miss Simmons," he addressed the intercom, "hold all calls. Galvin"—he gestured—"sit down. You're getting discombobulated unnecessarily. Let's talk it through."

Galvin sank into the plush leather chair and loosened his tie.

"Look," Hovington began, "Gammett and Universal are important clients. We don't give them a fast shuffle just because you almost got involved with the plaintiffs' side."

"Now, wait . . ." Galvin put both hands on the armrests and was about to propel himself upward.

"Please, Galvin. Hear me out. Then I'll listen to you."

Galvin slumped back into the chair. His jaw remained tight, but his ice-blue eyes seemed to soften.

"Do you realize how much money is involved in securing FDA approval for a new drug?"

"Hundreds of millions?"

"Try six hundred million. And that's not factoring in seven years of overhead, or living with the feeling that your product might not get the okay or some competitor might beat you to the draw."

Galvin listened.

"We have the best law firm in the city of Boston, maybe on the Eastern seaboard. Our litigation department, thanks to you, is second to none. Yet in a way we're all captives. We can't choose clients like some storefront practitioner. I can't turn down the Bank of Boston's business simply because I have a personal dislike for their vice president. Sure, sometimes I'd prefer to be on the other side of a case and champion the downtrodden. But that's not our lot. The well-to-do deserve a fair shake at justice, same as the poor. When we represent a client, we don't care if he's a philanderer or a rent gouger. That's irrelevant. A lawyer represents his client to the best of his ability. That's the mark of the true advocate. You guided Stone and Barr through the legal shoals and that was tricky.

"Do you think that Edward Bennett Williams liked defending Frank Costello, a Mafia boss, or Jimmy Hoffa? You bet your ass he knew where his own feelings lay. But he didn't quit on Costello or on Hoffa. He had ten blacks on the jury in the Hoffa case. And during the trial, what do you know? The great Joe Louis just happened to drop by and shake hands with Hoffa right in front of the jury. Now, Hoffa and Louis both came from Detroit. Maybe they were old neighborhood pals. Or just maybe Edward Bennett Williams, like the true advocate he was, saw an opportunity.

"Universal and Gammett Industries are now among our biggest accounts. They've asked us to defend them. That means we use every legal maneuver in our power to squash our adversary's case. If we don't, if we let something slip past us"—Hovington's gray eyes locked with Galvin's—"then, Galvin, I've seriously misjudged you."

The intimation stung. Galvin was going to argue, but he knew that Hovington was right.

"Okay, Carter," he said quietly. "I'll defend these guys, but I won't run with them."

11

Galvin boarded the firm's twin-engine D'Havilland for the Tuesday-morning flight to New Jersey. Stuart Trimble and Chip Hovington sat in the rear, sifting motion papers and screening case law.

Galvin settled next to the pilot, Ken Ritchie, and watched him go through his meticulous checklist. Ritchie read from a card, leaving nothing to memory or chance. He explained the maze of instruments—altimeter, transponder, ADF, DME, trim. Ever since Galvin's school days, the mystique of flying had held a special fascination for him. As the D'Havilland moved out onto the runway apron and commenced its roll, he recalled an earlier time when as a young boy he often visited nearby Squantum Airfield to watch the great aces and barnstormers that put in there: Wiley Post, Ruth Nichols, Amy Johnson, among others.

The D'Havilland whooshed into the milky gold of the morning sky and banked over Quincy Bay. Looking down, Galvin caught sight of the vestigial remains of the old Squantum Hangar, now converted into bayside condominiums. He recalled a day in 1937 when, perched on his father's shoulders, he had watched Amelia Earhart, clad in a brown flight jacket, leather boots, and jodhpurs, and wearing a wistful smile, wave to the crowd. She had looked right at him, nodded and gave a short salute. He had never forgotten that moment. He waved as the eagle disappeared from view. She was on her way to Howland Island and to eternity.

Galvin settled back, making mental notes as Ken Ritchie honed in on radials and vectors. The granite turrets and minarets of the Manhattan skyline glistened off starboard, and the murky haze of the Jersey shoreline loomed ahead.

For a brief moment Frank Galvin wondered where he was going. The steady drone of the engines, the slight rocking of the wings dipping gently below the horizon gave him a fictive sense of detachment, as if he were looking down on himself. He shrugged himself back to reality and glanced over his shoulder. Chip and Trimble were awash in yellow scratch pads, notebooks, and file cards. Galvin smiled; portal to portal, the meter was running.

Gammett Industries blended so unobtrusively with the landscape that one might not know it was there. Skins of bronze glass stretched over two-story elevations reflected the tranquillity of carefully tended gardens, manicured lawns, and sculpted evergreens. The season was days ahead of New England, and the star magnolias, Japanese cherries, and red azaleas were in full bloom. The crushed pea-stone drive coursed through arbors of pink and white dogwood. It was difficult to imagine that this industrial complex was one of the largest marketing divisions in the United

States. Except for groundkeepers and an occasional security guard, no one was in sight. Even the parking facility resembled a well-camouflaged bunker.

But once they were ushered into the vaultlike interior, all appearance of rural calm disappeared. Corporate ants with Lucite photos pinned to white smocks scurried along the corridors, pushing trays of multicolored bottles and stainless-steel canisters that glistened under antiseptic lights.

There was a frenzied order about the place. Elevator doors pinged open. Young men and women disembarked, alighted. The inventory was checked, then shuttled down gleaming white-tiled radials.

Galvin, Stuart Trimble, and Chip Hovington signed the incoming register.

"Just a formality, Mr. Galvin," said the chauffeur as he initialed each signature at the receptionist's station.

"Strange," Galvin mused.

"What?" Chip asked.

"Kind of weird," Galvin replied. "We came on this place just off the Garden State Parkway. It's so well concealed, I'll bet even the townspeople don't know it's here. Looks like a country estate somewhere around Marblehead."

"Even has the ocean," Trimble injected.

"But no one's smiling," said Galvin.

Chip and Trimble looked around.

"Jeeze, you're right," Chip said. "This's got to be the world's most somber corporation."

"And among the richest," added Trimble. "It registers seven point five on *Fortune*'s Richter scale."

Galvin spotted the trio coming halfway down the corridor. He played a game with himself. He guessed that Jerry Wilson, Gammett's general counsel, was the slightly balding middle-aged man to the far left. Earl Torgenson, the firm's president, was in the middle. He was the tallest in the group, neatly dressed in charcoal gray. There was purpose to his stride. He reflected the corporate image. To the right of Torgenson was Dante Corsini, the firm's associate medical director. Corsini had sloping shoulders, a certain bereaved look accentuated by black furry eyebrows, and a vest pocket full of fountain pens.

Galvin was correct.

Jerry Wilson zipped on a quick smile and extended his hand. "Mr. Galvin," he opened with professional enthusiasm, "heard a lot about you. Glad you're in our corner. Dr. Torgenson, meet the legendary Frank Galvin."

Torgenson nodded, gripped Galvin's hand firmly. The introductory protocol was played out. All shook hands.

There was something about Jerry Wilson that Galvin couldn't quite get a handle on. During lunch Wilson did most of the talking and Dr. Corsini, as if on cue, nodded agreeably. Neither Wilson nor Corsini were corporate types. Wilson had a slow, easy manner, a certain self-effacing charm augmented by a Southern drawl. He laid out the host table's academic and scientific credentials with deliberate care: Dr. Torgenson was a graduate of Penn and the Wharton School of Business, the recipient of numerous international awards. Dr. Corsini had several degrees from the Pasteur Institute in France, and he himself had received his LL.B. from Duke University, or as he put it with a tight smile, "the Harvard of the South."

Dr. Torgenson epitomized big business—square-jawed, handsome, holding middle age well at bay. He was even less talkative than Dr. Corsini, and although he seemed to listen intently, his glacial gray eyes constantly roamed the corporate dining room. He made a few tactless remarks about how groups of greedy lawyers had deterred the growth of the pharmaceutical industry over the past twenty years.

"Lyosin," Torgenson said thoughtfully, "is the greatest boon to mankind in the past century. And right now, gentlemen"—his voice lowered as if imparting a great confidence—"Universal's working with LaRoche Laboratories in Paris. We're on the verge of developing an AIDS vaccine, and the cure for cancer is just over the horizon." It was Wilson's turn to do the nodding.

Galvin made some quick assessments. Torgenson would be a difficult witness. He created the impression that his time was much too valuable for him to be involved with testimony. As if Torgenson could read Galvin's mind, he glanced at his gold Piaget wristwatch, patted his lips with the linen napkin, and excused himself, pleading an early-afternoon conference. He hoped the group would join them for dinner at the Southwick Country Club. He and Mrs. Torgenson would see them at eight.

The banter and pleasantries had ended. Chip and Trimble were to be closeted with Dr. Corsini to review the firm's history. Galvin wanted everything—investors, incorporators, directors, key personnel, chemists, technicians, analysts. Some weighty medical names had touted Lyosin even before FDA approval. He wanted a list of itemized disbursements from Gammett and Universal to such medical celebrities. When and where and how much.

Jerry Wilson sucked in his breath and rolled his eyes at Dr. Corsini. "It'll take some doing, Galvin," he said. "Not to mention the expense. Most records are in the archives in London."

"That's why we're here." Galvin smiled. "Time and money are luxuries we can *well* afford."

"You know," Jerry Wilson said as he shuffled through cartons of files marked CONFIDENTIAL in bold red type, "your own firm in Washington handled Lyosin's FDA approval. I'm sure you already have that data."

"We're rounding that up now," Galvin said. "But the files reflect only compliance with minimal standards. I want the raw data, the stuff that even the FDA doesn't go into."

"Even if available," Wilson sighed defensively, "I'm not so sure we can give it to you without clearance from London. From what I hear, Universal hasn't been legally served and the 'raw data,' as you say, will be privileged from discovery in any suit involving Gammett here in the States."

Galvin noticed that Wilson was losing his Southern drawl. "That may or may not be," Galvin said. "But in order to render a proper defense, we've got to cover all contingencies, and this stuff is important or may become important as litigation progresses."

"But if we don't have it *here*"—Wilson remained intransigent—"then no one can discover it. That's basic black-letter law. Even a graduate from a 'close cover before striking' law school knows that one."

"Look, Jerry." Irritation crept into Galvin's voice. "I don't give a good goddamn if Chief Justice Burger comes down with a mandate next week granting Gammett and Universal judicial immunity, or whether the stuff is gathering dust in some warehouse five thousand miles from here. What I sent Hovington and Trimble after has got to be produced. I'm aware of the legal restraints I can employ to prevent our adversaries from conducting a fishing expedition. I want it all—good, bad, incriminating. I'll decide what we need or don't need."

"I'm not so sure Dr. Torgenson will go along, let alone the boys in London."

"I'll have a little chat with the boys in London, Jerry." Galvin wanted to end the jousting. "Right now let's see the summons you received from the plaintiffs."

"Got it right here," Wilson said. "Came in yesterday. It was directed to be served by hand on Dr. Torgenson. The receptionist signed for it. That might make it defective."

"If we come up with that old defense, we'll have five sheriffs here next week hiding in the bushes waiting for Torgenson's limo. We'll agree to proper service. Stonewalling will only delay the inevitable."

Wilson nodded reluctantly.

Galvin perused the summons carefully. *Antonia Alvarez, Moe Katz, and Rhys Jameson, attorneys for the plaintiffs.* He read through the litany, the complaints of injury. He thought of the Ramondi boy.

"Now, count thirty-seven of the complaint states that Gammett is the United States agent for Universal. What's our position on that?"

"Preposterous!" Wilson snapped.

"Preposterous?"

"Gammett and Universal are as different as—"

"Chrysler and Revlon," Galvin interjected.

Wilson broke into a rictus smile and slid back into his drawl.

"Galvin, you ole houn' dawg," he bellowed, slapping his thigh.

The sparring was over. From now on the "close cover before striking" law school would be dictating to the "Harvard of the South."

○

Southwick Country Club sat on a hillock overlooking Raritan Bay. Galvin was struck by its quiet beauty. He had harbored misconceptions about the Jersey shore, perhaps because of Atlantic City. Southwick's rolling greens and white porticoed mansion resembled some Southern horse country estate, complete with white rail fences. Dr. Torgenson, wearing a white dinner jacket, greeted them on the balcony.

The clear twilight air had the pungent smell of the sea. The guests, all in evening wear, chatted, sipped cocktails, and selected canapés from silver trays carried by waiters dressed in colonial knickers and claret velvet jackets. Galvin noticed that the waiters and bartenders were all black.

Galvin felt out of place in his business suit, a feeling soon displaced by an effusive greeting from Dr. Torgenson. Wilson must have passed the word.

"Roxanne, darling," Torgenson said, turning to the young beauty at his side, "this is our counselor, Frank Galvin. Mr. Galvin, my wife, Roxanne."

Why was everyone so young, so stunning? Galvin wondered, quickly drinking in Roxanne Torgenson's silky golden hair, tanned bare shoulders, and crisp Main Line features.

"I'm pleased to meet you, Mr. Galvin." Her voice was as silky as her hair. She extended a white gloved hand. "You're from Boston, I hear. One of my favorite cities."

"Mr. Galvin has been retained to fend off the jackals," Torgenson remarked.

Galvin was annoyed and tempted to fire back. He counted to three. "We'll do our best," he said quietly.

"Roxanne, darling," Torgenson said, glancing at his watch, "I'll be closeted for a while with our marketing chief. Take Mr. Galvin around and introduce him to our guests. He's an Irishman, so make sure his glass doesn't become empty."

Temptation flashed for a scary moment, but Galvin said nothing.

The muted rhythms of a string quartet enhanced the conviviality of the guests as they mingled, chatted, and toasted the evening along. Galvin had been up since five o'clock that morning, and both he and the long day were slouching toward midnight. It was time to go. He suppressed a yawn. He declined a nightcap, made the necessary excuses, and contemplated a graceful exit when he saw her. She was at the far end of the dining room sipping brandy and talking with Dr. Corsini. She had black lacquered hair, high cheekbones, large almond eyes. Her skin, amber gold, reminded him of Tina Alvarez. She was Oriental, perhaps Thai or Vietnamese. A striking beauty. Galvin stood transfixed. He unconsciously accepted a drink from one of the passing waiters, holding it several seconds before placing it behind a spreading fern. He angled toward her, chatting briefly with a woman who grabbed his arm. When he finally reached the fringe of Corsini's group, she was gone. He hovered out of range for several minutes, but the Oriental lady did not reappear. He shrugged. He'd ask Corsini about her in the morning.

◘

Chip Hovington had skipped the formal evening and remained in his room at the Lord Burgoyne. Jerry Wilson had offered to pick him up at 6 A.M. the next morning for a four-mile row at the Gammett Boat Club. Chip had accepted and was now having misgivings about his oarsmanship, although he had made the varsity team at Princeton. He sat propped up on the bed, shoes off, tie loosened. Earlier he had skimmed the Importer's Agreement between Universal and Gammett with Dr. Corsini, and something about it disturbed him. He settled down, tilted the lampshade to get better light, and started again from scratch. He sipped a Scotch and water as he studied each word. Galvin had wanted to make sure Gammett and Universal were not one and the same.

The preamble had a lot of gingerbread.

Okay, Chip said to himself. What it boils down to is they trust each other. Universal makes the stuff. Gammett sells it.

Then came the negatives. Universal owned 100 percent of Gammett stock. Meetings were held each year in London, and English and Dutch nationals comprised the majority of the board of directors of both corporations.

It was beginning to look more like Max Factor and Revlon. No question about it, Chip thought. Gammett was the wholly owned subsidiary of Universal. But in the intricacies of corporate law, this was the structure of many businesses. Nothing yet to implicate Universal as the alter ego of Gammett.

The laws of the United Kingdom shall govern this agreement, to construct validity, interpretation, and performance.

Okay, Chip said again, a parent-subsidiary setup. The corporations were closely allied but separate enough to defuse lawyer Alvarez.

Each corporation keeps separate books.

And there was no getting around the language:

Gammett will transact all business pursuant to this agreement on its behalf and for its own account; it has no authority whatsoever to act as agent or otherwise for or on account or on behalf of Universal.

Then he spotted it squeezed into a paragraph on page 32.

All advertising, marketing strategy, product availability, price, and warranty policy shall be specified by Universal. Personnel hired or terminated by Gammett shall be subject to Universal's approval.

Shall. Chip tossed the word over in his mind. A mandatory, dictatorial, inflexible word, brooking no discussion, allowing no room for suggestion or maneuver.

He juggled it again. Personnel hired by Gammett or terminated by Gammett *shall* be approved by Universal.

He drained the glass of Scotch and reached for a pencil. He thought for a few moments. *Personnel hired by or terminated by Gammett shall be subject to Universal's approval.* This covered the clerk in the mailroom right up to Dr. Torgenson. No question about it, Universal had complete control over Gammett. Gammett was merely a cardboard corporation. Given such a contractual agreement, any fair-minded judge would rule that Universal was doing business in Massachusetts. Service of process on Gammett would bind Universal. Even Frank Galvin and all the legal talent at Hovington, Sturdevant, Holmes & Hall couldn't pull that one out.

Chip reached for the pencil, scratched out the word *shall*, and inserted *may*.

Nice—just a little cosmetic surgery, he said to himself. He held the document up to the light. He'd see Jerry Wilson first thing in the morning. No need to bother Galvin about this, or even Stu Trimble. He and Jerry Wilson had a rowing date at 6 A.M. Great time to discuss business.

Chip glanced at the digital clock on the TV. Fifteen past midnight. Might be too late, but he'd give it a try.

The phone in Chip's room rang at 4 A.M.

"Chip," said Carter Hovington on the other end of the line. "I got the information you wanted, came straight from Stan Frobisher in London. Use it in strictest confidence. Jerry Wilson's on his way out. He doesn't know it yet. Maybe has two months, then the axe. They're bringing in new talent. That's all Frobisher would tell me. Guess Wilson wasn't hardball enough."

"Fine, Dad." Chip suppressed a yawn.

"What's all this got to do with the lawsuit?" Carter asked.

"Let you know when we get back, Dad. It'll all fall into place."

12

Your clients ever get the impression that Galvin's not entirely on their side?" Jerry Wilson tossed it out casually as he negotiated his metallic-blue Mercedes in and out of the early-morning traffic on the Garden State Parkway.

"Oh, he's hard-nosed," Chip replied drowsily. He was slouched in the front seat, eyes half-closed, trying to catch up on a missing four hours' sleep. "Clients got to level with Galvin. That's why he comes off so good. No surprises on cross-examination."

"Have to agree with you there," Wilson said. "He's four or five questions ahead of me. But maybe it's the way he goes about it—his interrogation, I mean. He wants private records—patents, secret trade agreements, profit statements, confidential disbursements. Christ, even Torgenson isn't privy to that kind of stuff."

Chip was beginning to shake his early-morning lethargy. "Galvin's just thorough. Believe me, he knows what he's doing. There are counts in the plaintiffs' complaint for punitive damages. That means they're trying to sock you guys for a share of your net worth."

"That's ridiculous." Wilson accelerated past several cars.

"That's probably what the general counsel for Johns-Manville said when the first asbestos suit crossed his desk." Chip sat up. He was now wide awake.

"Just last week in Chicago," Chip said, "Scherring Pharmaceutical, the manufacturer of Coumadin, got whacked for thirty-eight million. And Cessna was damn near forced out of the airplane business when a Pennsylvania jury found against them for sixty-two million."

"The whole thing's gotten out of hand," Wilson shook his head. "The President's Committee on Tort Reform will see to it that national legislation puts an end to these legal crap shoots." He eased down from 85 mph as they approached the Red Bank exit.

"You're probably right," Chip agreed. "There'll be a hundred-thousand-dollar products liability cap before the year's out. Then guys like us, the corporations and the law firms, can get back to the more mundane pursuits of patent infringement, breach of contract, fighting Uncle Sam's antitrust legions, and making a handsome living."

Wilson forced a wry smile, then for several minutes concentrated on the roadway. He turned his car into a picturesque country lane that hugged the banks of the Shrewsbury River. "That's the Gammett Boat Club ahead," he said, pointing to a trim clapboard building, cylindrical wooden turrets at each corner, a heavily planked drawbridge slanting into the water. "We'll check out a two-man scull. Give it a four-miler this morning—two up to the Fort Monmouth bridge, two back. Dr. Torgenson's already on the river. He's the club singles champion. Even at forty-seven, he could make the varsity at Penn."

The security guard waved them through the gate, and Chip thought this was as good a time as any to broach the subject. If Jerry Wilson had an inkling he was going to be sacked, he'd react accordingly.

Wilson eased into a reserved parking space next to Dr. Torgenson's Porsche and leaned forward to shut off the engine.

"There might be a way, Jerry, to keep Universal from opening its vaults," Chip said.

"Oh?" Wilson leaned back. The motor kept purring.

"What's your guess as to Universal's take just on Lyosin alone?" Chip watched four young men angle down the drawbridge, a rowing shell hoisted over their shoulders. The river was metallic gray. The early-morning mist wisped in slow eddies from the water's quiet surface.

"You're talking worldwide net, after everything's factored in—R and D, personnel, marketing?" Wilson asked.

"All the rainy-day froth."

Wilson tilted his head, his eyes unconsciously checking right to left. "Perhaps three billion a year. It's a hot item."

Chip issued a low whistle. "You don't leave that out there for the government boys to tax, do you?"

"Hell no. It's disbursed carefully—amortization, salaries, certain benevolent funds in foreign countries, particularly Latin America, shareholders, repayment of loans. And a kitty's got to be stashed away for future research and development. No big corporation pays income taxes—if you follow me."

"Well, taking depositions under oath about financial expenditures can get sticky," Chip said.

"What you're saying"—Wilson removed his fingerless Swedish racing gloves and placed them on the cordovan dash—"is if we ain't in no lawsuit, Universal doesn't expose its backside."

"Precisely," said Chip. "No jurisdiction over Universal, no fishing expedition."

"Somehow I get the impression that Galvin doesn't share your optimism." Wilson reached forward and turned off the engine.

"Well, if I had to wager *right now*, Jerry, I'd bet that you guys are going to get saddled with jurisdiction."

"Even though Gammett and Universal are distinct corporate entities—separate books, personnel? And you know, of course, there's specific language in the Importer's Agreement prohibiting Gammett from acting as agent for Universal."

"That's just the point," said Chip. "Whoever crafted the agreement didn't leave Gammett a whit's worth of discretion. They can't do this, must do that. All dictated by Universal. Once our adversaries requisition the Importer's Agreement—and they will, on jurisdiction at least—Universal's a gone goose." Chip watched a few moments as a scull with eight young women glided past. A curly-haired coxswain with a megaphone bobbed in rhythmic cadence with her crew. Chip tingled inwardly as the silver oars clipped the placid water.

"That's the New Brunswick State varsity," Wilson said, then paused. "NCAA champs last year. I have a daughter on the J.V."

A daughter at New Brunswick State? Chip thought about it. Why not Radcliffe or some Main Line finishing school? It's not all that smooth going on a hundred-thousand-dollar salary. Hardly pays for the SL 500. And that would soon end. The Mercedes would be the last trapping to go. Nothing worse than a hack of a general counsel—fifteen or so years dousing company fires, trying to hang on until the golden handshake. Where would he go? No one wants an old house attorney who has lost his fastball. Corporations want kids two years out of law school, kids who churn eighty-hour weeks, the Stu Trimbles of the world.

Chip returned to the conversation. "If the Importer's Agreement demonstrated a little more flexibility, allowed Gammett some breathing room, then no jurist in the world would rule that Gammett was the alter ego of Universal. Say, if the word *shall* was softened a bit—buffered down to the word *may*. Then . . ."

"I see what you mean." Wilson stroked his chin. He squinted through the windshield as if he caught a glimmer of light in a dark tunnel. "Interesting," he said.

◘

Galvin waited in a cinder-block alcove outside Dr. Corsini's office and skimmed through Gammett's PR manual. He had been checked by security at varying intervals and a uniformed guard hovered nearby. The manual was impressively bound in blue leather with the firm's logo, a gold apothecary jar, embossed on the cover. Galvin had noticed this same emblem on tie clasps the bright young executives wore. The corporate world, Galvin observed, was not unlike the legal world. Cash flow was the common denominator. If billing was up, everyone prospered, and along the way some good was done.

Galvin studied an old photograph on the inside cover of the Gammett manual and was intrigued by several figures wearing jodhpurs and pith helmets standing at a dockside quay. "Dr.

Aubrey Ellison Gammett with Sir Rudyard Kipling, Rangoon 1909," the caption read.

Kipling. Galvin struggled to remember some long-forgotten lines. Something about pagodas and flying fishes and tinkly China bells.

"Mr. Galvin." Dr. Corsini's jaunty baritone voice interrupted his reflections. "I would like you to meet my colleague, Dr. Sabrina Bok-Sahn."

Galvin was startled to see smiling down at him the Oriental woman he had glimpsed at Southwick the previous night.

"Dr. Bok-Sahn is director of medical research and"—Corsini gestured toward the brochure Galvin still held opened at the photograph—"she's the granddaughter of old Aubrey, the lad you see there with the poet Kipling."

Galvin was surprised she was so young, early thirties at the outside, a sleek statuesque beauty. "I'm honored," he said, half rising.

"It is my privilege and honor, Mr. Galvin," she said, extending a delicate bronzed hand after withdrawing it from the pocket of her starched smock. Her voice had a tender quality, like soft summer rain. Lingering, caressing.

Galvin shook her hand gently.

"I've heard a lot about you." Again the dulcet tones. "Dr. Corsini tells me that Gammett is in trusted hands."

She had deep dimples in her cheeks, leaving the hint of a perpetual smile. Her jet-black hair was pulled taut from her forehead and coiffed in a tight bun. Any trace of old Aubrey was well hidden in the meld of three generations.

Curious, Galvin asked, "Did you grow up here?"

"I'm Burmese," she said pleasantly. "Actually, I've spent most of my life in London, where I trained. Dr. Corsini is showing me the ropes here. We've worked together now for three months."

"Oh, she's being modest, Mr. Galvin," Corsini said. "Dr. Bok-Sahn is a graduate of Oxford, and a Fellow, if I can use that chauvinistic term, of the Royal College of Physicians and Surgeons—all this at the tender age of thirty-three."

"I'm impressed," said Galvin.

Dr. Corsini ushered them into his office and asked them to excuse its appearance. Like the alcove, the office was gray cinder block, and devoid of windows. It was more a cubicle than an office and overflowed with ceramic figurines and other knickknacks, scientific memorabilia, and professional journals. Galvin surmised that the Gammett stockholders couldn't complain that money was being frittered away on opulent overhead, at least on the office of the associate director of medical research.

"Dr. Corsini has told me about your request, Mr. Galvin, and as I am the D.H.—"

"The what?"

"The designated hitter." Again the deep dimpled smile.

"Dr. Bok-Sahn will fill you in." Corsini was again quick to break in. "She'll tell you everything you want to know about Lyosin, even down to whether a single pill is worth the twenty-nine dollars the market commands."

Galvin took a seat next to Corsini, and Dr. Bok-Sahn sat in the tufted leather chair behind Corsini's desk. Galvin had assumed Corsini would lead the discussion. He needed to assess his mannerisms and attitudes as a potential witness.

"Okay, Doctor," he addressed Sabrina Bok-Sahn, "I just arrived from Mars and haven't the foggiest notion what your product is all about. You educate me. What is Lyosin, what does it do, and how does it do it? Do you chew it or put it in your gas tank? And who was old Aubrey Ellison Gammett and where do you fit in? As they say on Mars, my antenna is up."

Dr. Bok-Sahn paused. She reached into her smock pocket and pulled out a crumpled pack of cigarettes. With delicate care she extracted one and gestured an offer to Galvin, who declined.

"One of my bad habits." She smiled. "Cheroots. Been smoking them since I was ten. A few good puffs in the morning help me to get started."

Corsini quickly produced a lighter.

Galvin was puzzled. Smoking? A medical director? It went against the grain.

"Some things I'm going to relate I'm sure you already know, Mr. Galvin. It's common scientific knowledge." She took a deep drag on the cigarette, held her breath for a moment, then slowly exhaled. The smoke curled from her lips. "And some of what I tell you, only Dr. Torgenson, Dr. Corsini, and the top echelon in London are aware of." She inhaled again, then ground out the cigarette in a ceramic ashtray on Corsini's desk.

"I have Dr. Corsini's assurance that our talk and its subject will be in strictest confidence," she said as she uncoiled a metallic pointer that moments before had resembled a fountain pen clipped to her smock lapel. "Trust is important to me." Her large almond eyes fixed on Galvin. "Can I count on that assurance? Our competitors have four years left before cashing in on the market; that's when our patent expires. Lyosin will then be as available as aspirin. And at about the same price."

"What happens between us," Galvin said seriously, "is covered by the ethics of the client-attorney relationship. It's as sacred as the seal of the confessional."

"Fine," she said. "Parke-Davis, Schering, Richardson-Merrell, and some of the Silicon Valley upstarts knew the chemical ingredients of Lyosin even before we filed a new-drug application with the FDA. There are no secrets anymore. But there are a few kickers out there that the biotechs would love to get their hands on.

"What's the world's number-one killer?" she asked, more a postulation than a query. "Cardiovascular disease, Mr. Galvin. More specifically, coronary atherosclerosis." She answered her own question. "It accounts for more fatalities annually than all diseases, accidents, and wars put together."

She stood up and moved toward several anatomic charts pinned to a cork wallboard to the left rear of Corsini's desk. "I won't bore you with statistics, but this year coronary atherosclerosis will cause the untimely death of over one million Americans. And right now as I'm speaking, this insidious disease is laying down its sludge in the coronary arteries of all of us." She looked at Corsini, then pressed the pointer to her left breast and returned eye contact with Galvin.

"Although the Creator is usually provident," she said, "He's not always generous. Coronary arteries, even at their largest diameter, are about the size of soda straws, tapering to pinholes. The good

Lord simply made them too damn small. Every tissue or organ needs oxygenated blood to survive. If the brain doesn't get its supply within four minutes, irreversible damage sets in and cerebral tissue disintegrates and dies. Likewise, once you get necrosis of heart tissue, it's gone forever. It doesn't regenerate."

She pointed to a cross-section diagram of the heart.

"Here, running off the tip of the aorta, are the coronary arteries." She traced their course with the pointer. "These thread through the heart muscle, nourishing what we call the myocardium. The heart, despite being a great lyrical metaphor, is simply a pump about as big as my fist." She held up her hand. "It dilates and contracts, continuously." She opened her fist and closed it several times. "It does this seventy-two times a minute, a hundred thousand times a day. A remarkable organ. The engine of a Rolls Royce would burn out in four months if it had to duplicate this effort.

"Now look at this cross section of a *normal* coronary artery. This is like a pipe transporting life-giving blood to the myocardium. Its diameter is clear—no sludge, no corrosive plaques, nothing to impede blood flow.

"From age ten onward these small blood vessels build up sclerotic material that gradually occludes the diameter of the arteries. Why? That's the big medical mystery. Despite some intriguing scientific theories—diet, stress, smoking, obesity, what have you—medical science is still in the dark.

"See, here we have an atherosclerotic artery. Actually this specimen came from a thirty-seven-year-old male; the artery is ninety percent clogged. Only a trickle of oxygenated blood could pass this thrombotic area. The subject had what we call a myocardial infarction, a heart attack. Death was sudden, and without warning.

"Sometimes victims get a signal. Chest pains, shortness of breath. They make it to a hospital, undergo batteries of tests, go on a low-salt diet, take up programmed exercise, drug therapy, have a coronary bypass or even a heart transplant, and weather the storm, temporarily staying the inevitable. But most often the initial attack strikes unexpectedly." She snapped her fingers.

Galvin was impressed by Dr. Bok-Sahn's articulate delivery, particularly her ability to convert arcane medical data into layman's language.

"Now, up until the discovery of Lyosin, this buildup of sludge was inexorable. No known treatment or drug therapy could halt its invasive progression."

Galvin nodded acquiescence.

"Atherosclerosis is not a new disease like AIDS or Kawasaki syndrome. Nor is it endemic to Western man. It has been found in the coronary arteries of Egyptian mummies—some quite young—and in fetuses of unborn children. The big pharmaceutical giants—Bruenthal of Germany, Pasteur-LaRoche in France, Parke-Davis, Schering, Upjohn, and others—have been on the trail of this elusive killer for fifty years. Ten times as much money was spent on this project than was spent in developing the atomic bomb. And like the A-bomb, it was an all-or-nothing race. There was no second prize. In the end the gold belonged to Universal. They capitalized on the research and study of a young British medical officer assigned to Her Majesty's Expeditionary Forces sent to Burma in 1897 to protect shipping and mining interests of the East India Company."

"Old Aubrey?"

"Lt. Aubrey Ellison Gammett. None other. He had a liaison with my grandmother. Old Aubrey's books, manuscripts, and studies were passed down through my grandmother to my mother and, of course, that's where I come in.

"Burma is an ancient country," she said wistfully. "It was old when Marco Polo passed that way and when Kublai Khan pillaged it in the thirteenth century. The major races migrated from the Tibetan Plateau some four thousand years ago. The main tribes are the Burmans, Mons, Chins, Shans, and Kachins, with numerous offshoots. Each has a distinct language, culture, and customs. They may look alike, but they're as different as the French from the Dutch.

"Now, in Aubrey's day, heart disease wasn't discussed as it is today. People lived. Died. There were various epidemics and no one got terribly alarmed when someone clutched his chest and keeled over, least of all in Burma. Death was merely a transition, a reincarnation. But Aubrey, during one of his tiger hunts into the wild and remote Naga Hills—they have headhunters up there, even to this day—noted that the Changareet, an offshoot of the Kachins, seemed to live forever. As in Shangri-la, people survived to a ripe old age. By Aubrey's calculation, many lived well into their nineties. Keep in mind that this was at the turn of the century when the average Asian survived only to his mid-thirties. What, then, was so special about the Changareet?"

Galvin liked her story. She was the shaman around the tribal fire saying "Once upon a time . . ."

"Aubrey received a grant from the Royal Medical Society and camped with the Changareet for three years. He lived, ate, hunted, even cohabited with them, as my grandmother could well attest. She was Changareet. He was a mix of Father Damian and Albert Schweitzer, with a touch of rascality. He became fascinated at the Changareet's longevity and bribed the chiefs to allow him to perform autopsies on the most elderly when they died. The cause of death ranged anywhere from an encounter with a passing tiger to terminal pneumonia, but what amazed Aubrey was the state of the coronary arteries. Most were as smooth as a baby's bottom. In no case was heart disease the terminal pathology. Why?" Dr. Bok-Sahn recoiled her pointer and placed it carefully on Corsini's desk.

Galvin admired her timing. She had the raconteur's knack of arresting attention. Corsini sat with his hands clasped on his lap, a pleased smile upon his plump face.

"It's all in here," she said, reaching for a ceramic apothecary jar on a shelf just to the right of her shoulder. She opened the lid and spilled out several bean pods on the desk. Holding one between her thumb and forefinger, she examined it as if it were a rare jewel.

"This little brown kernel is the correiga, indigenous to the jungles of northern Burma, a kind of betel nut, one of the staples of the Changareet. They chew it, brew it, cook it, and smoke it."

"It gives them a buzz and a hard-on," Corsini offered, his full-moon face widening as he tried to repress a grin.

His humor was out of place. For the first time Galvin detected a slight flattening of the dimples in Bok-Sahn's amber cheeks.

She brushed an imaginary strand of hair from her forehead. "The propensity for increased libido from correiga extract is one of its interesting side effects. Also, it has certain opiate qualities."

If she was irritated by Corsini's intrusion, it was quickly dismissed. She would make an excellent expert witness, Galvin surmised, if the case ever got that far. He thought of Tina Alvarez cross-examining Sabrina Bok-Sahn. It would be quite a match. Also, he had the feeling that Dr. Bok-Sahn, despite her youth and corporate inexperience, was really running the Gammett show. Corsini was probably just a figurehead, window dressing for the stockholders and the board of directors.

"So, after these years of living in the jungle, like the good clinician he was, researching and running down medicinal herbs and exotic plants, Aubrey finally discovered the secret of the Changareet. It was this little nut right here. The correiga." She jiggled it in her palm as if it were a dice cube.

"So in a *nutshell*, Mr. Galvin, you have it. The Lyosin story, the Gammett connection—and where I fit in."

"Quite a story," Galvin said. He wanted to learn more about the actual formula, chemical ingredients, additives. How it was synthesized. He still didn't know how it worked. He wanted to know if old Aubrey's notes contained observations of deformities in Changareet offspring. But the initial briefing would do for now. The hard questions he'd leave to Chip Hovington and Stu Trimble. They would remain at Gammett for the rest of the week. Galvin had to be in their Washington office to get a rundown on the FDA approval.

"Here, gentlemen." Dr. Bok-Sahn crinkled her nose, and her dimples deepened into a seductive half-smile. "To your health." She handed a correiga to Galvin, passed one to Corsini, and placed one in her mouth. "It'll add hours to your love life."

◘

"Let me see if I have this straight." Dr. Torgenson poured some brandy into a crystal snifter. "You say, just by slightly amending the Importer's Agreement, we can avoid getting Universal involved in the lawsuit?" He walked from the rich walnut bar in his office and handed a glass to Jerry Wilson.

"I won't go into the legal ramifications," said Wilson, "but there's no question in my mind that that's exactly what can be accomplished."

Dr. Torgenson inhaled the amber liquid, toasted briefly, and took a sip. After a polite interval Wilson followed suit.

"Has Mr. Galvin authorized this procedural change?" Dr. Torgenson took a stronger sip.

"Absolutely," Wilson replied quickly. "It was proposed by Carter Hovington, Jr., and I might add it was a stroke of genius. When London drew up this contract, naturally they didn't have lawsuits in mind. No one did. Now this little maneuver can insulate London perfectly."

"Okay, Jerry," Dr. Torgenson said, "I'll attend to it. As you say, the document we send to our adversaries will be a photocopy. I'll discuss the cosmetics with London first thing in the morning."

Torgenson glanced at his watch. "I have to join my wife for dinner at Southwick."

Jerry Wilson lowered his half-empty glass. The discussion was ended. It was his cue to leave. He adjusted his tie clasp, fingering the replica of the gold apothecary jar. The little button behind the clasp was in place and the thin wire threading into the inside of his shirt was still covered by his tie.

"Have a good evening, Doctor." He nodded. "Please give my regards to Mrs. Torgenson."

Wilson hoped the hidden recorder had taped the entire conversation. It would be his insurance policy; indemnity against an unseasonable retirement.

13

The Prison Point Bridge loomed ahead and Rhys Jameson slowed the pace. For two miles he and Tina Alvarez had jogged shoulder to shoulder along the Harvard side of the Charles River. They kept up an idle chatter—the Red Sox, Whitney Houston, the upcoming weekend at the Cape, anything but the case. This was the mental and physical recharging, the brief respite before the workday gruel that would end well past midnight.

The cinder path was alive with joggers, bikers, and strollers, all trying to hold mortality at bay. "Okay, California!" Tina cried as they completed a 180 and headed back. "Race you to Beacon Hill."

"Gotta remind you," Rhys said. "I was on the track team at Pasadena High. Won a scholarship to UCLA."

"What event?" She adjusted her headband, and her shapely brown legs lengthened their stride.

"Trombone," he laughed. "Actually, my coach thought I'd make a fair hurdler, but I was too slow. Pretty swift on the horns, though. Made the marching band. You should have seen us at halftime against Nebraska."

They crossed Storrow Drive and headed up a grassy knoll toward MIT. Rhys accelerated and Tina met the challenge. Rhys had added a new dimension to her life. She relished the early-morning runs. She loved the rhythm of it, the crunch of cinders beneath her feet and the wind in her hair. But most of all it was Rhys Jameson. He was like no person she had ever met: intense, decisive, dedicated, yet still a boy, whimsical, as when he played reggae on the snare drum, sensitive when his agile fingers picked out something from Grieg or Debussy at the piano. They had become lovers as easily and as naturally as they had joined forces as colleagues. And last week Rhys had moved his gear into Tina's apartment.

◘

Moe Katz was frowning.

"These came by courier fifteen minutes ago." He pointed to a mass of documents on the conference table. "It's not only the Hovington paper chase, it's a goddamned blizzard. The defendant removed the case to Federal Court. Hit us with fifteen sets of interrogatories, all to be answered within twenty-one days. Thirty-seven notices to admit facts, twenty-five notices for depositions. And the kicker—you ready for this?—a motion to dismiss for lack of jurisdiction and failure to comply with Rule Eleven of the Code of Civil Procedure."

Rhys studied the papers carefully. He said nothing as he perused each page. Tina shared Moe's gloom, her thumb beneath her chin, her index finger tugging on her lower lip. Minutes dragged into what seemed like hours.

"All right." Rhys slapped the bulky papers down on the table. "Hovington's unleashed his killer bees—"

"Killer bees?" Moe sighed ruefully.

"Yes, fifteen litigation specialists who swarm all over you and chase you out the courtroom door. Okay. We'll hit them one at a time. Tina, I want you to start working up answers to interrogatories. Like right now. Moe, get book on Judge Baron—he's assigned to the case. From what I know, he's a stickler for protocol. That could cut both ways."

"What's Rule Eleven?" Moe tapped his forehead. "I must confess that to an old tort lawyer like me, these new procedures are confusing."

"Well, right now Rule Eleven is the least of our problems." Rhys picked up a pencil and scribbled some notes. "Briefly, it states that a litigant must have reasonable cause to commence suit against a defendant or he shouldn't be in court. In the old days, I could sue anyone, even the President, for anything—a fancied grievance, or just for the hell of it. No more. When I was with Hovington, Rule Eleven knocked out eighty percent of the cases before they even got started. Jurisdiction is the stumbling block. We have Gammett, no question about that. But Universal?" Rhys wiggled his hand. "And if we're out of court on Universal, we can forget them for all time. Gammett zips up its files, claims everything's with Universal. We'll hit the wall."

Moe's frown deepened. "I don't have to get a read on Baron," he said. "He's a blue-blooded sycophant. Been on the Federal Bench for five years and is bucking for an Appeals Court slot. He's no legal scholar—was a pedestrian lawyer for some fancy New York firm and they kicked him upstairs just to get him off the payroll. I know all about Chester Baron. Probably the worst judge we could have landed. He'll croak us. Not only dismiss the case, he'll whack us with costs, including defendant attorneys' fees."

Rhys tried to cut through the prevailing gloom. "Okay," he said, "so we got a battle on our hands. We didn't expect anything less. Tina, I want you to draft an affidavit listing facts and suspicions that implicated Lyosin at the time you started suit."

"I ran the cases by Dr. Rafael Meideros in New Bedford," Tina said. "He's a retired cardiologist, kicking eighty, used to be on the staff at St. Ann's Hospital. His wife was my mother's cousin."

"Oy," Moe cried. "A relative no less. We got problems."

"Look, we go with the hand we're dealt," Rhys said. "We have no choice. Tina, meet with Meideros tomorrow. Get his affidavit. If he thought that Lyosin caused the birth deformities, it should suffice. The judge can't look behind the opinion. At least not at this preliminary stage. His credibility is another matter, but that's for the jury to decide. Get me his CV, pack it to the hilt.

"Now, Moe, I want you to dig into that library of yours and get a brief together on the Hague Convention. I shot off letters rogatory last week to England and to Holland. I'll follow up what's happening on that front.

"Also, Tina, make an immediate motion for the Universal-

Gammett Importer's Agreement. This might give us the evidence we need to show they're essentially one corporation doing business here in Massachusetts."

"I've done it already." Tina snapped a token salute. "It has to be produced in three days."

"Fine. We might crash somewhere down the line, but at least we've pulled out of the station. . . . Let's see, today is Monday. The defendant motions are marked up in ten days. We got our work cut out for us. Tina," Rhys added, smiling, "you'll love London. What was it that Tennyson said? 'Oh, to be in England now that April's there.' "

"It was Browning." Moe's frown lifted. "And while you're packing, better check your malpractice insurance. I'm not so sure those Fall River families will be too happy to hear we're out of court because we blew the statute of limitations."

◘

Dr. Sabrina Bok-Sahn's eyes glistened as she read from the brown parchment of Aubrey Gammett's original journal.

She closed the worn binding and carefully tied the leather straps. "Aubrey noted an increased incidence in congenital defects among the Changareet and suspected the correiga nut. Keep in mind, Mr. Hovington, this was in 1902. There have been no studies since."

"That's what bothers me," said Chip. "No follow-up. Was this historical data transmitted to the FDA at any time?"

"Well, wait," Jerry Wilson interrupted. "This stuff has no medical significance. Hell, Chip, it was written almost a century ago. It was pure speculation, even then. The birth defects could have come from a variety of sources—malnutrition, stress at delivery, unskilled midwives, you name it. Aubrey didn't study other races and tribes. Could be the Kachins or the Mons had an even greater incidence of congenital defects than the Changareet. There was absolutely no need, medically or legally, to transmit this ancient scroll to the FDA."

"All right," said Chip, "I tend to agree. . . . Dr. Bok-Sahn, who has ownership of these notes?"

"They belong entirely to me. They'll be returned to a vault in my London office."

"Fine," Chip said. "Keep them buried."

Jerry Wilson's office was on the top level of Gammett's main building, overlooking an artificial lake. It was just down the hall from Dr. Torgenson's corner suite. Chip noticed the opulent fixtures, massive oynx desk, wall-to-wall Belgium broadloom, recessed bookcases. He compared it to Corsini's alcove. It was easy to see where Gammett's priorities lay.

"Jerry," Chip said. "What's the story on Corsini?"

"Corsini?"

"I mean, he doesn't appear to be all that swift."

Wilson grinned. "Oh, he's harmless. Been with Gammett for ten years, got all the degrees he claims on his résumé—University of Bologna, research chemist. I agree he's a little airy, but he never says the wrong thing, and he's well connected within the FDA. Obviously, we have other products besides Lyosin—Health Plus, the birth-control pill, and Saparine, an antidepressant. Next best seller to Valium. He gets out the 'Dear Doctor' letters, makes sure the medical complaints are properly edited and filed with the Feds. He's on a first-name basis with the director, Samuelson, and most of the Agency staff."

"And what about Sabrina Bok-Sahn?"

"Now you hit on it," Wilson replied. "She is so friggin' brainy, it scares me. Medically and politically, she's the real force behind Universal and Gammett." He leaned toward Chip and whispered, "She's got the juice in London and in Holland. We wondered why she came here. Even Dr. Torgenson treats her carefully. Ultra respect and deference. She could have us all canned at the snap of her fingers."

"The contents of Aubrey's journal disturb me," Chip said. "Here's the inventor of Lyosin himself suspecting that his product causes natal injuries."

"I'm aware of the implications. But what the hell, conjecture isn't legally relevant."

"What kind of person is Dr. Bok-Sahn? Can she be talked to?" Chip studied Wilson.

"I'll let London handle that."

"Well, I doubt if the lawsuit will be viable a month from now," Chip said. "But on the outside chance that it survives our motion to dismiss, it would be better if Aubrey's journal was retired to some dusty cellar in London, never to resurface." There was an edge to his voice.

"I'll talk with Dr. Torgenson." Wilson feigned concern. He looked as if he had just received a cancer warning. But somehow he couldn't recall when he had ever felt better.

◘

"Oy," Moe exclaimed, "Judge Baron denied our request for a thirty-day continuance." His hand trembled as he scanned the letter from the federal clerk's office.

"Now for the bad news."

Tina looked at Rhys Jameson apprehensively.

"The son of a bitch," moaned Moe. "The blue-blooded putz. This guy is giving us a judicial screwing, and I got a tight sphincter—excuse me, Tina—never saw anything like it in fifty years of practice. Look at this." He handed the letter to Rhys Jameson.

Rhys read it carefully and gave a low whistle. "Not good, Tina," he said. "The judge allowed the defense motion to subpoena Dr. Meideros and subject him to cross-examination under Rule Eleven." And his voice trailed. "Also you, Tina. . . ."

Rhys and Moe thought Tina would shrivel and melt away. She surprised even herself.

"Who signed the defendant motion?" she asked.

"Francis X. Galvin and Carter Hovington, Jr."

"Well, goddammit!" she cried. "If they want a fight, they'll get it!"

"Hold it," said Rhys. "There's nothing, I mean nothing, in the state or federal rules authorizing Baron to conduct such an inquiry. No lawyer should be subject to this indignity. We're representing our clients to the best of our ability. Our affidavit and that of Dr. Meideros should suffice. That's our position, on that we stake our entire case. If Baron holds us in contempt—well, that's up to him. But no one goes on the witness stand—not you, Tina, or Meideros."

"Okay, gang," she said. "No judicial coercion. Baron may threaten to incarcerate us, but we don't take the stand. Agreed?"

Moe sighed, a deep, tired, hand-wringing sigh, and let it out slowly, as if he'd been saving it up for years. "I think we'd better bring our toothbrushes," he said.

14

Mr. Galvin," the firm's Washington counsel, Colby Yaeger, said, "I want you to meet Dr. Fred Willis, former director of the Food and Drug Administration."

Galvin and Willis shook hands.

"I'm pleased to meet you, Mr. Galvin," Dr. Willis said. "Heard good reports about you. I'm certain we can work well together." Willis was tanned, well tailored, his thinning hair the color of dry ice. He wore a diamond ring on his little finger. Galvin assessed him quickly. The tan and ring would have to go.

"Dr. Willis has been retained as an expert consultant on the Lyosin litigation," Colby Yaeger said. "He's testified in many drug product liability cases all over the world. There's no one with higher credentials in the field of hematology and epidemiology."

Galvin took a seat in the bronzed mahogany conference room. Through the gossamer curtain there was a commanding view of Pennsylvania Avenue as it stretched out toward Capitol Hill.

"Tell me, Dr. Willis, were you director when Lyosin received FDA approval?"

"That's what makes it so perfect," Yaeger answered, "and why Dr. Willis will make such a credible witness. Can't be challenged on bias. Dr. Robert Gottschalk was director at time of approval. That was more than ten years ago."

Galvin didn't appreciate Yaeger supplying the answers. "Where's Dr. Gottschalk now?" He addressed Willis directly.

"Oh, Bob's senior vice president of Kettering Pharmaceutical in Chicago. We're extremely close."

I'm sure you are, Galvin wanted to say. He wondered who had authorized retaining Willis. It had been done without his knowledge. And at the moment it seemed like overkill.

"Dr. Willis has been here for the past week," Yaeger said. "He's been all through Gammett's new-drug application work-up, scientific studies, clinical trials—all stages. Everything's letter perfect. The drug's safety and efficacy are proven beyond the slightest doubt."

"Do you know anything about the correiga nut, Dr. Willis?" Galvin leveled a gaze at Willis.

Dr. Willis tilted his head back and eyed the ceiling. "The correiga? Let's see, the correiga. . . Does that come from South America?"

"No, from Burma."

"Oh, certainly." Willis snapped his fingers. "There are two biologically active components in the correiga nut, both alkaloids and therefore fairly easy to synthesize in the laboratory. The combination of the two makes up Lyosin. I'll bone up on the medicinal history of the nut as it was used by the natives before the advent of modern science. I'll also go over the pharmacology and the chemical synthesis process so it will be fresh in my mind."

Galvin made notes as he spent most of the afternoon interrogating Willis. The doctor had a keen mind and persuasive delivery, and knew his subject. And he enjoyed the thrust and parry of the exchange.

"Dr. Willis, what do you know about Dr. Sabrina Bok-Sahn?" Galvin looked directly at the doctor and motioned Colby Yaeger not to intercede.

"I don't know too much about her," he said cautiously. "I hear she's Gammett's new director of medical research. Comes from London. I do know Dr. Dante Corsini. He's well connected within the FDA and a knowledgeable spokesman."

Corsini's a dolt, Galvin said to himself. Probably doesn't know Charles Darwin from Charlie Brown.

"I'm due there tomorrow morning," said Willis. "I'm spending the week as Dr. Torgenson's guest. It'll be nice seeing Dr. Corsini again, and I'll certainly get to know Dr. Bok-Sahn."

"She's very pretty. . . ." Galvin's voice trailed off as he looked up Pennsylvania Avenue toward the gray fluted columns of the Capitol Building.

"What? I didn't catch what you said." Willis tilted his head toward Galvin.

"Nothing," Galvin said. "I was thinking out loud. Nothing relevant."

◻

"What in hell is all this!" Galvin slapped a blue-backed document he held in his hand. "I never authorized these motions to dismiss. And who's responsible for hiring Dr. Willis?"

Carter Hovington watched the second hand on his leather-embossed desk clock sweep for several moments. He examined his manicured fingernails for several more, allowing Galvin's anger to run down an embarrassed slope.

"Carter." Galvin's voice softened. "We've been away a whole week, and before firing off summary procedures we have to analyze what's been gathered. These motions could backfire. And I think retention of Dr. Willis at such an early stage in the litigation is . . . is . . ."

"Premature." Carter supplied the proper word.

"Yes. Premature. We enlist experts after the plaintiff articulates his medical position. That's basic."

Hovington swiveled a half-turn in his chair.

"Colby Yaeger called me while you were down at Gammett. He

said Willis was available, so it made no sense leaving the best expert in the world out there for the opposition. He's now in our camp and he can engage Dr. Gottschalk and others."

"Why wasn't I cut in? At the very least, it should have been run by Chip or Stu Trimble, then by me."

"Galvin." Carter Hovington's tone was soothingly professional. "That's why you have me, Colby Yaeger, and the firm. You're the general in the field, on the firing line. We, here at headquarters, can give you backup without bothering you with technicalities."

Galvin thought for a moment. Carter was always logical. Even when he was wrong. And in this instance, Galvin couldn't say that Carter was wrong. That bothered him.

"You know," Hovington added, "if we hadn't grabbed Willis, he wouldn't have lasted the weekend. Rhys Jameson made overtures to him. Colby Yaeger told me that Dr. Willis's secretary received a call from Jameson, so that's when we acted. I'm sure you would have done the same."

Galvin remained standing and Hovington was smart enough not to attempt further placation. He realized that standing gave Galvin a psychological edge.

"Okay," Galvin said. "I buy that. But this stuff—the motions to dismiss. I get back, nothing's coordinated with me, and bang, it's in court. Marked up for next Tuesday." Galvin placed the blue-backed document down on Hovington's desk and rapped it several times with his knuckles.

"Look, do you think we have worker ants or brownnosers around here?" Hovington put a little edge in his voice. "This is a law firm, a goddamned good one. You've got sixty-five lawyers in your litigation department. More than in any other section. They were all Law Review, number one or two in their class. They don't have to be told what to do. Actually, this was Andrea Schneiderman's work. She's aggressive, so goddamned smart we may have trouble keeping her. Okay, she went for the jugular. The only problem I see at present is that Judge Baron will grant our motion, the plaintiff cases will be dismissed, and the war will be over. That's the fundamental error. We haven't milked the case enough."

Galvin thought Hovington was being facetious. But he wasn't sure. He wanted to ask Carter if he was serious, but he let it pass.

Galvin picked up the blue-backed papers. His anger was completely defused.

"Well, in the future," Galvin said, delivering a final reminder, "on expert witnesses, I've got to be consulted."

"No question about it." Hovington allowed Galvin the parting salvo.

◘

Galvin arrived early at the twelfth floor of the Federal Building. Chip and Stu Trimble would be along shortly, but first he wanted to chat with Sheila Finnegan, Judge Baron's law clerk, to get an angle on the judge's inclinations. It was a practice he had picked up from Ed Concannon, whom he had bested five years ago in the St. Catherine Laboure case. Concannon always covered every contingency. He'd employ an elephant gun to kill a gnat, if need be. In a way, Galvin unconsciously emulated him.

The floor was deserted. Not even the clerical force had made an appearance yet. He wandered down the chipped-tile corridor, noted that the ashtrays next to the elevators had not been emptied and that the windows were badly in need of cleaning. The General Services Administration, the watchdog and guardian of federal properties, had begun to heed the President's austerity program.

He was about to push open the tufted leather door when, through the oval window, he spotted Moe Katz in his wheelchair, positioned at the counsel table. He opened the door a crack and saw Moe busily jotting down some last-minute notes. He wanted to rush to Moe, embrace him, kiss him, tell him everything would be all right. He felt an ache in his chest. Moe Katz would be pitted against him on the motion to dismiss. A brief shudder passed through him like a sudden chill wind. He'd wait for Chip and Stu Trimble, let Chip argue the motion.

"Never quit on those Yankee bastards." He recalled Moe's words during his apprenticeship. "Even if you know you're going to lose, let them know they've been in a fight. Maul them on the way down."

Galvin eased the door shut and backed away.

15

Galvin briefed his eager charges in the conference room. Andrea Schneiderman wanted to argue the motion. Chip and Trimble agreed. She had the cases, the legal citations, and the facts down cold. Galvin gave in. He had read her memorandum of law. It was scholarly and persuasive. The young woman lawyer would feel comfortable in front of Judge Baron. Although they came from disparate worlds—Andrea from the Bronx, De Witt Clinton High, and Hofstra University, Chester Baron from Hastings-on-Hudson (where there was no wrong side of the tracks), the Choate School, and Yale—both had received LL.B.s from Columbia Law. Andrea was number one in her class. Baron had just managed to graduate.

Moe was joined at the plaintiff's table by Tina and Rhys. He had been trying to decipher the Importer's Agreement, which had been supplied by a last-minute courier.

"Can't find a thing in this piece of gingerbread to hang onto." Moe leaned toward Tina and spoke in a stage whisper. "Title to the stuff passes in Southampton. Universal's responsibility ceases at the docks. Gammett then peddles it in the U.S. and Canada."

"Nothing in the Agreement gives Universal any indicia of control?" Tina asked.

"Nothing worth citing. Gammett is in charge of its own destiny.

I've underscored some minor points, but forget it. We'd be beating a dead horse," said Moe. "Even if we could find something, Baron would shoot us down."

"Okay, are you ready, Tina?" Rhys patted, then squeezed, her hand.

"Knees feel like gelatin," she said, "but ready as I'll ever be. And I got my toothbrush."

Moe checked off the case law. *"Turner versus the United States; Fisher versus Toyota; Henning versus Volkswagen.* Well, if there's a case out there we missed, it had to have been decided before the Mayflower Compact. I can't—"

"Hello, I'm Andrea Schneiderman," a voice behind Moe interrupted, "attorney for the defendants." Moe wheeled his chair to get a better view, squinting through his thick glasses. Tina and Rhys crooked their necks. Behind them stood a scholarly looking trio—Chip Hovington in a charcoal-gray three-piece suit, Stu Trimble, same charcoal, regimental tie, and Andrea Schneiderman, a darker tone of gray, white Lady Van Heusen shirt with lace tie, which Judge Baron might recognize as the right shade—Columbia blue.

Like professional pugilists, they shook hands and retired to their respective corners. It was obvious that Andrea Schneiderman would be arguing the case. The briefs and trial memorandums were stacked in front of her. Hovington, Sturdevant, Holmes & Hall were also stacking the psychological cards.

Tina wondered about the absence of Frank Galvin. She wanted to meet him head to head in the courtroom. She felt betrayed, and thought that her anger might carry her through. Now she was frustrated. There were no second-stringers at Hovington, Sturdevant, Holmes & Hall, but there were top dogs and Galvin was a top dog. Tina would hate to lose to an Andrea Schneiderman.

It was five minutes to ten. Clerk Sheila Finnegan entered from a side door, carrying a carton of files. She placed them on the judge's bench. "Good morning," she said pleasantly. The court stenographer set up her recording machine. The bailiffs filtered in and took their stations.

Galvin opened the door and eased onto a bench against the rear wall. A shiver went through him. Somehow he never got used to it. Veteran though he was, the courtroom was a special place and, as he viewed the lawyers sitting stoically awaiting the judge's appearance, a sense of awe overcame him. He was a lawyer. It was a badge of honor. The tradition went back to Runnymede Field, Cardozo and Bellarmine, night law school, his apprenticeship with Moe Katz, when he had such zeal and anger and was going to cure the social ills of mankind.

He looked around. Somehow the trappings seemed out of place—the stained-glass windows with their Justinian panorama, marble pedestals with polished figures in Roman togas, paintings of austere justices in wigs and cardinal robes. Even the gold-leaf eagle above the judge's bench seemed incongruous. It resembled a Nazi emblem, like a condor, a symbol of terror and oppression. He shook his head. Perhaps he was getting old. Even cynical. The law used to be his religion, the courtroom a sacred place. Now it seemed all wrong.

Then she looked at him. Tina Alvarez turned, perhaps feeling his presence. Her coal-black eyes held his. They should have mocked and taunted, or burned with hostility. But a faint smile pursed her lips. Then she looked away.

"All rise," bellowed the bailiff.

Judge Chester Baron strode briskly toward the bench, his black robe trailing. It was 10 A.M. One protocol Baron observed with an obsession was punctuality. Everyone was on time.

Baron slipped his horn-rim glasses toward the end of his nose and surveyed the sparsely occupied courtroom. The civil docket was almost empty. Friday motion sessions were always slow.

Baron signaled to Clerk Finnegan that a formal introduction of the case was unnecessary. He nodded in Galvin's direction. Galvin returned the acknowledgment. "I've read the briefs," Baron said. "Who will be arguing for the plaintiffs?"

"I am, Your Honor." Tina rose and braced herself against the table.

"And for the defendant?"

"Andrea Schneiderman of Hovington, Sturdevant, Holmes and

114

Hall for the defendants," came a crisp response. Her appearance and voice had the unmistakable resonance of confidence.

"All right." Baron teetered back and forth in his chair. "The court order required you to produce your medical expert and yourself"—he peered down at Tina—"for interrogation under oath. Are you prepared to go forward, young lady?"

"I'm ready to proceed," she said evenly. "However, I believe the burden is on the defendant to go forward."

Baron smirked. "Thank you Miss . . . Portia."

"Miss Schneiderman," he said. "I believe it is your motion. The court is at your disposal."

"Thank you, Your Honor." Andrea Schneiderman glanced toward the rear of the courtroom. "At this time I would like to call to the stand Dr. Rafael Meideros."

"Dr. Rafael Meideros," the bailiff again bellowed, looking around the empty courtroom.

"He's not here, Your Honor." Tina's voice had a hesitant glitch.

"Not here?" Baron realigned his glasses and viewed the court order. "Is he ill?"

"He's not ill. He's not coming."

"He's not what!" Baron's voice rumbled down at Alvarez.

"I advised him not to be here." Tina stood her ground. "We have his affidavit."

Baron motioned Clerk Finnegan to give him the court order.

"You received the court's order, Miss Portia?" Baron slowly removed his glasses.

"I did, Your Honor, and with all due respect, the name is Alvarez, Tina Alvarez."

"This was an order of the *court*, Miss Alvarez," Baron hissed. "You advised the witness not to comply with the court's order?"

"That's right, Your Honor," she said bluntly.

"Miss Finnegan," the judge said, motioning to the clerk, "give me the Disciplinary Rules, specifically Five, Subsection D."

Baron leafed through pages of the rule book as if he were about to deliver a sermon and was trying to find a Biblical quotation. Moe Katz's bony knuckles blanched white as he tried to sheathe his anger. Rhys Jameson leveled a hard gaze at the judge and Tina remained standing at the counsel table. An eerie stillness gripped the courtroom. The stenographer's hand was poised in readiness for the judge's pronouncement. In the rear of the courtroom, Galvin was feeling uneasy. He wanted to signal Chip Hovington to withdraw the motion, but it was too late. The issue was joined and it was now Baron's show.

"Yes, here it is." Baron smoothed out the page with great ceremony.

" 'Federal District Court Rule Five, Subsection D. Whoever files an appearance in any matter before the United States District Court shall at all times be subject to the rules and procedures of the court wherein such matter is pending.' Do you hear me clearly, Counselor?"

"Very clearly, Your Honor." Tina felt a surge of strength. Her knees had stopped shaking and she returned Baron's stare.

"Yes, well . . . and 'whoever disobeys, delays, or otherwise refuses to carry out the order of the judge or magistrate of said court, such person shall be adjudged in contempt thereof.' "

Baron again looked down. "Please listen carefully, Counselor. 'And shall be reprimanded, sanctioned, fined, or imprisoned for said offense as said judge of the United States District Court shall deem proper.' "

Baron closed the book with a resounding thud.

"Now, Miss . . ."

"Alvarez, Your Honor."

"You're quite young and apparently naive," Baron said with forced gentility. "Is this your first case before the Federal Bench?"

"First case, Your Honor."

"Hmm," Baron said. "I'll give you a chance to redeem yourself. This hearing will be suspended until two this afternoon, at which time you are requested to produce your medical expert for cross-examination, not only by the defense, but by the court. I want to get behind the doctor's affidavit. He signed it under the pains and penalties of perjury. I want to know what he said, what knowledge he had when he said it, and the factual basis for his conclusions. There'll be no spurious testimony in *my* court. Is that understood, Miss Alvarez?"

"With all due respect, Your Honor, I stand by my advice given to Dr. Meideros. I am an attorney safeguarding the rights of my clients. Again, with all due respect, it is *their* courtroom and they enter it seeking justice."

"You refuse to obey my present order?" Baron's pudgy face reddened. He looked as if he were about to ignite.

Tina said nothing. She remained standing.

"All right." Baron rose, placed both hands behind his black robe, and paced up and down. "Miss Curtis," he snapped at the stenographer, his voice hoarse with suppressed anger. "Please take careful note of all responses. I want to make sure Counselor Alvarez understands the gravity of her situation. All remarks from now on must be on the record."

Stenographer Curtis noted the judge's charge; her agile fingers skipped over the keyboard, capturing Baron's every word.

"We'll handle the testimony of your doctor at a later time," said Baron, still pacing. "He *will* be here! Mark my word, Counselor!" His voice trembled with all the threat and intimidation he could muster.

"You are here, Miss Schneiderman," Baron said, sitting down, his tone moderated to one of judicial restraint. "Please call your next witness."

Andrea Schneiderman rose quickly. "I call to the witness stand the plaintiffs' counsel, Antonia Alvarez."

"Antonia Alvarez," the bailiff boomed, "please approach the witness stand and prepare to be sworn."

Tina did not move.

"Miss Alvarez," Baron said benignly, "please step to the witness stand and be administered the oath."

"Again, Your Honor, with all due respect, I cannot and will not subject myself to such an indignity. I have no counsel. Anything I say might jeopardize the case of my clients. And I am legally and morally bound to protect their rights. That is my first duty."

"You have counsel, Miss Alvarez," the judge said curtly. "Mr. Katz is with you. He's an able trial practitioner and can fully protect your rights. And you, son, what's your name?" He gestured toward Rhys Jameson.

"My name is Rhys Jameson. I am also attorney of record for the plaintiffs. I stand with my sister. Her decision is my decision."

"Mr. Katz." Baron would try one last appeal. "I think you should act as counsel to Miss Alvarez and to Mr. Jameson. We now have an entirely separate matter. The integrity of the court is at issue."

Moe Katz backed his wheelchair away several feet to get a better look at Judge Baron. His gnarled hand adjusted his owlish glasses. He cleared his throat. "Your Honor," he said in a raspy voice, "I am, likewise, attorney of record for the plaintiffs. So that there'll be no mistake, I also stand with Miss Alvarez and Mr. Jameson. And meaning no disrespect to you, Your Honor, I think you misread Disciplinary Rule Five. My copy says, 'whoever disobeys the *lawful* order of the judge.' I think you left out the word *lawful*."

"Now, don't get cute with me, Mr. Katz. That was implied. You know that."

"No, I don't know that, Your Honor. It's my contention that your order is arbitrary, capricious, and totally lacking in legal precedent. There is not one case"—Moe held up a bony finger— "to support your present conduct."

Baron sensed he was on the spot, and he was unsure of his position.

"This court will stand in recess." He raised his gavel. "I will give you until ten o'clock Monday morning to reconsider. And if Dr. Meideros is not in the courtroom at that time, I will request that the United States Marshal's office issue a warrant for his arrest. This court stands adjourned." He banged the gavel and bolted toward his chamber.

16

alvin had left the courtroom before Judge Baron's abrupt exit. He took the elevator to the State Street level, walked four blocks to his office building, and gave Sid the doorman a twenty-dollar tip to take his briefcase up to his secretary.

He hailed a cab, loosened his tie, and rode in silence to Fenway Park. Milwaukee was in town against the Red Sox, and he joined the executives and the great unemployed taking the afternoon off to watch Roger Clemens have a go against the Brewers.

It was two hours until game time. He stood in line, bought a seat in the right-field bleachers, creased a score card into his wallet pocket, and ambled off toward Kenmore Square. He really didn't know what he was doing, or why. Baseball wasn't his game; it was pokey and lacked action. He hadn't attended a game in decades and could only take an inning or two on television, even when the Sox were in the play-offs.

At the intersection of Commonwealth Avenue and Beacon Street he watched the noontime bustle of college students lunching at sidewalk delis, browsing in bookstores and record shops, and lolling on the steps of the brownstones that lined the square. The area had changed little since he had attended Boston College In-Town, just three blocks away. He had been a brash, cocky ex-Marine then, consumed with the desire to prove himself. His father, Jack Galvin, a doctor, had died a miserable, forlorn death, in the end shooting codeine, dilaudid, finally heroin. Galvin owed the world a success. And in the ways that most people measure success, he had succeeded.

It had been forty years since Galvin last sat in the bleachers. Today he bought a box of popcorn and a Diet Coke, and settled in the stands near the right-field foul line. As much as he disliked baseball, he had a close affinity to Fenway Park. It was an archaic bandbox of a stadium, but it was Galvin's link to the past, to his father, who used to take him to these same bleachers. His father, in shirtsleeves and straw boater, would always sit in right field. "This is where the real fans are," he'd tell young Galvin, although in those days Dr. Galvin could have afforded the grandstand, even a box.

As Galvin watched the umpires take their stations and Roger Clemens go through his warmup, he thought back to the springtime of yesteryear when he would sit with his father for a full nine innings. The game seemed alive then. He'd hang on every pitch.

There was a gangling kid out of California, Ted Williams, who could tear the cover off the ball. And there was Bobby Dorr at second base and Junior Stephens at short and the Indian, Rudy York, at first. It was the great American pastime and, if the Sox were in town, Dr. Jack Galvin would be there every Wednesday. He'd send a note with a five-dollar bill to Sister Mary Joseph at St. Agatha's asking her to excuse his son, stating he was needed to work around the office.

Dark clouds now gathered over the light towers in center field, threatening to put an early end to the contest. It was warm for May and Galvin removed his coat and took out his scorecard. Fans applauded as Clemens retired the side and the Sox trotted toward the dugout.

The weather held. Galvin penciled in the strikeouts, the double plays, bought two bags of peanuts, another Diet Coke, and with the game deadlocked, took his seventh-inning stretch along with twelve thousand others. He couldn't recall when he had taken a day off in the last five years. No one knew where he was, not Carter Hovington, Julie Hedren, not even Courtney Evans, his secretary. It was a kids' game, and he was a boy again.

Mike Greenwall, the Sox' designated hitter, singled home the winning run, and the game ended. Galvin walked along Beacon Street and wondered how he could stave off the impending disaster. Moe and Tina and Rhys Jameson were on a collision course with destruction. Perhaps it could be avoided.

◘

"It's too late," Carter Hovington said tersely over Galvin's car phone. "We were wondering where you were. I know how you feel, especially about Moe Katz, but we couldn't withdraw our motion now even if we wanted to. Baron's pissed. The motion to dismiss is incidental. His authority is in question and he'll enforce his mandate no matter what. I hate to see any lawyer go down the tubes, maybe get disbarred, over nothing at all."

"Did it ever occur to you, Carter, that maybe Baron is wrong? Moe Katz has been around a long time. He's thought this whole thing through."

"That isn't the point, Galvin. A lot of judges misconstrue the law, federal judges included. But if Katz thought it all through, as you say, he's goddamned foolish. Baron's livid. He's not going to have some old 'slip and fall' lawyer and a Gypsy upstart tell him how to run his court. Maybe two years down the line Katz will win his point in the U.S. Court of Appeals, keep out of jail, and retain his license. Same for the Gypsy and Jameson. Then what? They can wrap up the little sheet of paper saying they were right and hit Baron over the head with it.

"No, Galvin, your friend Katz isn't thinking it through at all. He's forgetting the case and his clients. That goes for Alvarez and Jameson, too. You kiss Baron's ass if you have to—he's the trial judge. He still has to rule on our motion to dismiss. Forget about the contempt order. That's separate. But on the Rule Eleven motion, Baron will send them packing. And unless they can show an abuse of judicial discretion, that's not appealable."

Galvin listened. Hovington was right. "I have to agree," he said. "Look, I'll try to think of something. Moe's got to get back into Baron's good graces. There's no other way."

"Do what you have to do," said Hovington. "Regardless of what Katz does or doesn't do, Andrea Schneiderman, Chip, and Trimble are going to work well past midnight, just in case Alvarez and her medical expert have a change of heart and take the witness stand. And if I had to bet on it, I'd wager that's exactly what's going to happen."

Galvin drove along Atlantic Avenue and mixed with the late-afternoon traffic. He dialed the Federal Court's central number. "Hello," he said, "please connect me with Judge Baron's clerk, Sheila Finnegan."

◘

The call came through from Clerk Sheila Finnegan at five minutes to five. Moe Katz listened intently and motioned to Tina and Rhys to put everything on hold.

"I see, yes. Sheila"—his head nodded—"I agree it's a way out. We're not being obstinate, believe me. We just think we're right. If we cave in on this point, it'll establish a precedent that puts every practitioner who ever brings a lawsuit behind the judicial eight ball."

Moe stopped speaking and listened for a few moments. Little beads of perspiration formed on his forehead. He removed his glasses, took a crumpled handkerchief from his lapel pocket, and wiped his eyes.

"Uh, uh, okay, let me get this down. Tina Alvarez need *not* take the stand. Her affidavit will suffice. Dr. Meideros is to be there at ten Monday morning to be subject to cross-examination by the defense and if need be by Baron. . . . Yes, I agree it's a compromise, Sheila. You say if we don't go along, Baron will throw the book at us. . . . Yes, I understand. Sheila, you always were most kind. . . . Okay, yes, I speak for the others. We'll be there at ten with Dr. Meideros." Moe replaced the receiver.

"Well, Baron may not like to get overruled. Could hurt his chances for the Appeals Court. So we backed him off a little. But the crack is open. Do you think Meideros can handle Miss Snippywizard?" Moe looked at Tina. "She's a real ballbuster."

"He'll have to," Tina said.

◘

"All rise!" boomed the bailiff.

Galvin had difficulty getting a seat and found himself squashed in among lawyers, members of the media, and curious locals who had heard that Judge Baron was going to preside at an execution. Those assembled in the spectators' gallery, the smartly dressed professionals at the defense table, Tina Alvarez and Rhys Jameson at the plaintiff's table, the clerks, other court officers, and the stenographer all stood at attention as Judge Chester Baron, his head cocked at an imperious angle, bounced toward the bench. Moe Katz sat stoically, moving his wheelchair back a few feet so Baron could not miss seeing him.

"Be seated!" the bailiff cried.

Baron adjusted his glasses and carried on a muffled conversation with Sheila Finnegan. Both nodded in apparent accord. Baron busied himself for several more minutes, studying papers, opening a law book to a designated page, perusing it, then closing it with a resounding thud. He again nodded to Sheila Finnegan.

"The case of *Ramondi et al. versus Gammett Industries et al.* Case number 89653," Clerk Finnegan intoned. "The first order of business is compliance with United States District Court Order of May eleven, 1989. Are the defendant attorneys ready?"

"Ready, Your Honor." Andrea Schneiderman spoke for the defense.

"Plaintiffs?"

"Ready, Your Honor," Moe Katz, Rhys Jameson, and Tina Alvarez answered in unison.

"Fine." Judge Baron smiled, his voice cordial. "I have decided to allow the defense to cross-examine the plaintiffs' medical expert under Rule Eleven of the Federal Rules of Civil Procedure." He neglected to mention that he had reversed himself in his ruling to force Tina Alvarez to take the witness stand.

"Your medical expert"—Baron glanced at the affidavit—"Dr. Meideros is not ill today, is he, Miss Alvarez?"

The courtroom erupted in laughter. It was a humorous opening. Baron felt the apparent warmth of the spectators.

Not everyone was amused. Baron failed to hear Moe Katz's gravelly invective or to see the drained faces of Tina Alvarez and Rhys

Jameson, who remained standing. Galvin shook his head. It was an abrasive remark. Even Andrea Schneiderman, Chip Hovington, and Stu Trimble felt the levity was injudicious and demeaning.

"All right." Baron drummed his fingers together several times. "Miss Schneiderman, you may proceed."

Andrea Schneiderman was tall and slender, her dark brown hair cut short in a Joan of Arc–style pageboy. Her trim tailored suit was corporate beige with a splash of coral lace at the neckline. She picked up several papers from the defense table and positioned herself a few feet from the witness stand.

"I call Dr. Rafael Meideros." Her voice had the ring of supreme confidence.

Dr. Meideros wore a black suit, black tie, and crumpled white shirt. He looked as if he were going to Sunday Mass in the Azores. His somber face was chestnut brown, his curly hair a fuzzy white. He had a kindly look, one that would engender sympathy from a jury of peers. Judge Baron, however, was the sole judge and jury. He eyed Meideros curiously.

"Dr. Meideros." Andrea Schneiderman stood two feet in front of the doctor, put her papers down by her side, and established direct eye contact. "You are not *now* engaged in the active practice of medicine, is that correct?"

"Well, I . . ."

"No, please, Doctor." She glanced at her notes. "It's been seven years since you closed your medical office in New Bedford. Isn't that a fair statement?"

Tina Alvarez should have been on her feet shouting objections, but she waited. She had spent a full day prepping Meideros and was satisfied with his intelligence and his knowledge of the nuances of the legal environment. And during fifty years of medical practice, he had testified in court on many occasions. He knew what was expected.

"You have two questions before me, Miss Schneiderman," Meideros said calmly. "If you will bear with me, I will try to give you a responsive answer. I no longer engage in the active practice of medicine, as you say. Seven years ago my late wife developed multiple sclerosis and I felt that she needed my full attention, not

124

only as a doctor, but as a husband and companion. So I cut back on my practice . . ."

Schneiderman realized she had made a mistake. She had allowed Meideros room to ramble. *Confine the adverse witness to a yes or no answer.* The cross-examiner's cardinal rule. *And never ask a question unless you know the answer.* She waited for Meideros to finish his discourse. She wouldn't make the same error twice.

"Once a doctor, always a doctor," Meideros continued. "It's like being a lawyer. You never cease to give counsel. The same with a doctor. In the community, especially a small community like New Bedford and Fall River, you're always on call. I prescribe, see families, treat people at all hours, day or night. Pain and suffering has no office hours. But I no longer charge patients, nor do I list medicine as income-producing on my 1040.

"So as for question one: I *am* engaged in the practice of medicine, but not as actively as I used to be. As for question two: I closed my office in 1982, but my home is always open, for children, adults, or anyone needing aspirins for a headache or even a little hot buttered rum on a cold day. . . . I still prescribe."

Andrea Schneiderman didn't let Meideros's words settle. She had to regain momentum, get the witness in step with the cadence of her remaining interrogation.

"As to your formal education, Dr. Meideros, you attended Tortuga Medical School in Lisbon, Portugal, graduating in 1926. Is that correct?"

"That is correct."

"Tortuga is no longer in existence. Isn't that true, Doctor?"

"If you say so."

"No, Doctor, it's not what I say." She walked to the defense table, where Chip handed her a red-ribboned document with a gold embossed seal. She returned and leveled a gaze at Meideros. "Tortuga Medical School is defunct, isn't that correct? In fact, it went out of business four years after they issued you a diploma."

"That is correct," Meideros said quietly.

"Now, Dr. Meideros, you were admitted to practice medicine in the Commonwealth of Massachusetts in the year 1930, the same year Tortuga ceased operations?"

"Yes."

"You never were required to take medical board examinations to gain admission at that time. Isn't that correct?"

"Correct."

"You were admitted on a motion by letter from the Portuguese consulate."

"That is so."

Schneiderman omitted asking the doctor whether he had been tested and whether he had passed his national boards in internal medicine and cardiology. Schneiderman knew Meideros possessed these credentials.

"Now, Doctor, you are not an obstetrician?"

"I am not."

"You know, of course, that obstetricians deal with childbirths and birth defects."

"I'm aware that they do."

"You are not a gynecologist?"

"That's correct. I am not."

"You are not a neurologist?"

"I am not."

"Or a pediatrician?"

"I am not a pediatrician."

"Are you familiar with the testing procedures of the National Board of Epidemiology?"

"I am not."

"Epidemiology is the study of the origin of diseases, is it not, Dr. Meideros?"

"It is."

"Now, for the record, Doctor, you are not board-certified in obstetrics, gynecology, oncology, pediatrics, neurology, toxicology, or epidemiology. Isn't that correct, Dr. Meideros?"

"That is correct."

Schneiderman now shifted her attack and hit Dr. Meideros head on.

"I assume that when you signed your affidavit stating your conclusions, you were aware that you signed it under the pains and penalties of perjury?"

"Well aware," Dr. Meideros said calmly.

"And I assume you spent some time with Miss Alvarez in preparation of your affidavit?"

"Eight hours," he said.

"Eight hours?" The proper degree of incredulity crept into her voice.

"Eight hours," he reaffirmed.

From that answer, she quickly realized that Dr. Meideros probably knew in minute detail the medical background and history of the eight Portuguese families, and that he probably had exhaustively studied hospital records and pediatric reports. She would not allow Meideros to articulate his knowledge. "Were your conclusions known to you prior to the date Miss Alvarez commenced suit?"

"They were," he said.

"Dr. Meideros." She looked at her notes, paused a few seconds. "Do you know what country the correiga nut comes from?"

"The correiga nut?"

"Yes. I assume you are familiar with the correiga?"

Meideros glanced at Tina Alvarez. No help. He was on his own.

Schneiderman knew she had caught Meideros off base. She would now run him down.

"My question is not difficult," she said. "Do you know to what country the correiga nut is indigenous?"

"I do not," he said truthfully.

"Have you ever heard of the correiga nut?" she asked.

"I believe it has something to do with Lyosin."

"Aren't you aware that correiga extract is the primary source in the manufacture of Lyosin?"

There was a long pause. Meideros half-closed his eyes as if he were thinking. "It is not important," he began.

"No, please, Dr. Meideros! This calls for a simple yes or no answer, does it not?" She turned to Judge Baron. "If Your Honor please, could we have an instruction from the court that the witness be required to answer in the negative or in the affirmative?"

"Yes." Judge Baron turned to Dr. Meideros. "You will confine your answer to yes or no. If the question calls for a yes or no response, that's the way you are to answer. Do I make myself clear?"

Meideros was about to reply. He looked up at Baron, then back at Tina Alvarez. In that instant Tina picked up the subtle signal.

"Yes, Your Honor," he said almost meekly.

"Fine. Proceed, Miss Schneiderman."

"Did you know, Dr. Meideros, when you signed your affidavit that the correiga nut extract was the primary source in the manufacture of Lyosin?"

"I did not," he said evenly.

Schneiderman was now ready to roll Meideros out of the courtroom.

"Do you know how the correiga nut extract is processed?"

"I do not."

"Do you know anything at all about the chemical process by which correiga extract goes from plantation to drug capsule? Anything?"

These were cheap shots. Obviously the six or seven questions to follow would be grafted upon his lack of knowledge. Schneiderman exploited it like a seasoned practitioner.

"I do not . . ." There then came a series of embarrassing negatives. "I do not . . . I have no knowledge . . . I do not know."

Judge Baron leaned toward Meideros to catch every word, occasionally arching his eyebrows in disbelief.

"Now, Dr. Meideros," said Andrea Schneiderman, "since you know absolutely nothing about the correiga nut, nor its extract medically and scientifically, you must agree that you are in no position to postulate that a product containing correiga extract was the cause of the plaintiffs' injuries? Isn't that a fair statement?"

Her carefully crafted question allowed no digression.

"Well, let me put it this way," Meideros began.

Judge Baron banged his gavel. "No, Doctor!" he barked. "You are to put it in the context of which the question was framed. Again, I caution you, it's either yes or no. You either agree or you don't agree."

Dr. Meideros displayed no emotion. Inwardly he burned.

"In the *limited* context in which the question is framed," he said slowly, "naturally, I would be constrained to agree with Miss Schneiderman's premise."

"That you have no opinion on causation?" Judge Baron was going to administer the coup de grace. He removed his glasses and folded them with great ceremony.

"I didn't say that, Your Honor. My opinion is the same as that contained in my affidavit. The drug Lyosin was—"

"Please, Doctor, don't play word games with me! You've answered the question. That will be all!" The judge turned to Andrea Schneiderman. The Columbia Lion was roaring up and down the Hudson. "Miss Schneiderman," he said, "you may resume."

Andrea Schneiderman had the gut instinct of a seasoned cross-examiner. Quit now. Let the trial judge have the final word.

"Your Honor." She folded her notes. "I have no further questions of this witness."

"Fine." Baron again pounded his gavel. "I'll take the matter under advisement. The court will stand in recess."

Tina jumped to her feet. "Your Honor! I have the right to examine the witness. This is basic due process."

Baron was caught by surprise. He turned and glared at Tina Alvarez.

Tense moments went by. Members of the bar and the press, with their pens poised, waited. Tina was standing, her body charged with raw emotion.

Baron weighed a difficult situation. Tina was not intimidated. He would have to deal with her. "Yes," he said gruffly. "If you wish to question the witness, it's your prerogative. But as you well know, Counselor, you must confine yourself to areas of interrogation raised by Miss Schneiderman."

"The son of a bitch," Moe whispered to Rhys Jameson. "We're being fucked."

The defense table and Tina also heard Moe's earthy assessment.

Tina didn't hesitate. She addressed the doctor from where she stood at the counsel table.

"Dr. Meideros, the defense attorney, Miss Schneiderman, asked you whether you knew that the correiga nut extract provided the primary chemical ingredient in the manufacture of Lyosin. Do you recall that question?"

"Yes."

"And you started to say, and I quote, 'It's not important.' Then Miss Schneiderman interrupted you and there was a colloquy between Miss Schneiderman and the judge. Do you recall that?"

"I do."

"Now, would you please tell the court what you intended to say before you were interrupted."

Andrea Schneiderman jumped to her feet. "Objection, Your Honor!"

"Your Honor." Tina looked at Andrea Schneiderman, then up at the judge. "My sister was examining a witness that *she* called to the stand. I now have the right and the duty to cross-examine the same witness. I cite the case of *Hestor versus United States*, decided by our Supreme Court only last week. I have the case right here." She turned and reached inside a manila folder.

"That won't be necessary." Baron was unfamiliar with the case but realized that a call for Alvarez's proffered citation might make him look foolish. And, as to the principle of law, she was probably correct.

"All right," said the judge, "you may have the question."

Tina did not acknowledge Baron's ruling.

"Doctor," she said, "may we have your explanation. And please take your time so that His Honor will have your complete and unabridged testimony."

"Certainly," Meideros replied. He paused for several seconds. He knew that the entire case was on the line. "It is *not* important for *any* medical practitioner to have exact knowledge of the countless plants, herbs, or compounds that make up the vast array of pharmacologic drugs. In fact, such omniscience would be impossible. This knowledge is for the chemist and the pharmaceutical firms. Busy practitioners prescribing medications have to rely on the knowledge and integrity of established drug companies.

"I'm an internist and I prescribe digitalis to many of my heart patients to strengthen the heartbeat. Now, I'll wager that ninety percent of the prescribing physicians in the United States know nothing about the purple foxglove plant, let alone realize that it provides the chemical ingredients for digitalis. You see, the purple foxglove isn't important to the physician. It's there. It's been utilized as a heart stimulant since 1637. Knowledge of the efficacy and safety of the medicine is important, not the plant from which it is derived. The same is true for practically every drug in the lexicon of pharmacopia—penicillin from stale bread, curare, a muscle relaxant, from the Strychnos plant, South American Indian dart poison, aspirin from the willow bark, dicoumarol, the blood anticoagulant, from spoiled sweet clover.

"Now, simply because a doctor doesn't know that the purple foxglove even exists, doesn't mean that he can't prescribe digitalis to strengthen a failing heart."

Tina waited several seconds to make sure Meideros had completed his answer.

"Now, Dr. Meideros," she said, "in essence you were asked, 'Given the fact that you had no knowledge that the correiga extract constituted the chemical ingredient for Lyosin, how could you postulate that Lyosin caused the plaintiffs' deformities?' Would you please articulate your position and opinion, based on the limited scope of that question."

"Yes. Thank you." Meideros looked up at the judge. "The drug Lyosin is well known to me. I have prescribed it in the New Bedford and Fall River communities since it first came on the market some ten years ago. It was highly touted as a cure for heart disease. Now the drug companies—Gammett and Universal— know more about the drug, its efficacy, safety, side effects, and complications than anyone. They have inside information.

"In theory, Lyosin does the job it's supposed to do. It reduces cholesterol, one of the major risks of heart disease. Now, I don't know how Lyosin actually works. I don't even think the manufacturer knows. Medicine is not an exact science, like mathematics; it is an art, balancing probabilities, not weighing absolute certainties. Take the simple aspirin tablet. No one really understands how it cures a headache, or ameliorates cold symptoms. Maybe someday we'll have the answer. But that doesn't mean we shouldn't prescribe certain drugs simply because we don't understand the precise pathophysiologic mechanism that triggers the cure, or that people shouldn't take aspirin simply because they don't know how it works. We physicians can effectively treat a disease without actually knowing its origin. Dr. Walter Reed cured yellow fever before he realized its carrier was the anopheles mosquito. And after vaccination for smallpox was used successfully, scientists took another hundred years to find out why it worked.

"Now, an increased number of birth defects began cropping up in the communities of Fall River and New Bedford about six or seven years ago. To me, this seemed unusual, because the incidence seemed greater than the national average for a given population. So I started running my own tests at St. Ann's Hospital. I reviewed birth records and the medical data of all parents taking Lyosin in our area and compared them with those not on the drug. The results were inescapable. The incidence of birth defects was eighty percent higher in the offspring of parents consuming Lyosin than in nonusers. The percentage was too high to be ascribed to chance.

"I wrote to Gammett's medical director in 1984, advising him of my findings. I never received a reply. I also wrote to the FDA and received a terse response from that source, thanking me for my interest and advising that the drug was considered safe, and even efficacious. Period. I have copies of both letters with me."

"What did you do after that, Dr. Meideros?"

"There really wasn't much I could do. My suspicion and findings were never acknowledged by the manufacturer. And the top policing organization on prescription drugs refused to look into the matter. About this time my wife began developing symptoms of multiple sclerosis and I started to wind down my practice."

"A few more questions, if you please, Dr. Meideros." Tina moved from the counsel table and stood in the exact spot where Andrea Schneiderman had launched her initial interrogation. The late-morning sun filtered through the high arched windows and touched Tina's hair, giving it a satiny sheen. She was a poised, confident figure as she started her summary examination.

"My sister attorney, Miss Schneiderman, did not ask you

whether or not you were board-certified in the specialties of internal medicine and cardiology."

"I'll concede his qualifications in those respective fields," Andrea Schneiderman said, quickly rising from the defense table.

"Thank you for the concession, Miss Schneiderman, but for the record and for His Honor's assessment, I would like to have Dr. Meideros articulate his credentials as to how and when he attained his national board certifications."

Judge Baron nodded for Dr. Meideros to continue.

"I have been a practicing physician in New Bedford for fifty years. When I say I'm a specialist in internal medicine and cardiology, well, that's not entirely accurate," Dr. Meideros said modestly. "I'm really a generalist. In small communities like New Bedford and Fall River, you treat everybody. I've delivered babies, counseled single mothers, taken care of children, treated cancer patients, heart patients, patients with all sorts of acute and chronic diseases. I was the football team doctor at New Bedford High School for ten years and, of course, I mended my share of broken knees.

"About twenty years ago, with the influx of doctors into the community, I thought I should specialize. I took courses at Tufts Medical School in cardiology, angiography, and electrocardiography, and passed my national boards in internal medicine in 1972."

"How do you become certified in the specialty of internal medicine?"

"You take two days of written examinations and then you are quizzed—what we call 'boards' by professors in that discipline— and I successfully completed this testing and was designated a Diplomat in the Board of Internal Medicine."

"What is the specialty of internal medicine?"

"Well, we treat everything from the outer skin in." Meideros placed his hands on his chest. "All types of lesions and diseases."

"Now, at some time you were certified in a subspecialty— cardiology. Please tell His Honor what is cardiology and how and when you attained certification."

"Cardiology is a specialty branch of internal medicine dealing with diseases of the heart and vascular system. Again, you have to take board examination similar to those in internal medicine. I was certified in that subspecialty two years later, in 1974."

"Now, from 1974 to 1980, were you chairman of the Department of Internal Medicine at any hospital?"

"Yes. During that time I was chairman of the Department of Internal Medicine at St. Ann's Hospital in New Bedford, and chief cardiologist at the Veterans Administration Hospital in Fall River."

Tina could have asked several additional questions but decided to wind it up. She had done a superb job; like an efficient seamstress, she had stitched the holes, even added some embroidery.

"Dr. Meideros, one last question." She paused as Andrea Schneiderman had paused. "You signed the affidavit that His Honor now has in front of him. You stated your opinion that Lyosin caused the plaintiffs' problems. Are you of that same opinion today—right now?"

"Most assuredly."

A stillness settled over the courtroom.

Tina remained standing. No one moved for several seconds. Even Judge Baron was impressed.

17

Moe Katz spun his wheelchair in several circles and held the phone aloft. "We did it!" he yelled. "Tina, you did it! That was Sheila Finnegan. The judge ruled against the defense's motion. We're still in court—at least for now."

Rhys Jameson grabbed Tina in a bear hug, hoisted her off her feet, and whirled her around several times. She was sobbing.

"Okay." Moe feigned gruffness. "Maybe down the line we'll wish Baron ruled adversely. We got a taste of what it's going to be like, and believe me, we're picking our way through a minefield."

Rhys brought Tina to rest. The initial euphoria started giving way to hard reality.

"Baron's ruling only means that now Hovington and Galvin will bring in the heavies," Rhys said. "I understand that they've already engaged former FDA Director Dr. Fred Willis, also Miles McKenzie of Johns Hopkins, and Dr. Allison Wray, the epidemiologist from New Zealand. I tried to get all three into our camp. I was always a day late."

"Who's left out there?" Tina asked.

"Oh, there are always a few whores who will say anything for a buck. Don't get me wrong, Dr. Meideros did a masterful job. But the cross-examination was limited to a very small issue. Next time out they'll put him into the shredder. And round two," said Rhys. "There's a motion to dismiss our complaint against Universal for lack of service of legal process. Unfortunately, Baron might think he owes Hovington one. We may be hard-pressed to prevail on this score."

"And I'm afraid we haven't got the crucial connection between Gammett and Universal," Moe sighed. "The Importer's Agreement seems to spell out two autonomous organizations."

"I've been in touch with five London law firms," Tina said. "All want fifty thousand pounds up front as a retainer, with no guarantee that service on Universal can be accomplished so as to make it stick here. This is where the Hague Convention stuff becomes prickly."

"Fifty thousand pounds," Moe sighed, striking his forehead. "Did you say pounds?"

"That's seventy-five grand." Rhys whistled. "We're priced out."

"I've also talked with a solicitor, Penny Duncan," Tina said. "She's a solo practitioner, like me. Comes from Scotland. Just admitted to the English bar. Says she can file the necessary papers before Her Majesty's High Court, effectuating service of process over Universal. Barring that, she'd file letters rogatory for deposing Universal's executive officers. She said time may work against us, and Universal's legal beagles will be swarming like Spitfires, but she'll see what she can do."

"What about the rate?" Moe inquired.

"That's what's interesting," Tina continued. "According to Miss Duncan, contingency fees are banned by their rule of ethics. She'll bill us by the hour, but we don't pay unless we eventually prevail."

"What do you think?" Moe asked Rhys.

"Well, I get the impression that even at fifty thousand pounds, it's too small a matter for the boys from the Inns of Court. Penny Duncan sounds good to me, and price-wise you can't beat the arrangement. I say give her the go-ahead."

"Okay," said Moe. "I'll file a motion to continue the jurisdiction issue in Federal Court until we get some resolution in London. But it has to be done quickly—like tomorrow—and argued next week. If we get Universal into the suit, then we get our discovery and interrogatories under way. We start by deposing Gammett's medical director, then the presidents of both corporations. You never know what might turn up.

"I suggest both of you leave for London as soon as possible," he went on. "Keep in constant touch with Miss Duncan and with me. And while you're about it, do a little detective work. Try to see who's behind Universal. Check with the Royal Pharmacologic Society and the British Medical Association. Universal may have tweaked a few noses. You might come up with some unexpected friends."

◘

Moe figured it was late afternoon in London. He made several calls, got an answering machine, and left his name and home number.

He was getting ready to go to bed. He had consumed his warm milk and cookies when Miriam said he had an overseas call from Chumley Walker.

He wheeled back into his study, waited until Miriam partly shut the door, and picked up the phone.

"Chumley?"

"Moe?"

Moe's voice choked. "Chumley, is this really you?"

"Moe Katz!" came the voice. "Goodness. It's been—what? Twenty years?"

"Twenty-three, to be exact. That's the last time Miriam and I were in London. It was at that little hotel near Kensington Gardens, the twentieth reunion of the Moles."

"I say. Times 'as a 'abit o' flying. *Tempus fugit*, I says, Moe. Been forty-seven years now since we worked together. Seems like a fortnight."

"Chumley, are any of the old intelligence boys still around?"

" 'aven't seen 'em in eyeges, Moe, in eyeges. 'Tis me guess they're all gone. Our outfit disbanded. Never kept up me rating, Moe. 'Tis all under the MI-5. Military Intelligence."

"Well, I've a favor to ask, Chumley," Moe said. "I'm going to send you a narrative by post express. Outline what I need. See if you can round up some of the old boys or get in touch with someone who can do a little cloak work. Someone you can trust. It involves a lawsuit here in the States and a British-based outfit called Universal Multi-Tech."

"Uni? I say, Moe, 'at's bloody big timber."

"I know. That's why I'm calling. I need information. I'll outline what I'm looking for and I'll be in touch. I'll send you a retainer."

"No need fo' the reetyner, Moe. Ship the marching orders and let me see if I can be of service. On the quid pro quo, we'll work somethin' out later."

"How's Dottie?"

"Oh, she passed on several years ago."

"Sorry to hear that, Chumley. She was a fine woman."

"Thanks, Moe. 'at, she was. But now I go with a splendid lyedee. Seriously thinking of tying the knot."

"At seventy-five?" Moe shook his head. "Why in the world would you ever want to get married again?"

"Don't, Moe old chap. I 'ave to."

18

G alvin got out of the limousine at the same time that Tina and Rhys Jameson pulled up in a taxi. He had never figured they would be journeying to London. They'd be locking legal horns with Pillsbury & Mackay, the British solicitors retained by Hovington, Sturdevant, Holmes & Hall to quash service of process under the Hague Convention, and who had assured Galvin and Carter Hovington that the plaintiffs' claims were seriously flawed.

Galvin again glimpsed Tina and Rhys laughing and chatting at the check-in counter. They were dressed in brightly colored T-shirts, blue jeans, and sneakers, and more resembled backpackers than lawyers.

As he made his way to the first-class lounge, something gnawed at him. It was the sight of Tina Alvarez and Rhys Jameson, young, bubbly, both of whom he admired. They were embarking on a precarious journey. Two promising careers could go down the tubes over this case.

First class only had five passengers, and Galvin was tempted to send back for Tina and Rhys, but decided their paths would cross soon enough.

◘

"Yes, I spotted Galvin," said Rhys. "Got to believe something's up. Why Galvin? Is he going to tell Pillsbury and Mackay something about English law that they don't know? Just doesn't figure. Maybe we're scratching and the treasure's just beneath the surface."

Rhys adjusted his backrest and cradled Tina into his shoulder. She dozed off. He buried his head into the tawny swirl of her tousled hair. She smelled delicious. He had fallen for Tina Alvarez. Hard, like a schoolboy. She had beauty. No question about it. And she was primitive, sensual. But there was more to her than her physical charms. She had a simple honesty about her—idealism, qualities that could lead to her undoing. He would protect her. "Good night, Gypsy," he said softly. "Sometimes it takes all the running we can do to stay in the same place, Lewis Carroll." He caressed her smooth amber cheek ever so gently.

"Off with her head," she sighed contentedly, and with that she was sound asleep.

The case couldn't have been further away.

◘

Galvin was met at Heathrow Airport by Soames, one of Pillsbury & Mackay's chauffeurs, dressed in traditional black cap, black suit, and black leather boots. He was a taciturn master of efficiency, instructing the redcaps in proper placement of the baggage into the trunk of the Daimler, holding the door open for Galvin, and, during the twenty-mile ride to London, talking only when addressed through the intercom between the soundproof glass separating driver and passenger.

The limo was met at Browns Hotel by two similarly uniformed minions. From Heathrow Airport to his suite, Galvin never even lifted his briefcase.

The Pillsbury employees declined a tip. Soames would return at eight the next morning and take Galvin to meet with Derek Symes, the barrister selected to handle the Universal matter.

◘

Tina and Rhys rented a yellow stick-shift Austin from Hertz and managed with trepidation to drive on the left side of the roadway along the M4 Expressway. They veered through roundabouts loaded with traffic, shifted onto auxiliary roads, avoided near-collisions and shouts of angry pedestrians. They stopped, checked their map, stopped again at a petrol station, got hopelessly lost. After driving for the better part of an hour, they arrived back at the same petrol station.

If their plight seemed hopeless, they found a raw humor in it. They giggled and whooped, occasionally wiping away tears generated by the silliness of their predicament. On the car radio they listened to the Beatles singing "Penny Lane" and "Yellow Submarine."

"That's what we'll call our set of wheels," Rhys said, slapping the dashboard. "The Yellow Submarine."

"Okay, Cap'n." Tina gave a three-fingered salute.

"God, I thought the San Diego Freeway was bad." Rhys shook his head. "At least there I knew where I was going."

The Beatles had launched into "Eleanor Rigby" when a cabbie pulled alongside.

"You look lost, Guv'nr," came an ancient voice. A wrinkled gnome of a man, as old as Moe Katz, smiled a toothless grin.

"Looking for Wembly Court in Kew Gardens," Rhys said.

"Kew Gardens? Mate, this is Brixton, not a place to be when the sun goes down. The Garden's back aways. Follow me, Guv."

They coursed through market squares, down tight lanes, and past elegant crescents, finally arriving at a lovely cobbled street with Georgian brick townhouses. They pulled up in front of number 20.

"Nice nyebor'ood, Guv," the cabbie said. He tipped his cap, declined a tip, and sped off.

"God," said Tina. "Can you imagine a cabbie in Boston doing that?"

"Hard to imagine one in London," said Rhys. "Must be a Cockney. One of the earth's last great people."

He looked up at the townhouse, with its pink slate chimney pot, black iron railings, and bright red geraniums spilling from window boxes. Penny Duncan had arranged for them to sublet from a friend who was vacationing on the Continent.

"Come, my fair lyedee, as 'enry 'iggins would say. 'Tis a long way from Arruda Street. Let's see if our hostess left the key in the mailbox."

"Under the mat, ducks," Tina laughed. "And I do think we're just in time for a spot of tea."

Penny Duncan met them at the Bull and Flagon pub by the kiosk in Victoria Station.

"Thought you might like this place," Penny said. "It was Conan Doyle's favorite haunt. Most of his Sherlock Holmes stories were hatched at that table in the corner. Got an earthy clientele— dockworkers, masons, chimney sweeps. Not bristlin' with lawyers. In fact, maybe just us three."

They each hoisted a pint of stout and soon got swept up in the cheerful prattle of the surrounding patrons.

"We could use a Hawkshaw," Rhys said. "When the Dragon-wyck Corporation slams the door, not much can be discovered. They'll feed us just what they want us to know."

"Maybe it's prophetic that I picked this place to meet," Penny said. "Received a rather mysterious call earlier today from a chap named Archer. Said he'd been engaged by your associate Mr. Katz.

141

He wondered if Mr. Jameson had arrived, and wanted the phone number at Wembly Court. Everything was hush-hush. Told him to call you at my office tomorrow at noon."

"Funny," said Rhys. "Moe never mentioned it. Must be a paralegal, or someone Moe thinks can be of service."

Penny Duncan was about the same age as Tina, but plain-looking, rather plump, with stringy mouse-colored hair. She looked more as if she should be serving tankards of ale than pleading a case. But she was pleasant, had a slight Scottish burr, and there was a calmness about her that instilled confidence.

"On service of process under the Hague Convention, I think we're as cooked as a Guyenne goose," Penny said, "but we should prevail on being able to depose Universal's president, their marketing director, and two scientists whom I've learned were instrumental in developing Lyosin. They're still with Uni—Dr. Horst Brunner and Dr. Helmut Schindler—both expatriated Nazis, I might add, who migrated to London by way of Holland. Also, I learned that Uni's medical director is a Dr. Sabrina Bok-Sahn. She's a Londoner who comes from the Far East. Kind of a mystery lady, same general age as we are, perhaps a mite bit older. Seems Uni's placed her on a pedestal. I've done some preliminary checking. Even got a call from Derek Symes, the firm's key barrister, who wondered if I was serious in pressing the case. Thought I was barmy.

"I'll tell you right now, Pillsbury and Mackay may not be the largest law firm in London, but beyond a doubt, they're the most powerful. The Bank of England, the BBC, the London Stock Exchange—those are some of their *smaller* accounts. And what bothers me is the call came from Derek Symes instead of from some middling clerk or minor solicitor."

"Where do we stand legally, Penny?" Rhys Jameson drained his glass and signaled for a refill.

"Again, I'm wondering why the great Derek Symes would call an East End cipher like little Penny Duncan over such a trivial matter. I think we're headed somewhere, but to tell you the truth, luvs, I don't quite know where."

Derek Symes alighted from his white Bentley and greeted Galvin. Symes represented the essence of the Inner Temple: early forties, impeccably groomed, the proper touch of gray at the temples of his dark brown hair. He was dressed in a gray Windsor tie, striped Turnbull & Asser shirt, monogrammed gold cuff links, and a bright red carnation adorned the buttonhole of his dark-blue Saville Row suit. He carried a furled umbrella as if it were a swagger stick.

"My dear Mr. Galvin." He shook Galvin's hand with no-nonsense firmness. "Welcome to London. So glad you're with us. You brought the weather." He pointed his umbrella skyward. Shafts of sunlight filtered through coral-tinged clouds that seemed to pile one upon the other above the bosky grove of Hyde Park. "Up until today, we've had our usual fare of fog and drizzle."

The conference room at Pillsbury & Mackay was an eclectic mix of old murals, tiger rugs, antique maps, bookcases filled with leather-bound volumes and memorabilia from past wars. A painting of General Kitchener in martial pose kept watch over moldering canons, Zulu drums, and a brace of regimental colors.

Derek Symes introduced Galvin to the lead solicitors and barristers assigned to the Universal case, explaining that solicitors were practitioners who prepared cases for the barristers to try in court.

Aside from Symes and Leigh Pillsbury, a well-preserved octogenarian who sported graying sideburns and a white walrus mustache (he liked to be called "Major," especially when he lapsed into reminiscences of the "old brigade"), the firm's solicitors all appeared to be in their early thirties. Galvin soon became impressed with the quality of legal talent, noting that rather young lawyers were assigned to sensitive and responsible positions. He wondered if the pyramid theory (old guard at the top) was strictly an invention of the American law firm.

Derek Symes was the equal of any lawyer he had met in New York, Washington, or Boston. He was intuitive and articulate, could flush out sticky legal issues, and when it came to applying the law to the facts, he had instant recall. He was gifted with a keen sense of humor and was full of self-deprecating charm. Associates called him "Commander," but he confessed he was only the equivalent of a brigadier in the RAF reserve—"a weekend warrior," as he put it.

"Hope you don't mind the last vestiges of Empire," he said and grinned at Galvin. "The Major never throws anything away. We've some pretty dusty books in here, dating back to Blackstone, Lord Coke, and Sir Thomas More. Actually, it's a rather sobering environment, like a mausoleum."

Symes had three associates who worked with stacks of carefully indexed files. Yet he found it unnecessary to be briefed on the law or on the facts.

"Here it is in a nutshell," Symes said. He avoided the "old chap" and "blimey" clichés. His voice and manner were cosmopolitan. There was no Cockney in a background that embraced Eton, Oxford, and a military stint at Cranwell.

Galvin deflected the imperious gaze of Kitchener and listened.

"The plaintiffs are represented by a neophyte, Penelope Duncan. Nothing spectacular about Miss Duncan—no honors at Edinburgh, recently admitted to the Inns of Court, and just completed her two-year clerkship. But I never underestimate a novice. These are the ones that can catch you amidships when your guard is down. We have every angle covered."

"Letters rogatory were used in ancient Rome," Symes continued, as if lecturing at the Temple Bar. "Back then, a provincial, say from Gallia or even from here in London, engaged in a dispute with a citizen of Rome had to petition Caesar to obtain jurisdiction. If a Saxon merchant claimed the commandant of the Tenth Legion owed him for six wagons of wheat, Caesar's magistrate would screen the dispute to see if letters rogatory would issue.

"The modern process stems from the Hague Convention, an international agreement whereby foreign citizens can be sued or compelled to give testimony as if they were in the jurisdiction of the forum where the case lies. Under the Hague, signatory nations—and this includes Great Britain and the Netherlands—

agree to facilitate service and discovery in foreign lawsuits in return for similar privileges being granted its citizens in suits arising in their own courts."

"Sort of lets everyone play by a single set of rules," said Galvin.

"Precisely. An understanding based on comity. But comity is never a substitute for common sense. Like Caesar, the sovereign first screens the dispute to make certain that the local citizen or organization is not being unjustly harassed or shortchanged. And in our opinion, this is exactly the case with Universal.

"We're fighting service of process on several grounds. England has a three-year statute of limitations on lawsuits stemming from defective products, the Netherlands a one-year limitation. Universal essentially is a Dutch-English corporation established under the laws of the Netherlands. Its principal place of business and its shipping offices are at Bromley, just north of here.

"We maintain, and I think we will be successful, that at best, a three-year statute of limitations applies. From what I see, the inception of all of the plaintiffs' injuries occurred some six or seven years ago, well beyond our statute."

"Well, under the laws of Massachusetts, children can assert claims until they reach majority," Galvin interjected. "Their lawsuits, at least, would be viable in the jurisdiction where commenced."

"That's exactly the point," said Symes. "The rationale of the Hague is reciprocity. You see, a citizen in Holland would be at a disadvantage suing a United States corporation doing business here in England, because of our shorter statute of limitations. If the actual plaintiffs were English or Dutch, they'd be out. So, we're fighting issuance of letters rogatory on this ground, claiming that English law should apply and, thus, the action is barred."

"But won't Miss Duncan argue that the law where the injurious conduct occurred, in this case Massachusetts, should govern?" Galvin asked. "The French have a word for it—what is it?" He had it on the tip of his tongue.

"*Renvoi.*" Symes enunciated with the proper Gallic inflection. "In conflict of laws, look first to the law of the place of wrong and apply that law, even in your own venue.

"Miss Duncan undoubtedly will belabor that very precept," Symes said. "But keep in mind that your country consists of fifty different states, like fifty little sovereigns, each with distinct codes, statutes, and principles of law. So, if a dispute arose in Idaho, say, and the case were to be tried in Wyoming, Wyoming would look to the *lex locus delicti,* the place of wrong, Idaho, and apply that law. Not so here. From Land's End to John O'Groats, we have but one principle of English common law. It boils down to the difference between substance and procedure. The substantive law of the forum where the case is to be tried is Massachusetts. That covers the rules of evidence, damages, weight to be accorded expert testimony. We have no quarrel with that. But procedural law is another matter. Whether our citizens should be subject to a lawsuit at all because of our shorter statute of limitations is for our courts to say. After all, the plaintiffs are invoking our laws to drag our citizens before their forum. On that, our rules of procedure govern."

Symes continued his discourse, explaining the intricacies of English common law and marshaling cogent arguments embracing their defense strategy.

"The EEC, the European Economic Community," he said, "is vitally concerned in what happens here. France, Germany, Italy, Spain, Scandinavia, especially Sweden, all have filed *amicus curiae* briefs to prevent what they see as a fishing expedition to put their exports at a serious disadvantage. If jurisdiction is lost, everyone will parade to the United States to bring lawsuits, regardless of where the injuries occur. You lads in the States have an expression for it."

"Forum shopping," said Galvin.

"Yes, forum shopping. Not very sporting. I'm sure Master Lawrence might take a dim view of creating such dubious precedent."

"Master who?"

"Master Lawrence. He's the Master of the Queen's Remembrances, the Queen's designated magistrate who either approves or denies issuance of the letters."

"Assume we prevail on jurisdiction," said Galvin. "Just before I left, we were hit with requests that letters rogatory issue for depositions to be taken at the American Embassy of every official at Universal, from president right down to marketing personnel. Also included was the name of Dr. Sabrina Bok-Sahn, Universal's medical director."

Galvin noted a flicker of brightness in Symes's eyes at the mention of her name.

◘

The posh Bohemia Club in Covent Garden was full of old oak, old prints, and old waiters.

"The gathering place for the London bar," said Derek Symes as he snapped his fingers. A waiter in morning coat and striped trousers quickly appeared.

Galvin toasted with a bitters and soda, Symes a Glenlivet on the rocks. The camaraderie at 5 P.M. was clubby and chauvinistic. Galvin was becoming increasingly aware that the practice of law in London was a young man's game. Even the judges and the magistrates who mingled with the general bar seemed to be in their thirties. Derek Symes and a few others were, perhaps, the oldest. It was an exclusive men's club. Not one woman could be spotted among the young professionals. And Galvin was well aware that Derek Symes was the dominant presence.

"Robbie," Symes said, motioning to a young man standing at the bar, "come over and meet Frank Galvin, a barrister from the United States.

"Larry Robinson, this is Frank Galvin." They exchanged greetings and swapped good-natured collegial barbs before Symes and Galvin moved along.

"Robbie was in my command in the Falklands," said Symes. "We did a brief stint together. Flew torpedo bombers off the H.M.S. *Hermes.* We logged a few hits on the cruiser *Belgrano*, just before one of our subs finished it for good. Actually, Robbie is up for wing commander in my squadron."

"Does he practice law?"

"Sort of," said Symes, sipping his Scotch. "He's Master Lawrence."

19

Galvin left the Bohemia Club at five-thirty. It was still light out, and he thought he'd take the route along Victoria Embankment that coursed above the murky waters of the Thames. He could hail a cab at Westminster and be in Mayfair by early evening. Derek Symes had reservations at Annabel's at nine. He said he'd bring an interesting friend.

He stood on the quay, thankful for his topcoat. The evening chill and a misty rain made him reflective and moody. He could not see the rust-brick turrets of the Tower of London, but the thought of its grim keep did nothing to elevate his spirits. He shuddered as he remembered the poor souls who were held there before putting their heads on the executioner's block. He didn't know why, but women came to mind—Jane Grey, Anne Boleyn, Catherine Howard. He turned his back on these morbid reflections and made his way along the embankment. He watched lamplighters climbing ladders that leaned against antique lampposts. Quietly, eerily, through the enveloping fog, the gaslights flickered to life. Ahead he could dimly make out the spires of Westminster Abbey and the long purple outline of the Houses of Parliament. So much history, he thought, packed into one square mile. At Westminster he tossed coins into the Thames as the Romans had done; it was his votive offering to the Goddess of Justice.

A few steps beyond, he paused and examined a statue of some female deity.

"Aye, lad." A figure loomed out of the mist. " 'Tis a foine woman. She's Boadicea, Queen of the Celts."

"Oh?" Galvin was startled. "A memorial to the Irish? In London? Me dear grandmother from Sligo would never believe it."

"Bejaysus, yank," exclaimed the visitor, casting a furtive glance left and right. "Irish meself. Name's Faherty. Sean Aloyisous Faherty." He wore an olive-green knit sweater, dark corduroy pants, and a gray checkered visor cap, and in his hand was a small black suitcase. He had the pug face of Victor McLaglen, reminding Galvin of Gypo Nolan in *The Informer*, the classic movie on the Irish troubles.

"Sur'n b'gorra," Galvin mimicked. "Ne're would have guessed it."

" 'Tis me fav'rite place in London. Can see everything from here. The barges coming up the Thames, all the river traffic, Westminster Cathedral, and right over there, past the Abbey, is Scotland Yard. Now, if ever'n I plant a candle, lad, I'd begin there."

The visitor waited. It was an odd statement. If it was an insider's signal, Galvin failed to pick it up.

"Old 'Boady' here," the Irishman continued, pointing to the statue. "Fierce as they come, she was. Drove the Romans bloody crazy. Hit and run, hit and run." He jabbed the damp air with a closed fist. "Burned the bloomin' place down, she did."

"What finally happened to her?" Galvin was becoming amused.

"Sur'n she's 'ere right now, lad. 'Er ghost . . . She wouldn't buckle to the limey bastards. Only twenty-three, she was."

Somehow Galvin thought Faherty had his centuries mixed up. He looked at the benign features of the tribal Queen. In real life, probably big as a battle-ax, he thought, with the acid tongue of more than a few Irish women he'd known. But there she was, cast now in serene bronze.

Faherty disappeared into the mist as silently as he had arrived. Galvin turned up his coat collar and hailed a cab and headed for the fluorescent haze of Piccadilly. The ghost of Queen Boadicea was not far behind.

◻

Rhys Jameson sat down on a bench in Lambeth Park on the south side of the Thames, not far from where Galvin had encountered Faherty. He waited for half an hour and scanned the faces of several passersby, but no one made a move to sit next to him. Moe had called earlier to say that a man named Chumley Walker would be in touch. He was an old buddy from British Intelligence. Moe lamented that Judge Baron had granted only a week's continuance, and they now needed all the help they could get, from whatever source. He wanted to run down the courier who had delivered their registered letters to Universal; he had a hunch that something was funny about the whole setup. Rhys protested, but to humor Moe he said he'd go along. It seemed ridiculous. Penny Duncan's petition was to be heard by Master Lawrence the following day.

The park bench was damp and getting cold, as was his rear end. He was about to leave when an elderly man in a black trenchcoat with a tightly rolled umbrella under his arm stepped out of the darkness.

"Good evening, Mr. Jameson," he said. "Name's Archer."

Rhys felt he would burst out laughing. Good God, he thought. Moe's losing it. Playing cloak and dagger—and with this ancient. As if they hadn't enough problems.

"Real name's Walker, Chumley Walker. For the operation, it's Archer, code name Archer." He sat down, placed the umbrella vertically between his knees, folded his gloved hands on the staff, and peered straight ahead toward the Thames.

Rhys went along. Maybe they needed some comic relief. "Okay, Archer," he said. "How do you know I'm your contact?"

"Let's just say I know." Continuing to stare straight ahead, he pulled an envelope from an inner pocket, placed it on the bench, and slid it toward Rhys.

"I've got the initial information. Postman's name is Thomas

150

Gately. Works out of NW-3. Has the regular route to Uni's executive offices in Bromley. It's all in here. I'll be in touch."

He got up, snapped open his umbrella, and faded into the shadows.

Penny Duncan brewed some tea on a small stove in her office. She was her own secretary, answering the telephone, checking the mail, researching the law, and serving tea. Located on a ground-floor flat, not far from Blackfriar's Station, her office was small and tidy.

"Ordinarily," she said, "letters rogatory would issue as a matter of routine, wouldn't even be opposed. But we've kicked over a hornet's nest, and not every client has the clout of Universal or Pillsbury and Mackay. I must confess this is my first case before Master Lawrence." She handed a cup of tea to Tina, then one to Rhys.

Just as Tina took a strong sip, the telephone rang.

"It's for you, Rhys," Penny Duncan said. "Overseas." She handed him the phone. "Your partner, Mr. Katz."

Rhys tried to be as diplomatic as possible. "We've got our hands full, Moe. We go before the Queen's magistrate tomorrow and it's really iffy. The worst thing at this juncture would be to start tampering with witnesses, especially members of the British postal service. Moe, believe me, the whole issue may hinge on what the magistrate had for breakfast. It's that sensitive."

"This connection's not too clear," Moe said, "but I can't agree. I went to a lot of trouble getting Walker out of retirement. He's good. I know his work. If we can prove Universal signed for our registered letter, then we'd be home."

"Home where? For Christmas sake, Moe, that issue's done and gone."

"You know, Rhys, when Galvin and I were in private practice, we'd scour the countryside for witnesses in all our cases. Make sure we signed them up before the opposition even knew they were out there." It was a lame appeal.

"Moe, listen to me. This isn't a rear-end collision. Archer or Walker, whatever his name, wants to lean on the postal clerk. Moe, the war's over. We're not fighting the Nazis anymore. We're trying to have the guy in the wig give us the nod. This is delicate. We got to approach him with our hat in our hands."

"Well," said Moe, "do what you have to do. I thought I could be of help."

Rhys felt the hurt in Moe's voice.

As he hung up, Rhys emitted an exasperated sigh. He patted the telephone.

"I could use a Beefeaters in my tea," he said, flopping into a chair next to Tina. "I didn't tell either of you, but Moe Katz used to be in Army intelligence. Stationed here during the war. Worked with a group called the Moles. Now he's hatched up a scheme to put the mailman's feet to the coals, make him 'fess up to some conspiracy involving Universal." He shook his head.

"You know." Penny squeezed some lemon into her tea. "Give me the postman's name and address. I'll add him to my list of witnesses. Even if we're cooked on jurisdiction, I can't see the magistrate ruling against our procuring testimony by deposition. Universal might get out of the suit as a defendant, but we'll insist that their officers and employees are ordinary witnesses—like the postman—and we have the right to interrogate them under oath. When they spot the mailman's name, things might heat up a wee bit."

"What do you really think of our chances?" Tina leveled a concerned look at Penny.

"Not all that great," Penny said. "The Master of the Queen's Remembrances has the absolute say in matters of procedure, and this falls into that category."

"Can we appeal an adverse finding?" asked Rhys.

"Yes. In the event of a denial—even in part—of our petition, we can appeal to the Queen's Bench. There's a basic issue of international law involved. The shoe could be on the other foot someday. A British or Dutch litigant could be suing an American defendant. It's a two-way street. That's the entire foundation of the Hague Convention. I'm invoking a line of favorable cases—English common law, the law of the European Economic Community, the Commercial Codes of France and Italy. They all seem to spell out that letters rogatory should issue."

"Let's look at the downside," Rhys said. "Suppose we lose, even at the Queen's Bench level. What then?"

"Then we go to the House of Lords. That's our court of last resort. And failing there," Penny said, "costs, including counsel fees, are assessed against the losing party."

"Any other avenue?" Rhys asked.

"Then, my friends, it's Carey Street."

"Carey Street?"

"That's where our bankruptcy courts are located."

◘

Galvin was seated at the bar when he spotted them in the bronze-tinted mirrors. He watched as Derek Symes helped Sabrina Bok-Sahn out of her Russian sable and hand it to the hatcheck girl, followed by his white silk scarf, cashmere topcoat, and several pounds of sterling. She beamed a gracious thank you and the maître d' motioned to the bar.

The greetings were swift. "Thought I'd surprise you," Derek Symes said as he produced a silver Dunhill lighter and lit the cheroot that Sabrina Bok-Sahn had placed in a tapered gold cigarette holder. It complemented her gold earrings, strapless gold lamé evening gown, and her golden brown skin.

"We meet again, Mr. Galvin." Her luminous eyes gleamed. "Welcome to our fair city."

They were escorted to an elevated table overlooking the glamorous patrons by Lady Annabel herself. She bowed courteously as she settled them into place. Immediately, three waiters in gold-corded white jackets appeared. They rearranged the crystal, took cocktail orders, and one produced a light for another of Sabrina Bok-Sahn's cheroots.

There were ample servings of chilled Stilton soup, quenelles of smoked haddock, Dover sole, Guyenne duck, Yorkshire pudding, Cornish crab mousse. Lady Annabel stopped by several times to assure impeccable service.

They had promised not to discuss shop. The lawsuit was never mentioned.

The conversation centered on sights to see in London, the smart shops, the collection of ambers at Sac Ferrer's, and an unusual Hogarth at Sotheby's. Galvin had mentioned that Carter Hovington might like to buy the painting. Sabrina felt that the Hogarth at 638,000 pounds was overpriced. Symes thought the price was negotiable, and if Carter Hovington really wanted it, he'd see what could be done.

It was getting late. Galvin asked Sabrina if she had brought along some correiga nuts. Derek Symes looked puzzled.

"An in-joke." Sabrina smiled. "The correiga has certain aphrodisiac qualities. I'm sure neither you nor Derek is in need of it." She looked deep into Frank Galvin's eyes, her lips pursed in a seductive half-smile.

"Excuse me, Derek," Lady Annabel interrupted, "there's been a bomb scare in Trafalgar. You are to call Headquarters immediately."

"Goddamn peat farmers," Symes swore as he jumped to his feet and excused himself. "Slimey bogsiders. I'd like to bull-whip the lot of them."

◘

Derek Symes returned almost as quickly as he had left.

"It was really nothing." He retrieved his aristocratic delivery. "Someone planted a valise next to Lord Nelson's monument. It's been defused. A bunch of firecrackers. Alert's been called off. This is one of the reasons I continue to collect my reserve paycheck," he added. It was a minor conciliation.

Somehow the gaiety was off the evening. Galvin became introspective. He thought of the Irishman Faherty and his suitcase, and of his own father, a heavy contributor to the IRA, and of his grandfather Pradrig, who had marched with De Valera and sweated

154

at Mountjoy Prison with Connolly and Kevin Barry and who was with Michael Collins when he was ambushed at Béal na Bláth. Or so he claimed. In the Galvin household, lapses between fact and fiction had been easily forgiven.

"Okay," Symes said. "No more politics." He realized his initial outburst had been a mistake.

Lady Annabel appeared just in time to deflect further discussion. "Ah-hah." Symes rubbed his hands together. "The pastry cart."

He proceeded to pick out the delicacies—scones with clotted cream, Grand Marnier soufflé, Simpson's treacle roll, and custard—declaiming each with a gustatory flair.

A waiter appeared with the finest bottle of Napoleon brandy. Symes scanned the label with care and nodded approval.

After the glasses were filled, Symes raised his in a final toast, breaking into an embracive smile. "To us," he said.

In the fractured moment, Frank Galvin and Derek Symes shot glances at each other—across the crystal struck by candlelight, across the Irish Sea, across the peat bogs, and across the centuries.

Galvin returned the toast. "Yes, to my lovely hostess and gracious host." His smile was pure reflex.

2 0

Early the next morning, Galvin settled into the blue velvet of the limo and fingered the silver-foil wrapper of a Havana *primera*, compliments of Annabel's. The setting was conducive to a fine cigar. But after a moment he tapped the *primera* back into his lapel pocket. Smoking and imbibing were indulgences best left to memory.

Soames, his chauffeur, avoided the treadmills of Bond Street and the Mall and weaved through Mayfair's hidden alleys. They crossed Piccadilly and Galvin surveyed the tangle of cabs, cars, scooters, double-deckers, bicycles, and pedestrians converging toward the Circus. Soames maneuvered onto the Strand. Passing through Trafalgar Square, Galvin noted that Admiral Nelson's column still stood, all 167 feet thrusting skyward. He was reminded that a similar monument in Dublin had not fared as well. One night some lads wearing green ski masks dressed the Lord's obelisk in a wire necklace and spiced it with glycerin. Again, he thought about the Irishman Faherty and about his grandfather Pradrig. And he felt a little foolish over his flare-up with Symes.

The commercial sprawl of the Strand suddenly melted into Fleet Street, and as if by magic, the Daimler passed through a leafy zone into a green preserve of quiet bowers, manicured lawns, and ivy-laced towers. They glided into a parking area next to the Royal Courts of Justice. Bewigged barristers wearing black robes ambled toward their calls at the Old Bailey, the Temple Bar, and other halls of justice.

Derek Symes, in shoulder-length wig and with a satin sheen to his black robe, waited for Galvin on the steps of the Royal Court. Two barristers adorned in shorter wigs stood nearby.

"Squire Symes has taken the silk," Soames said, answering Galvin's inquiry as to the difference in attire. "Marks his rank and achievement before the bench and bar. The silk signifies that he only tries serious cases at"—he cleared his throat—"substantially augmented fees."

Greetings were quickly exchanged. Galvin ascended the granite steps, grooved by the feet of centuries, paused on the portico landing, and assessed the campus-like setting. Near the river was the Temple Inn with its diamond-pane windows latticed in lead, and beyond a leafy path were the Tudor brick patterns of the Gray and Lincoln Inns and the Old Bailey. He unconsciously looked for Tina Alvarez.

"Nice place you have here, gentlemen," Galvin said, addressing the group.

"Oh, we know how to take care of our own." Symes caught and

returned the humor. "Master Lawrence called this morning and said he'd be a bit late, so I thought we'd take the staircase to chambers and I'll show you around."

Galvin thought it was questionable in an adversary proceeding for a party litigant to be conversing so openly with the trial judge. The camaraderie between the English bench and bar would take some getting used to.

They ascended four flights of well-worn marble stairs, past medieval window slots, pausing at each level to look down stone corridors of legal history.

"Down this hall was where Lord Coke presided," Symes said. His silk robe rustled as he pointed.

" 'A man's home is his castle.' " Galvin spoke the rule of law laid down by Coke in 1582 in defense of a landowner who had killed an intruder.

"Say, that's good." Symes knew he had to mend some ethnic fences.

"Well, it all began here," Galvin said. "Concepts of equity and fairness, protection against royal caprice. Your common law is the foundation of our law in America. Justice is that soft bond that keeps us together."

They climbed another flight. "This entire floor is the Queen's Bench." Symes's arm swept in an encompassing arc. "Our trial and appellate court. Any adverse finding from Master Lawrence will be referred here."

"I suppose that's a two-way street"—Galvin was getting winded—"if the petitioners lose."

"Oh, I don't think the petitioners have either the wherewithall or the stamina to prosecute an appeal," Symes said. "Justice in the U.K. is expensive. Technically, they can appeal all the way to the House of Lords. But under our rules, costs are assessed against the losing party, *including* legal fees. Makes a litigant think twice about mounting an appeal."

Galvin didn't have to add it up. It would be exorbitant, a lot more than Moe Katz had managed to squirrel away.

They reached the top landing. From an expansive arched window, Galvin surveyed the setting below. "Over there," Symes said, pointing toward a collection of Gothic fieldstone buildings grouped around sculptured yews and flagstone terraces, "is Lincoln's Inn, sort of a university and residence for students and lawyers alike. Gladstone and Disraeli chambered there, and that's where Charles Dickens served his apprenticeship."

"I never knew Dickens studied law," said Galvin.

"Lasted only a few months." Symes motioned them to continue up the last flight. "At fifteen, he was a junior clerk at Lincoln's Inn. 'The law with its blank forms of legal process; its skins and rolls of parchment; foolscarp, brief, draft, and whitey brown' was not for Charles Dickens," Symes said, reciting some cynical Dickensian dicta. "In his brief legal stint, however, he did master shorthand and moved a few blocks to Fleet Street, where he plied his trade as a journalist. He portrayed lawyers as blackguards and Shylocks. And, perhaps in his day, they were. Dickens's London was a grim place, physically, professionally, and socially."

Galvin knew Dickens well—*Oliver Twist, Great Expectations, Bleak House.* In Galvin's formative years at St. Agatha's Grammar School, Dickens, with his railing against social injustice, was required reading. Galvin recalled that the great Victorian had little regard for the law and lawyers and never treated the old guild too kindly.

They walked along a granite corridor and were ushered into the Master's Chamber by a staff-wielding bailiff. The Chamber's stone interior echoed like the crypt of a medieval castle. Furniture was spartan; the Master's bench resembled a scrivener's desk, where quill, stamp, and royal seal were placed. A plain hardwood chair was reserved for the witness. Two rows of benches were filled with wigged barristers. Galvin spotted Rhys Jameson and Tina Alvarez seated next to their counselor, Penny Duncan.

The bailiff put his finger to his lips, signaling silence, and Galvin took his place next to Derek Symes. He would chat with Tina and Rhys after the hearing. Maybe they could get together for dinner. Then again, Galvin thought it wasn't such a good idea. Until their business dealings were over, better stay at arm's length.

"Hear ye! Hear ye! Hear ye!" intoned the bailiff. "All persons having business before his Lordship, Master of the Queen's

Remembrances, give your attention, draw near, and ye shall be heard. God save the Queen!"

The bailiff banged his staff three times. Master Lawrence's entrance had the air of judicial formality. His shoulder-length oyster-colored wig seemed to have a thousand periwinkled curls.

"Counselors." He extended his hands toward the group. "Please be seated. Rarely are we favored by such an impressive array of lawyers and visiting dignitaries. I acknowledge each and every one of you. Now, for the business at hand." He patted the red-ribboned parchments stacked on his desk. "I have read the legal briefs. The issues have been clearly set forth, and if all sides will waive oral argument, I will reach a decision."

Master Lawrence lifted a quill from its well and pointed it toward the barristers in a gesture of acknowledgment.

"M' Lord, in behalf of the governments of Sweden, Finland, Denmark, Norway, and Iceland, verbal argument is hereby waived," a barrister recited with aplomb. The only sound came from the squiggles of Master Lawrence's pen.

"Your Worship." Another rose stiffly and waited several seconds. "The Constitutional Governments of the Netherlands, the West German Republic, Belgium, Switzerland, Luxembourg, Spain, and Italy hereby waive argument and stand on their *amici curiae,* filed jointly."

Master Lawrence nodded and again wrote on a parchment with a great flourish.

"Honorable Monsieur," came another voice. "the Government of the Republic of France and the Principality of Monaco waive argument and submit on their brief."

"Respondent?" Master Lawrence flicked his quill toward Derek Symes.

"Respondent, Universal Multi-Tech Limited, hereby waives oral argument and submits to Your Lordship." Symes's voice was assertive, crisp, and confident.

"Petitioner?"

"Just a few words, Your Lordship."

The wigs and robes stirred with subtle displeasure as Penny Duncan rose. She adjusted her wig, which had become slightly dislodged. It was borrowed and she was unaccustomed to its fit.

"I will not recite the legal cases or judicial precedent," she said. "All are noted in my brief, and I will not belabor the premises set forth therein. What we are asking today is basic. A corporate entity is charged with dispensing into the mainstream of commerce a product unfit for human consumption. We may or may not be able to prove our accusations. What we are asking is not justice but a *chance* for justice—to allow a jury of peers to weigh the evidence dispassionately and then come to a decision." Her voice carried reminders of Bannockburn, Culloden Moor, and ongoing battles for acceptability.

"The respondent"—she nodded toward Derek Symes—"seeks to deny us the chance to go before an impartial forum to seek redress of our grievances. I note that in his brief the respondent argues that the three-year statute of limitations has expired in the United Kingdom and thus the action should be barred. And I am not unmindful of legal precedent cited by my adversary, Mr. Symes, and others representing vested interests. To be sure, most of the birth defects in the plaintiffs' children occurred some four to eight years ago. However, I respectfully submit that it was not discovered until quite recently that the deformities could be attributable to the respondent's product, Lyosin. And, since this is so, the statute of limitations is held in abeyance."

"Excuse me, Counselor Duncan," Magistrate Lawrence interrupted in a courteous tone, "but can you cite *one* case in the United Kingdom supporting such a premise?" He placed the quill against his lips and corrugated his brow.

"I have *no* case in the United Kingdom, Your Lordship," said Penny. Again she adjusted her wig. "But let me put it this way. . . . Suppose some brigand planted a time bomb under this very floor, like Guy Fawkes." She tapped her foot. "And for a year and a day it lay dormant, and then *boom!* it explodes!" Her hands flew in large arcs. "It causes injury and damage just twenty-four hours *after* our criminal statute for responsibility runs out." She paused to let the logic of her argument sink in. "Or suppose Your Worthy or Your Worthy's loved ones were fed some slow-acting poison that caused disastrous effects years later. I'm sure in those cases Your Lordship wouldn't care a whit about the statute of limitations.

"You see, it's not when the forces are set in motion, it's when the damage occurs. If no damage results, there is no crime, no necessity for redress, civilly or criminally. We maintain that Universal planted time bombs in unsuspecting patients. Some are still ticking. We ask that the Respondent be made to stand trial before the dock of civil justice. We seek only the chance to prove our case."

For an argument lacking legal citations, it was persuasive.

Master Lawrence waited several seconds. "Do you have anything further, Miss Duncan?"

"I have nothing further, Your Lordship."

"Mr. Symes, you have waived initial argument, but you may respond in rebuttal."

"I again submit to the wisdom of Your Lordship," Symes said.

Master Lawrence beckoned to the bailiff, who approached with a purple scapular and a floppy red beret resembling one worn by a university provost at commencement exercises. He handed the cap to the Master and placed the scapular around his shoulders. Master Lawrence adjusted the cap and frowned slightly as if he were deep in thought. Several seconds passed. Stillness settled in the vault-like interior like a pall.

"I find for the Respondent," he pronounced solemnly.

There was another stirring of robes and wigs. Symes remained impassive.

God, that was fast, thought Galvin.

"Please note my difference," said Penny Duncan, "and also register my appeal from Your Lordship's ruling."

"So noted," the magistrate said. Again came the sweeping flourish of the arm, the scratching of the quill. He removed his cap and scapular, then handed both to the bailiff.

"Now, issue number two." Master Lawrence folded his hands together.

"Is there any oral argument from learned counsel submitting *amicus curiae?*"

There was a negative shaking of heads.

"It is noted, learned counsel stand mute."

"Respondent?"

"Oral argument is waived."

"Petitioner?"

Penny Duncan rose, this time a little more slowly. She inhaled as if she were to launch into a lengthy dissertation. "The Petitioner submits," she said, a weary strain in her voice.

Again the bailiff draped the scapular about Master Lawrence's shoulders and placed the floppy beret on his head.

"I find for the Petitioner," he said. It was a surprise. "Letters rogatory shall issue. The list of witnesses submitted by Solicitor Duncan may be subject to deposition at the American Embassy come Monday next, to be continued daily until completed."

Symes jumped to his feet. If there was rancor in his voice or in his manner, it was well disguised. "Your Lordship," he said quietly, "kindly note the Respondent's objection."

"Noted."

"And appeal."

"Noted and recorded."

Galvin knew the ruling had surprised Derek Symes. But after reading the briefs on both sides, Galvin was also aware that equity and fairness had prevailed.

"Your Lordship," Symes continued, "since you have ruled that my client is not subject to the jurisdiction of the United States Court as *defendant*, I respectfully submit there should be no interrogation of postal clerk Thomas Gately. This is completely irrelevant to the issues."

Galvin's mind raced back to his initial conversation with Frobisher and Mallory and the 'sneaky peepy.' He held his breath.

"Granted," said Master Lawrence.

Penny Duncan looked at Rhys Jameson, who shook his head.

"Acquiesce," she said.

"And, Your Lordship," Symes followed it up quickly, "again, since you have ruled that my client is not a defendant and thus not subject to the United States evidentiary rules on discovery governing defendants, all personnel to be interrogated and"—Symes knew the names, but feigning a memory lapse, he read from a paper—"Dr. Sabrina Bok-Sahn, Dr. Horst Brunner, Dr. Helmut Schindler, Mr. Heath Mallory, the respondent Universal, respectfully requests that the deposition be presided over by Your Lordship or by an appointed designee, and that the interrogation be limited in scope to the manufacture of the drug Lyosin and not be a fishing expedition on extraneous matters such as sales, profits, losses, background of personnel other than those deposed, and further, that it be limited to complaints of complications and adverse reactions of the subject drug following approval in 1980 by the Department of Health and Social Security."

"I will preside at the depositions only if both sides agree," said Master Lawrence. "If not, I will request that the legal attaché of the American Consulate be the adjudicating officer. And," he added, "I will not order restrictions on the content of said depositions.

"Miss Duncan?" Master Lawrence flicked his quill in Penny's direction.

Galvin was beginning to like Master Lawrence. He would not be cowed.

"I think it best, Your Lordship," said Penny Duncan, "to have the consul's attaché preside."

"Mr. Symes?"

"I would prefer Your Lordship, but in the interest of expediting this matter, I will agree with my sister counselor."

"So be it," said Master Lawrence. "Letters rogatory will issue for interrogation to commence Monday next, to continue each day until completed. And I assume that since the U.S. Embassy is not legally a part of the United Kingdom, that the respective parties will be represented by American lawyers and the interrogation will be conducted by such counselors."

The bailiff took Master Lawrence's hat and removed his scapular. "All rise," he intoned.

The bailiff clacked his staff three times on the stone floor, and he and Master Lawrence departed in silent pageantry.

If Derek Symes was disturbed with the ruling, he concealed it well. There were no winners but also no losers. The assessment of costs had not been raised or mentioned. A judicial standoff.

Penny Duncan emerged with Tina and Rhys. They stood apart from the collegial banter and tried to assess their gains and losses.

Galvin pulled Derek Symes away from his fellow barristers and steered him toward their group.

"Hello, Tina, Rhys." He extended his hand and tried to produce a friendly smile.

"Hello, Mr. Galvin." Rhys shook his hand. Tina merely nodded. Only Penny Duncan and Derek Symes had a genuinely friendly exchange.

Symes did not try to patronize Penny Duncan by overpraising her performance.

"Well," Symes said. "A trade-off. A queen for a queen."

"More like a queen for a rook," she said pleasantly, implying it was she who had lost the regal piece.

Suddenly the conversation deadened. Symes jumped into the gap.

"Come, my dear Galvin," he said. "We must be going. Now, no cheating over the weekend, Miss Duncan. Trial preparation after hours isn't cricket."

Galvin wanted to tell Symes that he would join him later. He wanted to take Rhys and Tina and Penny Duncan to some out-of-the-way pub and tell them that somehow things would work out. He hesitated as he had done when he saw Moe Katz that day in the courtroom. But he hesitated only for a moment.

"Oh, yes," he said, turning to join Symes. "You three have a good weekend. You did a good job, Miss Duncan."

Tina watched Galvin descend the steps with the cadre of barristers, still wearing their wigs and legal finery. Some moments later she saw that they were joined in the courtyard by Master Lawrence.

"They're headed for the Bohemia," said Penny Duncan, noting Tina and Rhys's dismay at the relaxed bonhomie between bench and bar. "We can join them, if you like. Visiting lawyers, not to mention clients, are puzzled by this display of conviviality. The Bard put it well," she added. " 'Do as lawyers do in law, strive mightily, but eat and drink as friends.' "

"I'd prefer to stay at arm's length," Tina said, her expression grim.

"The Bull and Flagon it is, then." Rhys put his arms around Tina and Penny and led them in the opposite direction.

21

Neither side enjoyed the unusually warm spring weather tailored for a Saturday drive to the Cotswolds or a stroll in Hyde Park. Rhys and Tina skipped their early-morning jog and rode the tube from Gunnesbury to Victoria Station. They met Penny Duncan at a small bagel shop on Vauxhall Bridge Road, drank some strong Turkish coffee, and ate a full complement of shirred eggs with beefsteak pie before heading off to Penny's office.

◘

Stan Frobisher got on a conference call to Jerry Wilson and Chip Hovington. Frobisher's TelePrompTer signaled that only three were on the line.

"We appealed the Master's ruling on depositions," said Frobisher, "but he refused to stay his order until review by the Queen's Bench. I talked to Derek Symes just moments ago and he feels an appeal won't be successful, but we'll go ahead with it anyway. Depositions start Monday at the American Embassy, subject to our motion to strike all testimony if we eventually prevail."

"But you say that's unlikely," said Chip.

"Highly unlikely, according to Derek. Mr. Galvin will be handling the interrogation at the Embassy. He and Derek are meeting here all weekend with Dr. Bok-Sahn and the executive personnel to be interrogated. I'm scheduled to see the doctor in about an hour."

"Now, this is important," said Chip, "and Dr. Bok-Sahn can't let us down. You've spoken to her?"

"Our president, Ruuden Gore, flew in from Cairo yesterday. We met in executive session for several hours. Believe me, gentlemen, this isn't easy. She's, well, strong-willed and high-minded. Gore appealed to her humanitarian side and stressed how Lyosin aids the afflicted, alleviates suffering, prolongs life, and keeps a bloody lot of people off the welfare rolls. We employ over eight thousand at Bromley alone.

"You know, I think she's not entirely convinced that longevity is altogether a good thing. For someone with a 230 IQ, she's got some strange hang-ups. Stuff about reincarnation, how we get into the transition sooner or later—so why later? She's Buddhist but was educated by the Catholic Ursuline nuns right here in Maida Vale. Bad combination—the Ursulines were never that big on a long and happy life, either."

"Well, it's important." Chip's voice was firm. "She realizes the damage that could be done if Aubrey's journal surfaces. Especially since his initial findings were never mentioned to the FDA or to the United Kingdom Health Ministry. Eli Lilly got its rear end caught in the shredder for withholding just such information on the drug Oraflex. They were fined two million dollars, and their president and vice president got suspended jail sentences. And that's just the beginning. Their product was discontinued and lawsuits almost were their undoing. I'm sure you appreciate the delicacy of our situation."

"I read you," said Frobisher. "As I say, Galvin and Symes are meeting with the doctor shortly. I think she's mellowing."

Wilson spoke up. "Let me see if we have this clear, Frobie. Dr. Bok-Sahn is the last witness following Mallory, Brunner, and

Schindler, and you say there's no problem with those three? They don't even know about Sir Aubrey's journal?"

"Right-o," said Frobisher.

"And Sabrina Bok-Sahn, as it stands now, if interrogated, will deny the journal's existence?"

Frobisher suddenly became silent. He thought Wilson's recitals were oddly specific. He checked the TelePrompTer. Still only three on the line.

"Look," Chip said. "I think this is too sensitive to discuss over the phone. The next few days we'll be in touch by courier, back and forth on the Concorde. We won't even fax anything."

"We get the picture," Frobisher said. "It's now 2:10 P.M. London time. Galvin and Derek Symes have worked all morning going over masses of data. We deliberately left it a hodgepodge. We'll cart the stuff to the deposition in steamer trunks. It's up to the other side to decipher it, not us."

◘

Few knew of the existence of Aubrey Gammett's journal. One was Derek Symes. And Derek Symes was the real link to Sabrina Bok-Sahn. She seemed to trust him. They had holidayed together, attended the Derby at Epsom Downs, and boated off the Isle of Wight. Lately, they had been seen together at the best restaurants and at the smartest social functions in London. There were rumors that they were lovers. It was no accident that Pillsbury & Mackay had selected Symes to represent Universal Multi-Tech Ltd.

Symes had told Frobisher that Sabrina Bok-Sahn would deliver. Not even Chip Hovington was in on that. Not even Frank Galvin.

◘

Derek Symes introduced Galvin to Dwight Conover, legal attaché to the U.S. Embassy. He ushered them into the tiny conference room that had been reserved for depositions. Galvin thought the modest quarters indicated that the Ambassador to the Court of St.

James didn't consider the lawsuit one of his top priorities. Or maybe it was Symes's doing to underplay the importance of the proceedings.

Five witnesses were to be interrogated. Tina Alvarez would conduct the examination for the plaintiffs. She was to start with Universal Multi-Tech's president, Ruuden Gore, followed by Marketing Director Heath Mallory, then Doctors Brunner and Schindler, and finally Sabrina Bok-Sahn. But Symes had made sure that Gore wasn't available. He had advised Universal's president to go to Africa on a business trip. Gore was beyond the jurisdiction of any papers that might be served.

The preamble in the letters rogatory requested that witnesses produce "any and all documents, of whatever nature and whenever written, regarding the discovery and development of the drug Lyosin in all countries from its inception to the present. Also to be included were documents related to any and all complications encountered prior and subsequent to approval by the United Kingdom Ministry of Health and/or United States of America division of the Food and Drug Administration." The list was all-embracing.

Heath Mallory had been well prepped by Galvin and Derek Symes. Galvin had spent many hours with the witnesses.

"Don't volunteer information. A deposition is your present recall under oath," he had told them. "It effectively confines your testimony and can be used later at trial in front of the jury to impeach your credibility by highlighting inconsistent statements. Sections of the deposition can be read out of context, possibly dovetailing with evidence offered by our adversary on issues such as medical causation or negligent marketing. Keep this in mind. Brevity is the cardinal rule. Keep your answers precise and to the point. But don't be hemmed in by the examiner either. If you need to give a more complete explanation to avoid unfavorable inferences, don't hesitate to expand your answer so that it presents your position in the most favorable light.

"I'm not telling you *what* to say, but *how* to say it," had been Galvin's concluding advice.

◻

Tina Alvarez glanced up from her yellow pad when Galvin entered with Derek Symes. Her greeting was reserved. She thought back to the time when Galvin had spent the night with her in Fall River, how he had later steered Moe Katz and Rhys Jameson into her camp. She wondered what it all meant. Was Galvin playing some kind of cruel game with all of them, or was he, too, caught up in some inextricable force beyond his control? Already, in time and money, Moe had committed over a hundred thousand dollars, with no end in sight. She thought of Rhys Jameson's assessment of costs: two hundred thousand, maybe a million. A trifling amount to Universal and Gammett. But unless she could uncover some real dereliction by the defendants, she was headed toward a costly surrender. Like General Westmoreland in his fight with CBS, they'd simply run out of ammunition, the wherewithal to keep going.

Galvin watched Attaché Conover administer the oath to Heath Mallory, Universal's vice president of marketing. He was the officer designated by Universal as most knowledgeable of the corporate structure and was the official keeper of records.

There were preliminary background questions. Mallory was a native of Rhodesia but had been raised in Holland, had attended Juventus Schulen in Zurich, Freiburg-Inn-Bresgeau in Austria, and Queens College, Oxford. He was thirty-seven, married, had two children. He had served in executive capacities with three pharmaceutical firms since graduating from Oxford—LaRoche in France, Baer-Gruenthal in Germany, and Kingman-Sachs in Brussels, where he had been in charge of foreign marketing prior to becoming Universal's marketing director five years ago. His wife was a citizen of the Netherlands.

Mallory made a good appearance, spoke Oxbridge English with just the hint of a Dutch accent.

He parried difficult questions with the ease of a skilled fencer.

"I have no knowledge that Lyosin is capable of causing genetic damage in offspring of consumers. . . ."

"There was absolutely no indication in testing, in clinical trials, in animal and human studies, that Lyosin had or has such capability. . . ."

"The drug was studied in the United Kingdom, the Netherlands, the West German Republic, and in France, where it was subjected to the strictest testing procedures ever devised, and carefully monitored by physicians and scientists in those countries. It was proved to be safe and efficacious before the licensing agencies accepted it for distribution. The same care was applied in the United States and in Canada. Most recently, the Republic of China and Japan have authorized distribution by prescription."

After three hours of questioning, they adjourned for lunch.

Back from their break, Alvarez resumed her meticulous interrogation, but Mallory's computer mind took her through a jungle of scientific and medical data.

"There were some complications," he said at one point. "No drug is absolutely safe. These were recorded and reported to authorized agencies in all countries, including the United States, Canada, and the United Kingdom." He explained in minute detail the hows, whens, and wherefores "of the greatest medical find of the century."

Mallory was no academic ornament like Dante Corsini. He was a seasoned professional, knew the corporate structure intimately, and had the facility to assess each question quickly and answer it knowledgeably.

It had been a long weary day. Eight hours of cross-examination, identifying documents, going over clinical studies, the relationship between Universal and its worldwide markets, minutes of annual meetings, seminars, conferences. Galvin and Symes had done their homework.

Still, Alvarez persisted. She, too, had done her homework, and she knew the purpose of a deposition was to uncover information, not to belittle or confuse the witness. Sifting, weeding, and collating would come later.

Mallory was as adroit and articulate as Alvarez was relentless. He provided just enough information to be responsive, occasionally lecturing on the intricacies of research and development and techniques of international marketing. Everything he said confirmed that Universal was a colossus in this field. Mallory did not deny that in the pharmaceutical market they ranked up with Sterling, Upjohn, and LaRoche, and were as wealthy as any oil cartel. But what came through was the notion that Universal was a compassionate giant, sensitive to the ills of mankind. All of their products—asthmatic sprays, antipsychotic drugs, arthritic pain relievers—alleviated human suffering. The same could be said for some of their by-products—sleeping pills, hand lotions, hair tints, and Decasperm, a male birth-control pill that temporarily suppressed sperm counts "before, during, and after." In addition, they were deeply involved in cancer research and in developing a cure for AIDS. And the world's first official aphrodisiac, Ero-Plus (the correiga was the source), would soon be on the market. As Galvin listened to Mallory, Dante Corsini's words came to mind: "Not only will you live forever, but you'll go around with a perpetual hard-on."

Mallory had anticipated Alvarez's cross-examination and was totally in command. Each question he had seen coming. Except the last.

"Mr. Mallory." Tina Alvarez scanned her notes. "Do you know a Thomas Gately?"

"Thomas who?"

Galvin placed his pencil to his lips and glanced at Derek Symes.

"Thomas Gately. He's a postal clerk out of Knightsbridge Station. He has the regular morning route to Universal's offices in Bromley."

It was Mallory's turn to become curious.

"Why should I know him?" he asked.

Galvin leaned forward. Symes hunched his shoulders; Mallory was on his own.

"Let me back up a bit," Tina said. Penny Duncan handed her a document with several attachments. Tina passed it to the legal attaché.

"At this time, may this document with appendages be marked as an exhibit?"

"What is it?" asked the attaché.

Tina went out on a limb. "This is a letter dated January nineteenth, 1989, with a copy of a legal complaint that is the subject matter of this lawsuit. It was sent by me to Universal Multi-Tech Limited via registered post; that was a few months ago. It was returned unclaimed. Not even signed for."

"Why is it being offered as an exhibit?" the attaché inquired.

"To examine the witness as to whether or not it was received or signed for by any personnel at Universal at the designated address."

Galvin's stomach turned. *The sneaky peepy.* How in the world . . .

He was on his feet quickly.

"Your Honor." He addressed the legal attaché. "Any letter to Universal is completely irrelevant. The issue of jurisdiction has already been decided by the United States District Court sitting in Boston, Massachusetts. Further, the Master of the Queen's Remembrances has ruled that Universal is not a party to this lawsuit. The question of jurisdiction is *res judicata.* Whether or not Universal was served by registered letter under the Massachusetts long-arm statute is moot. Any evidence one way or the other is now completely irrelevant."

Derek Symes handed Galvin a copy of both orders, that of Judge Baron and that of Master Lawrence.

Tina Alvarez waited while Attaché Conover studied both documents.

"Yes," Conover said. "That issue has been decided. The exhibit will not be received and the question is excluded."

Tina conferred briefly with Rhys and Penny Duncan.

She should have made an offer of proof. Galvin was curious as to what information she had.

"I've finished with this witness," Tina said. "That's all I have."

"Mr. Galvin," the legal attaché said, "any re-cross?"

"We reserve the right to call Mr. Mallory at subsequent proceedings or at trial," Galvin said. "As for now, I have no questions."

"It is 4:30 P.M.," the legal attaché said as he started gathering up his papers. "We will commence with Dr. Brunner at 9 A.M. tomorrow, to be followed by Dr. Schindler and Dr. Bok-Sahn. Gentlemen, ladies, until tomorrow, these proceedings stand adjourned."

■

Galvin, Symes, and Sabrina Bok-Sahn had dinner at Universal's executive offices. They were joined by Mallory and Frobisher. Drs. Brunner and Schindler dined at a separate table. They would work well into the night, and Galvin felt it best to allow the doctors a peaceful meal.

"You did an excellent job today, Heath," he told Mallory. "Smooth delivery, articulate in your subject. Depositions alert either side that a particular witness may blow them out of the water or be vulnerable. They pinpoint inadequacies. Miss Alvarez, although young like Penny Duncan, knows how to compete in this male-oriented game. But I'm sure both are reassessing the posture of their case after today's testimony."

"Do you think they'll throw in the towel?" Frobisher asked.

"Uh . . ." Galvin caught himself studying the sleek beauty of Sabrina Bok-Sahn. "Unlikely." He cleared his throat. "They're really stuck. Alvarez built up too much expectation in her clients to back down now. But I can't see them denting any of our remaining witnesses. Doctors Brunner and Schindler are well versed in the subject of adverse reactions and side effects, none of which, incidentally, are of the type claimed by the plaintiffs."

Galvin dipped a crouton into the caviar bowl. "Dr. Bok-Sahn, you will be the last witness."

She nodded. Her eyes studied Galvin.

"I expect that you will be interrogated late tomorrow afternoon and well into Thursday," Galvin said. "We'll review the transcripts Friday and then I might head to Cornwall for the weekend."

"Where will you be staying?" Sabrina asked, extracting one of her long cheroots from her wafer-thin gold case. "I know a delightful guest house just north of St. Ives. Jane Austen used to summer there."

"Oh, I thought I'd rent a car and just head off into the countryside. Check into some small inn, relive some history. See Stonehenge, Berkeley Castle, search for Camelot."

"Berkeley Castle is a particularly sinister place." Derek Symes pulled out his lighter and lit Sabrina Bok-Sahn's cheroot. She nodded a thank you. That's where Edward the Second got it up his posterior with a red-hot poker. Simply ghastly way to end up. You can see the dungeon where the dastardly deed was done."

"We British have had our share of monstrous deeds," Frobisher chuckled. "They say that Jack the Ripper was a lawyer. Rumored to be Queen Victoria's nephew. Most of his victims ended up in the Thames, just around the bend from the Temple Bar."

"No ethnic group has a monopoly on goodness, and none are immune from evil," Galvin said quietly. "On second thought, I might just stay in London. Walk around. Somehow I need a holiday from violence and confrontation."

"Okay," Derek Symes said quickly. "No pastry carts tonight, Galvin. Let's suit up Brunner and Schindler in our finest chain-mail armor, maybe even stack some extra arrows for their bows."

Tina Alvarez's interrogation of Drs. Brunner and Schindler was exacting. She read from a series of prepared questions.

Dr. Horst Brunner traced his background. Born in Austria, graduated from Schoenhausen Medical School in Berlin in 1941, conscripted into the German Army as a medical officer the same year. (Galvin had Brunner emphasize the word *conscripted*. Schindler had enlisted but would use the word *served*.)

Brunner described his career for the next four years. In 1942 he was assigned to the German Sixth Army at Rostov and later at Stalingrad. He treated the wounded on both sides, Russian as well as German, including Hungarians, Serbs, Rumanians, Poles. "To a doctor," he said solemnly, "death and dying wear no uniform."

He retreated with the German Army, was captured by the Russians outside of Vienna and, together with German doctors and scientists, sent to Moscow, where he was held for five years before being released.

He bore no hostility to the Russians. He was treated civilly and had worked on a variety of medical projects—curbing epidemics, cholera, strains of influenza, malaria.

After his release, he returned to medical practice in Vienna, specializing in immunology, pharmacology, and internal medicine. He joined the staff of a Vienna-based pharmaceutical firm, Strachen-Hoer, was sent to Nice, France, where he studied under professors LaRoche, deClasse, and Freiberg on a host of diseases—cancer, venereal, neurologic. He joined the staff of Dijon-Schenlich in Amsterdam in 1965. When the firm was absorbed by Universal a few years later, he was named Chief Chemist, the position he now holds.

Like Mallory, Brunner traced the steps of Lyosin's development and testing, from arduous clinical trials to final approval by licensing authorities in Germany, the United Kingdom, France, the Netherlands, Canada, and the United States.

It was his duty to review complaints of side effects and adverse reactions and insure that they were properly recorded and brought to the attention of the health licensing authorities.

"No drug, not even the simple aspirin," he said, "is absolutely harmless. We expect an infinitesimal amount of adverse reactions to Lyosin, even fatalities. Some people may be hypersusceptible. Two individuals can be stung by a bee," he said, lapsing into a homey analogy. "One feels slight skin irritation, the other goes into anaphylactic shock and dies within seconds." He snapped his fingers. "The same toxin, same amount, but the hypersusceptible person has dormant factors that trigger a catastrophic reaction. Medical science doesn't know why.

"Fortunately," Brunner stated, "most Lyosin side effects are minor—skin rash, upset stomach, nausea, morning cramps, liquid stools. Fatal reactions were less than a half of one percent."

Galvin knew, as did Tina Alvarez and Rhys Jameson, that this percentage was well within the legal minimum.

Brunner ended his testimony on a strong note. "An estimated eighty billion Lyosin tablets have been distributed and consumed worldwide since the drug was approved in 1980. Not one case of genetic damage attributable to Lyosin has been reported."

Dr. Schindler was assistant medical director of Universal. His testimony was a duplicate of Brunner's.

Tina Alvarez was generating reams of tape but scoring few if any points. The evidence was unmistakable. Lyosin was the wonder drug of the century. The inferences were also there to be drawn: The pharmaceutical industry was big business, Universal's share of the market was astronomical, and many of Universal's top echelon were extraordinarily rich. But inferences were not evidence. The raw evidence that Lyosin had destructive capabilities was lacking.

Tina was ready for her final witness: Dr. Sabrina Bok-Sahn. The doctor was not only brilliant and articulate, but also strikingly beautiful and enormously wealthy. Yet, in the combination, Tina saw a mystery. She wondered just how far Frank Galvin would allow her to probe.

"Please raise your right hand, place your left hand on the Bible," Attaché Conover said to Sabrina Bok-Sahn. "Do you swear before God—"

"I do not recognize the Christian deity," she said quietly. She stood by the small table facing the stenographer. Her large almond eyes glistened with innocence, with a quality of naïveté. "If anything, I follow the precepts of Gautama Buddha. My allegiance is to no god, but to humanity. I *will* tell the truth."

It was obvious to Galvin and to Derek Symes that the trio of Tina Alvarez, Rhys Jameson, and Penny Duncan was thoroughly prepared. Tina's questions to Mallory, Brunner, and Schindler had proven that. With this in mind, Galvin had cross-examined Sabrina Bok-Sahn for four hours, as if in a mock trial, leading her into byways and traps favored by inquisitors. He had anticipated every avenue, every thrust of Tina's interrogation. Now, on the witness stand, Sabrina's answers, sometimes so gentle they were almost inaudible, had the clear ring of truth.

Sabrina recounted her beginnings in Burma, her formal schooling, her lineage to Sir Aubrey Gammett. She had connections in Burma. The Bok-Sahn family owned the Lyosin formula. They leased the patent to Universal. She candidly agreed that her job was part of the package and this was the main reason, not her IQ of 230, for her having been propelled into her present position.

She described the chemical formula of Lyosin in detail.

"Medicine is not an exact science," she said. "We can only

theorize as to how correiga extract dissolves blood clots, particularly in coronary arteries. It is probably due to two factors—lowering cholesterol levels and alterations in blood coagulability. While we're aware that many chemicals are capable of accomplishing this in the laboratory, Lyosin is the only formula known capable of dissolving atherosclerotic plaques in blood vessels of animals and humans at sites of thrombotic predilection."

She conceded that there were some people who should not use Lyosin—individuals with hyperglycemia, blood dyscrasias, anemia, those who already had an anticoagulating condition and other hematologic disorders. "These exceptions," she said, "have been carefully chronicled, catalogued, and computerized, and updated warnings are issued in package inserts in language understandable to physicians and patients alike."

"Do you have any knowledge from any source, whatsoever," Tina asked, "either past or present, that the drug Lyosin and/or its chemical components, including correiga extract, is capable of producing congenital deformities in offspring of those consuming either the drug Lyosin or correiga extract?"

It was the final question. Tina was exhausted. There was a strained weariness in her voice. Sabrina Bok-Sahn seemed as fresh as when the examination first commenced.

Galvin had been taking notes, but he knew Sabrina Bok-Sahn had handled the interrogation superbly. There would be no need for re-cross examination. He watched her brush a strand of dark hair from her bronzed forehead.

"No," she replied simply. "I have no such knowledge."

◘

"I'll have to take a rain check," Galvin said. He looked in at Derek Symes and Sabrina Bok-Sahn as Soames held the limo door ajar.

"I wish you'd reconsider." Derek's invitation seemed reserved. "We'll pick you up at eight, drive to Stonehenge and Salisbury Cathedral, and be back here at Browns in time for high tea."

If Symes's invitation seemed tentative, Galvin also sensed a certain pensiveness in Sabrina.

"Thanks again," Galvin said, "but I've got to catch an early plane out of Heathrow, 10 A.M. Brit Air."

"Well, my dear Galvin." Derek was smart enough not to belabor the invitation or the moment. "I think we concluded things quite successfully at this end."

Sabrina's eyes lingered on Galvin's, then moved away. Something in her eyes responded to his. Did he catch a faint signal? Her lips were pursed in her characteristic half-smile. Hard to tell what she was thinking.

"Yes, quite successfully," he said. "I'll be in touch." And with a slight wave of his hand he headed into the lobby of Browns Hotel. It was a polite lie. He'd have to move quickly. He hoped British Air wasn't sold out.

He dined quietly in a corner of the tearoom. It was as if he had stepped into a painting by Turner or Copley. And yet the muted tones—the brown carpeting flecked with gold, the heavy green swagged draperies, and the pale-yellow tableclothes—did nothing to elevate his mood as he picked at the crustless sandwiches. He thought of Sabrina Bok-Sahn. Her elusiveness gnawed at him. He tried to dismiss her, but it remained, a niggling pain in his lower gut. Sabrina Bok-Sahn was getting to him, this he knew. Maybe the little pangs of jealousy were honing in. She was Derek Symes's girl . . . forbidden turf.

◻

The first-class section on British Air's 10 A.M. flight was totally booked. After a wait as a standby, he shuffled on with a motley assortment of travelers—backpacking youngsters in Reebok sneakers, some hefting babies, a religious group of women with shawls, men with beards.

A pleasant stewardess with a crisp British accent smiled and passed him, together with the usual cellophaned mid-morning snack, the evening edition of the West Ham *News-Gazette*. It was a small-town daily. There were no copies of the *Times*. Galvin thanked her. He'd try his hand at the crossword puzzle.

The tea and biscuits were comforting, as was the journalistic mix in the *Gazette*—gardening, horticulture, animal husbandry, politics, soccer results, even the overseas baseball standings. The Red Sox trailed the Yankees by two and a half games. Oh well, he thought, the season is young.

From force of habit, he glanced at the obituary column. "The Irish sports page," as his grandfather Pradrig used to call it.

The name stood out:

GALVIN, EAMON IGNATIUS

He read the small print.

Grandson of "Billy" Galvin, late of Galway, Ireland, pugilist who fought Bob Fitsimmons for the world heavyweight boxing title in Brighton in 1897.

It was a distant relative. He remembered his grandfather talking of "darlin' " Billy, the Galway Gladiator, how the Boston strong boy, John L. Sullivan, ducked him constantly. He said a little prayer for Eamon and for Billy. He included Grandfather Pradrig and the great John L.

Then his eye inadvertently fell on the next name.

GATELY, THOMAS WINTHROP

Galvin's heart leaped.

Beloved of Catherine Simpson Gately, postal courier, died suddenly at home. The coroner ascribed the cause of death to heart failure. He leaves three children. John of Surrey . . .

Galvin lowered the paper. He began to shake.

22

Galvin awakened with a start. A cold sweat dampened his collar and he wondered where he was. He shook his head and wiped his eyes.

"Fasten your seat belts," came the announcement. "We'll be landing in thirty minutes."

Now he remembered. He was someplace over the Atlantic. The 747 had started its descent. He could tell by the pitch of the engines.

The flight attendant's bright blue eyes smiled down at him. "Are you okay, sir?" She had noticed the beads of sweat on Galvin's forehead. "You were groaning quite a bit, but I thought it best not to disturb you."

"The paper," he said almost incoherently. "Where's the *Gazette*?"

"The what?" She frowned in puzzlement.

I was reading the West Ham *Gazette*," he said curtly. "Where did it go?"

"I'll ask Cindy," she said. "She probably picked it up."

Now he started to come around. "I'm sorry," he apologized, resting his head against the seat and closing his eyes. "I must have been bushed."

"Do you want to see if I can round one up?"

"No, that's okay," Galvin said as he tried to think back. Had he dreamed this? No. He'd been working on the crossword.

Now things were coming into focus. *Gately, Thomas; postal*

courier; died at home. This had to be the mailman who delivered the registered letters.

Heart failure. Death occurred suddenly. Sudden implies unexpected. He wondered if an autopsy had been performed.

There was a gentle ping. A FASTEN SEAT BELT light came on. The wing flaps whirred into place and the landing wheels thumped into position. Galvin checked his watch. "Can you imagine," he said to the stewardess, "six hours to cross the Atlantic. I think it took Lindbergh a day and a half."

He had to forget about the death notice. He'd check out Gately when he got back, just to put his mind at ease. Probably a coincidence that his death occurred during the Magistrate's hearing. But he had to make sure. Then he'd get back to the Lyosin case and wrap it up. He knew he had been dragging his feet. He recalled Carter Hovington's lecture on advocacy. Edward Bennett Williams defending Jimmy Hoffa.

He thought of Sabrina Bok-Sahn. When would he see her again? Why couldn't he stop thinking about her?

◘

Jerry Wilson scrutinized the transcribed depositions from London. They had been indexed, summarized, and highlighted with a yellow marker. In all his years as general counsel of Gammett, he could not recall better testimony. Galvin must have prepared each witness to the nth degree, he thought. Almost too perfect.

He dropped off photocopies of the depositions for Dante Corsini and asked him to become familiar with the contents. He expected Alvarez's next move would be to depose Gammett's personnel.

Corsini liked the part where Sabrina Bok-Sahn spoke of the correiga's aphrodisiac qualities. He suggested changing the name of their new product Ero-Plus to Erecto-Plus.

"I'll speak to our marketing department." Corsini failed to detect the sarcasm in Wilson's voice.

Wilson had called Dr. Torgenson's secretary earlier for an appointment to brief the doctor on what had happened in London, to tell him about winning the jurisdiction issue and relate the superb testimony of Universal's personnel. He was sure Dr. Torgenson would welcome the news. Perhaps a reward would be forthcoming at his annual job performance review, now only weeks away.

As the afternoon dragged on, he became annoyed that he was still waiting for a response. At four-thirty Dr. Torgenson's secretary called and told him that the president would see him now. He spent another half-hour seated in the outer office, studying the new Federal bill designed to limit legal liability of manufacturers, particularly pharmaceutical firms. It had received bipartisan backing and was on the President's "must" agenda for legislative enactment. He would brief Dr. Torgenson on its contents.

At exactly 5 P.M. the secretary saw a red blip on her intercom and told Jerry Wilson to go in. He thanked her, gathered his documents, and gave one last tug to his apothecary tie clasp. Everything was in place.

Dr. Torgenson had always intimidated Jerry Wilson. Although he had been general counsel for thirteen years, Wilson was always unsure of his status. But today he pushed the heavy mahogany door open and walked in at full stride.

"Come in, Jerry," Dr. Torgenson said, a little startled. Wilson was practically upon him as he stood pouring from a decanter of Remy Martin.

"Sit down. Brandy?"

"Thank you, Doctor." Wilson accepted a snifter and settled into the leather club chair in front of Torgenson's desk. He stacked the depositions in a neat pile on the Persian rug near his feet and again fingered his tie clasp. He felt at ease.

Torgenson went through his ritual. He lifted the oversized brandy glass with both hands, like a priest at the offertory, and watched the amber liquid rotate as he shook it gently. He sniffed it, then sipped. Wilson waited in patient deference as he had done on countless occasions.

"Good news on all fronts, Doctor," Jerry Wilson said, toasting slightly, then taking a good swallow. The brandy sent a shot of warmth through his body.

"Senate Bill 1130 just reached my desk. It's designed to reduce legal liability on new products such as research drugs. Our message that litigation was inhibiting development finally got through. The Kalb Tort Reform Bill has Presidential support and should be the law of the land by November."

Torgenson took another sip of brandy. He knew all about the proposed legislation. The pharmaceutical industry's political action committee had heavily subsidized Senator Kalb's recent reelection.

"What are the financial limits on liability?" Torgenson asked, more to test Wilson's familiarity with the bill than to be given information.

"Only a hundred thousand per claim on new drugs approved on or after January first, 1980," Wilson said. "And, of course, that includes Lyosin."

"This is 1990," Torgenson said. "Any problem with the bill being declared unconstitutional? It is retroactive legislation."

"No problem," said Wilson. He was telling Torgenson something the doctor wanted to hear. "We went through the constitutionality bit last year on national malpractice, putting financial caps on damage awards against medical practitioners and health-care facilities. The key to the Supreme Court ruling is that the overriding social issue mandates enactment."

"Sounds good," Torgenson said. "And I understand things went well in London."

"Better than expected, Doctor." Wilson swirled the brandy, then drained his glass. "I have the depositions here." He nudged the stacked documents with his foot.

"And Dr. Bok-Sahn?"

Dr. Torgenson's self-assurance at times bordered on arrogance. But his job depended on keeping in the good graces of Sabrina Bok-Sahn. So Wilson's praise of Universal's medical director was not effusive. "She did a fine job," he said, playing to Torgenson's sentiments. "It was obvious that Frank Galvin had her well coached. Hovington Junior is sending the depositions to Dr. Fred Willis and Dr. Allison Wray, perhaps the leading epidemiologist in the world. He's soliciting their affidavits for a motion for summary judgment."

183

"Summary judgment?"

"Our next step is to get rid of the litigation, once and for all. We present affidavits to the trial judge, stating that there is no *reasonable* evidence for a jury to conclude that Gammett had knowledge that Lyosin is or ever was capable of causing the damage claimed in the lawsuit. There's really nothing for a jury to decide. With the environment created by the Kalb bill, and with Willis and Wray's testimony, this suit will be over within a matter of weeks."

"You've done an excellent job, Jerry," Torgenson said, "and I and London have been most appreciative of the fine services you've rendered over the last thirteen years."

Something pricked Jerry Wilson's insides. He sat erect as his hand gripped the brandy glass. He didn't like Torgenson's use of the past tense. This didn't sound like a lead-in to a pay raise.

"In the years we've worked together, Jerry," Torgenson continued, "you've known me to be strictly up front with you."

Wilson waited.

"Now we feel, and London feels"—Torgenson paused and inspected his glass—"that we have to bring in new blood as we enter the nineties. You're what, Jerry, fifty-eight?"

"Fifty-seven," Wilson replied too quickly.

"Have a daughter in college, I understand."

"A sophomore at New Brunswick State."

"Well, we're asking you to take an early retirement, Jerry, to become a member of the alumni."

"An early retirement?" The words stuck in Jerry Wilson's throat.

"We're bringing in Wyeth Richardson as general counsel as of June first."

"Wyeth Richardson? Why, he's with a New York law firm that just deals in estates and banking." Wilson's voice was beginning to crack. "Hell, Doctor, he knows absolutely zilch about the pharmaceutical industry. I mean *zilch!*"

"That's where you come in, Jerry. He can learn. You'll be retained as a part-time consultant."

Wilson sat stunned for several seconds. He knew argument was useless.

"Dr. Torgenson," he said, eyeing the president carefully. "What are the financial arrangements for my forced retirement?"

"Please," Dr. Torgenson said. " 'Forced' is an inelegant term. You are not being dismissed. I'm sure a person with your expertise will have little trouble latching on to something elsewhere. Letters of recommendation will be highly complimentary. London will make the necessary financial arrangements. It will be generous."

"How generous?" Wilson's said tersely.

Torgenson was getting annoyed.

"You will retire at twenty-five thousand a year. Any work done on a consultant basis will be paid at an hourly rate. Your life and disability insurance will continue, as will your boat club membership, just as if you were still an employee."

"That's not enough." Wilson's voice had a steely edge to it.

"What?"

"I said that's not enough. Twenty-five thousand merely pays me back what I contributed to my retirement plan. You know that. I make a hundred thousand a year on a job that commands two hundred and fifty thousand anyplace else. I've shagged and done the legal gut work for thirteen years." Wilson's voice rose. "Not once in thirteen years did Gammett ever get into trouble with anyone—Congressional Committees, the FDA—"

"Look, Jerry," said Torgenson, glancing at his wristwatch, "I've got to meet my wife at the club at seven. We'll have Personnel draw up the necessary papers."

Wilson made no effort to move. "I want a million dollars up front."

"You what?!"

"One million. And I'm gone. No alumni. No Blue Cross. No retirement. One million." Wilson mouthed the words carefully.

Torgenson had sensed a difference in Jerry Wilson from the moment he had entered his office. He had a certain calm and an unaccustomed sense of bravado. Wilson behaved as if he held some high cards.

"A million dollars? That's preposterous." Torgenson's voice was controlled. "What makes you think your termination merits that kind of money?"

185

"Well," Jerry Wilson said, crossing his legs, "I've been doing a lot of thinking lately. Sometimes as lawyers we do things to protect a client that aren't exactly ethical."

Torgenson eyed Wilson curiously. "Ethical?"

Wilson picked up a pencil and examined the point. "Like the present Lyosin litigation. London changed the Importer's Agreement. We represented to the court that it was the original and we prevailed on that basis."

Torgenson could see what was coming. He struggled to curb his fury.

"It was your recommendation—" Torgenson began.

"I know, I know," Wilson cut him off. He still studied the pencil, turning it in his fingers as if he were examining a rare gem. "But we all went along with it. You. London. Our law firm in Boston. It involves a lot of people. And as for the testimony of Dr. Bok-Sahn," he continued, assurance creeping into his voice, "it was outright perjury."

Torgenson's eyes narrowed.

"She professed no knowledge of genetic defects in offspring of correiga users," Wilson said. "Again, this complicity involves many important people. Bigwigs from the FDA, the British Ministry of Health. And, of course, you, me, London, Sabrina Bok-Sahn, our Boston law firm."

For the first time in his corporate dealings with Dr. Torgenson, Wilson sensed he was on a roll.

"You know, Doctor, sometimes a lawyer can't condone illegality on his own side. He has a duty that transcends the one to the client. Sometimes a lawyer feels constrained to call the adversary's attention to certain irregularities, especially when it substantially affects the outcome of the case."

Torgenson had it now. Extortion! Goddamned blackmail! If the price wasn't met, Wilson would get religion. "I see," he said evenly. "Well, maybe something can be worked out, Jerry, some compromise. I'll talk with London."

"The price is *one* million." Jerry Wilson was emphatic. "No compromise. Friday's my retirement day, Dr. Torgenson. You have until Friday."

186

Torgenson's voice was calm as he tried to sheathe his anger. "Okay, Jerry. But this doesn't change the fact that we still have to keep in shape. See you on the river in the morning?"

23

"My name is Williams," came the voice on Moe's answering machine. At least it sounded like Williams. "I'm calling about the Lyosin case. I'll be in touch."

And with that the message ended. Moe replayed it several times. It was a little faint. No hint of the caller's identity. There was no way to trace it. He was still peeved over the Archer reprimand, so he decided to keep the cryptic stuff to himself. Maybe the party would call back.

◘

Galvin was greeted by Sam, the black garage attendant, in front of the New England Tower Building. He gave Sam the car keys and a twenty-dollar bill.

"Congratulations, Mr. Galvin." Sam beamed a broad toothy-white smile as he jumped into the sleek silver Jaguar.

Galvin wondered about the salutation. He bought the *Globe* at the newsstand and nodded a few good mornings to tenants from other firms, briefly thinking it was odd that at 7:30 A.M. he failed to see anyone from his own staff. He took the private elevator to the fortieth floor, a solitary ride.

He stepped briskly from the elevator.

The surprise was more than a little staggering. At seven-thirty in the morning, the entire clerical force—paralegals, secretaries, analysts, computer specialists, librarians, legal interns—lined the black marble foyer. He was greeted with shattering applause. Julie Hedren, her green eyes glimmering their Nordic best, waited with a green carnation. Good God, he thought. St. Patrick's Day is two months past or ten months away. Then he spotted the sign newly inscribed in gold leaf above the heavy oak-grained doors:

HOVINGTON, STURDEVANT, HOLMES & GALVIN

Julie Hedren pinned the carnation on Galvin's lapel. The applause increased.

"Good morning, boss," she said. Her eyes were as misty as his. She kissed him, leaving lipstick imprinted on his cheek.

The inner-office doors swung open, and stationed within were the associates and partners. The applause continued as he advanced a few unsteady steps toward Carter Hovington and Cy Sturdevant, who waited at a podium where a microphone jutted out from a brace of green carnations.

Galvin was overwhelmed. The tough Irish kid from L Street had made it. Past events flashed through his mind like rainbow chips in a kaleidoscope. Mired in the blue-collar ghetto. The "close cover before striking" law school. The scruffy clients, the nickel-and-dime divorce cases. Years with the bottle. Now he looked into the bright faces of the partners and associates gathered around him. The ultimate tribute. It was a long way from brick bottom.

◘

"We got hit with the usual deluge," sighed Moe Katz as he opened the early-morning mail. "No checks, mind you, but plenty of bills and, of course, motions from Dewey, Screwem and Howe, for summary judgment."

"I was afraid that was coming," said Rhys Jameson.

"They're firing all the howitzers." Moe held up each document as he tolled them off. "Deposition notices on all plaintiffs, motions to produce hospital records, attending physician reports, a soup-to-nuts deposition on Dr. Meideros. All set for next week. And the summary judgment bit. Here's their brief." He lifted the document with both hands.

"What's the summary judgment piece?" Tina asked.

"A little like the motion to dismiss," said Rhys. "They contend that the evidence is so overwhelming in Gammett's favor that a trial is unnecessary. In essence, they maintain we have no evidence that Lyosin can cause genetic damage. It's accompanied by affidavits from a former FDA Director and an epidemiologist from the World Health Organization, stating unequivocally that there is no evidence, not even a suggestion.

"The CVs on the doctors, Willis and Wray, read like *Who's Who in the College of Saints and Cardinals*," Moe said, shaking his head. "We barely survived the motion to dismiss. This is the final zapper."

Rhys started skimming through the defense brief. "You know, I hate to say it," he said, "but in a way, if we go down the tubes on this one, maybe it's the best thing that ever happened to us. The case will be over."

"But what about Hector Ramondi and all the others we represent?" Tina asked.

"Life will go on," Rhys said. "It was a long shot to begin with. We gave it our best. It simply wasn't in the cards. The families have got to appreciate all you did for them, Tina."

"They won't," Tina sighed. "They'll always think I copped out. Galvin was right the day he met with all of them. I built up their expectations sky high. They thought I was sent by the Lady of Fatima and could fight City Hall. Galvin tried to be realistic about their chances. Oh, God . . ." She fought the need for a good cry. "He was so right."

"Okay, we had our shot," said Moe. "Now we've got to get our people ready for their onslaught." He tried to infuse some hope. "We can't just roll over. We still have Meideros and his letters to the FDA and to Gammett."

"Unfortunately, we're getting avalanched," Rhys said. "There's a national media blitz for tort reform, especially favoring manufacturers. They claim product liability insurance is forcing them out of business. The whole charade is being orchestrated by the insurance industry. Got to hand it to them, Madison Ave. sure knows how to be effective. Thirty-seven states have enacted ceilings on damage awards, and now the Kalb bill carves out the final sanctuary of privilege. Favors manufacturers of shoddy products, corporate polluters, drunk drivers. No one's going to be held accountable anymore."

"Well," said Moe. "I haven't played cards since Tina first walked into my office. Haven't even been in touch with my cronies. But before I buy the six-foot farm, we're going to give this one last broadside. They may beat us, but let's not go out whimpering and sniveling. If we fall, we go with a flourish. Okay?"

◘

The ceremony was short. A brief speech by Carter Hovington etched with just the right superlatives.

Cy Sturdevant was even briefer. He spoke for just a few moments, then shook Galvin's hand. "Now, back to work," he said. "Let's show our Irishman that even we Ivies can burn the midnight oil."

It was only 7:45 A.M., but already the computers were warming up and the phones were ringing.

Galvin was still overwhelmed. In his absence, everything had been taken care of—new letterheads and business cards, announcements to the general bar and the business sections of the *Globe*, *Herald*, and *Wall Street Journal*, all of which were on his desk. He shut his office door and sat for several minutes, incapable of getting into the swing of things. He went into his washroom, grinned when he saw the lavender splotch implanted by Julie Hedren. He took off his coat, undid his tie, and was about to wipe away the lipstick. He hesitated, then touched his cheek. There were the few society women he escorted to concerts and opening-night plays, but he had no steady girl, no one who shared his doubts or hopes. He touched the splotch again, then wiped his face clean.

He was putting on his jacket when Carter Hovington came in.

"I understand things went well in London," Carter said. "The depositions of Universal's personnel—a masterful job of witness preparation, Galvin. I've never read better testimony."

"I think we might be able to wind the case up shortly."

"Oh?" Carter evidenced a little surprise.

"Depositions are scheduled for next week for the families claiming genetic defects. Stu Trimble and his crew discovered similiar deformities in some of the related offspring, long before Lyosin ever came on the market."

"How in the world did he ever uncover that?" Carter was intrigued.

"Even Stu hasn't let me in on that one. Maybe he logged twenty-seven billable hours on an overnight flight to Lisbon," Galvin said and smiled. "I'll depose their expert, Dr. Meideros, the one who eluded Andrea Schneiderman. If he falters, as I suspect he will, we'll add this new information to our motion for summary judgment and the case will be history."

Carter liked Galvin's newfound enthusiasm. He suspected that Galvin had been dragging his feet.

"Have you looked at this piece of legislation?" Hovington reached into a manila folder and handed Galvin a thick document. "It just came in from our legislative service in Washington. It's the final version of the Kalb bill, ironed out by the Joint Commission on Tort Reform."

"Haven't had a chance to study it," Galvin said, "but I understand its general objective has merit. The pharmaceutical industry simply will not finance research and development of new drugs if it's going to be saddled with lawsuits at the end of the trail. I'm not so sure the bill will stand constitutional muster," Galvin continued. "It seems to violate the equal-protection clause in that it carves out a sanctuary of privilege for one group over another. In effect, it discriminates against those catastrophically injured by a manufacturer's product and favors the pharmaceutical firms, which are among the richest organizations in the market-place."

"Well, our job is to take the law as we find it and apply it to the maximum advantage for our client," said Carter. "If the Kalb bill becomes the law of the land, it will effectively thwart all litigation in this area. Claims against Lyosin or any other pharmaceutical product will be disposed of administratively, two cents on the dollar."

◘

Galvin was surprised to hear from Wyeth Richardson. "Mr. Galvin," he said, "everything I hear about you is terrific—like your handball match with Ted King. I was with Polk and Wardell in New York at the time. I've just joined Gammett Industries as general counsel. Thought I'd call and see how our motion for summary judgment is doing."

"But where's Jerry Wilson?" Galvin had swiveled his chair toward a view of Boston Harbor. He cupped the phone into the crook of his neck. At the same time, he was going over a checklist prepared by Stu Trimble for the Meideros deposition.

"Well, that's why I'm here," said Richardson. "He was such a nice guy and a good lawyer."

Galvin swiveled back toward his desk. His neck began to tingle and his shirt collar was getting moist.

"You know he was an avid rower," Richardson said. "Well, Friday morning he was on the Shrewsbury River in his shell. As you know, he was a little out of shape—overweight. And rowing's one of the most arduous physical activities in the world."

"Yeah. What happened?"

"He had a heart attack, right there on the river. The emergency techs were called, but he was DOA at Presbyterian Hospital."

"Did they do an autopsy?" Galvin was getting apprehensive.

"Yes. Coronary thrombosis of the left descending coronary artery. He had extensive atherosclerosis throughout his entire coronary tree. He was only fifty-seven, but they say he had the heart of an octogenarian."

Galvin felt relieved. "When was the wake?"

"No wake. A simple ceremony. He was cremated."

"Well, I'll send a note to his family," said Galvin. "He was a jaunty sort of guy. I liked him."

"Guess he wasn't on Lyosin," Richardson said.

24

Tina Alvarez and Rafael Meideros sat under the somber Caravaggio where four short months ago it had all started. Tina missed the chilly glare of Julie Hedren but not her officious tone when she said that Dr. Meideros's deposition would be taken in the tower conference room as soon as the court reporter was available. No salutations. No suggestion of coffee. It was enemy territory.

Dr. Fred Willis, Frank Galvin, and Chip Hovington had been closeted in the conference room for six hours. They had reviewed the medical literature, underscored the depositions, the courtroom pleadings, and the transcript of Dr. Meideros's prior testimony before Judge Baron. In preparation for Meideros's deposition, Galvin was leaving no forensic possibility uncovered.

They had narrowed the number of key questions for Meideros to fifteen. These were organized around lesser queries designed to set the stage for discrediting the doctor's testimony.

"We'll take excerpts from Meideros's deposition," Galvin said, "couple them with those of Universal's officials, and your affidavit, Dr. Willis, and that of Allison Wray. Then we move for summary judgment in Federal Court next week." He scribbled some final notes on his yellow pad.

"You mean there'll actually be no trial?" Dr. Willis asked. He had taken out his pipe and now tapped the bowl against the oversized marble ashtray he had managed to salvage from the clutter on the conference table.

"That's right," said Galvin. "It's a device employed by defendants when the evidence is so overwhelming in its favor that an expensive, protracted trial is unnecessary. It's addressed to the sound discretion of the trial judge. In this case, where the plaintiffs really have no evidence that Gammett, or Universal, for that matter, knew or had reason to believe that its product could cause genetic damage, I'm certain our motion will be granted.

"You see, the plaintiffs must not only prove that Lyosin caused the damage alleged—and here their case is terribly weak—but they also have to demonstrate that we had prior knowledge of the drug's potential danger, or that genetic disorders were apparent and we chose to ignore them."

Willis liked the way Galvin cut through the law's esoterica.

"We're sort of baiting a trap," Chip Hovington added. "The opposition thinks that this is just the first in a long series where we depose every expert or witness they list and every plaintiff bringing suit. Ordinarily, the plaintiff will insist that its experts—in this case, Dr. Meideros—give minimal testimony. No elaboration or lengthy explanations. These come later at trial. They'll give us just the bare bones. But at this stage that's exactly what we want. If Meideros gives us his name, rank, and serial number and professes ignorance of everything else, that's the way his deposition will read to Judge Baron."

Galvin wasn't too happy about the tactic, but it had to be done. It would save a lot of later grief. Yet such maneuvering always troubled him.

"How in the world did you ever come up with the data concerning the genetic disorders in blood relatives and the stillborn death in the Ramondi family?" asked Willis. "Isn't that information protected by the doctor-patient relationship?"

"That was Stu Trimble's stroke of genius," Chip said. "When Galvin was in London, Stu and his team were down in Fall River and New Bedford beating the bushes."

"They struck pay dirt," Galvin said. "The stillborn child in the Ramondi family had a severe cleft palate, and Trimble also got affidavits with attached medical data from four families, all related by blood to at least three of the plaintiff families, spelling out genetic disorders in four of their own children. The point is that all of those children were born before Lyosin was released to the public."

"That's amazing," said Willis. "But again, how did your man come up with this information?"

" 'Amazing' is an understatement." Chip grinned. "Trimble's the most innovative attorney we have and he's not letting us in on it."

"Oh, I don't mean to detract from my man Trimble," Galvin said. "But I've a hunch that it didn't take too much imagination. Birth and death certificates are matters of public record. Visit the County Registry and go from A to Z, say, over the past ten years. It's a boring day's work, but it's hunt and find.

"Now, if I were Stu Trimble," Galvin continued, "I'd know that a young Boston barrister with a Brahmin-sounding name, flashing around Fall River in a sleek BMW and asking a lot of questions, wouldn't get directions to the public library.

"There's an old Gaelic saying," he mused. " 'Success is seldom forgiven among the Irish.' Well, it cuts across ethnic lines. You see, the families bringing suit received a great deal of ink in the local newspapers. Everyone thought they were going to get millions of dollars. Some people can't stand to see others getting ahead, especially their own. Envy—it's one of the cardinal sins.

"And, if I had to guess"—Galvin looked at Chip—"I'd say Stu leafed through the Bristol County telephone directory—which, oddly, seems to be right here in the conference room." He picked up the yellow pages and thumbed through the book.

"Yes. Let's see. In Fall River, Ace Detective Agency: Lorenzo Almeida, proprietor. Or how about this. Cabral, Colon, and Carreras, private investigators."

"Alliterative," said Willis with a bemused expression.

"So, for a substantial fee," said Galvin, "why not enlist the services of Mr. Almeida or Senhor Carreras? Envy plus greed equals medical records."

Chip grinned and shook his head. "You see, Dr. Willis," he said, "we Young Turks think we invented champagne. There are no secrets anymore. But the important thing is that we have the records. I'm sure they'll take Meideros by complete surprise."

"Maybe, maybe not," Galvin said. "I have to figure that some of the confidential stuff has been leaked to the other side."

"You mean double dealing." Willis gave a contented puff on his pipe.

"Something like that. I've prepared for that contingency, and I'll know with a few soft questions whether Meideros has been tipped."

◘

Even Tina Alvarez was captivated by Galvin's incisive interrogation of Rafael Meideros. Galvin had long ago mastered the art of cross-examination. It came across as textbook-perfect. He led the doctor down seemingly innocuous paths, yet he left no room to maneuver, no means of extrication.

"Dr. Meideros," Galvin said matter-of-factly, "I trust you have reviewed your prior courtroom testimony?"

"I have." He eyed Galvin curiously.

"Now, you were asked whether you were an epidemiologist, and you answered at that time that you were not. That was a truthful answer, was it not?"

"It was."

"At that time, Doctor, you knew from your medical experience that epidemiology was the study of disease entities, their pathology, progression, possible causes or etiology, and, of course, cures or therapy. Is that a fair statement?"

"That's a fair statement."

"And as in the many disciplines of medicine—orthopedics, oncology, neurology, hematology—you will agree, will you not, Doctor, that epidemiology is a specialty in and of itself, having its own certification process, its national and international boards?"

"I'm not familiar with the licensing procedures, but yes, I'd agree with your premise."

"Fine. Now, Doctor, from your clinical experience as a medical

196

practitioner, you will concede that Frederick Willis and Allison Wray are doctors who are world-famous in the field of epidemiology?"

Meideros hesitated several seconds. "Yes," he said. "They are world-renowned."

"Have you had any lecturing experience in epidemiology, Dr. Meideros?"

"None."

"None?"

"None."

"Have you been granted any degrees in that field or any certifications?"

"I'm an internist," said Meideros.

"I appreciate that," Galvin said, "but may we please have your answer, yes or no."

"No," he answered quietly. Meideros could now see the tenor of the deposition. He had unwittingly endorsed Fred Willis and Allison Wray.

Galvin saw that Meideros realized what had happened and quickly moved to a new line of inquiry.

"Dr. Meideros," he said, "do you know how Factor Seven interacts with Factor Two—prothrombin—and other blood coagulation proteins to stop bleeding after injury to the human body? Please answer the question yes or no." Galvin threw it out as a trial balloon. As an internist, prepped for the deposition, Meideros must have known that correiga extract somehow altered blood coagulability, thus preventing or inhibiting coronary artery thrombotic disorders. If Meideros answered yes, then Galvin would again move to another field.

"I used to know. . . ." said Meideros.

"So your answer, at present, is that you do not know?" Galvin persisted.

"I do not know." Meideros's voice was scarcely audible.

Galvin now hammered away with the special questions prepared by Dr. Fred Willis.

"Isn't Factor Eight also known as the antihemophiliac factor, a large single-chain protein that regulates the activities for Factor Ten by protein enzymes generated in the body's own coagulation pathway?"

"That's not in my area of expertise."

"Do you know how Interluken affects the glands in the brain so as to cause the patient's temperature to rise and fall?"

"Not in my area of expertise."

Galvin could have moved to strike the answer as nonresponsive. He chose not to. "So, it's fair to state, Dr. Meideros, that you have no knowledge as to how Factor Eight works in regard to this clotting mechanism of the blood?"

"No present memory," Meideros replied.

"Do you know what chemical elements constitute blood Factor Six?"

"I'm not a hematologist." Exasperation was creeping into Meideros's voice.

"I appreciate that," said Galvin. "You know, of course, that not only is Dr. Frederick Willis known throughout the world in the field of epidemiology; he is also considered one of the leading authorities in hematology and has written several definitive texts on the subject."

"I would say his books aren't exactly classics," Meideros interjected quickly.

"I trust, then, that you have read this book?" Galvin picked up an impressive-looking tome. *Advances in Clinical Hematology*, by Frederick R. Willis, M.D.

"I wouldn't say it's the Bible," Meideros parried.

"Have you read it?"

"The Bible?"

"No," Galvin said seriously. "*Advances in Clinical Hematology*." Meideros's cavalier attitude and flippant responses would not go unnoticed by Judge Baron.

"I may have," Meideros countered.

"You may have?"

"Perhaps a few years ago."

"Hmmm, that's strange." Galvin looked at Madeiros. "It's a first edition published by Macmillan Company, New York and London, in February 1990. That's just two months ago."

Meideros said nothing. He would have his innings in front of the jury.

Galvin moved in for the kill.

"Dr. Meideros." he studied a document for a few moments. "In your prior courtroom testimony you said that you saw a pattern of genetic defects from studying medical records at St. Ann's Hospital in, I believe, New Bedford."

"Fall River," Meideros corrected.

"And it prompted you to write to Gammett Industries and to the FDA, and I have copies of your letters here marked Plaintiffs' Exhibits One and Two."

"That's right," said Meideros.

"Now, one of the plaintiffs' children is Hector Ramondi, isn't that correct?"

"That is correct."

"You studied the medical records of Hector Ramondi?"

"I did."

"He was hospitalized on several occasions at St. Ann's Hospital from 1981 through 1986, mainly to cure a septal defect in his heart, among other problems. And, in fact, you were called in as cardiology consultant during the initial septal surgery."

"That is correct," said Dr. Meideros.

"And you attribute this septal defect, somehow, no matter how remote the possibility, to the ingestion of Lyosin by Hector's parents."

"Absolutely." Meideros was now on firm ground.

"And you yourself prescribed Lyosin to your heart patients, including the Ramondis."

"I wouldn't do it now," Meideros responded.

Galvin let the answer stand. Again, the cavalier attitude would not escape Judge Baron.

"Now, when did you start prescribing Lyosin?" asked Galvin.

"As soon as it was approved for general prescription. It was heralded as a miracle drug."

"When was that? What date?" Galvin studied Meideros.

"I'd say sometime in 1980."

"It received FDA approval on March twenty-second, 1980. Would you say that you started prescribing it immediately after that date?"

"That's fairly accurate," said Meideros.

Galvin changed his tack.

"Where was Hector Ramondi born?"

"At St. Ann's Hospital."

"Who delivered him? If you know."

"Dr. Miguel Torres. He delivered practically half the population of Fall River."

"Have you discussed your theory on Lyosin with Dr. Torres?"

"I have."

"Where is Dr. Torres now?"

"I hope he's in heaven. He died a year ago."

"Did Dr. Torres share your belief that Lyosin ingested by Hector Ramondi's parents caused the child's septal deformity?"

It was an odd question. No one but Meideros would know the answer. Chip Hovington sensed that Galvin had made a gross mistake. Up until now the cross-examination had been flawless.

"He agreed with me one hundred percent." Meideros was emphatic.

Now there were two experts on the plaintiffs' side—Meideros and the deceased, Dr. Torres. And Torres couldn't be cross-examined.

Galvin didn't lose a beat in his rhythmic interrogation. "Dr. Meideros," he said, "during your study of the medical records, did you come across the birth at St. Ann's Hospital of a baby girl, unnamed, who was delivered by Dr. Torres on January sixteenth, 1979, unfortunately stillborn?"

"No name . . . Why should I know about it?" asked Meideros.

"Pardon me, Doctor," Galvin said courteously. "I mean no first name. The child was born to Thalia Tempesta Ramondi. The father was Manuel Ramondi; residence, 842 Weybossett Street, Fall River. Those are the parents of Hector, isn't that correct?"

"Correct."

No one but Galvin knew what was coming.

"I show you the birth record of St. Ann's Hospital," he said, "of baby girl Ramondi, delivered by Dr. Torres on January sixteenth, 1979. Would you please look at it?"

Meideros took out his black-rimmed bifocals and studied the record carefully. He knew then that he had walked into a mine field and that Galvin was about to push the detonator.

"Would you kindly read into the record, Dr. Meideros, the contents of the medical record that you now have before you?"

Meideros adjusted his glasses and read slowly. "Stillborn baby girl, Ramondi. Complications: fetal distress, ectopic arrhythmias during delivery necessitated Caesarean section. Baby ceased to breathe upon delivery. Mother sent to ICU in good condition. Baby six pounds, four ounces normal cephalic with the exception of bilateral cleft palate, severe. Hospital chaplain, Father Martinez, called to deliver last rites. No other complications."

"It was the Ramondi's first child, was it not, Doctor?" Galvin asked him.

"I believe so," Dr. Meideros said quietly. "It says prima one."

"And again, Doctor, when did you first start prescribing Lyosin to the Ramondis?"

No answer was required.

Galvin suspended his interrogation. He had what he needed. "Your witness." He turned to Tina Alvarez.

She studied her notes for a few moments. Forensically, Meideros had been destroyed. That was a given. She'd have to resuscitate his testimony before the trial. "No questions at this time," she said.

◘

Courtney Evans, Galvin's secretary, buzzed him at exactly 4 P.M.

"Mr. Galvin," she said, "don't forget the Governor Bradford law dinner tomorrow night at the Parker House. You're the guest speaker."

"I am?"

"I dug out one of your old speeches—the one where you

challenged the students not to become lackeys of the ruling class. I'm sure you can work around that theme."

"Thank you, Courtney," he said. "I'd forgotten all about it."

◘

It had been a tumultuous four weeks. The opposition wasn't giving up easily. Galvin, again, was tempted to arrange a meeting with Moe Katz. The case still bothered him. But Rhys and Tina were young, resilient. And from what he had heard, they had become partners in every way. At least some good had come out of the case. Somehow he'd find a way to make it up to Moe Katz.

His thoughts were interrupted by an exuberant Chip Hovington. Chip was always bouyant, and he wondered about that too, and about Chip's present romantic relationship.

"I'm meeting Dana Weatherbee at Logan at five, boss," he said. "She's coming to meet the family. Should be quite a week."

"Should be," Galvin agreed. "You can use my car, if you like," he said. "It's going to be a nice evening and you can put the top down. I was going to leave early, but canceled out. Call Sam and he'll bring it around front. Just be sure it's here in the morning."

"Great," said Chip. "I think Dana is over-limoed down there in the Big Apple. Time to get her used to how we Yankees manage to hoard all our money. One word says it all. Frugality."

Galvin loved Chip Hovington. A quiet bond had developed between them, strengthened over the past few months. Galvin was almost a surrogate father, yet more, perhaps like an older brother. Galvin stifled a grin and shook his head. He knew deep down that Chip was making a horrendous mistake. This wasn't California, where such liaisons might be possible, or even New York City. It was Boston, the bastion of crusty old-line civility. A mistress—fine. But marriage? For all of Chip Hovington's keen sense of reality, intuitive practicality, and shrewd analysis of the world swirling about him, Galvin knew that Chip had become entrapped in an impossible situation. Dana Weatherbee was a lovely lady. Beautiful. Stunning. And, from Galvin's short meeting with her, intelligent, with a prestigious job. But she was black, and not even the

Hovingtons, with all their social clout, could pull that one off. Nor was the legal enclave ready for it. Galvin knew also, and if Chip didn't know or didn't want to know, certainly Dana Weatherbee must be aware that nothing but ill loomed in their future.

Galvin tossed Chip the keys to the car. He wanted to say something, try to help Chip put things into perspective. But he held back. Let the Hovingtons handle it, he thought. The storm would blow its course. He'd stay out of it. He was so preoccupied, he forgot to tell Chip about Jerry Wilson.

Chip caught the keys behind his back. "Still got the old Princeton moves," he said. "See you *mañana*, boss."

"The name's Galvin."

"Okay, boss, Galvin, sir." Chip flipped a salute. "There's going to be a hot time in Tigerville tonight."

"I'd bet the farm on it," Galvin said inaudibly.

Galvin walked to the door and surveyed the incessant activity and listened to the staccato hum of the computers, music to the partners' ears. He said hello to Nancy Cosgrove, his night secretary, and glanced at his watch. Seven forty-five. It had been a crunching twelve hours. He'd grab a bite at Stella's, a hole-in-the-wall deli on Beacon Hill, and then go home and turn in.

◘

It was leaning against the cinnabar urn, half-hidden behind the bamboo palm. Hmmm, thought Galvin. Chip must have forgotten his gym bag. Not like Chip to forget anything.

He lifted it. Hefted it several times. Too heavy for sneakers and gym shorts. He thought he'd toss it into his closet so that the night cleaning crew wouldn't inadvertently take it for trash.

Before placing it on the closet floor, he unzipped it—he needed to verify that it really was Chip's. It could belong to anyone.

The bag was crammed with documents and letters. Again, more to establish identity than out of curiosity, he took the bag to his desk.

The papers appeared to have been sent by Federal Express. Galvin leafed through some letters, one dated only a week ago. All dealt with the Lyosin case and all were addressed to Chip, *Private and Confidential*, at his waterfront condo. The covering letters were signed by Jerry Wilson.

He buzzed his evening secretary. "Nancy, please have the evidence file on Ramondi versus Gammett sent down to my office. Also, get me the most recent Boston College alumni directory."

It was so subtle he could easily have missed it, had it not been for Jerry Wilson's memoranda. Wilson took care to enumerate critical transactions, recapping events on a daily basis. His was an odd style. *"As you stated . . . at your request . . . detailing the case thus far . . ."*

The names of Dr. Torgenson and Sabrina Bok-Sahn were mentioned frequently, as was London. *"London is working on it . . . London goes along . . . Dr. Bok-Sahn is proving difficult . . . The Aubrey journal is the kicker."*

Galvin compared the Importer's Agreement, the one that had been tucked away in the *Miscellaneous* file, with the one purporting to be the original that had been submitted to Federal Court. The two read word for word. Almost.

It appeared to be an innocuous change. *May* had been substituted for *shall*. But why had Chip communicated with Jerry Wilson without filling him in? It had to be London's show—the change was authorized by vote of Universal's board of directors, retroactive to the prior year. Legally, it might be a cure-all. But it was disturbing. He restudied the Importer's Agreement, holding a magnifying glass to each copy. The change was skillfully done. Not a space out of place.

He found the name he was looking for in the college directory. Bernard J. McCafferty had graduated with him from Boston College In-Town. They used to hang out together at the usual student dives in Kenmore Square. Bernie now headed the American Express office in London. He'd call Bernie early tomorrow morning, to catch him at his office, London time.

Then he put in a call to Buddy Roache at South Boston Quickie Print and made his request.

"Sure, I'll have the stuff by 10 A.M.," said Buddy. "I'll send it by special courier."

"No, I'll swing by and pick it up myself at nine-thirty tomorrow morning," Galvin said. He knew it would be close, but he'd be on Piedmont Air's 10:05 out of Logan to Philadelphia.

The last call was to Martha Ellen Kearney in Dorchester. She was an old friend, an account supervisor with New England Tel who could perform miracles overnight. In the past they had exchanged favors.

"Yes, I'd like the old number," he said. "Please install an answering service tomorrow for 1200 Beacon Street, Suite 1330, Brookline. The name's the same. Attorney J. Quentin Walsh. You're a peach, Martha.

He buzzed his secretary again. "Nancy, I won't be in tomorrow. Let Courtney know, and leave word to have Chip cover anything that comes up."

"Can I say where you'll be?" she asked.

"The ballgame," he said. "The Sox and the Phillies."

Nancy Cosgrove couldn't care less about the great national pastime, but there were a few basics that she did know. One was that Philadelphia and Boston could only meet in the World Series. They were in different leagues.

25

Galvin made Piedmont Air's flight to Philadelphia by a few minutes. He'd hope to catch the 6 P.M. back to Boston and get to the Parker House at the tail end of the Governor Bradford Dean's reception. He'd work on his speech on the return trip.

He checked the legal stationery he had picked up at Quickie Print—good-grade parchment, raised letterhead, scales of justice watermark in the lower right corner, even a fax number. He studied the business card:

J. Quentin Walsh
Attorney at Law
1200 Beacon Street
Suite 1330
Brookline, Mass. 02146
Telephone 266-1776.

Looked authentic. He'd call the number upon arrival in Philadelphia.

He scanned a memo pad noting his early-morning conversation with Bernie McCafferty. They hadn't been in touch for forty years, but it could have been yesterday. After the memories were exchanged, Galvin got down to business.

Sure, Bernie would check out Thomas Gately—get the death certificate, find out about the family. Being chief executive of American Express's London office gave him access to confidential sources. He'd call Galvin late tomorrow morning, London time.

At the Philadelphia airport, Galvin rented a Plymouth Valiant from Hertz and then called J. Quentin Walsh from a pay phone.

"You have reached the offices of Attorney J. Quentin Walsh," came the modulated voice. "We are in court and the secretaries are temporarily out of the office. . . . At the tone, please leave your name and number, and we will get back to you just as soon as we return. . . . Thank you."

Fine, Galvin thought, hanging up the phone. Martha Ellen Kearney is a positive jewel.

After studying his map, he maneuvered onto the Camden overpass. Factories, rail yards, and refinery tanks disappeared below. He turned north on the Jersey Turnpike. It was a thirty-minute drive to Trenton and then a pleasant ride on I-195 as he sped past serene dairy farms and dark loamy fields reminiscent of the Midwest. He arrived in Asbury Cove on the Jersey shore a little past noon and drove toward the beach, then back along the Shrewsbury River until he came to Jerry Wilson's house. It was a gray filigreed Victorian, badly in need of paint, set on a quiet street of moderately pretentious homes. Several late-model cars were parked in the driveway.

Asbury Cove was a small summer community. A large red-brick building on the main street housed the police department, municipal offices, and public library all under one roof. Galvin parked across the street in front of a drugstore, where he purchased a pair of dark tinted sunglasses and *The Trenton Daily News*. He sat down at the soda fountain, ordered coffee and a sliced ham on rye. It was a little after one. Plenty of time. But from here on in, things could get sticky. The lad at the lunch counter thanked him for the generous tip and gave him directions to Presbyterian Hospital.

◘

"I'm J. Quentin Walsh, an attorney representing the Northeast Mutual Insurance Company of Boston. Here's my card."

She was gray-haired, well into her seventies, one of those municipal servants who never really retires. She adjusted her thick-lensed glasses, studied the business card for several seconds, then placed it on her rolltop desk.

"We're looking into the possibilities of double indemnity in the death of Jeremiah T. Wilson of Asbury Cove," Galvin told her. "He died last Friday."

"I know," she said. "He was a fine man."

"I'll be needing a copy of the death certificate," Galvin said politely.

"Three certified copies were given to the funeral director, Thomas Fallon and Sons," she said, her tone heavy with authority. "I'm sure you can get one from them or from Mrs. Wilson."

"Aren't death certificates a matter of public record?" Galvin managed to look censorious.

She sighed and Galvin detected her irritation. "They are, but under town ordinance, they can't be released to third parties for thirty days. The charge is a dollar fifty per certificate. We will see to it that one is mailed to you, Mr.—?"

"Walsh. J. Quentin Walsh." Galvin opened his wallet and extracted two ten-dollar bills. "Pardon me, Mrs.—?"

"Grimshaw. And it's Miss."

"Yes, excuse me, Miss Grimshaw, I could of course see Mrs. Wilson, but she's obviously upset and it would really help us wrap up our investigation and enable us to authorize payments right away." Galvin placed the bills on the countertop. He saw that Miss Grimshaw knew he wasn't expecting change.

She slid the money from the counter into her purse in one motion. "Well," she said, "I know how slow insurance proceedings can be, and so's the Wilsons can get their money quickly. . . . Will one copy be enough?"

"One copy will be fine." Galvin nodded.

She disappeared, and a moment later he could hear the duplicator whirring in the next room. She soon reappeared, carrying a copy of the document.

He studied the certificate of death. It was a standard form similar to the one used in Massachusetts.

It listed *place, time, cause of death, onset of symptoms.*

According to the report, Wilson had suffered chest pains while rowing on the Shrewsbury River at 9 A.M. the previous Friday. The Garden State Ambulance Service had been called. Emergency medical technicians had administered artificial respiration. Vital and neurologic signs were absent. Pronounced DOA at the Presbyterian Hospital at 10:18 A.M. Autopsy performed by pathologist, Richard Stennes. Cause of death: *thrombosis of left anterior descending coronary artery, acute myocardial infarction, severe.* It bore the signature of Dr. Stennis, co-signed by James H. Pearson, M.D., Monmouth County Medical Examiner.

Galvin placed the document in his cracked leather bag, snapped the lock, and patted the faded gold initials J.Q.W. "Miss Grimshaw," he said and smiled, "you have been most kind. Many thanks."

Galvin bought a back copy of the *Asbury Cove Star-Journal* and left the Walsh card with the paper's receptionist. He clipped out the death notice.

Jeremiah T. Wilson, 57, general counsel of Gammett Pharmaceutical, died suddenly Friday morning. He was a member of the Odd Fellows Lodge, New Jersey Bar Association, past president of the Monmouth County Bar Association. Survived by his wife, the former Lillian Cormier, and two children, Laurie Wilson Henning of New York and Pamela, a student at New Brunswick State College. In lieu of flowers, please send donations to the Heart Fund.

The photo was vintage 1970.

Now he needed the emergency-room record and the autopsy protocol—confidential records released only on proper authorization. This could be tricky.

Presbyterian Hospital was a sprawling brick-and-glass complex set into the rise of a small hill. He pulled into the visitors' parking area and watched as a creamy-white ambulance with orange trim and the Garden State logo exited from the emergency area.

The lobby resembled that of a Hyatt Regency more than a medical facility. A glass atrium filtered sunlight along peach marble walkways that coursed alongside waterfalls and gurgling fountains edged by exotic plants and tropical fauna.

At the main desk he picked up a blank hospital authorization and signed the name *Lillian Cormier Wilson, Administratrix of the Estate of Jeremiah T. Wilson.* The forgery could get him into a heap of trouble. He tucked it into his inside pocket. He'd use it only as a last resort.

He left the Walsh business card with the nurse, and she directed him to Medical Records on the second floor.

"Can I be of assistance ta ye now, sir?" She was all of nineteen, curly red hair, freckles, round blue eyes, and a Gaelic lilt that stole Galvin's heart away. He had lucked out.

He quickly noted the name tag pinned to her white smock: Mary O'Donnell.

"Oh," he said in his finest simulated brogue. " 'Tis me lucky day. A lovely colleen from . . . let me guess . . . County Sligo?"

"Close." She smiled. "County Donegal."

"Ah, ah," Galvin said. "Of course, the dauntless O'Donnells from Donegal. Me dear grandmither talked about them often. 'The men were fierce warriors,' she'd say, 'the women renowned for their beauty.' She came from Sligo. 'Tis right next door."

Mary O'Donnell was a recent arrival, living now with a cousin in Red Bank. She would enroll at Rutgers in the fall and study to be a librarian. She loved Yeats and Joyce and Edna O'Brien. Oscar Wilde was her favorite. " 'Twas a frame-up by the Brits, him being queer and all that," she said. "He was a beautiful, sensitive man."

Galvin nodded agreement. "Sure'n, didn't they do the same to poor ould Roger Casement. God's curse on them."

"You sure know your history, sir, don't you?"

"Me sainted grandmither, Lord be good to her," said Galvin, "did not read fairy tales to us as kids, no sir, she read us the history of Ireland—Cuchulainn, Brian Boru, right down to Padhraic Pearse. But listen, my *Mary of the Curling Hair*, I am down here from Boston representing the Knights of Columbus Insurance Company." Galvin avoided her eyes, gleaming with childlike innocence. "I need the emergency-room record and autopsy protocol on Jeremiah T. Wilson, one of our fine policyholders, who passed to his reward here last Friday morning. My name's J. Quentin Walsh." He handed Mary O'Donnell his card.

"Well, the supervisor is at lunch," she said, "but let me check to see if his record is on file. Would ye be havin' a signed authorization, Mr. Walsh?"

"That I do, Mary." Galvin patted his briefcase.

She smiled and passed behind a row of shiny white metal cabinets that led to the medical records room where the latest in computers and microfilm equipment was housed. Galvin, waiting outside, saw several young women wearing white tunics saunter in. He hoped that none of them was Mary O'Donnell's superior. The room was moderately cool, but he felt little beads of perspiration gathering on his forehead. It could all blow right here.

"Ye're in a wee bit o' luck, Mr. Walsh." Her smile was filled with wistful Irish wonderment. "These were in Dr. Pearson's private folder," she said. "I made you a copy."

"Dr. Pearson?"

"He's the county medical examiner and Presbyterian's chief pathologist. Presbyterian? A funny name for a hospital, now, wouldn't you agree, Mr. Walsh? I don't mind telling you, it wouldn't be long standing where I come from, with a name like that."

Galvin's eye scanned the autopsy protocol.

"It says here, Mary, that the autopsy was performed by Dr. Stennis. Is he with Presbyterian?"

"No, he's a private pathologist connected with the Perth Amboy General. Not far from here."

"Mary, my dear, you've made me day. You're a colleen *deas ailing*, without a doubt, a beautiful sweet colleen." He patched his broken Gaelic with a broad Irish smile.

She smiled back with a flirtatious glint in her eye. *"Go raib mah agut, is mah an feal to fein.* Thank you very much, you are a good man yourself."

He slid his briefcase with the JQW initials off the counter and turned to leave. *"Slan agut.* Good-bye."

She wiggled her fingers. *"Slan leat, is go n'eirige an botair leat.* Goodbye yourself, and may the road rise to greet you."

He stuffed the medical record into his inner pocket next to the bogus authorization that fortunately hadn't been needed. In the corridor, Galvin passed a battle-ax of a woman. Somehow he sensed that she was Mary O'Donnell's supervisor. He quickened his pace.

After leaving the hospital and driving for a few minutes, he pulled into a Howard Johnson's parking lot to study the emergency-room record and autopsy protocol. It was a limited postmortem, confined to the thoracic cavity, at the family's request.

Galvin wondered about its forensic propriety. In cases of sudden death, especially DOAs at hospitals, the medical examiner, at least in Massachusetts, was empowered to perform the autopsy. Permission from the family was not needed. The medical examiner would perform a meticulous autopsy—head, brain, liver, heart, lungs, arteries, veins, microscopic section of all vital organs, and histologic analysis of the blood and blood chemistries. Traces of toxic substances were electronically screened. Galvin thought it odd that a private pathologist had been called in to make a limited examination.

Maybe New Jersey law was different. He'd have to check.

The gross examination of the body disclosed nothing alarming—appendectomy scar, no other abnormalties, no bodily ecchymosis, no signs of trauma. The cause of death was apparent. Two centimeters from the aortic orifice of the left descending coronary artery, there was a fresh thrombotic plaque occluding the artery's lumen, with a fresh infarcted area of myocardium five centimeters distal, with patchy necrosis of a major portion of the left ventricle.

Yet Galvin thought it strange that neither the left circumflex coronary artery nor the right posterior coronary artery, or their tributaries, were sectioned, and there was nothing to disclose arterial disease or lack of it elsewhere in the coronary arterial tree. Also, since the brain was not sectioned, there was nothing to disclose cerebral arteriosclerosis or cerebral pathology. He wondered where Wyeth Richardson had got the impression that Wilson had had the heart of an octogenarian. But maybe he was reading too much into the whole thing. The cause of death was readily apparent—a gross heart attack due to total blockage of a major coronary artery. And Wilson had been engaged in a strenuous activity when the attack occurred. Galvin recalled a pathologist telling him once that the left descending coronary artery was the "artery of sudden death" since it supplied the main pumping musculature of the heart. "Like stepping on a garden hose," the pathologist had said. "Once that artery is shut down, oxygenated blood is prevented from getting to the heart muscle, and like any other organ needing oxygen, it dies. If the left ventricle goes, you go."

The emergency-room record stated that Wilson had been seized with chest pains, called for help, and was found unconscious in his rowing shell. Galvin wondered who had provided this information and who had found him. The record didn't say. He read further.

EMTs Tom Gentile and Eric Wooden from Garden State Ambulance Service responded. No detectable heartbeat. Resuscitative efforts failed. Time from the locus to Presbyterian—15 minutes. Staff neurologist Dr.

Conroy called. No vital signs. B.P. zero/zero. Zero heartbeat, zero respirations. Subject cyanotic. Pupils unreactive to light and accommodation. Pronounced dead at 10:18 A.M. Body released to the custody of the county medical examiner's office.

Galvin checked the yellow pages. Garden State was also in the limousine and funeral business. They got the traffic coming and going, he thought. It was a short drive farther down I-195.

He placed a call to Ted King at Sterling & Moss in New York City. He knew King came from New Jersey.

The secretary told Galvin that Mr. King was in conference.

"Tell him Frank Galvin's in town," he said, "and I'll spot him five points, winner take all."

King came on the line immediately. "You old gyrene," he said, "where in hell are you?"

"Ted, I need some help. No, I'm not over at the New York A.C. It was a ruse to get past your secretary. Actually, I'm out in Jersey. Look, Ted, I know you have connections around here."

"Yeah. It's been years, but I do have a few contacts. What's up?"

"Can you get me a read on an outfit called Garden State Ambulance Service, operating in central Jersey from, say, Trenton to the shore?"

"Sounds like you're chasing ambulances again, Galvin," King quipped. "Okay, I'll see what I can find out. I take it you want the incorporators—names, addresses, the real owners behind the nominals."

"Yes. And, Ted, keep this confidential. Okay?"

"Yeah, you got it. And in our rematch, Galvin, as Goering said to Hitler, 'No nice guy stuff next time.' "

○

The ambulance dispatcher didn't look too friendly. He scrutinized the Walsh business card and studied Galvin, who had put on mirror-lens Ray Bans, with a measure of skepticism.

"Gentile should be in shortly," he said. "Can I get him on the transmitter and tell him what this is all about?"

"Just tell him that I'm an attorney and want to talk to him about the Jeremiah Wilson case. I understand that he and his partner transported Wilson to Presbyterian Hospital last Friday morning."

Galvin waited in the rented Valiant. He was not surprised when, after a short interval, the dispatcher came over and told him that Gentile had been called on an emergency and was unavailable.

"I'll wait," said Galvin.

"No." The dispatcher seemed a little flustered. "The run's down to Tom's River. They'll be gone all afternoon."

It was three-fifteen. As Galvin backed his car up, he saw the dispatcher copy down his license plate number. It would be traced to Hertz, then to J. Quentin Walsh. Buddy Roache's Quickie Print threw in the authentic-looking operator's license, encased in plastic, as an extra.

Galvin dropped the car off at Newark Airport and caught the six o'clock back to Boston. He had rented a room at the Parker House, and at seven thirty-five he got into his tux and headed for the elevator that would take him to the Dean's reception. It had been quite a day. He could expect Bernie McCafferty's call, maybe at 5 A.M.—midmorning, London time.

□

Except for the head table and some six hundred senior students who looked up at Galvin with expectant faces, he could count perhaps twenty or thirty graduates who could afford the one-hundred-dollar tab for the annual alumni dinner.

Governor Bradford Law was not Harvard or B.U. or Boston College or even Suffolk. It was an in-town diploma mill, mainly a night school, whose graduates always had difficulty passing the bar exam and thereafter making a living. The head table was a microcosm of legal mediocrity. There was Phil Fanning, a probate judge who had taken the bar eight times before passing and was presently under investigation for doling out lucrative guardians *ad litem* to his coterie of courtroom cronies.

"Rather than be the judge of probate," Dean Spellisey addressed the guests as he introduced Fanning, "I'd rather be the best friend of the judge of probate."

The audience roared. Galvin winced.

"And now," said Dean Spellisey, "the moment we've been waiting for. I take great pleasure in introducing our guest speaker, Governor Bradford's most renowned alumnus."

Galvin sat to the right of the podium, more than a little embarrassed by the dean's blandishments.

"In World War Two he was in the first attack wave at Iwo Jima," the dean said, getting caught up in the moment. "Wounded twice. Purple Heart. Combat Infantry Award. The Silver Star. When Frank Galvin landed, those Japs hightailed it clear back to Yokohama, believe me." The dean waited for the applause to die down. "And that's not all. He's had a distinguished career at the bar. Only a few years ago, he won the highest monetary award ever recorded in this country for a medical malpractice case. Nine million dollars." The dean held up two outstretched hands and nine fingers. "Nine million dollars. And I don't have to tell all you embryo attorneys here"—he looked at the graduating class with a mischievous grin—"that one-third goes into nine million rather easily—it's short division."

Laughter, then what seemed like endless applause. Galvin cringed. The priorities; they had it all wrong. He thought back to the late sixties, when lawyers marched and battled police and risked incarceration and disbarment in order to try and bring a halt to an ignoble war. There were heroes then. Daniel Ellsberg. The Berrigans. The Chicago Seven. Father Groppi. Angela Davis. Whatever happened to the idealism, the zeal?

"And now," the dean said, lowering his voice, "I'm letting you in on a secret. Only last week our honored guest was installed as senior partner in one of the most prestigious law firms in the United States—Hovington, Sturdevant, Holmes and Galvin. I present to you Governor Bradford's most illustrious son, and friend to us all, Frank Galvin."

Galvin stood up and walked to the podium, then waited for the applause to die down.

"Dean Spellisey, honored guests, members of the class of 1990," he began slowly. "I had prepared a talk. . . ." He pulled out a folded piece of paper from his inside pocket, then tossed it aside. It fell from the podium onto the floor.

"Oh, I was at Iwo Jima all right. I wasn't scared at all. I was petrified. I buried my head in the sand and made a lot of promises to the Almighty that I never kept.

"And as for having the enemy on the run, let me set the record straight right now. I've never witnessed a braver fighting man than the Japanese soldier. They were mostly young, seventeen or eighteen. Like you when you were in high school." He glanced toward the body of students. "But they were dedicated. They didn't run and they didn't quit. They fought until they died."

Dean Spellisey's smile began to fade.

"And while I'm on the Japanese"—Galvin's voice took on a solemn tone—"and this concerns all of you as lawyers and future lawyers, during World War Two we rounded up over a hundred and twenty thousand men, women, and children. Nisei, Japanese, second-, third-generation Americans. Born in this country, as American as you and me. And we stuck them in barbed-wire concentration camps for three years, in some of the most inhospitable terrain we have, the Nevada desert."

Dean Spellisey and Judge Fanning exchanged glances.

"We've wiped it from our memory. But it happened—right here, where the writ of habeus corpus is sacred. Where our Constitution guarantees that *no person* shall be deprived of life, liberty, or property without due process of law. These were our *own* people. We took away their homes, their farms, their meager bank accounts, and most of all, we stripped away their dignity.

"Do you know what it's like to lose your liberty? To have no rights? No counsel? No recourse?

"Where was the American Bar Association then? Where were those paragons of civil rights, Justice Hugo Black and Franklin Delano Roosevelt?

"And you know"—Galvin's voice took on new passion—"it was racism at its worst! We were also at war with Germany, Italy,

216

Hungary, Finland. No Caucasians were rounded up, just the Asians.

"And we fought that war—in fact, we've fought all our wars pledging to destroy dictatorial tyrannies that oppress and persecute minorities."

Dean Spellisey wondered how Galvin would tie it all together.

"The ultimate irony," Galvin continued, "was that some of the nisei were allowed to join the Army. They fought in Italy, the 442nd infantry. No outfit in our nation's history took as many casualties, or received more unit citations and Distinguished Service Crosses."

The graduating class sat in rapt attention.

"Okay." Galvin's voice came down a pitch. "What's this got to do with you and me and Judge Fanning here?"

The judge managed a feeble smile.

Galvin gripped the podium with both hands and glanced to his right, where most of the students were seated.

"Four years ago, I addressed this same event. I recall vividly what I said. I challenged everyone here to embark upon a crusade. There were four hundred and fifty inmates on death row, I said, and only fifteen had legal representation. Only fifteen lawyers really gave a damn."

There was total silence. Judge Fanning shifted uneasily. Galvin paused.

"What have we accomplished in four years? Not much. You are—what?" He turned toward the dean. "Six hundred and fifty law graduates?"

The dean brightened and gave an affirmative nod.

"Harvard has four hundred, B.U. five hundred, Boston College seven hundred or so, Suffolk six hundred and fifty, New England Law six hundred plus. That's a hell of a lot of lawyers spilling out into one small geographic area."

The dean began nibbling on his lower lip.

"We have more lawyers in the United States per capita than any country in the world," Galvin said. "A lawyer for every three hundred and fifty people. Can you imagine that? It seems incredible.

"Now, half of you will go into corporate law, you'll help the rich find legal loopholes to avoid taxes; you'll represent things, not people. And some of you will go to jail.

"The rest of you are wasting your time. You should be in business or in education or in the arts."

A pall settled over the assembly.

"Each of you," Galvin said, "will come to a crossroad. One way says do the right thing. There's more to this life than making a buck. It's not a road often taken, especially by lawyers. The other leads to a world of duplicity and inflated fees, the game where the only losers are the stiffs who are paying the bills."

Judge Fanning took a deep gulp of water.

"There are some things Dean Spellisey didn't say about me. Not long ago I was a drunk, a sleazy ambulance chaser, working funeral parlors and hanging around courthouses, like a jackal waiting for some probate judge to throw a few legal scraps my way. I was a man searching for a lost soul. My own!" He looked down into the sea of upturned faces. "And you know," he said quietly, "I'm not so sure I ever found it."

Galvin stopped. No summing up. No exhortation. No mandate. He simply turned and sat down.

There were several seconds of silence. Then from the back of the room came the thin sound of clapping. It spread across the student body toward the head table. The dean, who had felt betrayed, was quick to catch the rising swell. He stood and applauded vigorously.

Galvin rose, tipped his hand in a half-salute, and as his audience gave him a standing ovation, he headed toward a side door, not quite sure what he had said, but quite sure he had reached his own crossroad.

26

Galvin, Bernie McCafferty here. I'll bet it's four in the morning back in Beantown, but you told me to give you a ring."

"No, it's five," said Galvin, "and, Bernie, thanks for calling back."

"Well, I think I have the information you want. Our computers indicate that Gately lived rather modestly. Credit rating satisfactory for a postman's salary. Owned his own flat in West Ham. Mortgaged, but bank payments reasonably prompt. Died May sixteenth. Wife, Agnes, is a salesclerk at Harrods. Came home in the evening and found Gately slumped in a chair. He'd been reading the newspaper. Fifty-two years old, no major illnesses, under no active medical treatment.

"His wife called their physician, a Dr. Winston Carter, who viewed the body, did the necessary testing, filled out the forms, and consigned the body to All-Hallows Funeral Home in Blackheath for burial."

"Burial?"

"Well, not exactly. After the religious services, Gately was cremated and his ashes were scattered along his mail route."

"Boy," Galvin exclaimed, "talk about a postman going for a walk on his day off. Any autopsy?"

"No. The doctor certified the cause of death to be heart failure."

"Were the police called? Any coroner's inquest? Bernie, here's a fifty-two-year-old guy who walks miles on his route, in apparent good health, and for no reason at all, suddenly he cashes?"

"I know," said McCafferty. "I had our agent chat with Dr.

Carter. His explanation seemed plausible. Gately was in the age bracket where you can presume moderate arteriosclerotic heart disease. There were no marks on the body, nothing to indicate that Gately died from other than natural causes. The doctor was quite candid. He said that less than three percent of deaths in London go to postmortem. His opinion that Gately had a heart attack was an educated guess based on experience."

"Only three percent! Jesus," Galvin said, "people can get away with anything over there."

"That's London, lad. What with all the Arabs, Haitians, and boat people," McCafferty laughed, "they murder the King's English and sometimes each other. As Dr. Carter put it, Mrs. Gately could have adjusted a pillow over the old boy's head and not under it, and no one would be the wiser."

"Any payments, life insurance or otherwise, by any sources?" asked Galvin.

"Just the usual ten thousand pounds by Royal Globe Limited, and six thousand by Great Northern Indemnity. Mrs. Gately doesn't look like she's headed for the French Riviera. She still owes on the flat, and when he died, she only took a few days off from Harrods."

"Okay, Bernie, I think I have what I need. Would you send me the death certificate and a brief report and, of course, a bill?"

"Hey, Galvin. This one's on me. I take it you suspect that Gately left this world with a little push from his friends."

"I don't know," Galvin replied. "But yes, I'd say someone may have greased his path."

"Why in the world," McCafferty asked, "would an obscure postman who lives in a run-down flat in a Cockney neighborhood be that important to the great Frank Galvin?"

"It's a long story," Galvin said. "I'll let you know how things work out."

◘

On Monday morning no one was in a good mood. When Carter Hovington came in, he emitted a gruff hello and moved on. Galvin didn't have to guess why. In the 1840s, the enterprising Hoving-tons became seafaring squires by transporting slaves from Africa. Yankee merchants, they called themselves. Now things were coming full circle. Galvin noticed that Cy Sturdevant wore a bemused grin. Crusty Cy Sturdevant was enjoying Hovington's ethnic discomfort. But Galvin had other things on his mind.

He buzzed his secretary. "Courtney, would you ask Chip Hovington to come in to see me."

◘

"We've been *unga shoppt'd*!" Moe Katz cried, throwing down the latest packet from Hovington, Sturdevant, et al. "Absolutely fucked! We just got hit with a motion for summary judgment."

"How do they work so fast?" Tina was dismayed. "Meideros's deposition was taken only on Friday."

"I should have seen it coming." Rhys was so mad, he could spit. "Motion for summary judgment. This wasn't a deposition of Dr. Meideros, this was hunt and peck under Federal Rule Thirty. Christ!" He whacked his thigh. "I'll be a goddamn son of a bitch!"

"Those no-good pricks!" Tina exclaimed.

Even Moe Katz and Rhys shuddered at Tina's unaccustomed coarseness.

"We were mousetrapped," Moe said. "This summary judgment piece. Got to hand it to those lubricious bastards. There's no gentlemanly practice of law anymore."

"Are we going down the drain?" Tina looked at Moe.

"We're down the drain. But what the hell. I only lost two hundred grand, and for Christsakes, I had three hundred thousand dollars' worth of fun."

◘

"Come in, Chip." Galvin half-rose from his chair and beckoned to his associate. Chip hesitated at the door, then nodded to Courtney Evans. Chip's shoulders were slumped and he moved slowly, yet he put on his best manufactured smile.

"Shut the door, Chip," Galvin said. "I can tell things didn't go all that well at the Beacon Hill Chowder and Marching Society."

Chip flopped in the chair in front of Galvin's desk and loosened his tie.

"Want Courtney to bring in some coffee?" Galvin offered.

"No. No thanks, boss." Chip heaved a weary sigh. "I guess I was a hundred years ahead of my time."

Galvin wanted to get into other matters—the stuff in Chip's gym bag, his unilateral correspondence with Jerry Wilson. He'd work into it slowly.

"You know, Chip, things will work out. They have a way of righting themselves over the course of time."

"Time's not on my side," Chip said. "Dana's gone. She had me drive her to Logan last night. She's back in Manhattan. For good."

"Chip, I give a lot of credit to Dana Weatherbee. She's a sensible young woman, as well as beautiful. She knew it was impossible."

Chip sat trancelike, leaning forward, cupping his chin in his hands.

"And, Chip, give credit to your family. You had the blinders on. In a way I don't blame you. I'd have done the same. But it wouldn't have worked. Okay, it's not the end of the world." Galvin got up from his desk. "You're bruised a little. Big deal. You'll get over it."

"I suppose so." Chip's voice was as far off as his gaze. "You know, Galvin, I wanted to chuck this whole goddamn business."

"Yeah? So you jettison the law and your family. You think five years from now you'd be at the Princeton-Harvard game tailgating with Dana Weatherbee, and do you think Dana Weatherbee would still be enthralled because you write poetry, get the groceries at the Fifty-seventh Street Deli, and are pretty good in the sack?"

Galvin wasn't quite sure about the timing. He'd have to play it carefully. "Anyway, Chip, there's a couple of other things, if we can get back to more mundane matters. . . ."

"Sure." There was a wounded finality in Chip's sigh. He straightened his tie.

"Jerry Wilson died last Friday."

"I know," Chip said. "His daughter phoned last night. I was so

222

tired, I didn't quite take it in. I'll call his wife. I just haven't had the chance."

Galvin waited several seconds, then walked toward his closet. "You forgot your gym bag the other night," he said.

"Didn't even miss it," Chip replied. "Preoccupied, I guess."

Galvin lifted it from his closet floor, carried it to where Chip was sitting.

"Thanks, boss." Chip reached for the bag. "Got to get back in shape, start the roadwork again."

Their eyes locked for an instant. Each was aware that the other knew the bag didn't contain running shoes.

◘

The play-backs on the Quentin Walsh answering machine were exactly as Galvin had expected, except for the woman's voice.

Three calls, all from the same person. "Mr. Walsh, we're from Wellesley Hills. My brother and I would like you to handle our aunt's estate. It's quite large. We'll need to set up an appointment. I'll call later this afternoon."

No name. No number.

By the third call, the woman sounded irritated.

"Mr. Walsh," she said, "we've been trying to reach you, but no one's ever in. We are now inclined to take the estate elsewhere, maybe to one of the established firms, unless we can reach you soon. It involves a great deal of money. Well over a million dollars. I hope you're interested. We'll be at your office tomorrow afternoon at two."

Galvin was no Henry Higgins, but he was pretty good at placing accents. He could tell whether someone was from South Boston or from the north or south shore. This voice *should* have been from somewhere south of the Holland Tunnel, maybe around Bayonne or Secaucus, a place where some people knew where Jimmy Hoffa was buried.

The voice was soft and modulated, with a tinge of seduction, as if there was more involved than her aunt's estate, maybe a horizontal fee.

Ted King called later in the afternoon.

"Let me transfer this to my private line." Galvin pushed the necessary buttons. "Yes, that's better. Hope you're keeping the spin on the ball, Ted. I'll be down soon for the rematch."

"Eleven-zero's a shutout. You know that, Galvin. No gimmies this time. Well, I think I got the info you wanted. I'm not going to ask you why you need it, but you're playing with some real heavies."

"Oh?" Galvin got out his scratch pad.

"Garden State Ambulance and Livery Service Incorporated— that's the correct corporate name. They're owned by a straight-sounding group called Samana and Associates from Wilmington, Delaware."

"Wilmington. That's not far from Philly."

"That's right, my friend. Samana has a few corporate blinds, but at the end of the labyrinth is the Santigliano family out of Philadelphia."

"Family?"

"Yeah, not exactly the Swiss-Robinsons. Try the Gottis in Queens or the Luccheses in Chicago. Got it? Santigliano operates the largest trucking firm on the Eastern seaboard. Occasionally, a ten-wheeler runs over somebody. Funerals, stretch limos, ambulances are just a spin-off. Great Maytag for the green stuff." King paused for a moment.

"Galvin, be careful. These guys don't pitch underhand. If you're thinking of taking them on as clients, forget it. You lose a case, you wind up with busted kneecaps."

"Good advice, Ted. I'll keep it in mind."

At one-thirty that afternoon Galvin parked his Jaguar at the Beacon Street median strip alongside the MBTA tracks, about a hundred feet north of the 1200 office building. He had a clear view but carried high-powered binoculars in case he needed a close look. He fed the parking meter with quarters and smiled graciously at the Brookline meter maid tagging others around him who had tried to beat the system.

He kept an eye on traffic from both directions and jotted down license plate numbers of cars stopping in the vicinity.

He almost missed seeing two men wearing natty sport jackets, until they were just in front of 1200. They hesitated and talked for several minutes. It was now two-twenty. Where had they come from? He scanned the line of cars parked to his right and to his left. No additions since the last time he'd checked.

Using the binoculars, he studied both men. These had to be leg breakers. But they weren't stereotypes. They looked and dressed like Ivy League yuppies. One had on a gray herringbone tweed jacket and collegiate-gray flannel slacks. The other was similarly dressed in plaid and gray. Regimental ties. Perhaps in their early thirties. Slight builds. Certainly not enforcers with nicknames like Ball Cruncher or Snake. But he wasn't fooled. He laughed to himself. He could predict what would happen. The office building—the newest, highest, and most prestigious in Brookline—had twenty floors and rented at seventy-five dollars a square foot. And the ancient superstition still obtained: There was no thirteenth floor, no Suite 1330. And no J. Quentin Walsh. Galvin could even guess how long they would take. Ten minutes at the most. The men would check with other tenants, then with maintenance, finally with the building manager. No J. Quentin Walsh.

In exactly ten minutes the men emerged in an obvious state of agitation. Again Galvin viewed them through the high-powered specs. They both could have been from Wellesley Hills, but Galvin knew better.

He watched them stride briskly up Beacon Street, headed toward Coolidge Corner. From their gesticulations, he could read the thrust of their discussion. *Check the bar association, the telephone company.* That they'd do. And find that they'd been had.

About a hundred yards up the street a blue Toyota with Massachusetts license plates pulled up to the curb. One of the men got into the backseat, the other in the front.

Through the high-powered Bausch and Lombs, Galvin could see that an attractive woman was driving. She wore oversized sunglasses, looked to be in her early twenties. The Toyota crossed the MBTA tracks, swung left, meshed into traffic, and headed back toward the inner city. As the car swept past, Galvin hid behind his newspaper. He jotted down the license plate number: Z 8352.

He felt certain the car was registered to Hertz or Avis and was heading for Logan Airport. The trick would be in getting an ID on the driver.

27

You've got to be kidding!" Galvin's Jaguar swerved toward the median guardrail and only a quick jerk on the steering wheel brought him back into his lane. A motorist leaned on his horn, shouting expletives. A young girl in a low-slung red Camaro gave him the finger as she raced past.

"Are you okay?" came the voice over Galvin's Nynex receiver.

"Yeah, Skip, guess I wasn't paying attention. They tell you not to work these things while driving. Give me that again, slowly."

Patrick Emmett "Skip" McNeally was another of Galvin's Boston College classmates whom he hadn't seen since his drinking days. Skip had been a halfback on Frank Leahy's teams just after the war, earning the nickname Skip because he'd head for the sidelines rather than take a hit from defensive linemen. And it was Skip, senior detective, Precinct 3, Boston Police Department, to whom Galvin turned when he needed confidential information.

"That's right," Skip said. "It took some doing, but we have our ways. The car's registered to Avis Rental at Logan Airport. The operator who signed for the car is named Samantha Corsini."

"You said Corsini?"

"That's right, Corsini. She's twenty-two, listed her residence as Radnor Hall, Bryn Mawr, Pennsylvania. That's Bryn Mawr College. Must be a student there. Pretty snooty Main Line," said Skip. "Are you sure you got the right number?"

"Yeah. I'm afraid I have," Galvin replied. "Thanks, Skip." He felt weak. His stomach was churning and he thought he might throw up. He eased his car into a parking area along Storrow Drive. Maybe he'd take a walk along the Charles River embankment. He had to figure this all out.

◘

Rhys Jameson wheeled Moe Katz into the foyer of Hovington, Sturdevant, Holmes & Galvin. Both noted the gold lettering but said nothing.

"Oh, Mr. Katz." Julie Hedren's greeting was uncommonly effusive. "Please go right in. Miss Alvarez is already in the conference room with the Ramondi family and the court stenographer."

"Sorry I'm late," Moe said huskily. "Will Mr. Galvin be taking the depositions for the defendant?"

"No. It's a last-minute switch. Stuart Trimble will be doing the interrogation. Mr. Galvin's out of the office on other business."

◘

Galvin walked along the embankment toward the esplanade. The mid-morning sun was warm, and he loosened his tie and swung his suit jacket over his shoulder.

The rowing shells of Harvard, B.U., and M.I.T. glided over the placid surface of the Charles. Joggers, bikers, and strollers covered both banks of the river. Tennis players waited three deep by the Hatchshell courts, and frisbees, basketballs, and softballs filled the air. Galvin wondered if anyone went to work anymore or attended classes.

He picked up a discarded newspaper, sat on a bench, and checked the sports page. He was tempted to go to a baseball game. The Sox were in Detroit. Boston College was playing Holy Cross, but that was up in Worcester, and he felt that college baseball was about as interesting as watching the America's Cup races. He checked the movie guide. Nothing but horror stuff, although a new

Bob Hoskins movie set in Ireland was playing in Harvard Square. No. He was sick of intrigue.

Maybe he was reading too much into everything? And what was he supposed to make of the Corsini connection? By the end of the next week, the case would be over. Maybe things would settle down.

It hit him as he was sitting on the bench staring vacantly into space facing the Georgian brick buildings of Harvard University.

Settle. The case should be settled. Even if Katz, Alvarez, and Jameson appealed Judge Baron's dismissal, the Kalb bill would set a liability ceiling for eight plaintiffs. Galvin figured it quickly— eight hundred thousand dollars. A pittance to Gammett. The legal bill would be double that figure.

He'd recommend a three-million-dollar settlement. Gammett and Universal would go for it. He'd make sure they did. He could play hardball, too, particularly with his own clients. It was still only a drop in the cost-of-doing-business bucket. Alvarez's people would be bailed out. A settlement would repay a lot of debts.

Galvin arrived just as the depositions were breaking up. He headed toward his office. Through the gauzy curtain shielding the glassed conference room, he could see Hector Ramondi sitting on Thalia Ramondi's lap. His mongoloid grin was in sharp contrast to the fear and concern shown by his parents. And from the somber look of Moe Katz and the worried scowl of Rhys Jameson, Galvin suspected that all was not going well with the plaintiffs.

Tina was reviewing her notes, but she looked grim. He was tempted to make an appearance, to pat Hector Ramondi on the head and tell everyone that things would be all right. But he continued toward his office, picked up his messages from Courtney Evans, and asked her to send out for a sandwich.

Ten minutes later Stu Trimble bounced into his office. "Mr. Galvin," he cried, "we nailed them! Really nailed them!"

"Nailed who?" Galvin was squeezing some mustard onto his corn beef on rye.

"The Ramondis. Perjury. Even their attorneys were disgusted. They're jumping ship."

"Jumping ship? What are you talking about?"

"Right here!" Trimble was exuberant. He held up a sheet of legal-sized paper and slapped it several times. "A month ago we sent out interrogatories to all plaintiffs to be answered under oath. Okay?"

Galvin took a bite of his sandwich.

"Question Sixty-four." Trimble adjusted his rimless glasses. " 'Please list any and all genetic diseases, disorders, or bodily or mental infirmities in any children born to you at any time other than those claimed.' And the answer . . ." He paused. *"None."* Trimble spelled it out. "N—O—N—E. Signed under the pains and penalties of perjury. The Ramondis admitted during the deposition that they had kept the information about the stillborn with the cleft palate from Tina Alvarez—get this—since they thought it would hurt the case.

"Wahoo!" Trimble was about to jump in the air like the man in the Toyota commercial. "How do you like that for a case ender?"

Galvin continued with his sandwich. "You say the plaintiffs' lawyers are bailing out?"

"Miss Alvarez said they'd get back to me before we argue our motion for summary judgment this Friday. I know they want to drop the suit before Judge Baron lowers the boom."

"I see. You did a thorough job, Stu. I'll tell Carter and Cy. I'm sure they'll be more than pleased with the result."

◘

"We can't back out now even if we want to," Tina said to Moe and Rhys as they rode in Moe's specially equipped van, heading uptown to his office. "If we discontinue the Ramondi suit, what about the others?"

"I agree," said Moe. "And there's no telling what that putz Baron would do. I think we'd be worse off. We've just got to ride this out."

"You know, the Ramondis were duped," Rhys said. "I don't think they consciously tried to cover up anything. What do they know really about genetic disorders? And I'll take issue with that Trimble guy saying they committed perjury, and he'd seek sanctions. Technically, the Ramondi kid born in '79 wasn't viable at birth. The hospital record says the obstetrician was getting irregular heartbeats and then failed to detect a beat at all. This prompted the Caesarean. The baby was dead at birth. In fact, dead in the womb. The interrogatory said any child *born.* . . ." But even Rhys wasn't convinced that his premise was tenable.

"Well, maybe the Appeals Court will agree," Moe offered, "but Baron will go out of his way to box us in. He'll coerce us into discontinuing all suits or waive an appeal from allowance of summary judgment. In turn, he'll exercise his judicial leniency by not imposing sanctions against the Ramondis—maybe even against us." He sighed. "No telling what the bastard will do. He'll say we framed the interrogatory answer. We're dead in the water. But we go over the falls together. Agreed?"

"I love you, Moe." Tina leaned forward, grabbed his bony frame, and kissed his bald pate.

"Save your kisses," Moe grumped. "You know, Tina, you've added three years to my life. I want to stick around and see how this all turns out."

◘

"Are you back on the sauce, Galvin?" Carter Hovington couldn't believe what he was hearing. "Christ, everybody's talking about what you and Stu Trimble did to the plaintiffs. And that goes for Chip, too. You won the case. Period. I'll see to it Baron seeks no sanctions against the Ramondis or their attorneys. The case is over. Finished." Hovington slapped one hand against the other like a cymbalist during an orchestral finale. "Now you tell me you want to settle. Galvin, I really can't comprehend what in hell you're saying."

Galvin started to speak.

"No, wait," Carter interrupted. "I know how you feel about Moe Katz and the Portuguese girl, even Rhys Jameson. But our duty is to our clients, they pay us for one sole reason, to win, not to go around authorizing handouts for the other side. And believe me, you'd have one hell of a time convincing Gammett and

Universal to part with one dime. But three million dollars? For what? And they have to pay our fee on top of that. They'd seriously question our integrity, let alone our sanity. We'd lose them as clients and they'd sure in hell bad-mouth us with others we represent." Perspiration erupted at Hovington's silver-gray hairline.

"Carter," Galvin said. "The firm's litigation department is mine. I not only head it, but I take full responsibility for what goes on in it. I needn't remind you that I'm a full partner. And I know what I'm doing."

"In a pig's ass you know what you're doing," Carter shot back. "You're jeopardizing a client–attorney relationship. This decision of yours is completely irrational. You may head the firm's litigation department, but I own the firm!" Hovington rose from his seat, put both hands on Galvin's desk, and leaned forward. His face was beet red. "You're an employee working for me. You'd better get that straight, right now!"

"Okay, Carter." Galvin counted a few seconds. "Let me fill you in on a few things."

Hovington didn't wait to listen. He stomped out of the office.

Galvin shuddered as the door banged shut. Courtney Evans promptly reopened it.

"What was that all about?"

"Just a healthy difference of opinion, Courtney," Galvin said, brushing it aside. "Please have the Lyosin file sent down to me. I want everything—correspondence, pleadings, evidence, miscellaneous. And get ahold of Chip Hovington. I want to see him as soon as possible."

28

G alvin got on the phone with Wyeth Richardson. "I'm sure you're not up on everything that's been going on in the Lyosin litigation," he told him. "Suffice it to say we've prepared a motion for summary judgment. I'll argue it on Friday. It should be allowed by Judge Baron."

"The case will be over?" Richardson said.

"For all practical purposes." Galvin felt Richardson lacked the authority to make overtures for possible settlement. He would deal directly with Stan Frobisher in London, maybe even with Sabrina Bok-Sahn. He wondered about the memo from Wilson to Chip Hovington indicating difficulties they were having with her.

"Of course, the plaintiffs' attorneys can claim review of the judge's decision to the First Circuit Court of Appeals. Probably will. If they don't, the clients may hit them with a malpractice suit. Lawyers suing lawyers is the new legal pastime these days."

"Might be a better case for the plaintiffs than they had in the first place," Richardson quipped.

"Could well be," Galvin said. "That's why the attorneys have to run out the appellate string. A reversal of Baron is unlikely. They would have to demonstrate that his decision was patently erroneous and that he abused his judicial discretion."

"Well, from what I know about the case and appellate procedure, the plaintiffs have no chance at all," said Richardson. "And we should move against them for assessment of treble costs, including counsel fees, for mounting a frivolous appeal. It seems to me that the Federal Rules of Civil Procedure contain such sanctions."

"They do," Galvin said. "But they're seldom invoked."

"Seldom invoked? We did this all the time at Polk and Wardell."

"Sure, where IBM sues Xerox or vice versa, costs are a way of life. But here we're dealing with poor families of genetically damaged children and their case is being thrown out of court. We won't try to seek our last pound of flesh. We'll waive costs." Galvin was emphatic. "Oh, by the way," he said as if it were an afterthought, "is Dr. Corsini in?"

"I believe he's in conference with Dr. Torgenson. We've just received initial FDA approval on Ero-Plus. It'll be a blockbuster for the over-forty crowd—the world's first prescriptive aphrodisiac. Our marketing people predict it'll outsell Valium three to one."

"I hope you guys make a trillion dollars," Galvin said. "Tell the doctor to call me when he gets a chance."

○

The car phone suddenly buzzed. Galvin was surprised to hear Nancy Cosgrove, his night secretary, say that he had a call from Dr. Corsini. Galvin glanced at his watch: eight-ten. Corsini was working late.

"My dear Galvin," Corsini oozed with old-boy charm, "how are you? All I hear is what a great job you did for us in London. Sabrina tells me you're a superior barrister. And she thinks you're quite handsome."

"She has good taste," Galvin replied.

"She's got you on her mind, Galvin. She's not only beautiful, you know, but also very, very rich."

"A good combination," said Galvin.

"The reason I'm getting back to you so late"—Corsini's voice had a jovial bounce—"is that we had a little celebration in Dr. Torgenson's office to toast our staff. We just received final approval from the FDA for Ero-Plus."

"Probably will outsell Valium three to one," Galvin said.

"Say," Corsini laughed, "that's the exact prognosis of our marketing people. Boy, Galvin, guys like us will be walking around with a perpetual hard-on."

"That could be embarrassing—especially in church." He didn't wish to get involved in Corsini's brand of jocularity.

He wondered why Corsini hadn't mentioned Jerry Wilson's death. It was a time for condolences.

"I'm in a bit of a hurry, Doctor. You caught me on the turnpike heading to meet a client. I just called to wish you well and, of course, extend my sympathies on Jerry Wilson. Wyeth Richardson told me about it earlier."

"Oh, yes, a shame, Galvin," Corsini's voice switched to the proper tone of bereavement. "But I knew it was coming. He was overweight and hit the martinis too often. Typical coronary profile."

Galvin could almost lip-sync the next line.

"Jerry was only fifty-seven," Corsini went on, "yet he had the heart of an octogenarian. And the real pity," he added, "is that he was only weeks away from retirement."

"Well, I kind of liked him," Galvin said. "I understand he succumbed while rowing on the river last Friday."

"That's the ultimate irony," Corsini said, his voice now tinged with reproach. "Wilson always fancied himself an athlete of sorts. Rowing is the most brutal exercise in the world. More exacting than sex." Corsini sniggered. "He was a weekend rower. Not like Dr. Torgenson, who's on the river every morning."

"Well, I sent a letter and flowers to his family."

"That was kind of you." Corsini's voice softened. "I went to the services at Christ Church in Asbury Cove. Dr. and Mrs. Torgenson and several of our key officials attended. His wife and daughters were deeply touched by Gammett's outpouring."

"Well, best regards, Doctor, and congratulations on Ero-Plus," Galvin said, trying to sign off.

"Thanks, Galvin. It was my baby all the way. I knew from the outset that correiga extract would outdo shark-fin soup and powdered rhinoceros horn. Say, we're having a celebrity bash down here at the club this Saturday night to celebrate the FDA approval. Maybe you'd like to come. Some government people will be coming. All the FDA biggies. Mallory and Frobisher are arriving from London, and I understand Sabrina Bok-Sahn will attend."

A light flashed in Galvin's brain. His sensors were all in green. "She'll be there?"

"That's what the reservations say. Consider this a special invitation for you and a guest. But if I were you, Galvin, I'd come solo. You could escort Sabrina."

"Okay," said Galvin, "I'll check my trial calendar and let your secretary know. Meanwhile, say hello to everyone for me, especially your daughter."

"Which one?" asked Corsini.

"The one in college."

"I've two in college. Liat is at the Sorbonne."

"I guess I mean the one at Georgetown," Galvin said deflectively.

"Oh, you must mean Samantha. But she's not in D.C. Straight A's at Bryn Mawr. Into more things than Brooke Shields, and twice as good-looking. She's a real stunner, Galvin."

"I'll bet she is," Galvin said. "I'll try to make it down. I'll let you know."

"You know, Galvin," Corsini said, "I still think Ero-Plus should be Erecto-Plus, and how's this for a marketing slogan: 'Down one in the morning and you'll be up all night.' "

"Got to be the slogan of the nineties," Galvin said, eager to end the conversation.

"And how about—"

"Doctor, I've really got to run. I'll let you know about Saturday evening."

29

Dr. Hakar Jegalian, chief pathologist at St. Catherine Laboure Hospital, studied the autopsy report on Jeremiah Wilson. Galvin had developed a kinship with the doctor. The relationship had started with enmity, since Jegalian had testified as an adverse witness in Galvin's malpractice case against St. Catherine's. But professional respect had strengthened into a lasting friendship.

They sat in Jegalian's office, a white wallboard cubicle crowded with books, microscopes, and human tissue pickled in jars of formaldehyde. The room had an antiseptic scent; only a doorway separated it from the morgue, where cadavers encased in cool wet trays awaited dissection.

Galvin followed along on his photocopy, underscoring sections noted by Jegalian with a yellow marker.

"I've never seen such a limited autopsy in this kind of death," said Jegalian, adjusting his horn-rimmed glasses to peer more intently at the protocol. He ran a hand through his shaggy gray hair, which resembled the mane of an aging lion. "Obviously, Dr. Stennis knew what he was looking for. He only did two sections of the left descending coronary artery. Usually several are made, cutting through the heart as one would slice a peach or a pear."

"Dr. Stennis," Galvin said, "what kind of pathologist is he?"

"Well, there aren't any hacks in pathology, if that's what you mean. If you arrive at a mistaken diagnosis in a dead patient, no one really knows and seldom cares. You could goof on living tissue, but then if the diagnosis is questionable, you call in one or two others to cover your rear end.

"Most pathologists are M.D.s who can't cut it in private practice," Jegalian continued. "Too much overhead, the patients are a pain in the ass, whatever. They opt for a sinecure somewhere in the bowels of a state hospital at sixty thousand a year, no malpractice premiums and no heavy lifting. There's a certain elitism in medicine, and the other disciplines consider pathology the armpit of the profession.

"I've checked on Stennis through the American Board of Pathology. He's board-certified, chief of pathology at Perth Amboy General, a fairly big institution. He's up there—age seventy-three. But this is a business where an unsteady hand doesn't matter a hell of a lot. That's the beauty of pathology—no forced retirement. Of course, we like to say that pathology is the queen of the diagnostic sciences. All medical discoveries, cures, and treatments would still be back in the Middle Ages if it wasn't for guys like us carving up dead bodies.

"So to answer your question, Stennis is one of the deans down there in New Jersey. He occasionally teaches at Newark State Medical School, and he publishes a lot of articles in throwaway medical journals."

"Dr. James Pearson? How about Pearson?"

"I've checked on him, too. He's been the county medical examiner in Monmouth for some twenty years. And he's a mature sixty-nine. They have a lot of accidents—drownings, stuff like that, even an occasional shark attack during the summer months on the Jersey shore. I met Pearson at a pathologists' convention in San Francisco five years ago. He delivered a paper on amyotrophic lateral sclerosis—Lou Gehrig's disease. Again, you don't have to be Phi Beta Kappa to be a pathologist. So what we have is Stennis and Pearson, doctors with impeccable credentials. But I use that term with caution."

"Doctor," Galvin said, "an attorney friend of mine in New York knows the Newark district attorney, who says in cases of the sudden death of a person in apparent good health, the county medical examiner usually assumes jurisdiction of the deceased and performs a meticulous and exacting autopsy. Nothing is overlooked."

"The key word is *usually*," Jegalian said. "In New York City unexpected deaths, with no apparent foul play, seldom, if ever, go to autopsy. They simply don't have the staff. Someone views the body, makes sure the person's skull isn't bashed in, and certifies the cause of death, based on the person's age and medical history, or if no immediate history is available, comes up with the wastebasket diagnosis of heart failure. I'm not aware of the stats in New Jersey, but I'd wager they're similar to New York City. The law is the same here in Massachusetts and the same holds true—what usually should be done is usually not done."

"But you said you've never seen such a limited autopsy under the circumstances." Galvin was groping for some answers.

"Yes. I didn't say the protocol was a-okay." Jegalian looked up from the pages he was studying. "What bothers me is that the medical examiner did assume jurisdiction, then abdicated to a private pathologist, presumably brought in by the family. Permission for only limited autopsy was granted—section of the organs of the thoracic cavity. And bingo, Stennis hits the cause of death right on the nose. There can be no faulting his diagnosis even though the technique leaves much to be desired. In fact, except for a few sections of heart muscle, the other organs—lungs, liver, pancreas—were left untouched. Of course, it was co-signed by the medical examiner, but as far as I can tell, he never assisted in the autopsy. A pathology resident. . . . Let me see." Jegalian put on a stronger set of glasses. "A. R. . . . it looks like Benjamina. We Albanians are all over the place. I assume he's a resident at Presbyterian.

"Again, you can't fault the pathologic cause of death. 'Thrombotic occlusion of the left descending coronary artery with acute dependent myocardial infarction.' Wilson had a massive heart attack. Would have taken out a weightlifter."

"Would you say from your review, Doctor, that Wilson had the heart of an octogenarian?"

"No way to tell. The heart was not enlarged. It weighed three hundred and fifty grams. That's within normal limits for a person of

Wilson's build, weight, and age bracket. There were no areas of old infarction, which sometimes tips us off that he'd had past difficulties. And, of course, other than the site of the thrombosis, none of the coronary arteries or their branches were sectioned. I assume that Wilson, like all of us in his age bracket, had a moderate amount of atherosclerotic disease. So again, to answer your question, there's no way of telling."

"Any sign that Wilson was an inveterate drinker?"

Jegalian shook his head. "Again, the liver was not sectioned. Sometimes the liver's as big as a watermelon—a good indicator of a lifetime of imbibing. Here Stennis would have viewed the organs of the abdominal cavity, including the liver, but no mention was made of abnormalties, so we can assume it was not enlarged."

"Doesn't it seem strange that the lungs, pulmonary arteries, the aorta, and the carotid vessels were not examined? Not even the brain?"

Dr. Jegalian took out an old briar pipe from a pocket of his frayed smock coat. "You've been studying," he said, and smiled as he shook tobacco from a tin-foil pouch into the bowl, carefully packing it with his thumb. "No question about it." He lit the pipe and sent several puffs billowing toward the ceiling. "The technique was highly questionable. But keep in mind, permission was not given to open the head. Some families, particularly Roman Catholics, oppose any type of autopsy. They feel the body is the sepulcher of the Holy Spirit and shouldn't be mutilated under any circumstances, especially when everyone is going to be resurrected on the final judgment day."

"But Wilson was a Presbyterian and his body was cremated."

"I know," Jegalian mused. "The good Lord's got a hell of a lot of patching up to do. Wilson could have died from a pulmonary embolism, a ruptured aneurysm in one of the cerebral arteries, or from one of a dozen other causes. But the fact remains that the immediate cause of death was disclosed without question. And with that we can't argue. Everything else is mere conjecture."

"Okay," Galvin said, "now a few hard questions. Say I wanted to get rid of Wilson—forget about the thrombosis for the time being. Could he have been done in by methods undetectable by autopsy and toxicology?"

Jegalian puffed contentedly on his pipe, as if he had anticipated Galvin's question. "Sure," he said. "Some deaths defy pathologic diagnosis despite the most sophisticated postmortem. Wilson could have had an air or fat embolism travel from a vein in his lower extremity and lodge in a lung, causing a pulmonary infarct and death. Or similarly, a foreign substance could have been introduced into the carotid arteries, causing a cerebrovascular accident. As I say, there's no way of telling, since the brain and lungs were not sectioned."

"Again, forgetting the thrombotic lesion, Doctor"—Galvin looked at Jegalian intently—"could Wilson have been poisoned without it being detected?"

"The toxicology studies were negative. Not even a hint of alcohol." Jegalian held up a page of the protocol. "Ethanol, neg; acid/base scan, neg. But today there are many poisons, especially those used by espionage groups, that can be absolutely lethal without leaving a trace: botulinum toxin, curare—the South American Indian dart poison—a variety of snake venoms, the skin of the Kokoi frog. You can lick a postage stamp dipped in cyanide and be dead in ten seconds. And the best pathologists in the world and the most sophisticated electronic and spectographic studies probably won't detect it.

"But again, we come back to square one. Wilson died from a massive infarct in the left ventricle of the heart, secondary to a coronary thrombosis. And Stennis picked it up. No one can fault Stennis for hitting the diagnostic bull's-eye."

"Okay, now for the fast one," Galvin said.

Jegalian beat Galvin to the interrogative punch. "Wilson's coronary thrombosis and myocardial infarction. Could that have been induced by mechanical or toxic means?"

"Exactly," Galvin said.

The pipe lolled in the corner of Jegalian's mouth. He removed it and banged it gently against the Cinzano ashtray on his desk, stoking it for a few last puffs. Finally he spoke.

"Well, rowing, especially the first thing in the morning, could do it. Take the runner James Fixx, who succumbed while jogging.

The same happened to Jack Kelly in Philadelphia a number of years ago. Both were in excellent physical condition, both in their early fifties. Kelly was a champion rower. Expired while exercising. Stress, physical or psychological, is a well-known precipitant of thrombotic lesions. Look what happened to old Nelson Rockefeller. And then there's the fright phenomena. A person can literally be scared to death. Say, in the middle of the night some undeserving nephew lights a firecracker under the bed of his favorite uncle, the one with a bad ticker, who's leaving him two million in his will. *Bang!*" Jegalian slapped the bowl of the pipe into the palm of his hand. "Coronary thrombosis with myocardial infarction . . . and the nephew's a multimillionaire."

"How about drug-induced?"

"There are some interesting theories," Jegalian said. "The drug ergonovine can cause spasm of the coronary arteries. It's given to heart patients who undergo coronary arteriography to get X rays that show narrowing in the coronary arterial tree. It's risky. The radiologist has to have his malpractice premiums paid up. Even a few milligrams can cause a fatal spasm. There are other drugs, like potassium chloride, that can cause sudden cardiac death, and IV Thrombin can induce extensive intravascular clotting, which can lead to infarction."

"Would they be detectable?"

"Usually," Jegalian said. "If the pathologist's diagnostic acumen were specifically attuned. Especially if that's what he was looking for."

"Could they be overlooked?"

"Anything could be overlooked. The annals of forensic medicine are replete with cases of coronors and pathologists not doing their job."

"Or doing too good a job," Galvin said.

"That's happened, too," Jegalian agreed.

◘

Andrea Schneiderman sat with Chip Hovington and waited while Galvin perused the motion for summary judgment. Andrea had formulated the motion and had written the brief. Both were beautiful—articulate, persuasive, and firmly based on precedent. Chip patted Andrea's hand as he watched Galvin nodding approval with the turn of each page.

"It's the best legal brief I've seen since I've been here," Chip said.

Galvin tilted back in his chair. He rubbed his eyes with his thumb and forefinger for several seconds and gathered his thoughts.

"An excellent job, Andrea," he acknowledged. "If it's to be argued before Judge Baron, I'll see to it that you get the chance."

Andrea Schneiderman's head bobbed up as she tried to suppress a smile. Galvin was well aware that Tina Alvarez had given Andrea a shellacking in their first encounter. He knew how she must have smarted and brooded and prepared for the final showdown. He knew, too, that the summary judgment was airtight. It would be allowed by Judge Baron even if argued by a paralegal. For the plaintiffs, there was no escape. By Friday, Alvarez and the case would be history—along with the Portuguese families and Moe Katz.

"Okay." Galvin tilted his chair back toward his desk. "I want to check into a few things. Andrea, I'll let you know in time to prepare your argument."

Chip and Andrea got up to leave.

"Chip, will you stay. I want to go over a few other matters."

Galvin pushed the documents on his desk to one side. After Andrea was gone, he said to Chip, "You know, of course, that Carter and I have discussed possibilities of terminating the litigation by settlement."

Chip looked puzzled. "Carter mentioned something about it the other day. A passing remark. I got the impression that he didn't think you were really serious."

"Oh, I'm serious, all right." Galvin stroked his chin with his thumb and forefinger. "Chip, is there anything I should know about Sabrina Bok-Sahn's deposition testimony that maybe I'm unaware of?"

Chip sat cross-legged, resting his hand on his right ankle. He gave it a little tug. "You went through my gym bag?" There was a hint of dismay in Chip's voice.

"I did." Galvin offered no excuses.

"Well, what I was doing"—Chip looked past Galvin as if he were gathering his thoughts—"was working with Wilson to help the client. We've won the case all along—on jurisdiction, on the facts, and on the law. My duty is to the client."

"Chip, for Christ's sake!" Galvin stood up and leaned forward, his arms and two fists supporting his hunched shoulders. "Your duty is to the law!"

Chip eyed Galvin curiously. He cleared his throat. "Please, Galvin," he said. "I'm not some second-year law student with stars in my eyes heading for the legal peace corps."

Galvin felt he'd better hear Chip out. He wasn't sure himself where it would all lead—or end.

"We won the case on jurisdiction, okay?" Chip said. "Look, one thing I've learned in the firm, and especially from working with you, is that litigation isn't a nice-guy game. Our adversaries are trying to cut our balls off. We don't hand them the knife. When you're asked to defend a client, I don't care whether he's a mass murderer or a financial sleaze, you don't throw him to the wolves. Not if you're a real lawyer. You might not like the client, or what he does, but you don't let the system railroad him."

"Yes," Galvin cut in, "but you don't go around manufacturing evidence either!"

"Like what?" Chip shot back.

"Like changing the Importer's Agreement. We submitted a phony to the court—an absolute forgery!"

"Hey." Chip held up his hand, anger creeping into his voice. "You counsel a client. You tell him what the law is and what his chances are, depending on the facts of *this* situation or *that* situation. You don't want to know if he killed someone or stole from his employer. He then gives you a story you can live with, the one that leads to acquittal."

Galvin shook his head, but Chip continued.

"I didn't manufacture anything. I simply pointed out to Wilson the legal ramifications of the Importer's Agreement. The change was *theirs*, not mine."

Somehow it wasn't Chip talking. There was no contrition, no sense of regret.

"Okay," Galvin said. "Let's say for the moment I buy your story."

"Buy it? What are you talking about? What difference is there between my dealings with Wilson and Gammett and our manufacturing a new image for Judge Stone? Talk about a charade! And we made a deal in Robert Barr's case—suppressing criminal evidence of insider's information. Christ! Boesky and his Wall Street crooks went to the slammer, and Barr and his family are still playing polo at Myopia. If there's a difference, Galvin, I can't see it."

"There's a difference," Galvin said quietly.

◘

Galvin was alone in the broad expanse of his office when Nancy Cosgrove paged him that Dr. Corsini was calling long distance.

"Get the doctor's number," Galvin said. "Tell him I'll call him right back. Also, continue the Gammett motion for one week. Notify Chip's, Carter's, and Andrea Schneiderman's secretaries so there'll be no mix-up. I'll be down in New Jersey Friday, perhaps for the weekend."

Galvin stalled for a good ten minutes, called the number on his private red line, and reached Dr. Corsini at his home in Rumson.

"Mr. Galvin, you lead a charmed life," Corsini greeted.

"I do?"

"Sabrina," he chortled, "I talked with her this afternoon. She called from Amsterdam. Wanted me to let you know that she'd be delighted if you would be her escort for the evening of our gala. You're coming, aren't you?"

"Yes," Galvin said. "I'll be there, Doctor."

"Excellent," Corsini said. "I'll see to it that everything's arranged. I'll book you at the Rumson Inn. Sabrina will be staying there also."

"I'll arrive in Newark about noon, U.S. Air."

"Give me the flight number. We'll have you picked up."

"Oh, I'd rather just rent a car at the airport. I'll call you when I get in. See you Friday, Doctor."

"Believe me, Galvin, this is going to be the biggest bash central Jersey has ever seen. It's at the Boat Club, and the weather's supposed to be perfect. The guest list is stellar. Sonia Bassett is covering it for the *Washington Post* and don't be surprised if Vice President Quayle puts in an appearance. And, Galvin . . ."

"Yes?"

"Sabrina asked me about your marital status. A good sign, Galvin, a good sign."

3 0

Galvin purchased a roll of Certs at the gift shop of the Rumson Inn and peered down at the *Patterson Heights Times Star* at the bottom of the magazine rack. On page one a smiling trio of Gammett officials, Dr. Torgenson, Dante Corsini, and some marketing head, illustrated the lead story.

"You cut a handsome figure in your tux, sir," an elderly lady behind the counter told him as she went to hand him change from a five-dollar bill.

"I do?" Galvin returned her smile. "Keep it." He waved the change aside. It was a five-dollar compliment.

"No, please," she said, "maybe just a dollar, plus fifty-five cents for the Certs. It's more than generous."

She carefully counted his change.

"It's going to be quite an evening," she said. "Are you one of the Gammett V.P.s?"

He gave her a bemused look. "No," he said after a short pause. "You might say I own the company."

Sabrina Bok-Sahn had told him she would be ready within the hour. They were to meet in the lobby. He glanced at his watch—6:50 P.M.—then maneuvered toward a vantage point near the elevators. The burgundy carpeted hallway led to the foyer, where the exuberant guests paraded toward waiting limos. The Garden State Livery Service was doing quite a business tonight, Galvin thought.

He slipped a Certs into his mouth and watched a group of silver-haired men in black tie and exquisitely groomed women alight from the elevator. There was a sense of unreality to it all. He wondered why he was standing in the lobby of the Rumson Inn, light years away from brick bottom. The events of the past several weeks whirled in his mind, like a bad dream, and the spangled carnival of the evening ahead, a testimonial to a male aphrodisiac, failed to dispel his sense of foreboding.

But if the scene in the lobby had a surreal quality, it dissolved the next time the elevator doors parted. Leading the glittering guests was the bronzed and statuesque Sabrina Bok-Sahn. She was dressed in a white Russian fox cape and a silver lamé form-fitting dress slit slightly to reveal shapely legs. All eyes followed her as she glided into the lobby. She smiled her wistful, infectious smile.

"Mr. Galvin." She extended a gloved hand of shimmering silver. "I feel so honored to be in your company." A small group gathered around them, the men stealing glances in Sabrina's direction. More than a little envy was directed toward Galvin. And with good reason. Sabrina was stunning. Her black hair was tightly coiffed away from her toffee-hued forehead. Pencil-thin eyebrows curved in delicate crescents above her large almond eyes. Her radiance caused Galvin to catch his breath.

"Sabrina." He held her hand briefly, then kissed her lightly on both cheeks. "The honor is all mine. So nice to see you again."

Galvin ushered her quickly into a waiting stretch limousine. The driver looked familiar. And when he tipped his visored cap, Galvin was sure he was one of the men who had visited the phantom law office of J. Quentin Walsh.

As the limo pulled away, Galvin patted Sabrina's gloved hand. Then she gripped his hand with both of hers. Galvin could feel her warmth, her trust. She shifted closer. He felt a flicker of apprehension. This was not in his game plan.

The Gammett Boat Club had undergone a remarkable transformation. The rustic eaves and airy lofts had been converted into balconies, where graceful Greco-Roman statuary on terra-cotta pediments overlooked a leafy garden. Racing shells had been transformed into Venetian gondolas. A wall of water cascaded over volcanic rock into a pond where tropical fish flashed in swirls of gold, silver, and koki red.

Galvin's limo eased into line, crunching over the freshly laid pea-stone gravel toward the canopied entrance. A thirty-piece orchestra greeted the arriving guests with a medley of bouncy tunes from the club's veranda.

"What do you make of all this, Sabrina?" Galvin was quick to offer the lighter which Sabrina had deftly placed in his pocket.

She rubbed a cheroot with her thumb, then placed it between her lips. Galvin held the light for a few moments. Sabrina nodded a thank you, inhaling gently.

"Magnificent fakery," she said, exhaling slowly. "Four weeks ago, this was a dusty old boat house, a gymnasium for middle-management jocks. Now it's a Venetian carousel."

"Like a Hollywood set," Galvin said as he watched Dr. Torgenson alight from the lead limo with his wife and two daughters.

"Well, you and I are real, Galvin," she laughed, "and tonight you're my guy. And perhaps we don't have to stay for the last dance."

"Perhaps," said Galvin. The limo inched closer. The band leader looked like Mitch Miller, and his baton cut the air with a jaunty flourish. Galvin wasn't sure what the piece was, but it sounded like "Roll Me Over in the Clover."

"Rossini," Sabrina said, pressing her hands together. "The overture to *The Barber of Seville*. Dr. Torgenson remembered. It's my favorite."

The chauffeur opened the door. Sure, Galvin thought, this is the guy. He was slender, young, a little too good-looking to settle for being a driver of limousines. Or even ambulances.

"Thank you . . . uh?"

"Wooden, Eric Wooden, Mr. Galvin. It's an honor to be driving for such a handsome couple." He smiled at Sabrina Bok-Sahn. Sabrina smiled back.

There was no mistaking that Sabrina Bok-Sahn was empress of the Gammett realm, and she was treated regally. Galvin stepped aside deferentially as the Main Line patrons with the names of Du Pont, Mellon, and Wyeth paid homage.

"My dear Galvin." Dr. Corsini turned to Galvin after trying unsuccessfully to catch Sabrina's eye. "I want you to meet my daughter, Samantha."

Galvin nodded. It was the girl from Boston all right, the preppie with the oversized sunglasses. Tonight she was wearing sequined silver. She smiled demurely, a debutante, Main Line, year-at-the-Sorbonne sort of smile.

"This is the young lady at Georgetown?" Galvin asked. What he wanted to say was "We've met."

"Bryn Mawr."

"And you're right, Doctor. She is better-looking than Brooke Shields."

Galvin almost wanted to blow it all right now. What was it? Winston Churchill had put his finger on it when he wrote about the urge to destroy, to end it rather than carry on the fight. But why? You fight with yourself, even in good times.

The lights dimmed. A spotlight played on Sabrina Bok-Sahn and Dr. and Mrs. Torgenson. TV cameras whirred, and the orchestra segued into "The Road to Mandalay." Galvin eased out of range.

For the hostess and her guests, it was a heady moment. Everyone was here from the worlds of culture, business, politics. Maybe even Dan Quayle. Galvin knew he could be seduced by it all. Maybe he had it figured wrong.

Torgenson, Corsini, Frobisher, perhaps even Derek Symes. It was tough to imagine that any of them could be corporate hit men. Maybe Sabrina Bok-Sahn.

Dr. Torgenson approached the podium. The encomiums would be played out.

The limo passed through the check gate. The Dom Perignon in the silver bucket was just the right temperature. Galvin wrapped it in a white linen napkin and poured carefully into a long-stemmed crystal flute, then just as carefully drained some ice water into a glass for himself. He and Sabrina clinked a toast.

"To you, Mr. Galvin." Sabrina's half-smile was seductive. "For being the courtly gentleman you are."

"Sabrina," he said slowly.

"Yes."

He could delay it. Perhaps this wasn't the time. Why not enjoy the weekend. Sabrina wanted to go to bed with him. He knew that. And the idea wasn't all that unappealing. But if he did, he'd be lost. He knew that, too. Temptation passed through him like a sigh. Then it was gone.

"I'm still troubled about the Lyosin case," he said, looking out the smoke-tinted window to his right.

"I thought the case was over." She took a sip of champagne.

"As a practical matter it is." Galvin didn't want to get side-tracked. "What bothers me is that we may have won the case by subterfuge."

"Subterfuge?"

"Saying one thing when we know it's not actually true."

"You mean lying?"

"Under oath no less." There were several seconds of awkward silence. Galvin sensed Sabrina's introspection. For a moment he wondered if the limo was bugged. He'd have to run that risk.

"Why talk shop at a time like this?" she said uneasily.

"Sabrina." Galvin still stared out of the blue-tinted window. "I've got to. You see, I have this strange feeling that you didn't quite level with me in your deposition testimony."

"You could have called me in London and discussed all this," she said.

"That's right, I could have."

"You told me that my testimony was exactly the way you wanted it."

"Sabrina," he said bluntly, not wishing to lose momentum, "your testimony was excellent. I told you that. Derek Symes said it was superb. Perjured testimony generally is."

Galvin glanced through the glass partition at the driver named Wooden. The limo thrummed unerringly along the highway. "Let me be absolutely candid. You were asked if you had knowledge from any source whatsoever that correiga extract was capable of causing genetic damage. Do you remember that line of inquiry?"

"You *are* my lawyer," she hedged.

"I am."

"I certainly hope so. I've gone over all this with Derek Symes. Perhaps you had better call him in the morning."

"I intend to," Galvin said, "but right now, Sabrina, I want you to level with me. Did you answer *that* question truthfully?"

Galvin saw her bite her lower lip. A small tear gathered at the corner of each eye. She shook her head.

"Okay," Galvin said quietly. "Maybe we can straighten it all out. It's not the end of the world. Let's enjoy the rest of the festivities."

They rode the rest of the way to the Rumson Inn in silence. Even the gaiety, the laughter, and the exuberance of the other guests who'd arrived back at the inn couldn't resurrect the evening. Funny, Galvin thought, how Winston Churchill keeps coming to mind. "The old world at its sunset," the aging Lion had said, "was fair to see." And Galvin knew that some old worlds were coming to an end.

◘

"I'm authorizing a settlement of three million dollars in the Lyosin case," Sabrina Bok-Sahn said as she spoke into the phone at Dr. Torgenson's desk. "I'm here with Frank Galvin—and, Frobie, it's something we've got to do."

"Wait a minute!" Frobisher's voice came over the speaker

phone. "Sabrina, this is ridiculous! Put Frank Galvin on the line, and let me get ahold of Derek Symes."

The Monday-morning mood at Gammett Industries, still festive from the weekend, belied the pervading gloom in Dr. Torgenson's office. Torgenson studied his fingernails and sighs came from Corsini. Sabrina's gray tweed suit matched the seriousness of her tone as she explained her decision.

Galvin now moved to the speaker phone and signaled Sabrina to remain on the line.

"Galvin," Frobisher opened caustically, "what in hell's going on? We unfold the biggest pharmaceutical find since Lyosin and you're pissing on the parade."

"I have Dr. Bok-Sahn on the line," Galvin cautioned.

Frobisher's voice was steely.

"Wait a minute," he said. "Derek, are you there?"

"I'm here, Frobie."

"Okay, the snooper indicates we have four on the line. Me, you, Galvin, Sabrina, and Derek. The Lyosin case is over and now Sabrina calls me and wants us to ante up a three-million-dollar settlement."

"What?" Symes cut in. "We should be petitioning the court to assess costs and legal fees against the plaintiffs. I talked to Wyeth Richardson just the other day and he said it can be done under your Rules of Federal Procedure."

"Look, I know all that," Galvin said. He wondered about the advisability of a four-way three-thousand-mile call, but he knew he had to lay out the damage now, before the moment escaped. "I'm going over this just once and I don't want any stonewalling. We've a decision to make and it's got to be done today. We won all issues—jurisdiction, lack of knowledge of genetic defects—on *fraudulent* evidence!"

"Fraud? What are you talking about?" Frobisher shouted.

"Okay, here's exactly what I'm talking about," Galvin said curtly. "I assume you're taping this, so let me spell it out. I don't want any of you to miss a word. Frobisher, you sent me a phony Importer's Agreement, and you and London were well aware of it.

I represented to the court that it was the original. That's how we won on jurisdiction."

"Wait a minute now, Mr. Galvin! Wait just a minute!" Frobisher blared. "*Your* office devised the change. It came right from your law firm. Your associate, young Hovington, was in back of it. He suggested the changes and Wilson went along."

"Okay." Galvin could read the leverage. "So all our asses are on the line. But that doesn't explain Dr. Bok-Sahn's deposition testimony."

"Derek." It was Sabrina's turn to cut in. "I told Mr. Galvin. . . ."

"For Christ's sake," Symes blurted. "We counsel our people. I wasn't going to let Sabrina open up a can of worms. What in hell's so wrong about that? And don't forget, my dear fellow, it was your firm in Washington that handled the FDA approval."

"Maybe you guys aren't reading me," Galvin said. "We won the case on faked evidence and perjured testimony. I don't care who's involved."

"So what are you intimating?" Frobisher's voice suddenly became deathly calm.

"I'm counseling you to get up three million dollars. We settle this case."

"What guarantee do we have that three million ends it?" Frobisher inquired. "Won't your media pick it up, think it's bloody strange when we have the case won, we suddenly get rounded heels and keel over? And what about future litigation? There'll be a bloody parade of suits. You know what happened to Johns Manville. One of your country's largest corporations went belly-up in a situation such as this."

"Look," Galvin said. "I don't have all the answers. But I'll make sure any settlement will not be recorded on the court docket. In fact, there'll be a stipulation that the case be dismissed. We'll get the necessary releases couched in language that disclaims liability. I'll get agreements from the plaintiffs and their attorneys prohibiting publicity and press releases. That'll be part of the bargain. As an added precaution, I'll file a motion that all documents be impounded. The judge should go along."

Frobisher cleared his throat. "Supposing we want to tough it out. Let's say Ruuden Gore and our board of directors won't agree to . . . uh . . . hush money. What then?"

Galvin looked at Sabrina, then at Corsini and Torgenson.

"Derek Symes can answer the 'What then?' Frobie. He'll tell you it all began in your own backyard—a place called Runnymede Field."

Several seconds passed until Frobisher spoke. "Are you issuing a threat, Mr. Galvin?"

"Call it anything you like," Galvin said. "Get back to me after you confer."

"It'll take some time," Frobisher protested. "We haven't got that kind of money just sitting around.

"Fine," Galvin said. He caught the tight slide of Corsini's eyes toward Torgenson. "I'll wait right here for your call."

31

D r. Corsini lit a long Havana, then studied it for several seconds, his fingers caressing it as if he were touching an expensive flute.

"Smart, Mr. Galvin," he said, "getting us to pony up three million. One for the attorneys, two for the clients." Corsini tapped Galvin's knee, then sent several contented puffs billowing into the limo's interior.

"It's not over yet," Galvin said. He crossed his knees, shoe pointing toward Corsini, and pushed a button to open the window a crack. "The whole thing's got to go down. We don't put the entire three million on the table, not initially. Human nature is funny. People get greedy. They want more. Sometimes a lawyer can't control the client."

"Well, I'm sure you can put it all together, Mr. Galvin. You're one of those guys who can part the waters. Your ultimatum to Frobisher—talk about narrowing the options. It was, well, high drama. When you and Sabrina went down for lunch, Frobisher called Torgenson back and London threw in the towel. Not easily, mind you. There was kicking and screaming. Of course, having Sabrina in your camp was a factor Frobie had to reckon with, Torgenson too. You see, she's a little unpredictable, and right now we need her. The lease with the Bok-Sahn family runs another three years."

Galvin detected a subtle hint behind Corsini's affability. He didn't like the way Corsini used the words *right now*.

"And, Mr. Galvin, life will go on. We'll return to the pharmaceutical business churning out our golden pills, succoring the sick and saving lives, and you'll be back in Boston saving economic souls. Believe me, we'll miss you."

"I believe you," Galvin said. He had been apprehensive about the ride back to the inn, especially with Eric Wooden as driver. He had wanted to call a cab, but Corsini had insisted.

"Tell me, Dr. Corsini," Galvin said. "During the weekend no mention was made of Jerry Wilson."

"Well, as I say, Mr. Galvin, life goes on. We did have our initial period of mourning, and as you well know, you can't fly the flag at half-mast forever."

"I suppose not." Galvin wanted to probe deeper, but thought it best not to push his luck.

"You know, Galvin, it's nice to see that you're in with us." Corsini looked at Galvin through half-lidded eyes.

"I think that you, Dr. Torgenson, and London should get one thing perfectly clear." Galvin returned Corsini's stare. "I'm your attorney, but that's as far as it goes. I'm not in bed with you, if that's what you mean. And our position is still precarious. My job right now is to extricate everyone from a potentially explosive situation."

Corsini's dark squirrel eyes sprang wide open and he studied

Galvin with a gelid smile. "You intimated that unless London went along, you were going to blow."

"Blow?"

"The whistle. You know, as our counsel, you became privy to a lot of confidential stuff. It's like the priest in the confessional. The seal of the confessional is sacrosanct. You don't see priests running out into the street calling the cops."

Somehow the phraseology smacked of Chip Hovington. Galvin knew that when he and Sabrina had been in the executive lunchroom, the wires between London, Boston, and Patterson Heights, New Jersey, must have crackled.

The limo pulled up in front of the inn. Wooden hopped out and opened Galvin's door.

Galvin alighted, then looked back in at Corsini. "I'll call you within the next few days and let you know how I'm doing."

"You sure we can't give you a ride to Newark? We can take care of the rented car."

"No, thanks, Doctor." The door thudded shut and Galvin walked toward the entrance. He'd find his way back to Newark. He didn't know what the future held, but he was sure it was time to get out of Dodge. And he didn't want to end up alongside Jimmy Hoffa.

◘

"We have nothing to worry about with Mr. Galvin," Corsini assured Dr. Torgenson. "Our concern and London's should be with Sabrina."

Torgenson's jaw tightened. "I don't like the way Galvin won her over," he said. "And now she's asking questions about Wilson's death. Repentant sinners can do irrational things. She asked me if I knew the story about Henry the Second."

"Henry the Second? I don't understand."

"I didn't either." Corsini issued one of his strategic sighs. "Sabrina didn't elaborate, so I checked it out. It seems that King Henry ordered the murder of Thomas Becket, the Archbishop of Canterbury. Then he became so remorse-stricken that he confessed, donned a sack cloth, and had himself flogged publicly by local monks."

Torgenson measured some brandy from a decanter and handed a glass to Corsini. "Interesting," he said. "Maybe Counselor Galvin can end it all by the weekend. Right now, my dear Corsini, we're all climbing the mountain." Torgenson sipped his brandy. "And we've reached that portion where the going is most precipitous. One slip and we all may perish." He arched his wrist and motioned toward the floor.

"Galvin, too?"

"Especially Galvin. The ultimate hedge against disaster is Galvin. If we go, he goes. Like mountain climbers, we're tethered to each other."

◘

"Miriam," Galvin said, "I know it's late. I just arrived at Logan Airport and I'm heading toward the Sumner Tunnel. I've got to see Moe about something very important. Tonight, if possible."

"Well, he's had a difficult day, Galvin. This lawsuit has sapped him, but I'll get him up. What time will you be by?"

"It's now eleven. I'll be there within the hour. It's about the lawsuit, Miriam. I may have some good news."

"I certainly hope so, Galvin. This case has drained him and me. Don't let Moe know I told you, but he took out a hundred-thousand-dollar second equity on the house."

◘

"Moe, whatever differences we've had, we've always leveled with each other."

Moe sat in front of his tropical fish aquarium. Yellow and lavender minnows floated in fluorescent bubbles drifting lazily to the surface.

"Galvin, not only did we not bullshit each other, we had it going, you and me. We knew what the law was all about, why we were lawyers."

"I hope I never forget, Moe."

"For your sake, I hope you never do either." Moe rubbed his eyes. "The law was invented so people wouldn't throw stones at each other. Pure and simple."

"Do you believe in God, Moe?" Galvin pulled his chair closer to his host.

"Do I believe in God?"

"The God of Abraham is the God of Patrick, you know that, Moe? One and the same."

"*Oy vey,* Galvin." Moe sighed. "You didn't call me at eleven o'clock to get me out of bed and discuss theology. What is it?"

It was Galvin's turn to sigh.

"Maybe it's just my hedge against an approaching storm." Galvin cleared his throat. "Back when I was keeping bartenders in silk shirts, Moe, I had time to do a lot of thinking. When I wasn't sleeping off a hangover in my office, I used to go back to my old neighborhood church, St. Agatha's, and stow away in one of the pews. I'd wake up at two in the morning and see the eerie red glow of the sacristy lamp and I knew that Christ was on the altar, and I'd go back to sleep in my drunken stupor, feeling a secure contentment."

"Galvin, it's late." Moe stifled a yawn. "You Irishmen are all alike. You're banking on God having a sense of humor."

"Moe, next Friday we'll move for a summary judgment."

"I know all that."

"Gammett's house counsel wanted us to petition for assessment of costs, including legal fees."

"That figures."

"I shut the door on that one."

"You're charitable."

"Moe, I'm here to offer you and Miss Alvarez a settlement."

Another yawn was aborted halfway. Moe looked at Galvin in disbelief. "Gammett wants to settle? An apple for an orchard?"

"No. A legitimate deal. I have authority for three million dollars." Galvin signaled with three fingers. "And I'm putting it *all* on the table, Moe, every last dime I have. No time to play games. I want you to put it together and we'll present the settlement package for Judge Baron's approval this Friday."

Moe still was trying to comprehend what Galvin was saying.

"There are a few proscriptions, Moe. Gammett doesn't release that kind of dough without assurances. The settlement deal's got to be impounded."

Moe removed his thick-lensed glasses and rubbed his eyes again. He sat motionless for several seconds.

"Why are you doing this?" His voice began to wheeze as if he were trying to catch his breath. "I don't want charity, Galvin, nor does Alvarez. Especially Alvarez. If she thought for a moment this was a gratuity, she'd throw the money right back in your face."

For a moment Galvin toyed with the idea of letting Moe in on the entire story, but he thought better of it. The complicity was his alone and that of his client. He didn't want to brush his dear friend with that knowledge, and especially with his suspicions about the deaths of Gately and Wilson.

"You know my clients aren't exactly dumb, Galvin," Moe finally said. "They'll wonder why Gammett suddenly comes from zero to three million."

"I've thought of that, too." Galvin saw Miriam entering with a stacked tray from the kitchen. "Moe, that's where you're at your best—with clients, I mean. I never saw anyone close a deal like you. Tell them you tried for five but could only get three."

32

W ell, Galvin." Hovington quickly folded the *Racing Form* under the *Wall Street Journal* and reached for his early-morning coffee. "Nice to see you back from the Garden State. My spies tell me you whipped them pretty good down there."

"Your spies aren't too well informed." Galvin didn't even manage a half-smile. "Hope I'm not intruding, Carter, but we need to talk."

"Sure." Hovington glanced at his watch. "Cy and I have to be at Gillette Industries at nine. Gives us half an hour." He gestured toward a chair. "Sit down."

He flipped the intercom button. "Janet, hold all calls. Tell Cy"—he again checked his watch—"we'll meet at the State Street entrance at exactly eight-thirty. And have Cahill bring the car around front." He hung up.

"Coffee, Galvin?" Hovington motioned to the silver service tray near his desk.

"No thanks, Carter. What I have to say won't take long."

Hovington was prepared for Galvin, and yet he felt an inner disquiet that he hadn't experienced in years. He took another sip of coffee and eyed Galvin curiously. He felt it best to let Galvin broach the subject in his own way.

"I assume, Carter," Galvin began slowly, "that you've been in touch with Frobisher and Torgenson and have a complete printout of what transpired down at Gammett."

"I understand we've settled the Lyosin litigation." Hovington avoided a direct answer.

"Maybe. I'd say its ninety-nine percent settled."

"Well, thank God. Now we can move on to more important assignments."

"Carter, since you've been in touch with Frobisher, you're aware that Sabrina Bok-Sahn might recant her testimony."

"Recant? What in hell are you talking about? The case is settled."

"The civil case may be over. You and I know, as does Frobisher and the inner sanctum that runs Gammett and Universal, that we won our advantages on manufactured evidence and perjured testimony."

Carter steepled his fingers in front of his lips and rocked in his chair for several seconds. "Look, Galvin," he said defensively, "this is not a unique situation. It happens to every law firm. In the heat of battle the actors sometimes tend to become . . . well, overzealous."

"This isn't a soap opera, Carter, something we can turn off with the flip of the dial. This involves our clients, maybe the survival of the firm. It involves me. To revive a cliché, 'It happened on my watch.' "

"Okay, what's done is done." Hovington's voice was edged with impatience. He stood and moved out from behind his desk. "We settle the case Friday, pay the money, and lay it to rest." He checked his watch. "I presume you'll handle Friday's conference before Judge Baron."

Seconds seemed to drag into minutes. The only sound was the ticking of Carter's Bronzini desk clock.

Hovington reached into the silence. "You know, Galvin, you look a little drawn. You put one hell of an effort into this whole thing. Herculean. Everyone knows that. We should triple our fee for all the aggravation we took. Take a few days off. Go down to the Vineyard. Do some sailing and fishing."

Funny, Galvin hadn't thought about being tired. Suddenly he became aware of his old football knee. It ached. He was exhausted mentally and physically. He held his breath to stifle a yawn.

"I can handle Friday's settlement," Hovington continued. He was tempted to put his hand on Galvin's shoulder. "Hell, it's a gratuity any way you look at it. Baron's imprimatur will be pure reflex. The judge and I go back a long way."

"No." It was Galvin's turn to steeple his hands in front of his lips, as if in thoughtful prayer. "I'll see it through. I still need the word from Moe Katz that everything's agreed, and releases have to be signed."

Hovington sighed audibly. A gracious, professional, dismissive smile eased the tightness of his jaw. Galvin would put it all together, he knew that. By Friday noon, the case would finally be over.

□

Moe Katz called Galvin shortly before noon.

"It took some convincing," Moe said, "but everyone's agreed, including Tina. We cut our fee to twenty percent, ate the expenses. That was Tina's idea. Reluctantly, I agreed. When we slice it all up, Galvin, it isn't a hell of a lot, but I know, it's bailout time. Three million dollars is better than zero dollars."

"Fine," Galvin said quietly. "I'll send Stuart Trimble from my office over right now. You and he sit down with Alvarez and Jameson and draw up the necessary documents. All parties and counsel need to be signatories. Since minors are involved, the parents must sign releases indemnifying Gammett and Universal against future litigation—"

"Hey, Galvin," Moe interrupted, "you think I don't know the lingo? I was drafting releases before you were born."

It was a mild rebuke.

"Okay, Moe. Once Baron approves the settlement, it's final. All litigation, past and future, is expunged. The court documents will reflect that Gammett and Universal prevailed; there will be a finding for the defendants on all counts. That's the way they want it. And I've prepared a motion that I need signed by you, Alvarez, and Jameson, that all court papers are to be impounded."

"That's *de rigueur*," said Moe.

"And, Moe. All proceedings will be heard in the judge's chambers. No open court."

"Boy, it'll be crowded in there. But I understand."

"Everything must be strictly confidential, Moe. No leaks to the press. I can't tell you how sensitive and important this is. Alvarez has to control her people, make them understand that the whole thing will blow if just one reporter shows up."

"Hey, Galvin, you think I want that kind of publicity? When you spread it among eight families and twenty-four clients, each gets maybe a hundred fifty, two hundred thousand for a lifetime of pain and misery. Christ, everyone'll think I took short money."

◘

Derek Symes smiled at Sabrina Bok-Sahn as she emerged from the small variety store onto the cobblestone quay. A cold rain slanted in on the black-timbered storefronts, and she tried to cover her packages with her yellow slicker.

"Here, let me help!" Derek shouted as he opened the back door of the leased Renault and reached for the paper shopping bags, which Sabrina gladly surrendered.

"Careful with the sherry, Derek!" she cried.

She tossed her head back and unbuttoned her slicker as she slid into the bucket seat of the low-slung car. "Whew!" she cried. "It's kicking up pretty good."

Derek fitted the bags into a Styrofoam carton in the backseat. "Let's see. . . . French bread, Cheshire, Bristol Cream, and, oh yes, the old tar's delight—a fifth of Bombay. Should carry us all the way to Torquay." He undid his bright-orange jacket and climbed in next to Sabrina. He took off his knit cap, reached into the glove compartment, and removed a small towel.

"Here, dry your beautiful face. I've a complete change of clothing aboard the *Guinevere*."

"Do you think it's a good idea to put out in weather like this, Derek?" She laughed with childlike pleasure. "It could get rather nasty out there."

"Hey, these are the Sou'easters. Choppy. Challenging. But the wind's blowing strong from the Channel and the forecast calls for clearing. We'll plough at eight knots and be sipping marts at dockside by sunset."

"You're the skipper." She laughed again.

Derek eased the car out into the narrow street and edged through the holiday crowd—schoolchildren in parkas, vendors trying to compete with the wind, and the sailing set, men and women in yellow foul-weather jackets, turtlenecks, and stone-washed jeans.

Derek parked within a block of the Royal Yacht Squadron Marina. "We lucked out!" he exclaimed. "This has to be the last parking spot in the entire town of Cowes. A good omen."

Though the rain had slackened, the town's taverns and small neat houses were blanketed in a fuzzy mist. The wind whipped the bay into a pewter froth, and a sea of masts and spars bobbed and creaked at their anchorage.

Derek carried the bundles and Sabrina held onto the back of his jacket as they picked their way past fashionable yachts, schooners, and sloops, all gleaming white at their dockage, drenched clean by the dousing spray of the passing storm.

"Here she is." Derek stopped for a moment, assessing his yacht. A smile coursed across his square jaw, a smile of pride and power. "Sixty feet of sleekness. Wait until we start running before the wind, Sabrina. I'll give you a turn at the wheel."

He undid the cockpit tarpaulin and they scrambled aboard.

"Let's change into something dry," Derek said. "I'll check the radios and radar and brew some tea. We won't put out until we see enough blue sky to patch a sailor's pants. We'll throttle out past the bunker, then hoist sail when we clear the point." He consulted his watch. "Luv, I'd say in about twenty minutes."

The ship pitched and moaned, but the spacious inner cabin was warm and comfortable. The pegged floor planking glistened with fresh varnish that mingled with the rich aroma of old teak.

Derek mixed a batch of Bombay martinis and poured them each a glass.

"To the most remarkable young lady in the world," he said to Sabrina, "and the most beautiful." He clinked his glass with hers.

She nodded a toast in return.

"Oh, good God!" Derek jumped up. "The charts!"

"The charts?"

"My nautical maps. I left them in the trunk of the car. On a clear day, no problem, but with mist and fog, bearings can get a bit sticky out there."

"Well, why not wait it out? You say the storm will pass. We can have a few quiet drinks."

Symes snapped his fingers. "Won't take five minutes, Sabrina. Break out the brie and biscuits, and I'll be back quicker than you can say 'Pirates of Penzance.' "

"All right, Derek. But believe me, luv, I'd be content to loll right here."

"See you shortly, lovely lady." He cradled her in his arms, kissed her soft golden cheeks, and ran his fingers through her silky black hair.

"Hey," she laughed, pushing him off, "what's this all about?"

She saw a faint glistening in Derek's eyes.

He kissed her cheeks again. Once, twice. Softly.

Then he was gone.

Sabrina was in a giddy mood. She kicked off her boat shoes and rested her feet on the burled teak table in front of her. She reached for the ship phone, hesitated, foraged through her purse for a slip of paper, then dialed the overseas operator.

In no time, the call went through. It was as easy as ringing her London office.

"Hello," came a weary voice.

"Hello, Mr. Galvin?"

"Yes. Who is this?"

"Galvin, it's Sabrina, Sabrina Bok-Sahn."

"Sabrina?"

"Yes. I'm calling from England. Did I wake you? You sound as if you've been catching some zee's."

"Oh, no. It's 3 A.M. here, but it's time I got up and walked the dog."

Sabrina laughed. "Oh, good God. The time difference. Got it reversed. Called on a whim, Galvin. How is everything going on the Lyosin case?"

"Oh, fine, just fine. Should be resolved within the next few days."

"Well, you won't guess where I am, Galvin. I'm on Derek's yacht, *Guinevere*. Just the two of us. Isn't that . . . snuggly?"

"What?" Galvin sounded wary.

"Yes. We're putting out to sea down to Daphne Du Maurier country."

"Where's Derek?"

"Went to get his charts."

"You're sailing, just the two of you? No captain or crew?"

"Galvin, luv, you don't sound too enthusiastic."

There was a short silence. Then a burst.

"Sabrina, trust me! If you *ever* believed anything in your whole life, *ever*, please dear God, Sabrina, trust me now!" It was a shout. A command. "Get off that boat! Quickly!"

"Galvin, you're joshing!"

"Get off! For Christ's sake! Go! Now! Please, Sabrina, I know what I'm talking about! You're in grave danger! Goddammit! Sabrina, get off that fucking boat and call me in an hour. Go!"

"Galvin," she said. "I think you've had a wee bit of the creature, as you Irish would say." She hung up the receiver.

□

Derek looked up at the clouds rolling in over the chalk hills beyond the town. The weather seemed to lighten. He ducked under an awning and lit a cigarette.

He picked up his attaché case and made his way along the quay, exchanging greetings with the holiday crowd as they converged toward their yachts for a weekend of sailing.

He reached Morey's Dock, perhaps a hundred feet from the *Guinevere* when it happened. The blast was deafening, the concussion staggering. The *Guinevere* simply evaporated. A huge fireball tore through pillars and planking and showered the dock with a hail of charred splinters. All that was left of the *Guinevere* were bits of smoldering debris and oil burning on the water's dark surface. Then silence. Not even the gulls screeched.

Those on the pier stood transfixed, unable to speak. Some fell to their knees sobbing, thankful to be alive, knowing they had escaped death by seconds and inches.

"Oh, dear God!" Derek broke the deadly calm. He bolted from the group and raced toward the devastation.

"Get back, man!" A burly sailor caught up to him and held him fast. Another wrapped him in a bear hug. "There's nothing you can do!"

"Bloody bastards!" Derek sobbed in the man's grasp. "Oh, Sabrina! Sabrina! Oh, dear Christ in heaven! Fucking dirty bastards!"

The *London Times* carried the story in a special edition. IRA ON RAMPAGE OF TERROR, screamed the headlines.

Fifteen stations in London hit; Scotland Yard, the London Museum, Lloyd's, Charing Cross Station. Prominent barrister Derek Symes, wing commander in RAF Reserve, narrowly escapes death. Yacht totally destroyed. Dr. Sabrina Bok-Sahn, executive and socialite, feared lost. Emergency alert declared by War Ministry. Prime Minister appeals to Dublin.

Galvin received the news when he called on his cellular phone to tell Courtney Evans that he'd be in late—eight instead of seven-thirty—that he had been up working since early morning.

"You had a call from Dr. Corsini." She paused. "He said that IRA assassins tried to kill Derek Symes on his yacht this morning, London time."

"What! Oh my God! Dear God! Jesus, this is terrible! Did he say anything else?" Galvin stammered and his voice trembled. "Was anyone hurt?"

"That's the entire message, Mr. Galvin. The doctor said he'd be taking an early plane to London, that you could call him at Universal."

◘

Galvin reached Bernie McCafferty in London five minutes after arriving at his office. He called direct on his red line.

"Bernie, I understand there were some fireworks around London this morning." Galvin struggled to compose himself.

"Yeah, Galvin. Some old Fenians were at it again. Oddly, it was early Saturday morning. No one was hurt. Innocuous targets. A pillar at the British Museum took a beating, but other than some broken windows, nothing unusual. We've come to expect this sort of thing, like earth tremors in California.

" 'Symbolic strikes more than anything else,' " McCafferty told Galvin, quoting from the *London Times* article, " 'just to let the people know that the old Emerald Hill gang didn't expire with De Valera.' "

"Symbolic strikes? Schoolchildren could have been at Charing Cross Station."

"Not early on a Saturday morning. Most everything was wrapped up tight as a drum, even the pubs."

"How about the yacht of lawyer Symes?"

"Well, that sort of figured. Symes was RAF, served three years as commandant of the Brits' air base in Derry."

"Any word on his passenger, Sabrina Bok-Sahn?"

"There's nothing left of the yacht, Galvin, absolutely nothing. The *Daily Mirror* carried pictures of the site. The blast incinerated everything. It's a wonder no one else was hurt. Boats moored nearby were totally destroyed." McCafferty spoke quietly, as if it were an afterthought. "And the IRA claimed responsibility for all attacks."

"Okay, Bernie, many thanks. Dr. Bok-Sahn was a client and friend of mine."

Galvin was feeling sick. It was Iwo Jima all over again—the paralyzing fear, the darkness ahead. But now there was grief as well as anger. He had to act. He put his hand to his forehead and shielded his eyes. "She was an extraordinary person, Bernie."

"I'm sorry. If there's anything I can do . . ."

"Yes. There may be. I'll let you know."

◘

Galvin sat in a rented Toyota parked in the shadows of the Chelsea gas tanks on Constitution Wharf. Across the Mystic River, the Boston waterfront shimmered in quivers of white and neon red.

He flicked the overhead light to check the time: eight twenty-five. Sure enough, on schedule, a small cabin cruiser without navigation lights slid out of the darkness, the engine throttling back to a muffled thrum. Galvin got out of his car and walked to the edge of the pier. Two men in dark jerseys, black knitted caps, and faded chinos scrambled onto the wharf, quickly wrapping a rope around a sagging timber.

"Mr. Galvin?"

"Yes. Frank Galvin."

"I'm Declan Haggerty." A huge ham of a hand gripped Galvin's. "And this is Sean O'Reilly." Galvin exchanged another tight handshake.

"Sorry to meet like this," said Haggerty. "Watch your step. This place hasn't been repaired since the Navy pulled out ten years ago."

Galvin picked his way in the dark, following the men, who ducked into a crumbling brick-walled alley.

"Sean and I work the trawlers off Newfoundland," Haggerty told him. "Also make a few runs to Cork and Galway. Thought it best to meet here. We feel it's a little closer to home."

Declan Haggerty was throwing out assurances. Galvin had been checked. The trust was there.

They climbed a rickety staircase. A thin sliver of light faintly outlined the dilapidated warehouse landing. Haggerty knocked. A door creaked open. A burly uniformed security guard beckoned them to enter.

Galvin faced Haggerty across a small table illuminated by a dull overhead light. A Vargas Girl poster from the fifties was pinned to a slat-board wall, along with a yellowing photograph of Ted Williams with his arm around an aging Babe Ruth.

O'Reilly and the security guard stood in the shadows, sullen and watchful. Galvin came right to the point. "Yesterday the IRA acknowledged in four London newspapers that they were responsible for blowing up the yacht of a reserve commander, Derek

Symes, at its mooring on the Isle of Wight, also detonating bombs at various locations in London. It never made the Boston papers, not even the *New York Times*, but in London it created quite a stir."

The men listened. Haggerty scribbled some notes.

"Oddly, apart from the yacht, there wasn't much damage—chipped concrete, stuff like that—and again, but for the boat, no injuries or loss of life. But a prominent London doctor, Sabrina Bok-Sahn, was on board Symes's yacht. Symes supposedly left minutes before the explosion. Sabrina Bok-Sahn wasn't so lucky."

"How do you know all this? I mean about Dr. Bok-Sahn?" Haggerty looked at Galvin through the thin light.

"Because I spoke to her on the ship's telephone, maybe seconds before the yacht blew. I warned her. Apparently she didn't take me seriously."

"And Symes was the target?"

"I have reason to believe that the target was Dr. Bok-Sahn."

"Why should the Brotherhood wish to harm Dr. Bok-Sahn?" Typically, Haggerty was following an ancient Gaelic custom, answering questions with questions.

"That's why I'm here. I want to know if the IRA was *really* responsible. The *whole* thing doesn't add up."

"Okay," Haggerty said quietly. "We'll check it out. We'll be in touch."

◘

"Hello, Mr. Galvin," the voice came over Galvin's private red line. "Father Paul Dwyer here, assistant pastor at St. Agatha's in South Boston."

"*St. Agatha's?*" Galvin sensed that this was his contact but was surprised at the ironic turn of events. St. Agatha's had been his boyhood parish, where during his parochial-school days the Sisters of St. Joseph had drummed into him the stolid rituals of Irish Catholicism and fears of eternal damnation.

"Yes," came the voice. "It's about your annual contribution to the Emerald Society. Could we get together, say, this Friday?"

"That will be fine, Father," Galvin said. "Friday it is."

"Make it about noon," the voice said. "We'll meet inside the church."

South Boston was a fifteen-minute drive from Beacon Hill, but for Galvin it could have been as far away as Milwaukee. Even in his drinking days he had kept "Southie" and the old neighborhood at a distance. It was a mental block mainly, a return to past embarrassments, when his father was escorted home in police cruisers. Friendly South Boston cops would usher Dr. Jack Galvin up the front steps of their home on upper Broadway. Young Galvin would hide on the banister landing and watch his mother stand in pained silence as his father staggered into the study and collapsed into a worn leather chair.

"He'll be all right now, Martha," Officer Twomey would say. "Just a wee bit o' the creature. 'Tis the strong man's failing. But seriously now, 'twould be best to have him admitted."

Martha Galvin was beyond regret. Gaunt, haggard, prematurely gray, she still tried to cling to an aristocratic past. A world of summers at Nantucket and Newport, piano recitals on Sunday afternoons, festive weekends at the Dartmouth Winter Carnival and in Montreal, a trip to Paris. But the world had gone wrong. The young physician, chief of the Surgical Service at Carney Hospital, had been handsome, compassionate, a healer. The erosion was, at first, barely noticeable. Then came the long hours, death watches buffered by alcohol, liaisons with willing nurses, mild opiates, finally the shots of heroin. Dr. Jack Galvin had died at thirty-eight.

All that remained for Martha Galvin was a heavily mortgaged brownstone, a 1941 Packard, and not much more. And Martha Galvin was an exhausted slattern, beyond remarriage. Her aristocratic good looks had withered from too many fretful nights and rumors of other women. She was a year younger than Doctor Jack.

Frank Galvin had tried to lay the bad memories to rest, departing for Camp Lejeune a week after his father's death. The country was at war and he had chosen the toughest of the services. The Marines.

He had returned only once—to his mother's wake at Scanlon Brothers Funeral Home two years later. He left the same day. The

270

South Pacific beckoned—Iwo Jima, the tough Texan lieutenant, Red Beach, the young Jap soldier.

He owed the world a success. And success never allowed him to dwell on the past, or on defeats, or on embarrassments. Not even on victories.

Now, as he backed his Jaguar onto the cobblestone driveway and eased past the ivy-laced portals into Louisburg Square, he knew it was time to confront old ghosts, rekindle a lost courage. And perhaps in South Boston he would find an answer, or at least tie up the loose ends.

He drove toward the Northern Avenue Bridge, past Rowes Wharf, where the commuter boats slid into rubber-tired moorings and disgorged smartly dressed executives who carried *Wall Street Journals* and furled umbrellas. Overhead, gulls swirled in noisy spirals. He snapped the sunroof open and sucked in the warm spring air and the briny smell of the sea. The day augured well, and he looked forward to seeing old landmarks, maybe even finding a face or two buried in the hazy distance of forty years.

He parked near a crosswalk on "L" Street, inching in between a dusty mix of Chevys, Ford sedans, and Plymouth station wagons. It was a short walk to St. Agatha's. Old sycamores, leafy lindens, and maples still lined the brick sidewalk every hundred feet. A road crew was contemplating how best to fill potholes, the scars of winter.

He hesitated at the chain-link fence to St. Agatha's Academy and smiled as he watched grade-school children—girls in green-plaid uniforms, boys in gray flannel pants, white shirts, and regimental ties—being herded up the steps by vintage nuns. The uniforms, the nuns, the ragged columns of children were as unchangeable as the Catholic Church itself. Galvin thought about it. The rigidity, the archaic theology, the arcane Irish customs always went against his grain. But the old values remained. And he thought about that, too.

St. Agatha's was not a pretty church—not like the brisk Byzantine patterns of Sacred Heart on Dorchester Bay or even Holy Redeemer out on the Point. St. Agatha's was a moldering Gothic monstrosity. A squat granite belfry covered with the droppings of nesting gulls topped its graying hulk. It loomed above the school-yard, a stanchion of intransigence, mostly blocking out the sun, especially during recess time. His grandfather Pradrig had been given a Fenian's farewell from this very church. As Galvin mounted the steps beveled by the tread of countless parishioners, he recalled the casket draped with the Irish tricolor. The priests, even Monsignor Lally, had worn emerald-green vestments, and from the choir loft an angelic voice had sang Pradrig's favorite song, "The Breastplate of St. Patrick," in Gaelic. And not long afterward, his father, then his mother, had ascended the same granite steps encased in coffins.

The somber cloister hadn't changed—maybe a little less gold leaf above the pulpit, some brightening to the toffee lacquers of the alabaster pillars, and the burgundy carpeting on the center aisle was badly frayed. All else was the same. The Aeolian-Skinner dom-inated the stygian gloom of the choir loft, probably still out of tune. The votive candles flickered their melancholy light. Stained-glass windows depicting the Stations of the Cross bore the names of donors. The risen Christ, arms outstretched, was sculptured above the Italian marble altar.

As if by reflex, Galvin reached into the vestibule font and blessed himself. The church was deserted. Only shafts of sunlight that splayed into soft lavenders and teal greens disturbed the cool darkness. The garnet glow of the sanctuary lamp signaled Christ's presence on the altar. Galvin partly genuflected and moved into the last row of pews. He sat motionless for several minutes, occasionally glancing up at the plaster countenance of St. Agatha. Even when he was a youngster, her enigmatic gaze had been hard to avoid.

Galvin had been drifting. He realized a strange inner quiet and was startled as the click of an opening door resounded in the domed sacristy.

He watched as a priest wearing a black cassock genuflected, busied himself with rearranging placards on the altar lectern, then peered back into the darkness.

Galvin half-rose, giving a hand signal. Father Paul Dwyer motioned Galvin to approach.

They shook hands and exchanged greetings.

"Tell you what, Father, maybe the house of God is not the proper place to discuss politics. Want to take a walk?"

"Fine." Father Paul seemed relieved. "Let me get out of this attire." He gestured toward his clerical garb. "Meet you outside the rectory in five minutes."

They hesitated at the iron-grill gate to the schoolyard. Father Paul had a boyish face, dark brown hair, was perhaps in his late thirties. He had on a loosely fitting green satin jacket, ST. AGATHA'S GALLOPING GAELS scrolled in gold lettering across the back. A nun was directing a kickball game, and she and several participants waved in their direction.

A soccer ball rolled under the gate and Father Paul quickly retrieved it. A carrot-topped youngster, obviously playing center field, yelled "Two bases," signaling a ground rule double, and ran toward the gate.

"Here," said Father Paul, holding the ball on his outstretched hand.

When the boy reached for it, Father Paul flicked his wrist and the ball spun up his arm, across his shoulders, down the other arm, and landed on his index finger, where it kept spinning. The lad gasped, his eyes turning into blue saucers.

Several others playing the outfield raced toward the show Father Paul was putting on.

"You'll break up the game, Father!" the nun yelled good-naturedly. She uncoiled a whistle from around her neck and was about to exert her authority.

"No need, Sister Margaret." Father Paul smiled back. He handed the still-spinning ball to the boy and gave a benedictive pat on his head.

Galvin was impressed. "You missed your calling," he said as they moved on down "L" Street.

"Oh, I grew up in Jersey City," he said, "a gym rat. I toured with the Harlem Globe Trotters—you know, the white clowns who made the black boys look good."

They crossed Columbia Road onto Day Boulevard and walked along the seawall overlooking Dorchester Bay.

Father Paul sensed Galvin's uneasiness. "You're questioning my credentials, Mr. Galvin?"

"Well, I am a little, shall I say . . . chagrined. Haggerty and O'Reilly, fine. But a priest of God? St. Agatha's no less."

"Oh, we've come a long way since the old Victor McLaglen days. I don't care who you are—pauper, priest, whatever. Unless you become involved, do something about injustice, then you might just as well live out your life as a subservient clone."

Galvin remained silent. He had never quite shared the sentiments of his grandfather about the IRA. They were wrapped in an eight-hundred-year-old time warp, as far as he was concerned. And then there were the killings, drugs to support mercenaries, the day-to-day cruelties on both sides.

He looked at Father Paul. Political sophistry was as foreign to him as false gods.

"The information, Father. The explosions in London. Dr. Bok-Sahn. Can you help me?"

"You know, Mr. Galvin, we have a certain protocol in our organization. Declan Haggerty. Me. Now I must pass you on to the top. Believe me, you can trust him like we trust you." It was Father Paul's turn to level a gaze at Galvin. "This is his card. You are to meet in his office at 2 P.M. Tuesday. What he tells you is gospel."

Galvin took the card, winced as he glanced at it, and inserted it into his pocket.

"My grandfather Pradrig is probably turning over in his grave right now, Padre." Galvin tried to conclude with the Irish cliché.

"I doubt it," said Father Paul, extending his hand. "*Slan agus bennacht*, as we say in Gaelic."

"Yes. Thank you, Father." They shook hands. "I think I'm headed in the right direction."

◻

Galvin was ushered into Dr. William Prescott's office suite by his nurse.

"Dr. Prescott," she said, "this is a new patient, Frank Galvin."

274

She smiled, backed away, and closed the door with a discreet click. Galvin quickly took in the decor—clean, antiseptic, professional journals stacked neatly on a side table, a shelf of imposing medical texts serving as a backdrop to Dr. Prescott's desk.

Prescott was wearing a white linen coat; the obligatory stethoscope dangled from a pocket. He had ginger-brown hair, a chunky build, and his nose, dented and flattened across the bridge, showed signs of earlier athletic encounters. A Scarsdale, New York, socialite, Cornell, Harvard Med, chief of Vascular Surgery at Boston General Hospital. If one needed a coronary bypass, Dr. Prescott, the leading surgeon on the Eastern seaboard, was the man to do it. He was booked solid for six months. He was also the provisional head of the Brotherhood, the American wing of the Irish Republican Army.

The incongruity of it all made Galvin uneasy. Father Paul and Dr. Prescott weren't exactly stone-killers. And he knew he had called in a lot of favors.

Prescott had an easy, engaging smile. "I would love to get you into the movement, Mr. Galvin," he said. "We need people like you."

Galvin sat in front of Prescott's beveled walnut-grain desk. "I'll make monetary contributions," Galvin said. "The Emerald Society always has been one of my favorite charities. Goes back to my grandfather, who chauffeured General Michael Collins—or so he said."

"Collins's motorcade was ambushed at Béal na Bláth." Prescott frowned slightly.

"I know," Galvin said. "That was Grandfather's day off. So where did you get that nose?" He thought it best to digress.

"The same place you got your knee. On the playing fields."

Galvin knew that Prescott was aware of everything in his background, particularly his Brahmin affiliations. The knee was the password.

Galvin was still perplexed. Prescott had the ultimate cover. And Galvin had been let in on it.

"You're wondering, Mr. Galvin, why a mainliner like me is mixed up with guys like Declan Haggerty and Sean O'Reilly?" Prescott eyed him carefully, his tone reassuringly confidential.

"The thought crossed my mind. They're not exactly the Irish Rovers."

"Well, I'm not a double agent for the Brits, if that's what you're thinking."

"I must confess I had some reservations. I take it you're not Catholic."

"Far from it." Prescott laughed. "I'm as white Anglo Saxon Protestant as you can get. My father is vicar of St. George's Episcopal Church in Flushing Meadows, Queens. But it's not a question of religion, Mr. Galvin. Some of Ireland's great martyrs—Wolfe Tone, Robert Emmet, and Padhraic Pearse—were Protestants. When you come right down to it, it's simply a question of right versus wrong. Every man has to add something of value to his life, something beyond the humdrum of his profession."

Prescott lowered his voice. "Today we don't speak of the IRA. We call it the Liberation of Northern Ireland. In any event, Mr. Galvin, we have the information you requested. *We* had absolutely nothing to do with the Royal Yacht Squadron bombing nor those in London."

"You're sure?" Galvin looked Prescott square in the eye.

"You have my word. Whoever claimed IRA responsibility had some ulterior motive. We get blamed for a lot of things. The source will be checked. We have a few friends in Fleet Street."

Prescott placed his stethoscope around his neck and pushed the intercom button for his nurse.

"Take your coat off and roll up one sleeve," he said to Galvin.

The nurse entered with a stainless-steel tote board.

"Okay, button up, Mr. Galvin," said Prescott, "and see me in five weeks." He scribbled out a prescription. "Fill this at the pharmacy and keep off the liquor. No fatty foods and maintain a salt-free diet." He looked up at the nurse. "Linda, book Mr. Galvin again for some time near the end of June.

"Good luck, Mr. Galvin. Treat your heart right and it'll last a lifetime."

"Yes, thank you, Doctor." Galvin glanced at the prescription as he left the waiting room: *Lyosin. Four times daily.*

33

My dear Galvin." Dr. Corsini's voice was heavy with bereavement. "I'm here in London with Frobie. It was a terrible thing, the accident with Sabrina."

"I know," Galvin said.

"Derek is devastated, simply torn apart. He's under sedation. But you know Derek, he didn't earn his wings by not being—"

"Resilient," Galvin interjected.

"Precisely, resilient. Well, as you can imagine, things are topsy-turvy here in Bromley. We've closed the plant for two days in remembrance of Sabrina."

Galvin wondered how many others were on the line.

"We're having a memorial for her Monday afternoon."

"Was her body recovered?"

"Heavens, no! The blast destroyed everything. Dr. and Mrs. Torgenson will be here, and select staffers from Gammett and Universal, Frobie and Heath Mallory. Ruuden Gore is coming in from Amsterdam. We'll repair here at the office after the services for a small get-together."

Galvin could guess what was coming.

"We would like you to attend. You can be Derek's guest at his place in Belgravia."

"You've checked with Derek?"

"Oh, yes. He's a ballsy guy. No one's safe anymore. The terrorism—it's barbaric, monstrous."

"I know," Galvin said.

"You'll attend, of course."

"Well, we have the settlement this Friday here in Federal Court."

"Oh yes, the settlement. We'd almost forgotten. But you can still fly over on Saturday, no? We'll make all the arrangements at this end, have you picked up at Heathrow and so on. We'll be expecting you."

"I'm sure you will," said Galvin cryptically.

There was a slight pause.

"Ah . . . ah . . . yes." Corsini cleared his throat. "Hope to see you Sunday, Galvin."

"Tell me, Doctor." Galvin suspected the call was being monitored. "Why do you think Derek Symes was singled out by the Irish Republican Army?"

"Well, he was . . ." There was a muffled background conversation. "Ah, who knows?" Corsini adjusted quickly. "Short time ago it was Mountbatten, then Margaret Thatcher. I for one stay out of politics. Bad for business."

◘

"Oh, Jesus." Carter Hovington shook his head. "Christ, when was this decision made?"

"I just received word from Wyeth Richardson, Gammett's new counsel," Chip said. "His orders came straight from London. The three million is off the table." Chip made a sweeping gesture with his hand. "We're to prosecute our motion for summary judgment."

Carter was visibly shaken. He stood at his desk hunched forward, supported by both arms extended, his hands balled into chalk-white fists.

"Does Galvin know?"

"You're the first to know. Galvin is out of the office."

"Where is he?" Carter was impatient.

"I have no idea. Neither his secretary nor Julie Hedren has the foggiest idea where he went."

"When he left, did he say when he'd be back?"

"Apparently not."

"Unlike Galvin," Carter fumed. "This is going to blow everything. Goddammit, what in hell does Frobisher think he's doing!"

Carter jabbed the intercom. "Janet, get Stan Frobisher on the line!"

"Dad, calm down," Chip said. "I was just as upset as you when Richardson called. But let's think the whole thing through. The real force behind Universal and Gammett was Sabrina Bok-Sahn. She's dead. There's a state of uncertainty. Puts everything on hold. Same thing would happen here if Cy Sturdevant died."

"No, it's not the same. We had a commitment. An offer was made. It was accepted. It's a bona fide contract. That's black-letter law. Any first-year law student knows that."

"Dad, I helped prepare the releases. The agreement isn't binding until it's signed by Gammett and Universal. We only have the plaintiffs' signatures."

"Chip, you've got to be kidding. What kind of nonsense is that!" He pushed the intercom button again. "Janet, what's holding up that call to Frobisher?"

"I'm getting through to London now, Mr. Hovington."

"Frobie?"

"Yes."

"Carter Hovington here."

"Carter, my dear fellow. I'm sure you're calling about Dr. Bok-Sahn. We are all terribly shocked."

"Frobie," Hovington said curtly, "what's this I hear about the offer in the Lyosin litigation being withdrawn? We bargained in good faith. We made an offer. It was accepted. The settlement conference is scheduled for Friday."

"I understand," Frobisher said calmly.

"You understand? Well, for Christ's sake, what is this about our reneging on the offer? Am I hearing correctly?"

"Your hearing is perfect. We did extend an offer. It was subject to final acceptance by Gammett and Universal. To make it legally binding, it required the signatures of Torgenson and Gore."

"*We* are authorized to sign for Torgenson and Gore," Hovington said angrily.

"You have something in writing spelling out that authority?"

"Frobie." Carter bristled. "Don't get cute with me. This is

standard operating procedure with all our clients. Sometimes we have to make split-second decisions. We negotiated in good faith. Offers were extended on that basis. A deal is a deal. We're not going to welch."

"Now, you listen to me, Carter." Frobisher's conviviality suddenly disappeared. "You are our counsel. *We* are the client. Your job is to advise, recommend. You carry out *our* wishes, not your own. *We* are the ultimate arbiter of whether we pay or don't pay. We've had a terrible tragedy here. A death in the family, so to speak. Everything's on hold."

"You can't do this, Frobie," Carter said, his voice weakening to a raspy whisper.

"You're taking orders from us, Carter. Don't misconstrue the relationship. Now, I also take orders and my orders say withdraw the offer. Do I make myself clear?"

"Frank Galvin isn't going to be pleased." Carter tried to buy some time.

"I don't care tuppence whether Frank Galvin likes it or not." Frobisher sensed Carter's capitulation. "The deal's off. You're to press for summary judgment and we expect you to prevail. Wyeth Richardson says you can't lose. Now, do you understand me?"

Carter trembled. His complexion was turning the color of his pearl-gray rug.

"Yes," he said quietly. "I'll relay the message to Galvin."

"You do that," Frobisher said. "In fact, we're expecting Galvin in London this weekend."

Carter was confused. "You are? Does he know about the withdrawal?"

"He will."

"He'll be upset, believe me."

"He'll get over it," Frobisher said with finality.

Carter hung up the phone, then slumped into his chair and shook his head.

Chip walked over to him and placed a hand on his shoulder. "Dad, Galvin once told me that the practice of law would be great if it weren't for the goddamn clients."

Carter tried to smile.

"Hey, we have a quirky client. Christ, look at the crazy people we've represented in the last few months. I'll get ahold of Galvin. We still have twenty-four hours. Things can change."

"I'm not so sure." Carter sighed. "There's a lot more to this whole thing than you know."

"Dad, I've worked on this case for months. I know more than you do. Right now, it's push versus shove. Egos are involved. Galvin dictated the settlement. Frobisher and Torgenson were forced to eat crow. Now they're making us squirm a little. I'll see if I can run down Galvin. I've a faint idea he'll be sitting somewhere in Fenway Park"—he checked his watch—"just about now."

◻

Galvin had completed his seventh-inning stretch.

The P.A. announced that Stone, Reed, and Boggs would be the batting order for the Sox, who were playing against the Royals. Saberhagen toed the mound and went through his warm-up throws.

A roar started in the deep center-field bleachers that reverberated along both ends of the grandstand as Stone laced a drive between two Royal outfielders. It was a close play at second, but when the dust settled, Stone was safe and the fans who had been ominously quiet for seven innings now sensed a rally.

Reed laid down a bunt. Twenty-two thousand fans held their collective breath. The Royal third baseman charged the ball, whirled, and with deadly accuracy threw out Stone as he slid into third. Quiet again descended.

"How did you score that?" Galvin smiled at the little old lady to his right, who, like Galvin, had her scorecard pock-marked with dots and glyphs that only the true baseball fan could decipher.

"Five to six, Reed reaching on an F.C.," she said as she inserted the proper squiggles on her card.

"You don't think he had the ball beat?"

"Makes no difference," she said smugly. "Still a fielder's choice. Reed's B.A. dipped two points. He's now hitting two forty-three—down eighteen points from last year at this time."

"He's still the best second baseman we've ever had," Galvin said.

"You gotta be kidding." The little old lady looked sharply at Galvin. "Reed couldn't hold Bobby Dorr's glove. Two hundred nineteen chances without an error."

The little old lady was right. The announcer ruled it five to six, third to short, Reed reaching first on a fielder's choice. Galvin marked it on his scorecard.

There was a lull in the game. A conference on the mound. The Royals manager motioned to the bullpen for a right-handed pitcher to face Wade Boggs.

"Well," Galvin said, crossing both arms in an authoritative stance, "there was never anyone around here like Wade Boggs."

"C'mon." The little old lady smirked. "You ever see the Kid play?"

"The Kid?"

"Williams. The Splendid Splinter. Ted Williams. Why, Boggs couldn't fill his jockstrap. And what about Lefty Grove? Now, there was a ballplayer."

34

Carter Hovington paced the library with his hands behind his back. So many volumes. Corpus Juris Secundum. *American Law Reports. Harvard Law Review*. Stacks upon stacks. It was late evening and the library buzzed with junior associates assembling briefs, culling precedents, and weaving loopholes through legal thickets. Carter used to think that the burgundy-covered tomes contained all the answers to human behavior. Now he nurtured doubts. Was it all a horrendous waste? So much time, so much untold energy ground up in the hungry maw of litigation.

Chip had briefed Andrea Schneiderman, Stu Trimble, and the others on the sudden shift in plans. The case would be prosecuted to summary judgment. Andrea Schneiderman checked the brief for typos. The legal content was pluperfect.

Carter addressed the group in one of the quieter alcoves.

"I alerted Judge Baron's clerk that settlement negotiations had collapsed, and we're now pressing for final resolution. The judge cleared his docket, and ours is the first case to be heard Friday morning."

○

The game had gone into extra innings. The Fenway arcs came on, and what had been a rare daylight game droned into the night. It was a one-to-one deadlock as the Sox came to bat in the bottom of the thirteenth inning.

Galvin missed the game-winning homer by Tony Pena. He was trying to reach Moe Katz on the pay telephone and felt the stomping and roar of the crowd, the concrete understructure vibrating above his head as he listened to the ring at Moe's office.

"Hello," came a gravelly voice.

"Moe, it's me, Galvin."

"Don't try to soft-soap me. I've heard. I don't think there's anything more we have to say to each other."

Galvin waited for the stomping and thunder to die down, glancing upward toward the shaking cement beams. "Moe," he shouted. "I'm at the ball game, Fenway Park. I've been here all afternoon. Are you telling me something about Friday's settlement conference?"

"There is no settlement conference."

"What in hell are you saying?"

"I'm saying that you guys welched on your bargain."

"You're kidding me!"

"Don't get cute with me, Galvin. Sheila Finnegan, Baron's law clerk, called this afternoon. Said settlement negotiations had evaporated and that Friday's conference would be as originally scheduled, defendant's motion for summary judgment . . . *Evaporated*. Those were her exact words."

Galvin bit his lower lip as the roisterous fans spilled into the exit ramps in varying states of euphoria.

"Moe!" Galvin shouted. "This can't be true! There's some mix-up!"

"You should have called." Moe's voice dissolved into a weary hurt. "Our people signed releases. We even cut our fee back to make it work."

"Moe. I'll grab a cab and be there in fifteen minutes."

"No. I think all dealings from now on have to be at arm's length. I've never experienced anything like this before. Never."

"Moe, I'll straighten this out."

"Even when I deal with the apple-for-an-orchard insurance companies and sleazy adjusters, once you have a deal, it's a deal. Hell, even the corner bookie pays off when he's hit."

"I can't hear too well!" Galvin shouted. "Let me get out of here and I'll call you back."

"No, you needn't bother, Francis." Moe's voice became funereal. "We'll cover our ass as best we can."

It was the ultimate rebuke. Larded with Jewish-Irish guilt. Moe never called him Francis.

"Moe . . . Moe?"

The crowd was getting unruly. Beer spilled over Galvin's lapel. He listened for Moe's reply but the click was ominous.

◘

Galvin arrived at the office a little after eight. Nancy Cosgrove recited his messages. "Dr. Corsini called from London. You're scheduled on the Concorde Saturday at noon from Kennedy, arrive at Heathrow 10:30 P.M. London time. They'll pick you up. He'd like you to call."

Galvin merely nodded.

"Mr. Hovington is in the library. He'd like you to join him when you arrive. They're working on Gammett's motion for summary judgment."

"Thank you, Miss Cosgrove." He charged into his office, removed his suit coat, and threw it on the chair in front of his desk.

◘

Moe's bony hand trembled as he worked the buttons on his wheelchair.

"I just couldn't believe it when Sheila Finnegan gave me the word. I still can't believe it. This time we've really been *unger schtopped*!"

"It's fucking ridiculous." Rhys Jameson's lip curled in anger. "Never, I mean never, in my tenure at Hovington, Sturdevant did we pull a stunt like this. We've been suckered."

"I don't understand." Tina furrowed her brow. "Galvin extends an offer of three million. We accept. Releases are signed. It's a binding agreement. We can't go back to our people now and say it was all a charade. What kind of cruel joke is Galvin playing?"

"I don't . . . I don't know." Moe's head bobbed. "I can't figure it out."

"Trimble said the releases had to be signed by Gammett and Universal, but that it was a mere formality. I helped draft the releases." Rhys's finger stabbed the tabletop.

"Unfortunately," Moe offered, "it was subject to the defendants' signature."

"That's a bullshit maneuver!" Rhys seethed. "This isn't the armistice in Tokyo Bay. We signed and shipped it back for their signatures."

Tina's dark eyes smoldered with pent-up anger. "Did the other side call? Did Galvin give some explanation?"

Moe sighed, a long, disconsolate sigh. "Galvin called from Fenway Park, of all places, four hours after I get it secondhand from Baron's law clerk. Our house is collapsing down around our ears, and Galvin's off eating popcorn and watching a ball game."

"Well, what did he say?" Tina looked at Moe.

"He mumbled something. Wanted to come over."

"I think we better get him on the phone right now," Tina said. "We've got to know what's going on. Our clients are going to go ape. There'll be malpractice suits flying all over the place."

Moe thought for several seconds. "Galvin said he'd call. We'll wait."

"For Christ's sake, Moe!" Rhys barked. "This is no time for protocol! We're not talking edge or bargaining position. We're running on E, can't you understand that?"

"I agree" Tina looked at Moe. "We've got to know what gives before we approach the clients."

Moe thought again. "No, if Galvin calls, fine. He owes us an explanation and a damn good one. But I'll be goddamned if I'm going to make the initial overture."

Rhys picked up the phone and started to dial.

"Put down the phone, Rhys." Moe trembled, his voice a smoldering whisper. "This is my office and you'll use my equipment when I say so."

It was an angry split, a breech that had been festering since the Chumley caper.

"Moe." Tina tried to stitch the moment. "Rhys is right. Let him make the contact."

Moe said nothing. Inwardly he burned.

Rhys dialed.

"Hovington, Sturdevant, Holmes and Galvin," came a pleasant salutation. "Good evening."

"Is Frank Galvin in?" Rhys held his breath. His fingers drummed the table.

"His secretary says he's not to be disturbed. May I say who's calling?"

"Jameson. Rhys Jameson. Tell him to call me the moment he's free. He has the number. Is Chip Hovington there?"

"Yes, but he's in conference and also can't be disturbed."

"Well, tell him that Rhys Jameson wants to speak with him. It's urgent. Same message to Mr. Galvin."

"Galvin!" Carter greeted him as if he had seen a ghost. "I'm glad you're back. Now, I know you're upset"—he raised his hands as if to ward off some verbal blow—"but . . ."

"Hey." Galvin smiled. "These things happen. Right? London's CEO dies. All bets are off."

"Yes. That's what we've been told." Carter's voice was hesitant. He cast a bewildered look in Chip's direction.

"So," Galvin said, "the deal wasn't consummated. No meeting of the minds. Contracts must be in writing signed by all parties and supported by consideration. One of Williston's basic tenets. Christ, I even knew that at Bradford Law."

"Yes, but I thought you'd be disturbed. I was upset, Galvin. When Frobisher called me from London, I gave him a tongue-lashing, believe me. They put us in an awkward position."

Galvin clapped Carter on the shoulder. "No one said practicing law would be easy. But it's not the end of the world."

"Well, what do you advise? London wants us to press for summary judgment."

"So? The client is the captain of the case. They're paying the freight. They want us to press, we press."

Carter shook his head. Galvin astonished him.

"Okay." Galvin turned to Andrea Schneiderman. "Let me see the brief. We'll be ready Friday morning."

Galvin tried to reach Moe at home.

"It's after ten, Galvin," Miriam sighed. "Moe's sound asleep. He doesn't look good at all. I gave him his medication and he went out like a light. Is anything wrong?"

Galvin wanted Miriam to awaken Moe, but he thought better of it.

"No. I'll call him first thing in the morning. Tell him to look at an old case, goes back to the eighteen fifties. *Dodson versus The Great Northern Railway*. It's at Forty-five *Illinois* three eighty-five.

"Wait, let me write that down. What's that again?"

"Volume Forty-five of the *Illinois Law Reports* at page three eighty-five. The defendant attorney was a pretty good lawyer. First name was Abe."

"Abe . . . ? My goodness, Galvin. One of our own?"

"One of our own," said Galvin.

◘

Galvin was running into a lot of negatives. Miriam said that Moe had left for the office. "No, he didn't leave a message."

Calls to Moe's office were met with busy signals. He deliberated taking a cab over there, but felt it would be awkward; he'd probably run into Alvarez and Jameson. He needed a one-on-one.

A little after 9:00 A.M. Carter Hovington walked unannounced into Galvin's office.

"This isn't my idea, Galvin," Hovington began defensively, avoiding eye contact.

Galvin sensed what was coming. "I'm being relieved as trial counsel in the Lyosin case."

"Uh . . . uh," Carter stammered. "Let me explain. . . ."

"Marching orders. London gave you my marching orders."

Hovington smiled weakly. "Galvin, you're absolutely clairvoyant." It was a lame compliment.

"That's the Irish in me, Carter. Did you know my remote ancestor Maeve of Connaught was a Druid priestess?"

Hovington sidestepped the banter. "I'm to present the argument before Judge Baron."

"Mind if I sit in?"

"Of course not." Hovington suddenly turned jovial. "You know, Galvin, I haven't argued a case in two years." He removed his glasses and chewed on the stem. "Yes. Two years, Galvin." A faint smile crossed his lips.

288

35

It looked like another law book mixed in with the clutter of morning mail. Moe glanced at it as he sorted the bills and throwaways. The handwritten script misspelling his name caught his eye. He hefted the package, then with a letter opener grasped in his shaky hand proceeded to pry it open. Jim had gone to the Federal Law Library to photocopy the Illinois decision, *Dodson v. The Great Northern Railway*. He wondered why Galvin had indexed it.

With great effort, he unwrapped the package's several inner layers and removed a gray audiocassette. There was no message, no instructions. He shook the box several times and scoured through the wrappings. Nothing. Just the cassette. He looked at the postmark: *E. Caldwell, N.J.* The date was illegible.

Moe had resisted the electronic invasion into the practice of law; his typewriters were antique Remingtons and Royals. He had only agreed to rent computers, word processors, and a tape deck for the Lyosin case.

Now he was thankful to have the sophisticated equipment. He inserted the cassette in the tape deck and pressed the START button.

"We've never met, Mr. Katz," a solemn voice began, *"but in a sense we have. We're on opposite sides of the Lyosin litigation. My name is Wilson, Jeremiah T. Wilson, general counsel of Gammett Industries. I tried contacting you last week. . . ."*

Moe sat entranced, his bony fingers gripping the wheelchair. His mind shuttled back to Coney Island in lower Brooklyn. *He was a frail and frightened kid in the front seat of the Giant Dipper with his Uncle Saul. There was laughter, squeals, straw hats, and a concertina playing in the distance.* He returned to the present. Sure, the mysterious caller. Unconsciously he peeked around. He was alone. Jim would return momentarily, and Tina and Rhys were overdue. He pushed a button on his wheelchair and moved closer. *There was a thud and the roller coaster moved down the ramp.*

"I've reason to believe, Mr. Katz, that my life is in jeopardy. This is why I'm dictating this message. In the event this terminal event comes to pass, I've taken steps to ensure that this tape reaches you."

Moe's hands began to tremble. *There were muffled squeals behind him. Looming ahead, the track went into the sky, held aloft by the fragile grip of a white-trestled skeleton. Uncle Saul's arm hugged his shoulders.*

"You and your clients are being defrauded," the voice continued. *"First of all, you obtained proper jurisdiction over Universal by registered letter. Universal's general solicitor, Stanley Frobisher, received your letter, bribed the postal deliveryman into leaving it without the necessary endorsement, had the contents read by a special monitoring device and returned it as if it were never claimed.*

"All defendant's counsel are involved. Myself. Frobisher. Universal's personal barrister, Derek Symes. Trial counsel Carter Hovington, Jr., and Frank Galvin—especially Frank Galvin. That, Mr. Katz, is only the start."

Moe clicked off the recorder and shuddered. *The coaster was hurtling into an uncontrollable descent.*

Wrapping his arms around his thin upper torso to quiet the heaving, he sat for several seconds in limp disbelief. He pushed the EJECT button and slipped the cassette into his coat pocket.

◘

"The judge didn't elaborate," said Carter. "Our motion for summary judgment has been kicked over for a week. Baron said something about a judicial conference. If I had to bet"—Carter slipped into a half-smile—"he'll probably be at Rockingham Park by post time."

"Fine," said Galvin. "It'll give us more time to polish our brief."

"The brief is perfect," Carter said. "Believe me, I'm impressed with that young Schneiderman girl. She'll be up for junior associate in August, Galvin. First Jew we've allowed into the firm."

"Yeah. The whole world's gone crazy, Carter. An Irishman makes partner."

Galvin walked toward the window. Below, the city melted into the vapory haze of early summer.

Carter wasn't quite sure how to end the conversation. "Take the week off, Galvin. Go to London tomorrow."

" 'Go to London tomorrow.' " Galvin laughed.

"Something wrong?"

"No, not really. The idea just overwhelmed me. Maybe it's my parochial background, Carter. You know, the kid from Southie."

Carter looked at Galvin quizzically.

"I'll say this, Carter. It all worked out pretty well." Galvin crammed his hands in his pockets, still standing at the window.

"What worked out?"

"The judge's continuance, Sabrina Bok-Sahn's memorial on Monday. I think I will go and pay my last respects. But let's keep it on the Q-T. I'd rather not let anyone know I'm coming."

"Nonsense! For Christ's sake, Galvin, our number-one client right now is Universal. Stop acting like some goddamned schoolboy! You'll represent the firm. I'll call Mallory and tell him you'll leave on the Concorde at noon tomorrow, just as they suggested."

◘

Galvin's cab pulled up at Logan Airport about an hour before Swiss Air's midnight flight. He made his way to the main lounge, sipped a soda and lime, and watched the eleven o'clock news. President Reagan was riding horseback in retirement on his Santa Barbara ranch. Boston Mayor Flynn announced his reelection plans in the upcoming Democratic primary.

If all went well, he'd be in London a good twenty-four hours before he was expected.

He sat in tourist class next to a nun as the DC-10 droned into the night sky. He napped on and off, and each time he woke up, the nun was smiling at him.

"I'm Frank Galvin." He extended his hand.

She was young, early thirties. Not bad-looking for a nun. "I'm Sister Veronica." She seemed full of smiles.

The stewardess came by. Galvin ordered a Diet Coke.

The nun studied the wine card. She said quietly, in almost a whisper, "Let me see. Maybe Chardonnay." Her voice was soft as down feathers.

Galvin tried to catch the accent.

She looked like the quintessential nun—black habit, square-rimmed headdress, starched white wimple—all of which struck Galvin as rather odd. Nuns didn't dress this way anymore, did they? He glanced around. The plane was half-empty.

"What order sends a lovely emissary of the Lord to the town of London?"

"The Sisters of St. Joseph." Her cheeks had deep dimples and her soft gray-green eyes matched her soft misty voice. "Actually, I'm going on a teacher's holiday. I have to attend a lecture or two at Cambridge."

They sipped their drinks in silence, Galvin and Sister Veronica. Some time later the stewardess announced that they would be landing at Heathrow in thirty minutes. "Tell me, Sister," Galvin said as the light flashed FASTEN SEAT BELTS, "where is your Mother House?"

"My mother's house?"

"No," he laughed, "I mean your home office. Headquarters." He waved an arm toward her black garb.

"Oh." She smiled with white even teeth. "Baltimore. Mother Elizabeth Seton was our founder."

Galvin made his way to the lavatory. He was feeling queasy and it wasn't from the descent in altitude. The Sisters of St. Joseph had taught him in grammar school. They had black habits all right, but Sister Veronica wore no crucifix; all Sisters of St. Joseph wore small black crosses on their white starched bibs. And Mother Seton had founded the Sisters of Charity. That he knew. His cousin Mary

Doherty had left the order but still considered herself one of Mother Seton's daughters, even after two divorces.

He looked at himself in the mirror. He was drained white and shaking. He rinsed his face and dried it with a paper towel.

No one, not even Carter or Courtney Evans, knew that he was taking an earlier flight. And Bernie McCafferty had arranged the flight through his London office. He looked again in the mirror. He'd put some distance between himself and Sister Veronica, exit down the opposite aisle, not even pick up his bag in the overhead bin.

No, that would be foolish. He'd have to stand in line at Customs. No way to avoid Sister Veronica, at least for now.

He smiled at the nun as he buckled his seat belt. Maybe he was getting paranoid. Surely she couldn't be a hit man.

"Where are you staying in London?" He turned slightly toward her.

"It's my first trip. I'm staying with friends in Mayfair. Their driver is picking me up. Say . . ." She tilted her head toward him. "Can I give you a lift to wherever you're going? Traffic from Heathrow is horrendous. I understand the M5 to London is hectic at this hour."

Now he was sure . . . or was he? Mayfair, the M5? For a first-timer in London, Sister Veronica certainly seemed to know the territory.

After the plane landed and they'd gone through Customs, Galvin walked with Sister Veronica on the pedestrian tram escalating them toward the parking area. He carried her garment bag, having slung his own carry-on over his shoulder.

They were met just outside the electronic glass doors by a uniformed driver who alighted from a black Rolls-Royce. For all her vows—poverty came quickly to Galvin's mind—Sister Veronica appeared to travel in rather posh circles. Mayfair wasn't exactly Soho.

The driver, an Oriental, perhaps Thai, tipped his cap and grinned a welcome. He had a trim black goatee flecked with gray and eyes button-black like a stuffed tiger.

"You must be Soong," Sister Veronica said.

"Yes m'lady," he replied with a crisp Edwardian accent. "The Achesons will be ever so glad to see you."

"Oh, Jesus! Excuse me, Sister!" Galvin slapped his fist into his hand, then fumbled through his pocket. My passport! Holy smoke! Left it back at Customs! Put my bag in the trunk. I'll be right back." He patted Sister Veronica's hand and dashed off.

He did catch the Rolls's license plate. Y705N. He ran into the main entrance, where the flags of foreign nations dipped like pennants in the great room of a medieval castle, raced down a flight of stairs, and melted into the flow of travelers headed toward a street exit.

Galvin boarded a double-decker bus marked KINGSTON UPON THAMES and soon was headed down a side road. Heathrow, Soong, and Sister Veronica were well behind him.

Y705N. He jotted the number down in a notebook. Sister Veronica would be pissed. She and Soong would soon realize he'd given them the slip. At some point the Rolls with Galvin's bag in the trunk would head into London. But he was not alongside that luggage. At least for now.

36

The drizzle misted Galvin's view of the procession slouching toward the gray-draped bandstand. He sat concealed in a cluster of pink rhododendrons on a grassy knoll just across the duck pond in St. James's Park. He wiped the binoculars with the lining of his parka, then searched the canopy of black umbrellas for familiar faces. He spotted Corsini standing in the front row with Gore and Dr. Torgenson. Others he could not place. His eyes swept back and forth, half-expecting to find Sister Veronica and her Oriental chauffeur. He was thankful for the olive-drab rain gear and the rumpled tweed cap. They provided camouflage and also served as a sturdy buffer against the English weather.

A gong sounded. Along a crushed-gravel path, sandal-clad monks gowned in saffron silk swayed and chanted to the tinkle of China bells. A Buddhist priest, head bent, hands pressed in prayer, shuffled behind tonsured clerics. Several women wrapped in red silk saris completed the procession. Galvin surmised that they were of the House of Bok-Sahn. Trailing at a respectable distance were Derek Symes, as well as Mallory, Frobisher, and their spouses.

The ceremony was brief. The priest delivered the incantations—propitiations to Quan Yin, the goddess of compassion. The joss sticks were burned, malevolent spirits laid to rest, and prayer beads invoked the Gautama Buddha, a diety that Galvin thought had as much reality as the Holy Ghost. And of course, Guan Yin was the Virgin Mary, or vice versa. Galvin shook his head at the futility of the moment. Somehow the gods and goddesses, whether East or West, seemed an enormous fiction, one of man's last great follies.

Derek Symes mounted the rostrum. He stood bareheaded in the rain, declining an umbrella.

"I had penned a few simple remarks," he began. He held a paper aloft, then crumpled it in his fist.

"I need no literary appendage when I remember Dr. Sabrina Bok-Sahn." Symes paused. "The Guatama Buddha"—he grasped the podium with both hands—"was an emissary from God—the God of Abraham, the God of St. John."

"The God of St. Patrick." Galvin mouthed the omission cynically and lowered his binoculars.

"Dear members of the Bok-Sahn family . . ." Symes's voice trailed off into a solemn whisper. "She was young, so . . ." He began to choke; his Edwardian cool was deserting him. "So . . ."

"Great in bed." Galvin again mouthed the words.

Derek Symes cleared his throat. He lowered his head and wiped his eyes. The rain seemed to pause. "*Oh God*, how I loved her."

It hit Galvin, like a blow beneath the heart.

Just then the dark clouds parted, and through the cerulean breech sunlight dappled the group in pinkish approbation.

Symes struggled to continue. "That's all I can say." He moved from the podium and wiped his eyes with his handkerchief. Galvin followed him through the binoculars.

No one spoke. Only flashbulbs fractured the stillness. A gong tolled solemnly from some distant space. He wondered. Could someone fake all this? Histrionic bullshit. The old onion-in-the-handkerchief trick. Symes was orchestrating one great charade with mesmerizing perfection. Or was he?

Galvin bought some flowers at a sidewalk stand, then caught a cab at Queens Gardens as Big Ben tolled three. He'd call Bernie McCafferty later that evening for an update on Sister Veronica's car registration.

"Shoreditch," Galvin said, settling into the rear seat. "One eighty-eight Appleton Quay, just off Knightsbridge Road."

"Got us a bit of a ride, Guv. 'Bout arf-'our, I'd say."

"Fine." Galvin removed his cap and glanced at vehicles to the rear. At a stop light, two leather-jacketed bikers with spiked pink hair idled alongside. Then they revved their Harley-Davidsons and sped off. Hard to tell if anyone was following. Traffic was packed in on all sides.

"Got relatives in Shoreditch, Guv?" The driver looked at Galvin in his rearview mirror.

"No, just staying there."

"Shoreditch's a bit run-down, Guv. I'd take you for staying in Belgravia or Bloomsbury."

"Times are tough," Galvin replied curtly.

The cue wasn't missed. The remaining distance was covered in silence.

When they arrived, Galvin paid the fare. He checked the deserted street, waited until the cab drove off, then opened a creaky iron gate and rang the bell at Mrs. Crocker's Bed and Board.

"For you, me lovely colleen." Galvin handed Mrs. Crocker a spray of forget-me-nots.

Mrs. Crocker smiled a sly cockney smile and put her heavily jowled face into the bouquet, inhaling deeply.

"Now, you shouldn't 'av," she said, smelling the flowers again. "Me number-one boarder, you are, Mr. Quinlan. Ye Irish are so romantic."

Galvin was about to turn toward the staircase.

"Oh, ye 'av a message, Mr. Quinlan. A Sister Veronica called."

"What!" Galvin suddenly lost his Gaelic brogue.

"Did I say some'im wrong, luv?"

"No! No! It's . . . 'Tis an old friend." Galvin fought to regain composure and rekindle his Barry Fitzgerald veneer. "Sure'n didn' I tell her I'd be a staying here a few days." Galvin tapped his forehead. "The old memory," he said. "When did she call?"

"Ye know me, Mr. Quinlan. I ain't be given out no information now to no one. Me place 'ere could be the French Foreign Legion, if ye get me meaning? Says she is lookin' for a gentlemin. Described you to a tee, she did—ruddy good looks, salt 'n' pepper 'ansome, she says." Her arms swept in a large arc. "Aye says that ye 'ad checked in this morning for a fortnight. Mercy, did aye do wrong?" She breathed a deep wounded sigh, pressing both hands into her breasts.

"No, Mrs. Crocker. 'Tis me aunt's niece now, a Sister of Charity from Kilkenney."

"Call 'er at this number." Mrs. Crocker produced a slip of paper from beneath her shawl.

"Thank you." Galvin took the note, glanced at it, and crumpled it into his coat pocket.

◘

Galvin called Bernie McCafferty from the pay phone in front of the pharmacy just up the street. A cold sweat bathed his forehead. "How in the world . . ." he muttered to himself.

"Bernie, Galvin here."

"Yes, Galvin. I've reached a dead end. Y705N isn't registered to anyone. Sure you got the right number?"

"No, I'm not sure, Bernie. But this Sister Veronica?"

"The nun with her novitiates screwed up?"

"Well, I think I'm being set up, Bernie. No one in the world could possibly know where I'm staying. Hitler could hide out here. No one followed me. I didn't rent a car. Used a fictitious name. And when I get back, I find out this phony nun had called."

"There are ways, believe me," Bernie offered.

"I believe you. But right now I've got to get my stuff and get the hell out of here." He began to shiver.

"Forget the stuff," said Bernie. "Have you got a pencil and a scrap of paper?"

"No, but I've a good memory. What's the drill?"

"Take a taxi. Fifteen eighty-one Kensington Mews. That's in Blackheath. I'll meet you. It's a little pad I use when I can't make it home."

Galvin hung up the receiver and looked cautiously up and down the fog-bound street. The tenement rows were shrouded in a gray shawl of mist. The street looked deserted. Hard to tell.

He walked past Mrs. Crocker's B&B and must have covered eight blocks before coming to a major intersection. He reached a roundabout where signs pointed to Bromley, Crystal Palace, Bexley. There was a hack station just up the road, and he stood under a leaky Plexiglas shelter to hail a cab. Miraculously, one swerved toward him, then pulled to an abrupt stop.

"Fifteen eighty-one Kensington Mews, Blackheath," Galvin said with authority.

It was a forty-minute drive. The rain had picked up and Galvin settled back and wondered how he would handle the next few days. He'd have to get his third set of clothing, that was for certain. And thank God he had a friend like Bernie McCafferty.

It was a quiet street of middle-class tenements with rows of identical cement steps edging the sidewalk. The cab pulled up and stopped. A dim porch light faintly illuminated a stained-glass and oak door.

"You sure this is Fifteen eighty-one?" Galvin asked as he paid the driver. "I can't see any number or street sign."

"Fifteen eighty-one it is, guv. 'At's it with the light."

Galvin got out, and as he pulled up his parka collar against the beating rain, he watched the cab speed off into the darkness.

He mounted the stairs, peered in vain for an address number, then pulled on a brass knob, triggering a carillon of chimes in the interior.

An ocular peephole moved, then the door slowly opened.

"Good evening, Mr. Galvin. Nice to see you again."

Galvin was about to bolt, but his legs were lead weights riveted to the porch. "Jesus Christ!" he swore audibly. It was Soong, Sister Veronica's chauffeur.

37

Dodson versus *The Great Northern Railway*. Moe read it carefully. The defendant had secreted evidence and the trial judge angrily reversed a verdict in Great Northern's favor, assessing triple costs and punitive damages against the transgressing railroad. The defense lawyer was a country practitioner from New Salem, Illinois, named Abraham Lincoln.

It was a fiery decision. "Such egregious conduct," the judge bristled, "not only undermines the very fabric of our judicial system, but goes against the grain of basic concepts of fair play."

Moe fingered the cassette in his coat pocket. "Defendant's counsel claims he was unaware of the deception. Such may be the case. Yet the defendant cannot hide behind the attorney-client privilege. And I dare say," the judge added, "if counsel had known of the subterfuge, which I'm not saying he did, his duty is not to his client, but to the court and to society."

Moe placed the cassette on his desk, but quickly slipped it back into his pocket when Tina and Rhys arrived.

"Supposing, just supposing," Moe said to Rhys Jameson, who was indexing their counterbrief, "a litigant fudges on the evidence. What sanctions could be imposed against the wrongdoer?"

"Fudges?" Rhys eyed Moe quizzically.

"Well, you know. Say on a motion to produce certain documents, someone loses the stuff or maybe it gets caught in the company shredder. Accidentally."

"All depends," said Rhys. "Are you in Federal Court?"

"Uh, yes, let's say I'm in Federal Court." Moe examined his fingernails.

"Rule Thirty-seven," Rhys said. "At the moment the subsection escapes me. A litigant could be in a pack of trouble."

Moe furrowed his brow. "How much trouble?"

"Well, the trial judge could assess severe penalties, punitive damages."

"Punitive damages?"

"Sure. The defendant not only gets tagged ordinary damages, but gets whacked for a portion of its corporate hide. The idea is punishment on top of civil redress. It's the harshest remedy in the law."

"Do you know of such cases?"

"Matter of fact, this very thing happened in the Dalkon Shield litigation a few years back. Sent the manufacturer, A. H. Robbins Company, a mega-bucks corporation, scurrying for Chapter Eleven. One of Robbins's trusted in-house counsel blew the whistle; said he was ordered by superiors to shred incriminating evidence. Some heavy legal hitters, guys like Griffin Bell, Jimmy Carter's A.G., tried to bail Robbins out, but to no avail."

"What happens to the transgressor's counsel?" Moe removed his glasses and inspected the lens.

"Maybe nothing. In this case, the court pinned a medal on Robbins's counsel for having the 'courage' "—Rhys wiggled two sets of fingers—"after ten years of wrestling with his conscience to come forward. Sanctions can range from a judicial slap on the wrist to censure, disbarment, or criminal charges—contempt, obstruction of justice, even mail fraud. You could end up wearing the denims. Depends on the environment, the political times, and, of course,

300

the judge. No one treats errant attorneys too kindly these days. What case do you have in mind?" Rhys was curious.

"Oh, Murray Friedman—he's just down the hall. Seems that one of his cronies got himself into a jam in the bankruptcy court. Murray was in here this morning trying to pick my brain."

Rhys had a hunch that he wasn't telling Moe Katz anything that Moe didn't already know. "Anything to do with our case?" he persisted.

"No, of course not." Moe replaced his glasses and began to shuffle through some blue-backed papers. "I'll tell Murray."

Tina had overheard the conversation and wondered, as did Rhys, if Moe's hypothetical was a little closer to home than he was admitting. The last two days Moe had seemed subdued, introspective. She assumed it was because of the impending summary judgment. Or his deep disappointment that Galvin and young Hovington had not returned Rhys's calls.

"I met with the families last night," she digressed. "Quite a crowd. Father Correira was there and Dr. Meideros. I gave them the downside right away. Portuguese expect candor from their own even when it hurts. I could have been talking to the wall. They wanted to know where the money was. I said it wasn't coming." She shook her head.

"Do they realize that come Friday they'll be out of court?" said Rhys.

"Sure. Nothing like saving the best for last. Like I got bad news and worse news. In a way they expected it. Life was delivering the final cruncher. I insisted that everyone attend Friday's hearing, children included."

"But Baron's holding the motion in chambers," Moe said. "He'll resent a mob scene."

"They'll pack the courtroom anyhow," Tina said. "They want an open forum and I agree. Too much stuff with Baron is held behind closed doors."

"Might not be a bad idea," said Rhys. "Let's file a motion that everything be held in open court."

"No." Moe shook his head. "Baron will read it as intimidation. He'll bury us."

"There's going to be a hell of a lot of lawsuits," Tina said. "Against me, mainly. I've checked my malpractice policy. I carry only a hundred thousand."

"I've got the best defense possible," Rhys said. "No home. No car. No bank account. Save for my set of drums and horns, my net worth is less than zero. As they say along Bankruptcy Row, I'm judgment-proof."

Neither mentioned Moe, who could lose it all—his home, his savings, his wife's future, the scrapings of a lifetime.

"Forget malpractice," Rhys said. "We poured our souls into this case. No jury in the world would say we lay down on the job."

But the specter of malpractice remained, and they all knew that Moe was the one who was most vulnerable.

"Okay." Moe clapped his hands. "We're acting as if we've got a touch of the swine flu. Right now we map our appeal. Baron'll deep-six us, that's a given. But it's not over till it's over!"

"Well." Rhys brightened. "Our brief is as ready as it'll ever be. Summary judgment is an extreme action, not readily granted."

"Listen," Moe said, "why don't you two go to a movie or something. Let me be by myself for a while. I want to think."

◼

It was the craziest surprise in a series of crazy surprises. Soong assured Galvin he would not be harmed.

Galvin stood in the middle of the Victorian drawing room knowing that Sister Veronica, by whatever name, would make an entrance. She did.

Sister Veronica dismissed Soong.

"Mr. Galvin." She extended her hand, a slight smile pursing her lips. "Please understand—"

"Oh, listen." Galvin poised warily, like a sprinter in a standing start. "I understand perfectly. And I know you went to all this trouble just to make sure I got my clothes back."

Her voice suddenly lost its gentility. "I was assigned to look after you. I'm afraid I took too much for granted. Our driver was waiting for you at the hack stand in Shoreditch. You're in Woolwich now—but I believe you're safer here than where you planned to go."

Galvin wanted some answers. What was her connection, who tipped her off about his flight on Swiss Air, and who was she? But for now he decided to listen. "Hear out the opposition," Moe had schooled him years earlier, "even if you want to land on them hard. See where they're headed. While they lather in their strengths, you might detect a weakness."

"Your clothing is upstairs"—she gave a long upward roll of her eyes—"and you can take a shower." She checked her watch. "We're scheduled to leave in exactly three hours."

"Leave? For where?"

She gave him a look that offered no openings. "I'm charged with assuring your safety," she said tersely. "This time I intend to succeed."

◘

Moe inserted the cassette into the recorder, reread the instructions, pushed a few buttons, and, after several frustrating efforts, got the tape to play.

"You will only receive this, Mr. Katz, if I am deceased. There is no copy, so treat this with utmost care.

"Let me get to the point. Dr. Sabrina Bok-Sahn lied in her testimony in London. I refer to page one forty-one, line fifteen of her deposition.

"Quote. Counsel Alvarez to Sabrina Bok-Sahn. 'Do you have any knowledge from any source, whatsoever, either past or present, that the drug Lyosin and/or its chemical components, including correiga extract, is capable of producing congenital deformities in offspring of those consuming either the drug Lyosin or correiga extract?'

"Quote. Sabrina Bok-Sahn. 'No. I have no such knowledge.'

"You will note that her counsel on that occasion was Frank Galvin. He prepped her. He knew, and I knew, as did Hovington, Jr., and Gammett and Universal's VIPs, that her testimony was perjured. And perjury isn't a very nice word, Mr. Katz.

303

"There's a manuscript by Aubrey Gammett, discoverer of the correiga nut; that's how Gammett Industries got its name. Aubrey married Bok-Sahn's grandmother; 'shacked-up' would be a better word. The manuscript is known as Sir Aubrey's journal.

"In a nut shell, no pun intended, Aubrey was aware that correiga extract generated birth defects. If he did not know with scientific certitude, he was aware of the strong probability. And as you know, Mr. Katz, probability meets the legal test. This data was never delivered as requested by your motion to produce documents. In fact, its existence was categorically denied. The journal's contents were never communicated to the FDA when Lyosin underwent that agency's new-drug investigation.

"Correiga now is a potency pill. God knows what will happen down the line, say five or ten years from now. It could well affect the next generation, similar to the drug diethylstilbestrol—DES—causing cancer. Took a generation for the latent defects to develop. One thing for certain, Mr. Katz, Lyosin should be off the market. It could well be the thalidomide of the twenty-first century.

"My time is short. There's a photocopy of Aubrey's journal in a public locker at the Port Authority bus terminal, Forty-second and Eighth Avenue in Manhattan. Locker number Eight-five-six-L. I repeat, Eight-five-six-L. South-side location. I've discarded the key, so you'll need a court order to open it. That, Mr. Katz, I leave to you. Make sure the media is invited.

"Don't involve my family. They know nothing of the complicity. I leave this to your sense of honor.

"You may ask why, as Gammett's chief counsel, I tolerated this fraud, why I'm coming forward at this late date.

"Well, quite frankly, Mr. Katz, I lacked the balls.

"So, Mr. Katz, the burden now rests with you. I trust for your sake and for the sake of your clients that you will not be as weak and cowardly as Jeremiah Wilson. Goodbye."

Moe sat limp for several seconds. A sudden tightness in his chest threatened his breathing. His immediate thoughts were of Frank Galvin, his spiritual son. He loved him now more than ever.

His hands trembled as he extracted the cassette. Moe wheeled into his library and gazed at the rows of buff-colored law books. He stopped at Volume IV of *Williston on Contracts*, conveniently placed at waist level. He removed the text, opened it, replaced a flask of Chivas with the cassette, tucking it into the nook cut conveniently into the pages. Then he tapped the book back into place.

Somehow he had to get in touch with Frank Galvin.

▬
3 8
▬

S oong stood by the small black Citröen as Galvin, carry-on slung over his shoulder, descended the unlit stairwell. The dank darkness was punctured by gaslights that sputtered from neighboring tenements. Sister Veronica, wearing a black beret, gray woolen jacket, and corduroys, locked the back door and signaled to Soong. He quickly relieved Galvin of his baggage and stored it in the trunk and opened the rear passenger door.

Galvin climbed into the cramped backseat and was joined by Sister Veronica. The Citröen slid out into the wispy fog.

They drove the small back roads heading northwest from London. In the stillness of the early-morning hours, no one spoke. Sister Veronica sat alert and attentive. Galvin pretended to nap. They passed through stone villages and moldering market towns: Stowe-on-the-Wold, Shipton-under-Wychwood. Faint traces of dawn brightened the eastern horizon.

Sister Veronica broke the long silence. "These are the Cotswolds," she said. "Perhaps the loveliest countryside in all of Britain, certainly the quaintest."

Galvin sat up, rubbed his eyes, and stifled a yawn.

"I used to come here on holiday." A wistful melancholy crept into her voice. "These hamlets haven't changed in hundreds of years. This is how England used to be—half-timbered houses, village greens, coaching inns."

"I take it, Sister," Galvin said, looking at his companion, "you're English, but forgive me, the nun's garb and the accent sort of took me. I still can't place the accent."

"I travel quite a bit," she said evasively. "And please, the name is Veronica . . . Veronica Smith."

They reached Birmingham by late afternoon. Soong negotiated the tight grid of narrow streets as if it were familiar territory. They passed rows of red-brick warehouses, cinder-block factories, and stockyards, bumped over stone bridges and railroad crossings.

"This is where we part." Veronica studied the serried row of tenements. They reminded Galvin of a side street in Baltimore.

Soong idled into a pebble-dashed driveway. Except for occasional passing vans and small cars parked diagonally in the roadway, the inhabitants seemed to have taken a holiday.

"You've been most helpful," Galvin said with a tinge of sarcasm. "I mean, I really enjoyed the scenery, not to mention the conversation."

"I'm afraid I wasn't much of a tour guide." She glanced back through the rear window. "But some things are best left unsaid. You'll be accompanied from here to Liverpool by someone who'll fill you in. They'll see that you're safely aboard the ferry to Belfast."

"Belfast?"

She stared straight ahead. "From there, your return to the States is assured."

Soong turned off the engine, opened the driver's door, and walked back toward the street. Galvin saw him check in both directions.

Veronica smiled at Galvin and extended her hand.

"My traveling companion from here on in," Galvin said, patting her hand gently as he helped her out into the small courtyard, "*she* wouldn't be Burmese, would *she*, like Mr. Soong?"

She gave him a long, slow slide of her eyes as she left him with a minor conceit. He wasn't as stupid as she thought he was. Galvin watched as she walked toward a tram stop.

The Birmingham residence had not aged gracefully. Weeds sprouted through the cracked cement driveway, and the stucco around the black-iron hitching post had eroded into a chalky pile. Yet for a way station, it was not without advantages—unobtrusive, blending easily into the sooty brick warrens that crowded the street.

Inside, Galvin sat on an ancient sofa, its faded floral pattern spilling stuffing onto the pegged wood floor. Green rice paper peeled from the walls, and the gold satin draperies had faded to a jaundiced yellow. He stared through a cracked mullioned window, trying to piece together the hazy shards of the kaleidoscope, when Soong entered with a woman whom, for a moment, he mistook for Veronica Smith.

She was dressed in a black beret, a worn woolen jacket, baggy corduroys, and her hair was cut short. For a few moments he was stunned. Speechless. "Oh, Jesus!" he erupted. She rushed to him. He held his breath and reached for her, folding her soft body into his arms.

He kissed her cheek gently. She was sobbing. He could feel her eyelashes quiver.

Sabrina Bok-Sahn looked up at him. Suddenly she seemed waif-like, vulnerable. No smokey mauve eyeshadow accentuated her Oriental visage, her tear-stained face was devoid of makeup. She buried her head into his shoulder. "Galvin," she breathed softly.

He strengthened his protective embrace.

◘

Sabrina Bok-Sahn was sitting against the bedstead, a white negligee clinging to her bronze shoulders. She was smoking one of her ever-present cheroots. Galvin shut his eyes for several moments. A slow, easy smile softened his chiseled features. It had been many months since he had smiled so genuinely, many years since he had cared so deeply. And he knew she felt as he did. "You saved my life, Galvin," she had moaned during the roiling spasms. Was this merely a repayment? If he had harbored any doubts, they had vanished during the night.

He saw Sabrina in a new light—a simple girl, shorn of her dragon-lady image, desperate for love. As desperate as he. And there was a calmness about her now. When he spoke, she listened as if what he said were the most important thing in the world.

"Some lover," he laughed, propping himself up alongside her. "I went out like a light."

"Oh, you were good, my friend." She smiled, her dark eyes crinkling at the corners. "No Ero-Plus for you."

In the eternity of the next few seconds, neither spoke. But each knew that this out-of-time idyl was soon to end. Sabrina smoked slowly, sending eddies of blue smoke curling toward the ceiling. Sunlight peeked through frayed runs in the worn silk drapery and speckled the salmon-colored fabric of the bedroom in little fits of light.

Each sensed the other's introspection. The moaning, wrenching, and thrusting was over. Reality was setting in. The case. The law. The desperate course. Symes. Corsini. Choices.

Sabrina smoked in silence. Her brown sculpted fingernails traced lazy patterns on his chest. There was intimacy in the silence—something within each of them reached out to the other.

His arm circled her bare shoulders. Reality could wait. She held a finger to his lips. Her eyes shimmered.

She rolled almost on top of him, reached across and ground the cheroot into a cut crystal tray on his side of the bed. She didn't roll back.

◘

They stopped at a roadside stand at a honey-colored village nestled above the River Trent. In the distance the granite screes of the Pennines beetled on the lavender skyline. There was the smell of lush pasture in the air, the drone of cicadas, grazing sheep and languorous cows.

Soong ambled away, and Galvin and Sabrina sat at a small picnic table exchanging sips of coffee from a thermos cap.

"What is this all about?" Galvin looked deep into Sabrina's eyes. "The yacht explosion, all this stuff?" His hand swept toward the Citröen. He had saved her life. She owed him some explanations.

She closed her eyes as if trying to gather her thoughts, then looked at him, her doe eyes glistening. "Bear with me." She reached for his hand, hesitating halfway.

"But Symes tried to kill you. And Corsini, Gore, the whole pharmaceutical crowd. How did you ever get mixed up with that bunch?"

"I know." Her gaze shifted toward the Pennine Hills. "I'll deal with the situation in my own way. Derek and I were professional lovers."

"Professional lovers?" Galvin shook his head.

"We extracted from each other; a *quid pro quo*, you might say. It was a volatile situation. The lawsuit got in the way. You just happened into the crossfire."

Galvin poured more coffee into the cap and offered it to Sabrina. She shook her head.

"I think they saw a weakness in me," she said.

"Or a strength." Galvin drained the coffee.

"No. Everyone thinks I'm in total control." Tears welled up in her syrup brown eyes. "I'm not. I'm as brittle as they come. For all our trappings, the Bok-Sahns are of peasant stock. I'm just a small-time girl from the Rangoon River, the bastard progeny of a freebooting colonial."

"Yes," Galvin interrupted, "but your family isn't exactly on food stamps." He screwed the cap back on the thermos and noticed that Soong had reappeared in the lane. "Where does Sister Veronica fit into all of this? I take it she never took her final vows."

Sabrina smiled, shaking her head. "She's my best friend here in London. We went to school together. Her name isn't Smith, of course. She used to be an actress. Still does commercials for the BBC."

Sabrina nodded almost imperceptibly to Soong, who stood at a respectful distance.

"You could have called and let me know you were all right."
Galvin also eyed Soong, who was now leaning against the car with his arms folded.

"I know. I should have. After I left the *Guinevere* and it blew apart, I just kept running. Everything hit me at once. . . . Derek Symes, I still can't believe it. And I had to see you again. I knew I could trust you. That's when I brought in Veronica. The nun's outfit was her idea."

"How well do you know Soong?" Galvin again eyed the chauffeur, who hadn't seemed to have moved in the last ten minutes.

"Soong is my watchdog. He's Changareet like me and has worked for our family for years. Been with me since my convent days. I trust him like I trust you. And he has contacts everywhere. Even with American Express." Her demure smile held a glint of mischief.

He studied Sabrina for a moment. She had a girlish quality, a disarming candor. She was either the loveliest, most sincere person he had ever met in his life—or the deadliest. He wasn't quite sure.

"The lawsuit," Galvin said, "the one back in Boston, it's got to be settled."

"It's too late for that. What's done is done. Besides, I'm dead," she said. "I couldn't interfere now even if I wanted to, and the other Bok-Sahns can't influence policy."

Galvin searched for an opening. "What's the future hold for us? I mean for you and me?" It was a question he wished she had asked.

"I'm going back to Burma." She signaled Soong that they would depart soon. "I can disappear for a few years. Maybe then . . ." Her voice trailed off. Neither spoke.

But in the awkward silence, both knew it was hopeless.

They reached the Liverpool docks by early evening. Soong stood by the Citröen, a sullen sentinel, as Galvin and Sabrina, arms interlocked, walked toward the Belfast ferry.

"What do you intend to do?" Sabrina asked as they stood by the creaking gangplank.

"I haven't got the foggiest idea." He shook his head.

"Do what you have to do," she said softly.

A small tear glistened, welled, then shuddered down her amber cheek. He held her. Then she turned and walked into the darkness.

◻

Galvin leaned over the stern rail and peered down at the black waters swirling in the ship's wake. Perhaps it was the throb of the engines or the occasional moan of a foghorn mingled with thoughts of Sabrina, but a tremendous calm seemed to settle over him. Sabrina's last words tumbled in his mind. *Do what you have to do.* Below, the dark froth seemed to beckon. He could end it.

"Wind's kickin' up, lad. Once past the Mersey, gets bloody mean. An' this 'ere ain't the *Queen Mary*. Best we both be inside."

Startled, Galvin lurched back.

The intruder was dressed in a black pea jacket and boatswain cap. "One slip, boyo, an' we'd ne're find ya in this 'ere soup."

"You're right, Cap'n." Galvin steadied himself against the ship's roll.

"She's a stunner," the stranger said.

"A stunner?"

"The Oriental lady, mate. I see'd ya from the foc'sle. 'Ad a China girl m'self once, from Sumatra."

Galvin merely nodded and groped his way along the deck. He thought it best from now on in to keep his own counsel.

39

After making a call to Bernie McCafferty and only half-explaining his predicament, Galvin headed toward the single-engine Beagle that waited on the rainswept tarmac at Eglinton Airport, just north of Derry. The Customs official quickly checked his passport and nodded. The same expeditious treatment sped Galvin on his way from Shannon aboard an Aer Lingus jet to Boston.

Like the midnight flight on Swiss Air, the Aer Lingus DC-10 was half-empty. No suspicious-looking nuns, just the usual complement of Irish-American tourists, sentimental, with more than a share of fermented farewells. The captain announced that flying time to Kennedy International would be seven hours, ten minutes, adding that the trip was *nonstop*.

"Jesus, Mary, I should hope so." A grandmother type seated across the aisle clucked audibly. It drew nervous titters from the nearby nonsmoking section.

Galvin tried to nap.

Sabrina kept reappearing—tender, warm, doe eyes glistening. The lovemaking. The intimate silence. The contentment. Some lines from Kipling came to mind. A poem of long ago. How did it go? Yes, he had it.

> By the old Moulmein Pagoda, looking lazy to the sea,
> There's a Burma girl a-sittin'
> And I know she thinks of me . . .

Yet what was he thinking of? She was still his client. With that relationship came an irrevocable trust.

"Never pick up a horizontal fee," Moe Katz had admonished during Galvin's formative years. "A client will have you by the balls. And there's nothing worse than a falling-out between two whores. You'll crawl to keep your license."

Everyone on the plane seemed to be asleep. Even the perky green-suited stewardesses had retired to some slumbrous recess. Only the thinly lit EXIT signs illumined the quiet darkness.

Galvin tilted his head back and tried to sort the jumble of events that kept spiraling in bizzare kaleidoscopic patterns. If he ever entertained the thought of sacrificing Sabrina on the altar of justice, others would have to go—Chip Hovington, the firm, God knows who else. The whole thing was beyond contemplation.

He adjusted the air spigot above his head and closed his eyes.

Shit, he swore to himself, he should have aborted the goddamed case the very moment Frobisher mentioned the "sneaky peepy." A lawyer has a right to choose his clientele. He had hesitated. He recalled a frightening newsreel he had once seen. It was a long time ago. Pathé News. Lowell Thomas narrated. A young sailor held guidelines to an atmospheric balloon. It was someplace in New Jersey, maybe Lakehurst. Suddenly the balloon jettisoned its moorings and bolted skyward. The sailor held on and was carried aloft. Two hundred feet. Five hundred feet. Six hundred. The camera followed as the swabbie's grip weakened, then caught the stark horror as he hurtled to his death. Poor bastard. Just trying to do his duty. Like the doomed serviceman, Galvin had held on too long.

40

Rhys Jameson stuffed the trial bag with last-minute documents. "It'll be kind of nice getting back to the clarinet," he said. "Wonder if I remember 'Harlem Nocturne.' "

Tina Alvarez bit on her lower lip to hide her apprehension. "I'm sorry," she said to Moe.

"Sorry." Moe emitted a cackle. "Sorry for what?"

"You didn't need the aggravation. She cupped his hand in hers. "Or the expense."

"Hey, Tina. Look, you gave me back my life, my reason for being a lawyer. If it wasn't for you, I'd be sitting here drying up, listening to crazy dames with whiplashes trying to get something for nothing."

Moe dismissed any further lament with a wave of his hand. "I haven't felt this great since the day I tried my first case in Boston Municipal Court. Tripped over my bag when I got up to argue to the jury. They felt sorry for me, gave me three thousand dollars—a lot of dough back in the thirties. Been tripping over my bag ever since."

Tina managed a faint smile.

"Jim." Moe wheeled toward his outer office. "Bring the wagon around front. It'll take some doing, but we'll squeeze everything in—props, documents, even the lawyers."

They rode to the courthouse without conversation. The only sound was Jim braking for pedestrians. They inched down Beacon Hill, swung onto Tremont Street, then drove through the Washington Mall.

"That your clarinet in the window, Rhys?" Moe tried to part the gloom as they passed a pawn shop cluttered with brass horns, glittering rings, and white-gold watches.

"Could be, Moe. Traded it in for smoke and mirrors." Rhys's glib response was deflected by a flat smile.

"Tina." Moe looked over his shoulder from his front-seat harness. "Put that checklist away and enjoy the view. Do you think Marie Antoinette was crocheting on her way to the guillotine? Hey, when you haven't got a Chinaman's chance, the case is easy. We'll try it nice and loose. And you never know what a jury will do."

Moe wanted to let them in on the Wilson tape, but he didn't know quite how to broach it. There had to be a proper opening. It was blatant hearsay. And Wilson was dead. But the Aubrey journal—that was something else. Despite his gallows humor, down deep Moe was agonizing. Loyalty to an old friend. Duty. The two were in conflict. Moe knew it came down to a question of basics. He had to present every shred of credible evidence he could find on behalf of his clients.

They arrived at Post Office Square expecting an armada of stretch limos from Hovington, Sturdevant, Holmes & Galvin. A mild disappointment. Their adversaries alighted from cabs or walked. Carter Hovington carried his own bag. They caught sight of Stu Trimble, Andrea Schneiderman, and others. A galaxy of talent descended on the gray granite portals of the Federal Building.

"Carter is a master of the ploy," Rhys observed. "Potential jurors will be checking in and he wouldn't be seen dead in a limo. They hoof it, down dress. The brie and Chardonnay come later."

Moe wondered where Galvin was.

Two charter buses stopped in the Square and discharged a full complement of passengers. The Portuguese families—grim-faced men in dark rumpled suits, women in nondescript dresses, some carrying babies, others leading children by the hand.

Tina shook her head as she watched retarded children being helped from the bus. In their innocence they looked strangely happy, as if embarking on a Sunday outing.

"I suppose a person has a right to attend his own trial," she observed lamely. "I'd have preferred just the parents, and maybe have them bring the children, briefly, for shock value. Having them hanging around, sniffling, coughing, crying, will turn the jury off."

"That's the least of our worries," said Rhys. "If we don't survive Hovington's motion for summary judgment, we're dead. There'll be no jury. It'll be over before the morning recess. We got enough evidence to at least put in a *prima facie* case," he added. "Sure, evidence is weighted so much in Gammett's favor the scales damn near hit the bottom. But there's always the issue of credibility. Any factual conflict, pro or con, has to be resolved by the jury. They're the ultimate arbiter of the facts. Thank God."

"But that putz Baron—excuse me, Tina," Moe said. "Even if he rules in our favor, it's still no bed of roses. He'll string us out. It's the luck of the draw, winding up with that judicial lackey." Moe shook his head. "Too bad we didn't pull Judge Roberta Quinlan. Now, there's a broad with heart. She'd find for Faust."

◘

Courtroom 12 was as somber and austere as it was meant to be. A bronze American Eagle incised in walnut paneling above the judge's bench glowered down with an imperial stare.

The uniformed bailiffs directed the families to their hardwood seats with as much bluster and authority as they could muster.

Moe wheeled himself inside the enclosure reserved for members of the bar. Tina and Rhys followed.

"We'll lead with our best witness," Tina said. "I've worked with Dr. Meideros for three solid days, gone over every inch of the depositions. He's got a photoretentive mind and knows what's expected. Most important, he's been in front of Baron before. Won't get sandbagged this time. He'll set the stage for the parents' testimony."

Andrea Schneiderman, Chip, and Carter Hovington came in, exchanged polite nods with the plaintiffs' lawyers, then settled at the table reserved for defense counsel. Rhys could see the Hovington entourage dispersed strategically among the spectators and the families—lawyers, analysts, psychologists, notepads at the ready.

And Rhys knew that Hovington's hirelings would have done their homework and investigated each prospective juror. Nothing was left to chance in selecting or eliminating the six jurors who would sit in judgment. Those finally seated would best reflect Gammett's mercantile philosophy. And then the defense could sit back and wait, witnesses on call. The plaintiffs had the burden to go forward. Also, the burden to persuade. Hovington could test and sift, rebut and cross-examine, expose weaknesses, sidestep traps, introduce motions to exclude or to strike, grinding the plaintiffs' evidence until it was threadbare. And Hovington had the world's best experts at his beck and call. If it got that far.

"There is no such thing as impartiality," Carter Hovington had admonished his group. "Pick jurors who are business-oriented—penny-pinching housewives, law-and-order Caucasians. We'll make their prejudices work to our advantage. If you get stuck with a black, make sure he's Uncle Tom. No Latinos. No collegians. No *chip on the shoulder* mentalities."

And the defense psychologists would study every mannerism of those selected—crossing of arms could signify rejection, soft features might characterize sensitivity toward the plaintiffs' plight, or some stern young visage might signal defiance, a railing against the status quo.

Moe glanced back. The courtroom was packed. But he failed to see Frank Galvin. And that was strange. Galvin was still listed as the defendant attorney of record, and there had been no motion to strike his appearance.

"Quiet, please. Quiet!" the chief bailiff barked toward the spectators. "Any further talking or disturbance, and all of you will be cleared from the courtroom. This is a court of law, not a public meeting house."

There was a muffled stillness. Even the children sensed the reprimand.

Clerk Sheila Finnegan looked up from her desk in front of the bench. She nodded toward a side entrance, a cue that the judge would make his heralded appearance.

317

"All rise," intoned the bailiff.

Judge Chester Baron entered in full stride, nose angled toward the ceiling, his black robe trailing.

"Look at that imperious cretin," Moe whispered.

"Hear ye, hear ye!" The bailiff chanted. "The United States District Court sitting in Boston is now in session, the right honorable Chester L. Baron presiding. Give your attention, draw near, and you shall be heard."

"Your Honor," Sheila Finnegan read from the court docket, "the first order of business, civil case 88-454: *Ramondi et al., plaintiffs versus Gammett Industries and Universal Multi-Tech Limited, defendants.*"

"Gentlemen," Baron said amicably, "and, ah yes, ladies"—he looked at Andrea Schneiderman, then at Tina Alvarez—"I think you have all been before me on past occasions. Now let's determine at the outset who is trying the case for the plaintiffs and who's going to represent the defendants. Mr. Katz?"

Moe wheeled his chair squarely in front of the bench.

"I will try the medical aspect for the plaintiffs, Judge," Moe said.

For a moment the judge looked beyond Moe and took in the crowded spectator section, obviously perturbed at the overflow of visitors. He leaned forward to Sheila Finnegan and whispered, "Miss Finnegan, there'll be no standees in my courtroom. This isn't Boston Garden. And the potential jurors, where are they to sit? Tell the bailiffs to *clear* the courtroom."

"Your Honor," Sheila said in her soothing way, "just a thought. Why not dispense with the preliminary stuff?" She held up a blue-backed document. "Defendants' motion for summary judgment. We may not need a jury."

Baron rubbed the end of his nose. "That means I'll have to make an immediate ruling."

"Not necessarily," she replied tactfully. "Perhaps Your Honor could listen to arguments on both sides. Receive the briefs, then declare a recess. Have the law clerks check the case citations, research the law, then prepare a memorandum and final order for your signature. Whole thing should be over by noontime."

"Uh, yes, Miss Finnegan." He cleared his throat. "But tell the bailiffs there'll be *no* standing. I don't want a stampede."

Moe was still sitting in front of the bench. He waited for an opening. "And, Your Honor—"he began.

"Please, Counselor!" the judge boomed. "I'm discussing an important matter with the Clerk."

"I thought you were finished, Your Honor."

The judge glared down from his perch with a coldness designed to intimidate counsel and witness alike.

Moe removed his glasses and returned the icy stare. Awkward seconds went by.

Then Baron said, almost in a conversational tone, "Do you feel up to it, Mr. Katz? Trying the case, I mean?"

"Well, Your Honor, my colleague Miss Alvarez will handle the opening statement to the jury and interrogate the lay witnesses, and I'll handle the medical and cross-examination. You are aware of my associate." Moe swung his glasses toward Tina, who rose quickly.

"Yes. A competent young Portia." Baron oozed with chauvinistic cordiality.

"And, Mr. Hovington?" Baron said crisply.

Carter Hovington snapped to his feet. There was an imperceptible exchange of glances, but nothing to hint at the fact that the senior Hovington had been the swing vote on the judicial nominating committee that had landed Baron his federal judgeship. The bond was there and it could be made manifest in subtle ways.

"Your Honor." Carter Hovington addressed the judge. "Frank Galvin, who has handled this case since it started, has been detained on other serious matters." Hovington slowly approached the bench. He was dressed impeccably, with a dark-blue suit, white button-down shirt, discreet pale-blue tie. With his pearl-gray hair and perfect posture, he cut an impressive figure.

"I therefore solicit this honorable court to accept the withdrawal of Mr. Galvin's appearance and substitute it with those of Carter Hovington, Jr., who will be lead counsel, and Andrea Schneiderman as first assistant."

Chip and Andrea Schneiderman stood.

"I, of course, will assist at the defense table and will plead defendants' motion for summary judgment."

Hovington gave the substitution notices to Sheila Finnegan, who handed them to the judge. Baron studied them with furrowed brow.

"Fine." The judge looked up. "Any objection, Mr. Katz?"

It was a surprise to Tina and Rhys, but Moe had half-expected it. Galvin had been giving him signals all along. Moe looked back into the sea of faces. Still no Galvin.

"No objection," Moe said quietly.

"Okay," said the judge with a slight smile. "The first order of business is defendants' motion for summary judgment. I think this can be best handled in chambers. Miss Finnegan, tell the court reporter to bring in her equipment so we can formalize the record."

"With all due respect, Your Honor," Moe interrupted the bailiff, who was about to declare a recess, "all matters pertaining to this trial should now be held in open court."

The defiance had been laid out on the table for all to see.

Baron commenced a slow burn. His face reddened. His neck muscles tensed and his beefy jowls worked heavily. He closed his eyes tightly. But when he opened them, the little Jew boy was still there—a cinder in his eye that wouldn't go away.

"If that is your desire, Mr. Katz." He rocked in his chair, fighting to curb his indignation.

"That's the plaintiffs' request, Your Honor."

"All right." The judge removed his glasses, inspecting for some minuscule spotting. "Please call the case, Miss Finnegan. We shall proceed."

◘

Galvin made three unsuccessful attempts to telephone Sabrina Bok-Sahn. He called the BBC, but they knew of no one named Veronica Smith in their commercial department. He tried to call the Bok-Sahn family in Rangoon, but the overseas operator couldn't understand him and the call did not go through. Finally, he reached Bernie McCafferty's secretary at his London office, but she said Mr. McCafferty was on holiday.

Everyone seemed to be on the dark side of the moon.

∎

He left his car with the doorman, purchased a spray of green carnations at the lobby florist, and took the express elevator to Hovington, Sturdevant, Holmes & Galvin.

He paused in the hallway. The inner foyer never ceased to impress, with its rich fruitwood paneling, the priceless Caravaggio. The glistening black tiles echoed as he walked toward Julie Hedren's station. She smiled as she always had.

"For you, Julie." He produced the spray from behind his back.

She gasped. He had never addressed her by her first name before. "Oh!" she exclaimed, her cool Viking veneer suddenly deserting her. "My, aren't they beautiful. Green's my favorite color."

"Matches your eyes." Galvin broke into an easy smile.

Galvin reached for his messages and noticed a diamond on Julie Hedren's left ring finger.

"So." He rotated her hand, the blue ice shimmered in the glint of the overhead light. "Who's the lucky guy?"

"While you were away." She smiled lamely. "A lawyer at Bingham, Thorndike, Crane, and McCauliffe."

"Fine old Brahmin firm," Galvin said. "My best to you, Julie."

"You have tons of calls." The secretarial timbre returned to her voice. "Courtney has most of them."

He flipped through the messages hoping for a note from Sabrina. Nothing.

"Lot going on," she said. "The Gammett case was called for trial."

"I know," he said, still leafing through the pink slips.

"Will you be going up to the courthouse?" she asked.

"Unlikely."

And with that he kissed Julie Hedren's hand. "Congratulations," he said.

In his office, Galvin removed his suit jacket, loosened his tie, and sank wearily into his chair. He tilted his head back, propped his feet up on his desk, and closed his eyes, remaining motionless for several minutes.

"Cy Sturdevant is here to see you," Courtney's precise voice came over the intercom.

Galvin had half-expected it. "Send him in," he said, both hands bracketed behind his head, his eyes still shut.

Cy was an incessant company man. Nearing eighty, he had boundless energy, and he was a match for the junior associates in logging business hours.

"Galvin, my boy," he greeted as he entered with a brisk stride. "Glad you're back. We lost touch for a few days. I trust you were on the clock."

"No. The meter wasn't running this time, Cy." Galvin opened his eyes, but his unprofessional posture remained the same.

Cy was quick to detect a weary catch in Galvin's voice.

"You look a little tired," he said, searching for a clue.

"Just sitting here doing a lot of thinking."

"The Gammett case?"

"Perhaps."

"You know, Galvin." Cy started cracking his knuckles and rocking heel to toe. "I agree with Carter. You've worked night and day on that litigation. You got too close to the case. Step aside. We've got more important stuff."

Galvin sighed but said nothing.

"I think I'll run down to the courthouse and see how Carter is doing," Cy said cheerily. "He expects a favorable ruling from Baron. They go back a long way, you know. Want to come along?"

"Think I'll skip it, Cy. Knowing the right judge sure as hell beats having a good case."

◘

Carter Hovington never was lacking in eloquence. When the occasion demanded, he could switch it on like a thermostat. And now his argument was cogent and persuasive. Even Moe Katz was impressed. Judge Baron seemed to hang on every word. Carter outlined the gaping holes in the plaintiffs' offer of proof, reciting gross deficiencies in the quality of expert testimony, noting that the vast compendium of medical literature failed to cite a single instance of congenital deformity due to Gammett's product. "Not one case. Not one!" Carter shook his finger.

"As you know, Your Honor, the plaintiffs' burden is two-fold." As he began to sum up his motion, his voice was on an ascending roll. "They must prove by a fair preponderance of the credible evidence that Lyosin is causative of their injuries, and this, I respectfully submit, they cannot do. Moreover, they must prove by the same quality of evidence that the defendant Gammett was aware or should have been aware of the likelihood of its product to cause the incurred damage.

"The plaintiffs' entire case lacks such proof. It is as flimsy as the paper upon which their affidavit is written." Hovington slapped the lectern in front of the jury rail, sending several papers spiraling to the floor. The *thwack* resounded ominously throughout the hushed courtroom.

"Your Honor." He removed his glasses, folded them, and tucked them into his vest pocket. "I ask you, most respectfully, to grant the defendant's motion for summary judgment and to dismiss the plaintiffs' case."

The families leaned forward. They had no legal training, but they sensed that their day in court hung in the balance.

Carter Hovington remained in place, allowing the weight and acuity of his words to settle. He then pivoted like an officer on dress parade and walked at a jaunty clip toward the approving glances of his associates.

The judge paused for several seconds, then said, "Thank you, Mr. Hovington. Mr. Katz?" His voice was suffused with "Top this if you can" affability.

Moe wheeled into position and lowered the microphone to his level. It sputtered and coughed; loud staccato sounds punctured the awesome calm left by Hovington's persuasive delivery.

"Your Honor." Moe bent into the microphone, cocking his head, birdlike, to peer up at the judge. "As you well know, if there is *any* evidence, no matter how slight, favoring the plaintiffs' premise on causation, then it suffices to establish a *prima facie* case. The same is true on prior knowledge."

"I'm aware of the law, Mr. Katz." The cordiality suddenly drained from the judge's voice. "Mr. Hovington set forth cogent arguments stating that your proffered evidence is so lacking in merit that it creates no factual issue for a jury to decide."

Moe sucked in his breath, pushed away from the microphone, and wheeled as close to the bench as he could, still retaining Baron in his sight. "I stand by my affidavit," he said. "Dr. Rafael Meideros will testify on causation."

"Is Dr. Meideros also going to address the subject of the defendant's knowledge?" Baron's challenge came rumbling down.

Moe glanced around and cleared his throat, then refocused on Baron. "We will prove," he said slowly, "through the defendant's *own* witnesses that Gammett, its agents, servants, and employees, had *actual* knowledge of the propensity of its product to cause the *exact* harm suffered by the plaintiffs."

Carter Hovington smirked. Even Rhys and Tina held their breath.

"I'll hold you to that, Mr. Katz," Baron said. Moe was as far out on the legal limb as he could get. "With that in mind," the judge went on, "I am constrained to allow the plaintiffs to go forward. But you can, Mr. Hovington, renew your motion at the completion of the plaintiffs' evidence. I will deal with it at that time in the form of a motion for a directed verdict."

Baron was obviously displeased. Moe Katz, temporarily at least, had boxed him in.

"I will deny the summary judgment. The case will proceed. We shall impanel a jury." The judge banged his gavel. "Bailiffs, clear the courtroom."

◘

It was well after six when Hovington's briefcase brigade entered through the outside foyer and streamed down the corridors to assemble in the law library. Galvin stood by his office door and watched them troop in. They had to be all of thirty strong. He nodded to Chip and Carter. There was a clubby buoyancy about the group but not one of final victory. Galvin could read their faces and demeanor and it was one of guarded optimism. Galvin retreated to his office. He would leave them to their tomes and documents. The chef had already made the sandwiches and snacks. There would be no dining at the roof garden. It was an evening for work.

A little after eight, Cy Sturdevant came into Galvin's office. "Superb," he said. "Carter was superb."

"Oh?" Galvin said. "He won the summary judgment?"

"Heavens no. Hell, if the case went down that easily, our dog and pony show would be over. The meter would stop running." Cy chuckled.

◘

Galvin stopped at the lobby newsstand for the evening paper. He was about to head toward the underground garage when he spotted Mallory, Frobisher, and Symes coming through the revolving doors. He watched them in the mirror over the cash register.

A young man, whom Galvin couldn't place, followed, carrying two briefcases. They studied the lobby directory and made their way toward the brassy gleam of the elevators.

Galvin had heard that they were staying at the Parker House. He and his liaison, Katie Doherty, chief reservations clerk, went back a long way. No one else from England was registered there. She had also checked the other major hotels. No. Dr. Corsini. There were several Orientals but no one named Bok-Sahn and no one fitting her description.

Sabrina had his number, office and private line. Where was she? She should have called.

41

G alvin was startled to receive a call on his cellular phone. He had switched to a new service the previous day. Even Julie Hedren and his secretaries didn't know the number. He had to write it down so he wouldn't forget it himself. There was a temptation to let it ring. Rush-hour traffic and telephonic discourse didn't mix.

He pushed a button to enable him to talk without detaching the receiver.

"This is the overseas operator. There is a call for a Mr. Frank Galvin." The voice was precise British, as clear as if it came from the corner drugstore.

"Tell me, operator, what's the locus of this call?" Galvin asked cautiously.

There were a few seconds of silence.

"Staffordshire, Coventry Township." The enunciation was "rain in Spain" perfect.

Galvin did some mental gymnastics. Now 7:05 A.M. in Boston, about noon back in England. Sensing that he would need a tape of the conversation, he flipped the recorder button.

"Yes. This is Frank Galvin."

More silence.

"Galvin? Sabrina." It was a morning for surprises. He could recognize her satin-laced voice anywhere. But this morning it was pensive, uncertain.

"Sabrina, are you okay?"

There was hesitation.

"Look," he said, "just answer yes or no. Let me do the talking."

"No! No!" she said too quickly. "Really, I'm fine. I'm here with Soong and . . ."

"I see." Galvin was getting edgy. "Just a tea-and-crumpets call from the Midlands."

He stopped at a pedestrian light in Government Center and tried to gather his thoughts.

"Galvin." Sabrina became solemn. "I think you are about to do something very, very foolish."

The traffic light turned green and he started forward.

"The case in Boston." A dragon-lady quality replaced the velvet. "If you truly have feelings for me, you'll do nothing to impede the logical outcome of that trial. The repercussions could be most unfortunate."

"What repercussions?"

"Mr. Galvin." A new voice came on the line. It was crisp, button-down Anglo-Saxon. "Don't perjure yourself to the court just to spite your client. Sabrina took you into her confidence. Don't be a cad toward a lovely lady by now misrepresenting your involvement and placing your clients in a dangerous position. Not very sporting, my dear fellow. Unethical, not to mention criminal ramifications."

No overt threats. He was dealing with people who knew their craft.

"What kind of perjury am I about to commit?"

"Come, Counselor. Right now I'd say you're being rather precious. It will be your word against that of reputable people. And one never likes a turncoat, an informer. You Irish should appreciate that."

"Put Sabrina back on." Galvin bristled. "I want to make sure she's all right."

There was a long pause. Interminable seconds.

"Yes, I'm here Galvin," she said. "I wanted you to come with me. You should have. I must say good-bye. Again, don't do anything foolish. Think of yourself, your career. And, if you really care, think of me. You're a sweet guy, Galvin. As we say in Gaelic, '*Kara makree, is lor dun oluck.*' "

A decisive click.

Galvin punched the operator number several times. Nothing. *Kara* meant *dear*, he knew that. Maybe even went beyond—an expression of ultimate affection. But, save for a few household greetings, his knowledge of the language was almost nonexistent. *Kara makree, is lor dun oluck.* He repeated it several times.

He replayed the final portion and jotted it down phonetically. He'd get a read from Lee Maguire, professor of Irish Studies at Boston College.

What irony. Perjury. Fraud on the court. Turncoat. *Your word against that of reputable people.* He thought about it. On this he'd lose.

And they'd have some embarrassing garbage to spill onto the floor. He shook his head in disbelief. Some tides aren't worth swimming against.

Kara makree. He churned the phrase over in his mind. A term of endearment? A fond farewell? Perhaps. But why Gaelic?

As he drove past the Federal Building, something caught his eye. He noted Moe's station wagon parked in a handicapped parking area next to the front steps. Jim, Moe's chauffeur, was in the driver's seat talking with someone who was standing alongside the car. It shouldn't have been unusual—but the man at Jim's window was ambulance and limo driver Eric Wooden.

Galvin pondered the odd connection as he rode the courthouse elevator to the twelfth floor, arriving shortly after the judge had declared the morning recess. But he soon forgot about Wooden and Jim when he saw the families with their children gathered in morose huddles in the corridor. From the looks on their grim faces, he knew that their case was not going well.

He recognized Hector Ramondi and his mother. Despite the boy's size, she held him up to the water fountain, trying to find the spigot handle. Her face was distraught and dark circles had formed beneath her eyes.

"Here," Galvin said. "Allow me."

The boy gulped voraciously, splashing water on his poplin windbreaker and blue flannel pants. He grinned and giggled and his lidded mongoloid eyes oscillated wildly.

"Mrs. Ramondi?" Galvin said quietly. He continued to hold the handle while she in turn took a drink.

"*Obrigado.*" She dabbed her mouth with her thumb and forefinger, then squinted. "Aren't you . . . ?"

"Yes. I'm Attorney Frank Galvin. We met quite some time ago, at your home in Fall River."

She said nothing. The silence was awkward. Galvin patted Hector Ramondi on the head. The boy's eyes were now wide open and his grin broadened.

A buzzer sounded throughout the gray corridor. "Court is coming in," the bailiff at the electronic check-in station barked. "Please take your seats. There'll be no standing."

Galvin filed in with the others, squeezing into the last row at the end next to the jury rail.

Moe Katz's wheelchair faced the judge's bench. Rhys and Tina assembled documents on the counsel table. Carter, Chip Hovington, and Andrea Schneiderman sat nearby awaiting the judge's entrance.

"All rise!" the chief bailiff cried. There was a muffled clack in the spectator section. The judge came in, his robe billowing.

"Be seated," the bailiff commanded. Again the muffled clack.

"Now, let's see where we were." The judge's voice was filled with boredom. "We'll resume the direct examination of Dr. Meideros. Counselor"—he looked down at Moe Katz—"you may proceed."

Galvin searched the faces of the jury as Meideros made his way toward the witness stand. Six jurors and two alternates, all middle-aged, Caucasian. Three women and five men. It was a defendant jury. Galvin could read it. They were bored stiff and couldn't wait to conclude and be on their way. There was a lot of eye rubbing and stifled yawns. And it was only eleven in the morning.

Moe wheeled to the lectern situated just to the right of the last juror. He adjusted the microphone and watched Dr. Meideros take his seat.

"Remember," the judge said, leaning down toward the doctor, "you are still under oath, and your testimony is being recorded under the pains and penalties of perjury."

"I understand." Meideros looked up at the judge.

Moe didn't appreciate the admonition. Especially in front of the jury. From now on in, the judge would get rougher. He brushed an invisible strand of hair from his bald pate. A nervous preliminary. Like an athlete going through a superstitious ritual.

He glanced back at the spectators.

And there he was. Frank Galvin. Seated on the outside in the last row. Their eyes met. And Moe caught something else. An imperceptible nod. Or was his imagination playing tricks? No. The communion was there. Was he reading this correctly? He hoped so. He took a deep breath and faced Meideros.

Dr. Meideros fidgeted in the witness box while awaiting inter-rogation. As soon as things got under way, the doctor knew that his testimony was being lost on the jury. He sensed their inattention. Moe asked the right questions, technically and legally correct, but the disquisition lacked spontaneity, the germinating spark of credibility. Any sympathy toward Moe was diffused by his bron-chial voice and gnome-like appearance. He failed to instill confi-dence. Meideros envisioned Carter Hovington not even gracing his testimony with cross-examination—it sounded that wooden.

Moe had to have sensed it, too. "With your honor's indulgence," he addressed the judge, "I would like to suspend with Dr. Meideros at this time and call, as part of my case in chief, the defendant's medical director, Dr. Sabrina Bok-Sahn."

Carter Hovington snapped to his feet. "Objection, Your Honor! This maneuver is highly irregular."

"Yes." Baron seized the opening. "Mr. Katz, you commenced with this witness this morning. There is sequential protocol that must be observed. The doctor will conclude his testimony. Mr. Hovington is entitled to the right of *immediate* cross-examination."

"Judge"—Hovington waved his hand cavalierly—"I have no objection to suspending at this time, if the witness will resume the stand later today and my rights of cross-examination will in no way be abridged." Hovington was not being generous. His concession curried favor with the jury, and he too needed time to prepare the final cross-examination or decide to waive it.

"As your honor knows," Hovington said, resting his hand on the jury rail, "and as Mr. Katz is aware, the Federal Rules of Civil Procedure do not allow an adverse party to call an officer of the defendant if, in fact, such officer is not domiciled within a hundred-mile radius of the court. Also, Mr. Katz did not list Dr. Bok-Sahn on his list of witnesses that your honor requested be submitted prior to trial. Dr. Bok-Sahn *was* a resident of London, England. She has been missing since a boating accident several weeks ago. Mr. Katz *knew* all this. He is out of order making such a request in front of the jury, the implication being we are somehow making her unavailable. I strenuously object to this conduct."

Before the judge could start his judicial chastisement, Moe turned from the lectern and wheeled toward the document table.

Judge Baron waited.

Tina and Rhys exchanged baffled glances.

Moe selected a black-cased deposition from the pile of documents and wheeled back toward the lectern.

"I assume you want to read the deposition testimony of Dr. Bok-Sahn." The judge's voice was pinched with impatience.

"Excerpts, Your Honor."

The judge looked at Carter Hovington. "Well, I suppose he has that right, since the witness is unavailable."

Carter was now going to box in his opponent. Moe had accepted his concession, but it came with a condition. "No question about that, Judge," Carter said, "but if we dispense with the logical sequence of testimony to accommodate plaintiffs' counsel, then I respectfully submit that he *must* read into evidence *all* of Dr. Bok-Sahn's testimony, not merely tailored segments."

The jury moaned as Hovington held up his deposition copy— three inches thick, give or take a centimeter. Their collective displeasure was directed toward Moe Katz. Exactly as Carter Hovington had planned.

The judge rocked in his chair. "Mr. Katz? I think Mr. Hovington's request is well taken. An *accommodation* for an *accommodation*."

Moe fingered the deposition. He had underscored the few pertinent sections he intended to read. It would have taken only ten or fifteen minutes. But three or more hours of canned testimony would be a tiring and ineffectual monologue. The jury would be turned off in half an hour, asleep by noon. The judge and Hovington had successfully deflected the thrust and timing of Moe's case.

Moe glanced back in Galvin's direction. Again the slight nod.

"All right," Moe surrendered quietly, "but with your honor's permission, may I read the questions and have my associate Miss Alvarez take the witness stand and read the response, as if she were Dr. Bok-Sahn?"

"Again, this is highly irregular." The judge frowned.

"It's done every day, Judge. Roberta Quinlan allowed this procedure just a few months ago."

"Do I look like Judge Quinlan?" Baron barked. "Your request is addressed to the sound discretion of the court. I can either agree or decline. Mr. Katz, are you saying that you're not quite up to reading an hour or two of deposition testimony to this jury?"

"Yes, Judge, that's what I'm saying."

"Mr. Hovington?"

"I have no objection, Your Honor." Again, the generous concession.

◘

The day droned on; it was late afternoon. Moe was laboring. He constantly patted his bald head with his handkerchief and his glasses kept getting fogged. His raspy monotone dwindled at times to inaudible queries. Tina tried to stress comments she deemed important, to establish eye contact with the slumberous jury.

"One last question," Moe said.

The jurors emitted a collective sigh of relief.

Moe left the lectern and positioned his wheelchair in mid-center of the jury rail. He waited two, three, four . . . seven, eight seconds, until Moe felt his stop-and-go tactic had sufficiently roused the jurors from their lethargy. He assessed each one, front row and back.

" 'Question to Dr. Bok-Sahn.' " He cleared his throat. " 'Do you have any knowledge from any source, whatsoever, either past

332

or present, that the drug Lyosin and/or its chemical components, including correiga extract, is capable of producing congenital deformities in offspring of those consuming either the drug Lyosin or correiga extract?' "

Tina, still puzzled at Moe's tack, read the final response. " 'No. I have no such knowledge.' "

It was the end of the road. Moe was a tired, aging wizard who had run out of pulleys and mirrors and the green smoke of money. He had a sense of tragic defeat and started to shiver. He clamped both arms around his frail body to keep from trembling.

◻

Galvin called Professor Maguire during the afternoon break. "Give me the spelling again, Lee, I must have had it wrong."

Galvin jotted it down. *Charia mo chroi, is leor nol don eolach.*

Galvin looked at the note. "You sure of the translation, Lee?"

"Positive."

"And you say it comes from someone proficient in the Celtic tongue."

"It's an ancient expression."

"Thanks, Lee. My path is now downhill."

"And may the wind be at your back. *Slan abhaile*, good-bye and safe home.

"I'll need it, Lee. Much thanks."

42

"I call to the witness stand Mr. Frank Galvin." Moe Katz's voice was a whisper.

It took a while for the stratagem to register. There was a hush, an apprehensive stillness, then a muffled rumble, like distant thunder.

"Your Honor, this is preposterous!" Carter Hovington jumped to his feet. He shot a glance over his shoulder. He had not seen Galvin enter the courtroom.

The judge was caught by surprise. Tina Alvarez and Rhys Jameson were equally baffled. The trial and Moe were grinding to a beleaguered and ironic end; they were sure of it.

"Your Honor," Hovington said, quickly assessing his adversary's tack; he had to regain control of the trial. "I think you will agree that this morning I allowed Mr. Katz every accommodation, every courtesy. Now he's engaging in utter nonsense. Mr. Galvin is attorney of record defending Universal and Gammett. He's not subject to call as a witness in any proceeding, let alone this one. There is no rule, absolutely no precedent in my vast experience as a member of the bar—and, Your Honor, that goes back forty years—for such breach of protocol. You simply can't call as *your* witness the other side's counsel. That's so basic, it defies argument!"

Hovington should have requested a bench conference out of hearing of the jury, but he had to get his shots in now and put the clamp on Moe Katz, who, like an outclassed club fighter, was disturbingly resilient.

The judge looked amused. He grinned and shook his head as if he were recalling an old joke. "Mr. Katz." He was on the verge of a chuckle. "Are you serious?"

"I am, Your Honor."

"Can you cite any precedent whatsoever for calling your adversary of record to the witness stand?"

Moe wheeled toward the bench. "Excuse me." He flapped his hand toward Carter Hovington. "You're in my way. I can't see the judge."

Hovington stepped aside, sweeping his hand toward the bench in mock courtesy.

"To answer your first question, Judge, I don't need a case citation or rule of law to call a witness. Mr. Hovington here mentioned something about basics. Well, this goes back seven hundred and fifty years to the Magna Carta. I can call *any* witness in my client's behalf. This is a hearing before a jury of peers. To answer the second part of your question, Judge, Mr. Galvin is *not* the attorney of record. Everyone seems to have developed a short memory. Mr. Galvin's appearance was withdrawn. That was the first order of business."

Andrea Schneiderman passed Carter a note. He examined it quickly.

"Now," Moe continued, "if a witness has relevant information—"

"Your Honor," Hovington interrupted, "there are two Circuit Court of Appeals cases—*Vacarro versus United States*, reported at 258 Federal 2nd, page 1153, a 1983 case, and *Bangor Freight Lines versus Interstate Commerce Commission*, decided only last week in our first circuit. The adverse party in the *Vacarro* case sought to summon the U.S. Attorney as a witness." Carter glanced at the note again. "It was not allowed. Any information gained through investigation, or otherwise, during the pendency of litigation was deemed attorney's work product, specifically privileged from interrogation. The court quashed the summons. That was a criminal case, Your Honor. The latter was a civil case, wherein the plaintiff sought to call as a witness the chief litigation attorney of the U.S. Justice Department. Same result."

The judge peered down over his glasses. "Mr. Katz, is Mr. Galvin under summons?"

"He is not, Your Honor."

"Is he even in the courtroom?" the judge inquired.

"I am here, Your Honor." Galvin stepped out from the last row.

Tina, Rhys, the defense personnel, the spectators—everyone in the courtroom issued a collective gasp, then an excited murmur.

Carter Hovington's face turned bright pink as he eyed Galvin.

"Mr. Galvin," the judge said, trying to regain control of his courtroom, "you are associated with the defense law firm, are you not?"

Galvin advanced several paces. "I am, Your Honor."

"And you worked in the preparation of this case since its inception. Is that a fair statement?"

"It is, Your Honor."

"Then I rule"—Baron reached for his gavel—"that you are privileged from being called as a witness in behalf of the plaintiffs. This is consistent with the law in this jurisdiction and, I dare say, in all jurisdictions throughout the United States. Mr. Galvin, you may return to your seat."

Carter Hovington tried not to show emotion, particularly relief.

Moe spun his chair around so he was positioned at an oblique angle to the jury. He looked at Galvin. Behind his thick-lensed glasses, his jelly-bean eyes danced quizzically. The jurors leaned forward. Raw voltage had jolted the case; no eye rubbing now.

"To the extent permissible, I choose to waive the privilege, Your Honor," Galvin said evenly. "I stand ready and willing to testify."

"Objection, Your Honor! This whole thing is absolutely absurd!" Carter Hovington looked up at Judge Baron. His eyes narrowed, his jaw tensed, and he folded his hands behind his back. Baron did not mistake the stance. Carter Hovington was calling in all the chits.

Moe Katz waited. Nothing could be heard but the echoes of Hovington's dissent.

The judge emitted an injudicious sigh. "Mr. Katz, do you seriously wish to proceed along these lines?"

"Most seriously, Your Honor." Moe felt a tightening in his chest and a numbing sensation spreading down his left arm. He needed his medication. But the case would stall if he requested a recess or showed any sign of weakening.

Tina and Rhys saw beads of perspiration popping out on Moe's forehead, and under the arms of his gray tweed suit widening sweat stains became evident. Tina started to rise.

Moe waved her off.

Andrea Schneiderman passed Carter Hovington another document. He scanned it quickly.

"Your Honor," he blurted, "here it is." He shook the paper. "*The Code of Legal Ethics.* The privilege belongs to the *client*, and to no one else. I'm quoting from the Code. The attorney is under an ethical duty *not* to disclose privileged communications to anyone and *must* claim the privilege unless the client waives it. . . . And, Your Honor," Hovington added with a tone of finality, "the clients here aren't waiving a thing."

"I agree." The judge reached for his gavel to end the day's proceedings. "That's black-letter law, right, Mr. Katz?"

"I've been around a long time, judge, maybe too long. I'm well aware of the Code. But the Code has two important exceptions. If Mr. Hovington will read a little further, it says that a document which preexists the attorney-client relationship does not become privileged merely because it's handed over to a lawyer . . . and when an attorney condones perjury, the privilege can't be invoked."

Baron smiled wearily. "Mr. Katz, you're not saying that Mr. Galvin condoned perjury or that there is some preexisting document out there that might help your case?"

Moe waited several seconds. "Judge, that's precisely what I'm saying."

The judge looked at the courtroom clock. Four-thirty. The late-afternoon sun slanted through the splotched windowpanes, and eddies of dust floated in lazy circles. It was time to adjourn. He didn't like what was happening.

"How long do you intend to be with this witness, Mr. Katz?"

"Ten minutes, Judge. Fifteen at the most."

Baron was on the spot. During three trial days, he had hurried Tina Alvarez's and Moe Katz's presentation, forcing their witnesses to testify without interruption until six o'clock. Adjournment this early would look patently biased.

"All right," Baron exhaled. "But my main concern is the jurors. They've been working overtime. Again, Mr. Galvin, do you wish to take the stand?"

"I do, Your Honor."

The judge looked at the jury, arching his eyebrows to signal his displeasure, then glanced at his watch. "For the record, Mr. Hovington, I am constrained to allow the testimony—but you may renew your objection at a later time. Fifteen minutes, Mr. Katz. Proceed."

Galvin seemed at ease, the corners of his mouth curled slightly upward in a look of relaxed contentment. His chiseled features were complemented by his charcoal-gray suit, white Oxford shirt, and plain navy tie. His fingers rested momentarily on the jury rail.

The bailiff approached. "Raise your right hand. Do you swear to tell the truth, the whole truth, and nothing but the truth, so help you God?"

Galvin gave the rail a squeeze as if taking leave of an old friend, then raised his hand with solemn deliberation.

"I do."

Moe Katz wasn't quite sure where he was headed or what questions he was supposed to ask. He would be flying by the seat of his pants.

The jurors leaned forward. Carter Hovington sat ramrod stiff, his mouth drawn in a tight thin line, his eyes locked on Galvin with dark intensity.

Galvin sat down in the witness box, impassive; his face betrayed no emotion. Inside he was dying. More than a few fates were on the line.

"Mr. Galvin." Moe packed his failing voice with every ounce of energy he could muster. "Were you here today when Miss Alvarez and I read the deposition testimony of Gammett and Universal's medical director, Dr. Sabrina Bok-Sahn?"

"I was."

"Did you hear the entire testimony? I think it covered some three, three and a half hours."

"I did."

"Now, so that the jury and his honor will understand your role in this case and the nature of your testimony, and that of Dr. Bok-Sahn, and the role of my colleague Miss Alvarez—is Miss Alvarez the same person who conducted Dr. Bok-Sahn's deposition in London, England, that was read here today?"

"She is."

"What were your responsibilities?"

"I was defense attorney for Universal and Gammett. I counseled Dr. Bok-Sahn during her testimony on that occasion."

Carter Hovington was doing a slow countdown, ready to explode. Galvin couldn't be doing this, he thought. The fucking ingratitude. But he didn't want to erupt in front of the jury. With a half-century of lawyering instinct, he scribbled Galvin's responses and started to formulate his cross-examination. Galvin would not get off unscathed.

"Did you know Dr. Bok-Sahn very well?" Moe inquired.

"Yes, I did." Galvin's voice was calm yet authoritative, like an airline captain telling passengers to fasten their seat belts.

The judge shook his robed sleeve and studied his watch.

"Now, Mr. Galvin, I'm again going to read excerpts from Dr. Bok-Sahn's testimony." Moe placed the acrylic-bound deposition on the small shelf of his wheelchair and adjusted his glasses.

"By Miss Alvarez: 'Question: Do you have any knowledge from any source, whatsoever, either past or present, that the drug Lyosin and/or its chemical components, including correiga extract, is capable of producing congenital deformities in offspring of those consuming either the drug Lyosin or correiga extract?' Dr. Bok-Sahn. 'Answer: No. I have no such knowledge.' Was that Dr. Bok-Sahn's testimony, under oath, that you heard in London?"

"It was."

"The same testimony that was read here today?"

"The same."

"No doubt in your mind?"

"No doubt."

Moe hesitated. His voice was a death-watch whisper. "Is that particular testimony of Dr. Bok-Sahn's true?"

"No, it is not," Galvin said slowly.

Only the ticking of the courtroom clock could be heard. The jurors continued to lean forward, their eyes riveted on Galvin.

"At the time it was taken in London"—Galvin looked intently at the jurors—"I thought it was true. I subsequently learned that it was not."

It was now black or white. No legal subtleties. Someone was lying.

"Let me explain." Galvin spoke with steady assurance. "About a month after Dr. Bok-Sahn's deposition in London, I learned that she did not tell the truth." He waited several seconds. "I came across information plainly indicating that correiga extract, the source of Lyosin, the drug in question, was capable of producing birth defects in the offspring of those who consumed the raw material.

"A journal written by Dr. Aubrey Gammett, the discoverer of correiga in 1902, contains graphic descriptions of the consequences of the extract's consumption among the Changareet people, a tribe in the country of northeast Burma, the geographical source of correiga. Gammett Industries had this journal in its possession. Neither its contents nor the information concerning possible adverse side effects were communicated to the Food and Drug Administration as required in the investigation of any new drug. In fact, its existence was categorically denied, as you just heard from the deposition testimony of Dr. Bok-Sahn. And, as attorney for the defendants, after I became aware of this information, I failed to supplement our response to the plaintiffs' request for documents as required by the Federal Rules of Civil Procedure. In fact, I did nothing."

Moe cleared his throat, then pretended to study his notes. Now, most important, the final question. *Why?* Why come forward at this late date? Why the delay? But the old rule was sacrosanct. Never ask a question of a witness unless you know the answer. He'd let it go.

Moe's eyes were blurred. He felt as if he was about to collapse. And if he did, he was afraid the jury might think it was all a ploy. They might not be buying Galvin. And Carter Hovington was coiled and waiting. Moe wasn't sure how it would all end. Yet even if Hovington's cross-examination dented Galvin's story, he still had an ace in the hole, the Wilson tape and the bus locker.

"Your witness, Mr. Hovington." Moe's voice faltered, and he wheeled away so the jurors wouldn't detect the welling mist in his eyes. Galvin was destroying himself.

"Mr. Hovington, it's now five o'clock." The judge gathered up his papers. "Do you wish to suspend until tomorrow morning, at which time you may commence your cross-examination?"

Carter underlined some notes on his yellow pad.

"Dad." Chip bent toward his father. "We need to talk this whole thing out with our people. Wrap it now."

Carter Hovington scowled. "Adjourn? That's exactly what Katz thinks we'll do. A twelve-hour reprieve and they'll have every conceivable response down cold. Galvin has to be destroyed—now! And I intend to do it!" Carter grabbed his notepad, and rose to the attack.

"Thank you, Your Honor." He disciplined his voice to a conciliatory tone. "If the court and the jury will be indulgent, I'd like to continue with this witness at this time. My interrogation shouldn't last long."

"You may proceed."

Carter Hovington squared his shoulders and slowly walked toward the witness stand. He stopped near the jury foreman. His manicured hand rested momentarily on the jury rail, then he tapped it lightly. He waited. The jurors waited. The spectators, the bailiffs, the judge waited.

When Carter faced Galvin, his eyes were smoldering cinders.

"Mr. Galvin, you *are* my law partner, are you not?"

Galvin braced for the fire storm that he knew was coming.

"I am."

"And, let me see, you've been with my law firm how long?"

"Five years."

"Five years. Yes. Five years." Carter put his hands behind his back, tilted his head toward the ceiling, and closed his eyes as if he were pondering some elusive equation.

"And you are a *full* partner in the firm, are you not?"

"That is correct."

"Where is your residence, Mr. Galvin?"

"Eighteen Louisburg Square, Boston."

"That's known as Beacon Hill, is it not?"

"It is."

"It's fashionable up there."

"It's a nice area."

"You own your own residence at that location?"

"I do."

"A three-story townhouse, is it not?"

"It is."

"You also own a summer place in Osterville on Cape Cod?"

"I do."

"And a fifty-eight-foot yacht?"

Carter had stretched it by five feet, but this was no time to quibble over fractions.

"Yes. The *Emerald Isle*," Galvin added.

A slight smile from a juror named Callahan did not go unnoticed by Hovington.

Tina leaned toward Moe. "Object to this whole line of questioning. It's not relevant. And those working stiffs on the jury—you can hear them gulp."

"No," Moe whispered. "Galvin knows what he's doing."

Carter Hovington removed his glasses and tapped the stem at the corner of his mouth. He stepped closer to Galvin.

"What was your gross salary last year?"

"I'd say in the vicinity of seven hundred thousand dollars."

"Seven hundred thousand?" Carter replaced his glasses and looked at the jury, his eyebrows raised, his lips pursed in a silent whistle.

"That is correct." Galvin also looked at the jury.

"Now, you were assigned by me to defend this litigation as chief counsel right from the start."

"I was."

"So, any information gained about this case came from that assignment?"

"That is correct."

"And you took this assignment with the understanding that you would *fully* and *faithfully* defend your clients."

"That *was* and that *is* my understanding."

Hovington smarted. It was Galvin's first departure from the "yes" and "no" rote the examination sought to elicit. He'd have to tighten the interrogation, leave Galvin no room for digression.

"Let me see," Hovington said casually as if it were an afterthought. "Prior to joining my firm, you were associated with Moe Katz, the same gentleman who questioned you this morning, isn't that correct?"

"That's correct."

"As a matter of fact, Mr. Galvin, Tina Alvarez, that young lady seated alongside of Mr. Katz"—Hovington motioned with his glasses—"came into your office to see if you would take on the very case that she and Mr. Katz are prosecuting here at this moment. Isn't that correct?"

"She initially approached me with that idea, which I turned down after I learned that our law firm had been involved in securing FDA approval for Lyosin. There was a conflict—"

"Yes," Hovington interrupted. "There was a conflict of interest. You'd be playing both sides of the case."

"Is that a question?" Galvin tried to appeal to some sense of fair play.

"Strike it." Hovington now picked up the pace. "Do you see the young gentleman seated with Mr. Katz?"

"I do."

"He's plaintiffs' associate counsel, Rhys Jameson, is he not?"

"He is."

"Now, Mr. Jameson also worked for *my* firm under you in the litigation department, did he not?"

"He did."

"And you subsequently discharged him, did you not?"

"He resigned."

"Okay, but by whatever mode, he became disengaged from the firm, and now shows up working for your old associate Mr. Katz and with Miss Alvarez, who initially tried to peddle you the case."

"Again," Galvin replied evenly, "I'm not sure you are asking me a question."

Hovington paused. From the corner of his eye he tried to gauge the jurors. Hard to tell how they were reacting. They were listening—that was a certainty. He was satisfied with the tactical web he was weaving, planting seeds of doubt.

Tina and Rhys were apprehensive. Hovington was lacerating Galvin. And the judge was allowing him free rein.

Carter thought it best to alter the line of interrogation so that Galvin wouldn't detect a pattern.

"Now, you say that you became aware of a parchment from someone named Aubrey Gammett that was written when?"

"It was a one-hundred-and-twenty-page journal. Written in 1902."

"My," said Carter, a cynical edge to his voice, "that was before the *Titanic*'s maiden voyage. Before World War One. Nicholas the Second was Czar of Russia. That was a long time ago."

"It was."

"You're not saying that I had anything to do with concealing this so-called journal, are you?" Hovington pressed his notes against his chest.

Galvin looked at Chip Hovington. Chip averted his gaze. "No," Galvin said solemnly, "it was solely *my* responsibility."

"Fine." Carter cleared his throat. Galvin was taking the fall. The firm wasn't involved. For a moment he hesitated. But he was an advocate. He was defending a client. Gammett, Universal, Jimmy Hoffa. It made no difference.

"You said that Dr. Bok-Sahn did not tell the truth; in essence she lied, perjured herself, about the existence of an antiquated journal."

"Yes."

"Dr. Bok-Sahn was an honorable young lady, was she not? In fact, quite religious—wouldn't you agree with that assessment, Mr. Galvin?"

Galvin could see it coming—each question packed with innuendo, the question more important than the answer.

"She still *is*," Galvin said.

"*Is?*" A red sensor flickered. Carter's head snapped backward. "You are of course aware that Dr. Bok-Sahn met with a fatal boating accident in England"—he scanned his notes—"in May of this year."

"That's not correct."

"Not correct? Are you trying to tell this honorable court and jury that Dr. Bok-Sahn did *not* die in an explosion aboard a yacht on the Isle of Wight in May of this year?"

"That's what I'm saying. Your information is incorrect."

Carter's face flushed. He replaced his glasses and again inspected his notes.

"I show you a newspaper clipping from the *London Times*." He passed it to Galvin, then stepped back as Galvin studied it.

"It states, does it not, that Dr. Bok-Sahn was killed in an explosion aboard the yacht *Guinevere* at the Royal Yacht Squadron, Isle of Wight, isn't that what it says?"

"That's what it states."

Carter's eyes left Galvin. He leaned on the rail and looked in at the jury. "Are you saying that the *Times* is incorrect?"

"That's what I am saying."

Something was wrong. Galvin was too confident. Carter shot a glance at Frobisher, Mallory, and Symes. Symes seemed to be signaling, crossing his fingers in the shape of a T, like a basketball coach requesting time.

"*Cross-examination is like a bayonet. You can use it for anything but sitting*," Hovington often lectured at trial seminars. He now had to leave on a high note—make sure the jury knew it was the witness who was impaled, not he.

"When did you last talk with Dr. Bok-Sahn?" He removed his glasses, still eyeing the jury, his voice couched in skepticism.

"This morning at around seven o'clock." Galvin glanced at his watch. "She called from England and told me to do the right thing. That's what I'm doing."

Symes passed a note to Chip Hovington. Chip caught Carter's attention.

"Excuse me, just one moment, Your Honor." Hovington feigned clearing his throat, then walked unsteadily toward the counsel table. His hand trembled as he removed his glasses from his vest pocket and scanned the message.

SUSPEND NOW! SABRINA BOK-SAHN IS EN ROUTE. SHE'LL PUT THE LIE TO GALVIN!

Hovington was visibly shaken. "Your Honor," he said, struggling to regain his faltering composure. "The hour is late. May I suspend interrogation of the witness and resume first thing in the morning?"

"Yes." The judge too was unnerved. "The court will stand adjourned until ten tomorrow morning." He banged his gavel and bolted from the bench.

◘

Carter and Derek Symes were closeted in a private session in the conference room. Even Chip, Mallory, and Frobisher were excluded.

"Let me get this straight." Hovington bristled. "You knew that Sabrina Bok-Sahn did not die in the yacht club explosion, yet you didn't tell me?"

"Look, Carter." Symes's voice was controlled. "When the blast occurred, we were all in a state of shock. I was the IRA target. They missed me by seconds. We all thought Sabrina had perished."

Carter paced back and forth as Symes continued.

"No one knew she didn't survive. Everything disintegrated. When I received the monthly bill for the ship's telephone, I was surprised to see the last call was placed to Galvin's Boston residence. That's when I started checking. Sabrina's whereabouts came from a tip of a friend who does telly commercials for the BBC. And we never expected Galvin to take the stand. That wouldn't be allowed in Britain."

"Goddamn it, Symes, the case is being tried *here!*" Carter wrapped his knuckles on the conference table. "Baron gave us all the breaks. We were coasting until Galvin bushwhacked us. Imagine me, head counsel, not knowing that my client's key officer is not only alive and well, but daring, I should say inviting, our side to throw in the towel. Galvin sure stuck it to us, pouring in all sorts of hearsay. Symes, the jury got *one* impression, and at the worst possible time—the tail end of my cross-examination. Galvin challenged me. And I had to back off! You put me in one hell of a hole."

Derek Symes thought for a few moments. "What's done is done," he said calmly. "That's why it's so important to have Dr. Bok-Sahn rebut Galvin's testimony." He extracted a tapered cigarette from a Dunhill gold case, then offered one to Carter, who refused with an abrupt shake of his head.

With steady assurance, Symes took out a platinum lighter from his suit-coat pocket, flicked it, and lit his cigarette. He puffed decorously for a few moments, then eyed Hovington. A thin smile coursed his lips.

"Dr. Bok-Sahn is an unusual person, Carter. Intelligent. Beautiful. You've never met her. She has a way about her. Engaging, mesmerizing. She'll be believed."

"No. Let it go." Hovington's hand chopped the air. "You bring her on and it'll lend credence to every goddamn thing Galvin said. He said she was alive. She's alive. I was wrong. Can you imagine what the jury's thinking?"

Symes ground his cigarette into the green marble tray, removed a paper from his inside pocket, and handed it to Carter.

"Here," he said matter-of-factly, as if he were ordering lunch. "I mapped this out while listening to Galvin. It's a series of questions for tomorrow's cross-examination. You stick to this script, dovetail it with Sabrina's testimony, and the jury will run Galvin out of town."

Carter perused it quickly. "You've got to be insane!" His voice snapped like the cracking of frozen leather. "This is sleaze! Goddamned garbage!" He slapped the paper, his anger mounting. "What kind of lawyer do you think I am!"

Symes leaned toward Carter, his voice still steady, like an

admiral trying to stem a mutiny. "Galvin stabbed you in the back. Have you forgotten that, Carter? You—Hovington? The lion of Boston? You made him a partner. An equal. This stumble-bum lawyer."

"Don't give me that crap!" Carter scaled the paper onto the floor. "No, Symes, it's over. We're bailing out. I don't give a goddamn if it costs two hundred million. I'm going to get Moe Katz on the line. I think he'll be reasonable."

"Before you do anything rash, Carter"—Symes still had the faint smile, but his voice was now as cold as Siberia—"your son Chip was in on this whole thing."

"What the fuck are you talking about?" Carter's voice quavered. "Galvin accepted sole responsibility."

"I'm fucking talking about Chip tampering with the Importer's Agreement so we won on jurisdiction. Changing critical contents. And he and Jerry Wilson buried the Aubrey journal. Maybe you'll all end up in jail." Symes's Etonian courtliness had completely disappeared.

Hovington paled as if he had been told he had terminal cancer.

Symes retrieved the paper from the floor and handed it to Carter.

"How sure are you of Sabrina Bok-Sahn?" Carter's voice was now bereft of all anger, replaced by the whine of fear.

"Very sure. You just stick to the script."

"But what about the journal?" Carter gazed off into a middle distance. "Suppose Katz has a copy?"

"We've got every contingency covered. There's no journal. No copy."

"All right, but I don't want any more surprises." Carter tried to rekindle his sense of indignation. "When do I see Dr. Bok-Sahn to go over her testimony?"

"You don't. Leave Sabrina to me. I'll give you a list of five or six questions to ask her. Bang. Bang. Bang. Keep it short. Sabrina won't equivocate."

Carter tried to force a smile, but his face was grim. "You know, Symes," he said, "our fee is going to be so outrageous, it'll make you guys quake. Believe me!"

"I believe you." It was Symes who smiled.

◘

"I've got something to show you." Moe chortled as he reached for Volume IV of *Williston on Contracts*. "Rhys, you thought I was off my rocker with Chumley."

He patted the green leather text as Tina and Rhys exchanged perplexed glances.

"This'll corroborate Galvin." His bony fingers pried open the pages as his grin added another crease to his face. He held the gray cassette aloft. "We got the bastards right by the *cajones*! I know some Portuguese too, Tina." He cackled. "Unfortunately, it compromises Galvin. But what's done is done."

He inserted the cassette, punched the ON button, and watched the tape begin to roll.

They listened. Ten seconds. Twenty seconds. Nothing but the slow whir of the sprocket.

"Something's wrong." Moe's hands began to tremble. "Oh, no!" he wailed. "Dear God! What have I done! It must be the recorder!" But Moe knew it was the tape. It had been erased. And he hadn't the foggiest notion of the locker number in the Manhattan bus station. Only he and Jim knew of the bogus Williston volume. Could someone have gotten to Jim? No. Jim had been with him for thirty years. It was absolutely unthinkable. Oh, shit! He sighed.

"Well, what's this all about?" Tina broke the silence.

"Oh, just a little piece of hearsay that we wouldn't be able to introduce anyway. Forget I even brought it up."

◘

Moe called his chauffeur's apartment in Mattapan. "Jim, sorry to bother you so late."

"No problem, boss. I'm still up. Reading my Bible."

"Did you get to the one about the thirty pieces of silver?"

"Thirty pieces of silver? Is that in Deuteronomy or Genesis?"

"I think you'll find it in Matthew," Moe said dryly. "Listen,

349

Jim, drop by the office early tomorrow and pick up Volume Four of Williston."

"Volume Four?"

"Yes. It's in the library. *Williston on Contracts*. You know, the book where I hide the schnaps."

Jim hesitated, then blurted, "Okay, boss, will do. And I'll be by to pick you up at eight."

Somehow Jim sounded like Rochester on the old Jack Benny show. And Moe could detect voice inflections like a polygraph.

43

I re-call to the stand Frank Galvin." Carter Hovington glanced at his checklist, then watched as Galvin nodded to the jury and took his seat in the witness stand.

"Mr. Galvin," Judge Baron said, squinting into the morning sunlight filtering through the east windows, "you are still under oath, is that understood?"

"Yes, Your Honor."

"Mr. Hovington, you may proceed."

Carter Hovington was no longer the floundering lawyer of the previous day. Dressed in a conservative dark-blue suit, white shirt, and navy tie, his gait was bouncy as he proceeded to the counsel table and picked up an indexed manuscript. "Mr. Galvin," he said, "let's back up a minute. Yesterday you made a categoric statement. So there will be no mistake as to what was said, I will quote from a transcript of your testimony." He waved the document with a slight flourish. "Your Honor, to ensure accuracy, may I approach the witness?"

"You may." Baron was curious.

Galvin anticipated some sort of surprise. He looked over the packed courtroom. The British contingent was absent.

Hovington walked to the witness stand and positioned himself over Galvin's left shoulder.

"Now follow along with me on line five," he said. " 'Question. Dr. Bok-Sahn did not tell the truth; in essence she lied, perjured herself, about the existence of an antiquated journal.' 'Answer. Yes.' "

"Now, Mr. Galvin." Hovington eyed the jury. "Have I read that correctly?"

"You have."

"Do you wish to recant that testimony?"

"I do not."

"You said, and again I quote, 'Dr. Bok-Sahn is an honorable person.' Was that your testimony yesterday afternoon?"

"It was."

" 'Honorable' denotes utmost veracity and credibility, does it not?"

"One can be honorable and still be overwhelmed by events," Galvin countered.

Hovington smarted but moved on quickly. "What was the exact conversation you had with Dr. Bok-Sahn wherein she told you, as you say, 'to do the right thing.' "

"It was in Gaelic."

"Gaelic?" Hovington's expression hovered between astonishment and disbelief.

"I sensed Dr. Bok-Sahn was being coerced and that is why she spoke in Gaelic."

"Are you proficient in Gaelic?"

"No. In fact, I needed a translation."

"So you say she lapsed into some sort of linguistic code—you went off, got it deciphered, and then inferred that she had given you the green light to call her a perjurer."

"I'm not sure what you're asking me."

"Let me withdraw it." Hovington felt satisfied. He scanned his notes, then walked slowly in front of the jury box, paused and placed his hand on the rail.

"Mr. Galvin," he began casually, "when you traveled to London to counsel Dr. Bok-Sahn, you were aware that she was the medical director of Universal?"

"I was well aware."

"She was your client."

"She was my client."

"And with that relationship came an element of absolute trust. Would you agree with that premise?"

"I would."

"And while you were in London, as you say, counseling the doctor, you were in her company socially as well as professionally. Is that a fair statement?"

"That's a fair statement."

"As a matter of fact, Mr. Galvin, you escorted Dr. Bok-Sahn to a cocktail reception in New Jersey several weeks ago, did you not?"

"I did."

"Stayed at the same hotel?"

"Yes."

"In separate rooms?"

"Yes. Of course."

"Let me be perfectly blunt." Carter removed his glasses and pointed them at Galvin. "Did you go to bed with Dr. Bok-Sahn?"

It came with dagger swiftness, catching Galvin off guard. His mind raced. Carter couldn't be this insensitive. There were time-honored rules of the game. You won above the belt or you didn't deserve to be in the courtroom. It was the trial lawyer's code.

"In the name of decency, Your Honor!" Moe tried to bolt from his wheelchair.

"Mr. Katz." The judge cleared his throat. "*You* put the witness on the stand. When an attorney calls a witness, he implicitly vouches for his veracity. In essence he says to the jury 'Believe him.' Now, *your* witness made some broad accusations. Mr. Hovington not only has the right, but also the duty to test this witness's credibility." Baron peered down at Galvin. "The objection is overruled. The witness is instructed to answer the question."

Again Galvin surveyed the courtroom.

"Come, Mr. Galvin. Do you need time to think about it?" Hovington's fingers tapped a little dance on the jury rail.

"Yes, I went to bed with Dr. Bok-Sahn," Galvin said quietly.

"You went to bed with *your* client." Again the eyeglasses, the lawyer's prop, was used as a pointer.

"That is correct."

Hovington faced Galvin, poised like a matador for the final wounding. "*Why*, Mr. Galvin, knowing that you were Dr. Bok-Sahn's attorney"—his voice was a mounting crescendo—"knowing that she trusted you, that she was a person of honor and integrity, *why* did you take advantage of her and subject her to sexual relations? *Why?*"

A few jurors shifted uneasily.

Galvin thought carefully. *Why?* He had an opening. Tell them about his suspicions. Wilson. The jurisdiction question. The death of Postman Gately. Symes's complicity in the yacht explosion.

He hunched forward. No eye contact with the jury. He gazed straight ahead.

"Because I loved her," he said quietly. "I still love her."

Hovington waited for the follow-up. There was none. It was late-show stuff. A cliché.

"That's all I have," Hovington said. He shook his head, his lips pursed in disapproval.

"Mr. Katz?" Baron was now a paragon of judicial restraint. "Any re-direct?"

"No questions, Your Honor." Moe signaled with a resigned wave of his hand.

"Have you completed your case?" Baron inquired.

Moe looked hesitantly at Tina and Rhys. He avoided Galvin, who remained seated in the witness box. Galvin had been skewered. No question. But hard to tell what the jury was actually thinking. "Yes, Your Honor, we rest our case."

"Mr. Hovington." Baron addressed the defendants' table. "Do you wish a brief recess before commencing your evidence? I assume you'll make an opening to the jury."

Hovington rose slowly. "Thank you, Your Honor. Most respectfully, I feel we should proceed. I will waive my opening to the jury, and the defendants will call only *one* witness." His voice was firm, confident. "I call to the witness stand Dr. Sabrina Bok-Sahn."

○

Galvin left the stand as Sabrina approached. She was understated elegance, trim gray suit, a Victorian cameo pinned to white lace at her slender throat. The jurors regarded her intently.

As Galvin and Sabrina were about to pass, their eyes held, then slid away as if by agreement. Something in her eyes responded to his. Was it regret?

Galvin walked to the rear of the courtroom and squeezed into a seat.

The bailiff stepped forward to administer the oath. "Raise your right hand," he said.

Surprisingly, Sabrina Bok-Sahn did as directed.

"Do you solemnly swear to tell the truth, the whole truth, and nothing but the truth, so help you God?"

"I do," she said softly.

Now Galvin could see it coming. He had been a fool. Sabrina with her Buddhist ties, her proclamation that she recognized no deity but humanity—that wouldn't play in Boston. So suddenly she gets religion. Symes was her Svengali—or maybe she had been the Dragon Lady all along.

"Dr. Bok-Sahn," Hovington began slowly, "you were requested to appear here today because of the, uh, unusual circumstances that occurred in this case, is that correct?"

A leading question. Legally objectionable. A lawyer is not supposed to guide his witness. But the jurors would resent Moe's interference now.

"That is so." Sabrina's voice was like the stirring of mountain snow. Her calm demeanor reflected sincerity.

"When did you arrive in Boston?" Hovington glanced at the prepared script.

"About ten last evening."

Hovington checked his watch. "Did you have a chance to read the transcript of Mr. Galvin's previous testimony?"

"I did."

"Now, Dr. Bok-Sahn, were you here in the courtroom this morning when Mr. Galvin resumed the witness stand?"

"I was."

"Did you hear his testimony?"

"I did."

"Mr. Galvin called you an honorable person and said he was in love with you. Do you recall hearing that?"

"Yes," she said almost inaudibly, her head slightly bowed.

"Now, in your capacity as medical director of Universal, working with Mr. Galvin, both here in the United States and in England, you got to know Mr. Galvin quite well, did you not?"

"I did."

"Socially and professionally; isn't that a fair assessment?"

"It is."

"Did Mr. Galvin escort you to a rather grand party in New Jersey, say two months ago?"

"He did."

"As a matter of fact, you stayed at the same hotel, isn't that correct?"

"We did."

Hovington was surprised at how smoothly it was going. Like Galvin, Sabrina could have added, "In separate rooms." She didn't. Symes had kept his promise. Sabrina was delivering.

"And, Doctor, you spent time together last week in the English countryside, isn't that correct?" Hovington peered at the jury to gauge their reaction.

"That is correct."

From his position near the rear of the courtroom, Galvin looked at Symes, whom he noticed for the first time. He could see the tacit approval. And oddly, Sabrina was telling the truth. So far.

"Dr. Bok-Sahn, did you hear Mr. Galvin say a few moments ago that you gave perjured testimony in your London deposition?"

"I did."

"Now, Doctor, Mr. Galvin was your counsel during that testimony, was he not?"

"He was."

"How long did Mr. Galvin spend with you in preparation of that deposition?"

"Well, we were together for a week in New Jersey. All told, perhaps ten days."

"Ten days? That was thorough preparation."

"It was."

Hovington creased the script and placed it in his inner suit pocket. He paused.

"Dr. Bok-Sahn, you have taken an oath before God Almighty to tell the truth." Hovington's voice was sepulchral. "Have you done so?"

"I have."

"You read Mr. Galvin's testimony. You heard him here this morning relate your conversation. He said you spoke in Gaelic. Is Mr. Galvin telling the truth?"

"I did speak to him in Gaelic."

Hovington quickly put on his glasses and reconsulted his notes. "Are you proficient in Gaelic?" His voice was cautious.

"I speak several languages. Gaelic was required by the Ursuline nuns during preparatory school."

Hovington had several more questions, but felt it best to wind up her testimony. "Dr. Bok-Sahn, Mr. Galvin represented to this honorable court and to this jury of peers that you knew of the existence of a so-called Aubrey Gammett journal, and that you *perjured* yourself in your deposition. You're aware of his testimony on that point, are you not, Doctor?"

"I am."

"Now, as a matter of fact, Doctor, there is *no* journal. *No* such journal ever existed, and Mr. Galvin is the one who is perjuring himself—isn't that the real truth?"

Sabrina looked at the jurors, then at the sea of faces in the spectators' section. Her eyes surveyed the mongoloid children and their haggard mothers.

"Mr. Galvin told you the truth." Her voice quavered and her eyes brimmed with tears. "I was the one who lied."

Hovington's knees sagged and he held the jury rail to keep from falling. There was not a sound. The judge, jury, spectators, counsel, bailiffs sat frozen, locked in the amber of early-morning sunlight.

◻

Judge Baron wanted the case settled. "It's too bizarre to let it go to the jury," he said, throwing up his hands as he paced about his chambers.

"We've reached a tentative agreement." Hovington's voice was as disconsolate as his slumped posture.

"Twenty million," Moe Katz said.

"Well, subject to Lloyds giving the okay," said Symes with artificial bravado. "I've got a call in to them now."

"Twenty million's a bargain." Baron addressed Symes with an authoritative scowl. "And I don't want any niggling. This goddamn case is going to be closed! Today!" He pounded a fist onto his desk. "If it isn't, I'm calling in the U.S. Attorney!"

"It'll be settled," Symes said without hesitation.

◻

Galvin drove Sabrina to Logan Airport. She rested her head against the leather upholstery and closed her eyes. They rode in silence.

He carried her luggage through the check-in. She snapped open a suitcase and handed him a small package. "Here," she said, her voice misty. "The Aubrey journal. You may need it."

She looked at him for a moment. "It's hopeless, Galvin, it's hopeless."

Galvin said nothing. Inside he was dying. She touched his cheek briefly with her fingertips, then turned and melded with the passengers moving toward the aircraft gate.

Galvin stood at the observation window and watched the Air India jet skim down the runway and disappear into a cloud bank out over the Atlantic. He knew she was now beyond the reach of Symes and the Uni crowd. He also knew she was disappearing from his life forever.

He walked back along the white-tiled concourse toward the main terminal. Suddenly he felt a great emptiness. He was alone. There had always been a woman, even in his drinking days. Someone to share the lies.

He thought of Sabrina—her soft brown shoulders, her faraway look as if she were fixed to another time. Like no woman he had ever known, she had given him the hint of immortality.

He checked his watch. Two o'clock. He hesitated, then turned toward the lounge. He needed a drink.

Galvin ordered a double bar Scotch—no need for a fancy brand—and stared into its tawny depths. But he saw no solutions there. He'd been down that road. What were his options? Damned few. He couldn't return to the firm. Brahmin Boston would politely close the door to his future among their elite. And wherever he went, whatever he did, Derek Symes would be out there, poised and waiting. Symes wouldn't lose the second time around.

He pushed the shot glass aside. Get going, he said to himself, you're back to square one. He left the lounge and headed for the newsstand to pick up the *Globe*'s classifieds. Find new office space.

That would be a start.

ACKNOWLEDGMENTS

Carolyn Blakemore, whose fine editorial hand guided the book through a long but rewarding journey.

Peter Matson, my agent and friend, for his help, professionalism, and perseverance.

Betty A. Prashker, my editor-in-chief, for her support, perception, and kindness during many drafts and revisions.

My superb secretaries, Elaine DeFosse and Catherine McDonald, who labored untold hours in perfecting the script.

John Balsdon, Esquire of London, England, for his insight and commentary on the judicial topography of the United Kingdom.

And to the memory of my father, Clement Barry Reed, who nurtured in us a deep affection for the Irish race.